The BELLE OF WINCHESTER

BOOK TWO
THE ELLSWORTH ASSORTMENT

CHRISTINA DUDLEY

Cover design: Kathy Campbell, www.kathryncampbell.com

ISBN: 978-1-963408-07-2

William Ellsworth = (1) Henrietta Baldric
= (2) Catherine Catchway
= (3) Anne Fielding
= (4) Miranda Gregory

- (1) Florence = Robert Fairchild
- (1) Lily
- (2) Tyrone
- (2) Araminta
- (3) Beatrice

Charles Ellsworth = Jeanne Martineau

- Benjamin
- Austin

The
Ellsworth Assortment

CHAPTER ONE

In the midst of life we are in death.

— The Book of Common Prayer, *The Burial of the Dead* (1662)

Miss Lily Ellsworth's mind wandered.

It was not the dullness of the sermon, though Mr. Pennyworth's sermon was indeed dull. The curate, besides being at least 130 years old, kept losing his place in his notes and then starting over again with a line already delivered a minute earlier. As a result, Lily's father William Ellsworth was fast asleep, bald head hanging off to the side and mouth open, and Lily's stepmother had already twice nudged him when he began to snore. Lily's younger brother Tyrone had insinuated a small volume from his pocket and was happily reading, while his twin Araminta knotted her handkerchief in a tight ball and batted it back and forth along the pew with Beatrice, the youngest of the Ellsworths. Nor were they the only members of the congregation lost to spiritual edification that morning. When Lily peeped from under her bonnet brim, she counted four other parishioners asleep and two nodding. Several other congregants stared up at St. Eadburh's familiar hammerbeam roof and several more at the just-as-familiar stained-glass scenes from the saint's life.

No. Mr. Pennyworth's dullness might plumb untold depths, but he was not responsible for Lily's lack of attention. Her mind wandered because she was *delighted.* Positively *triumphant*. For the day before she had attended her very first horse races. Added to which, at the races themselves she experienced an even greater thrill, that of making her first conquests. Several of them, to be precise.

These two achievements alone would have been enough, but there was yet one more. For, among the conquered, Lily was certain she had also met the man who would do very well, eventually, for a husband, when she was done having her fun. Because, truth be told, Lily pictured marriage as a far-off, somewhat dull and featureless country which she was in no hurry to arrive at. The chief source for this belief of hers was her father's history. Mr. William Ellsworth's repeated unions (four of them to date) did not, she thought, make up in quantity what they lacked in quality. *He* always appeared content with the matches, but Lily did not envy the lots of her mother or her three successive stepmothers. Yes, by marrying they lived comfortably, with a husband who did not beat or browbeat them, but that was as much as could be said. And in return they must share his bed and manage his lot of mismatched offspring and smile upon his bald, spotted head and know that any heart pangs of their own would go unnoticed. (It will be plain from this summary that Lily loved her father mildly and dutifully, but no further.)

Therefore—marriage. Something inevitable, but best pushed off as long as possible.

In any event, when the novelty of eligible spinsterhood wore off, or advancing age forced her hand, she had selected the man who would do as well as any other, and likely better than most, to accompany her into hidebound middle age.

Mr. Gilbert Wright.

Lily repeated the name in her head, suppressing a complacent smile. Mr. Gilbert Wright, proud owner of Slapbang, the five-year-old who soared ahead of the field to take the hundred-guinea purse of the King's Plate.

It had taken some doing to be among the witnesses to the victory. Attendance at the races required her father's presence, which in turn required two things of its own: the end of their season of mourning for the third Mrs. Ellsworth, and the fruition of a season of steady urging by Lily and Araminta. But he had yielded at last and ordered the barouche landau brought 'round: "Let it be a treat to celebrate Tyrone returning from school." Lily knew her bookish brother would prefer a history to a horse race any day, but she was too glad of her father's capitulation to point this out.

Tyrone returned to Hollowgate for the long vacation to make one of the party, along with his father, Lily, and Minta, while the fourth Mrs. Ellsworth remained at home with Beatrice. Poor Beatrice begged to go along, but Lily ruthlessly told her, "Nonsense. There might be drunken gentlemen about and rough language.

That's why Papa has to come. Besides, if any of the horses are lamed and have to be shot, you know very well you'll cry your eyes out, and I haven't patience for that."

"I won't cry, Lily. I haven't cried in—a fortnight!" protested her youngest sister. "You're just afraid I'll sit on your new gown."

"And so you would," retorted Lily. "If you come it'll be a crush, and now that I may finally wear whatever I please, I don't intend to be sat upon. That's why Minta's friend Aggie can't come either. It's bad enough Minta can't be made to stay behind. She is sure to get in some scrape."

"You are the unkindest sister in the world. I can't wait for Flossie to return," complained Beatrice, not for the first time. Indeed, their eldest sister Florence had married the attorney Robert Fairchild recently, and the Fairchilds were not expected back from their honeymoon until August. For most of Beatrice's seven years, it had been Florence who played the maternal role in her life, a role now filled by her new stepmother, the former Miss Gregory. (Because Miss Gregory had been a lifelong neighbor, the Ellsworths still accidentally addressed her thus with some frequency.) As stepmothers went, the former Miss Gregory was exemplary: kind, forbearing, tolerant, not insistent on remaking Hollowgate in her own image. But Beatrice still missed Florence. Lily was no substitute. Not in the least.

Lily was *not* maternal toward her younger half-siblings. She soon forgot Beatrice's wishes and woes in the excitement of the outing, excitement that began as soon as the barouche landau turned up Race Way toward Worthy Down where the course lay.

In addition to the carts of showmen and vendors and the flocks of trampers to be found at every racecourse and fairground, there were scores of more respectable gentlemen en route. In carriages, in phaetons, on horseback. And if they weren't all handsome or young, they were at least all well-dressed for the occasion. All of them—every last one of them—turned to admire her and to bow to her father. And such was Mr. Ellsworth's standing in Winchester (some wags might call it his notoriety) that the Ellsworths did not need to squeeze for purchase between gambling tents or gingerbread stalls, but instead had space open magically for the carriage at the home straight, within sight of the post.

And there Lily held court.

Gentleman after gentleman approached, having buttonholed some acquaintance of William Ellsworth, in order that an introduction to him—that is, to *Lily*—might be achieved. There was Mr. Caxton, whose hair was so flaxen that his eyebrows and eyelashes blended entirely into his forehead. Mr. Trimp, whose tailor seemed to think he was a slenderer man than the tape showed, for he looked in danger of bursting his waistcoat buttons and (Lily suspected) the seat of his trousers. Sir Basil Longworthy, whom she paid little attention to, despite his baronetage, because he was nearly as old as her father; and, after a lifetime of watching her papa marry and then marry again, Lily had no patience for men she thought would do better to nurse their rheumatism than dreams of remarriage.

Gentleman after gentleman! And most of them lingered as near as they could during the races, reduced to making up to Tyrone or Minta if they could not speak with her. At first she allowed Mr.

Walter Dailey to take the place to her right hand because he was far and away the handsomest of the lot, but he proved so deeply tedious, droning on and on about his own stud of horses and why this, that, or the other one would have carried the day had it been entered, that Lily eventually turned her back to him and began to favor the flaxen Mr. Caxton. And then both men—all the men—were forgotten in the thrill of the second heat of the King's One Hundred Guineas Plate. The bell was rung; the course cleared. All waited in breathless excitement.

Or nearly breathless.

"If Wright's Slapbang takes this one, there'll be no need for a final heat," Mr. Dailey informed her. It was difficult for him to keep silent more than two minutes together.

"Slapbang nearly eliminated Kingdom Come in the first heat," put in Mr. Trimp, sucking in his midsection when she glanced at him. "So I imagine this will do the trick."

"Well, why didn't he eliminate him?" Lily asked. "He won that heat, after all."

"To eliminate him, he would have had to beat Kingdom Come by a 'distance,'" droned Mr. Dailey. "That is, Slapbang would have had to reach the finishing post before Kingdom Come reached the distance post. A matter of 240 yards."

"It was close, it was close," murmured Mr. Trimp. He rubbed his hands in excitement, having visited the betting post to put money on Slapbang. "That horse has bottom!"

"Perhaps. But when my Midwinter is another year older you'll see him here," declared Mr. Dailey. "Midwinter is a tail male descendant of the great Herod, you know, Miss Ellsworth. Just like Tattersall's famous Highflyer. Talk about bottom! Some swear by the Eclipse line, but I say if it's good enough for Tattersalls, it's good enough for me. And when one considers the training my horses undergo—! There is nothing like my estate of Crossdown for building stamina and strength, for the land has an incline in the western half of some two to three degrees over two miles, followed by a steeper slope, and my man starts Midwinter at an easy gallop for, say half a mile, before urging him faster on the incline —"

Lily patted a yawn from her mouth and let him deliver the rest of his speech to her shoulder. "How long is the home straight, Mr. Caxton?"

"Oh—er—"

"Six furlongs," Mr. Dailey answered loudly. He went on to describe the course in painstaking detail—not furlong by furlong but almost inch by inch, and Lily was certain that, if the horses had had to carry Mr. Dailey and all his knowledge on their backs, the race would have seemed six *hundred* furlongs to them.

"I say, here comes the leader," shouted Minta after a time, leaping up and making the carriage bounce. "Give me the glass, Tyrone. I want to see."

"You've had it this whole time."

Before the two could resolve their struggle for it, Mr. Trimp hollered, "By gum! That's Wright's horse! Out in front! Confound me, if that isn't Slapbang!"

"His lead is increasing," cried Tyrone, getting as caught up as the rest.

"What a beauty!" Lily exclaimed, clapping her hands.

It was Slapbang indeed, black and shining, flying down the straight with his diminutive jockey crouched above the saddle, both wearing shining blue and silver silks. The cheers which erupted were swallowed by the thundering hooves of Slapbang's pursuers, but the sixth furlong was far too late to catch him, and the five-year-old handily sailed to the finish.

"Oh, Papa! He won! He won!" Araminta sang, jumping up and down, the carriage creaking and lurching like a ship in a storm, "I want to be a jockey! May I become a jockey?"

William Ellsworth gave his characteristic beatific smile and pretended not to hear her, leaving Lily to step significantly on her sister's foot and Tyrone to elbow the girl until she resumed her seat with a huff and a bump.

"Ah, Miss Araminta, I'm afraid your ambition can never be satisfied," Sir Basil Longworthy wheezed at her. "There are no female jockeys, you know. But I admire good horsemanship in either sex. Do you and Miss Ellsworth ride often?"

"Florence never rides at all," Minta replied shortly, vexed to have her aspirations so roundly crushed.

"He means Lily, you blockhead," groaned her twin. "Lily is Miss Ellsworth now."

"Oh," said Minta, unperturbed. "Well, Lily never rides either. But do look! Do you suppose they will come this way? I hope they come this way! They will—they are! Slapbang and the jockey and some other gentleman! Give me the glass again, Tyrone."

The baronet threw a look over his shoulder. "It's Wright with the horse. Gilbert Wright of Meadowsweep. The horse's owner."

"Mere beginner's luck," said Mr. Dailey. "Can't say Wright's entered more than a handful of races. I doubt Slapbang will repeat such a performance at Stockbridge, much less Newmarket. Fortunate the creature didn't come up lame, the way his rider took those last furlongs. My own jockey Carter always says..."

Lily sat forward, silencing Mr. Dailey in her mind, if not in reality. She held very still and—after one sharp glance—kept her eyes demurely lowered. But beneath her lashes she studied the approaching victor.

He was above average height and strongly built, carrying himself with jaunty confidence and encased in tailoring that put other gentlemen to shame. A beaver hat covered hair of middling brown, and as he drew closer she decided he was handsome. Not quite as handsome as Mr. Dailey, but Mr. Dailey's handsomeness came at far too high a price. And while Mr. Dailey might talk of his talented stud, it was Mr. Wright whose beast had made him one hundred guineas richer that day.

She could have kissed her father when he called out to the champion of the hour, "I congratulate you, sir!"

Readily, Mr. Wright paused before their carriage, straightening sharply when his gaze touched on Lily.

The onlookers soon crowded the rail for a better look at Slapbang, many reaching to pat a flank, some offering compliments to the wiry jockey still atop him.

"Dailey, will you perform the introduction?" Mr. Wright prompted.

Grudgingly, Mr. Dailey said, "May I introduce Mr. William Ellsworth of Hollowgate? And Miss Ellsworth, Miss Araminta Ellsworth, Mr. Tyrone Ellsworth. This is Mr. Gilbert Wright of Meadowsweep."

"Outside Romsey," put in Mr. Wright.

"Why, we live off the Romsey Road," declared Minta. "May I pat your horse?"

Mr. Wright gave another bow and held out a hand to assist her from the carriage, a hand which Minta didn't even notice as she bounded out. He turned to Lily. "Miss Ellsworth...perhaps you might like to meet Slapbang as well?"

While Lily didn't particularly want to stand beside a horse that was sixteen hands if he was an inch, and who was even now swishing his tail in annoyance to have so many pressing close, she did very much want to be handed out by Mr. Wright and have a better look at him. Therefore she extended a delicate little gloved hand, felt it taken in a grip which lingered perhaps an instant longer than it needed to, and found herself beside the victorious Slapbang. Minta was already petting and patting away, and Lily ventured one stroke right after her sister's, hoping the horse would think they came from the same person. Then she stepped back and raised her blue eyes to Mr. Wright's hazel ones. "He's a beauty," she told him.

He stared at her with frank admiration. "Coming from you, Miss Ellsworth, that is a compliment indeed."

She lowered her lashes. "Nonsense. I don't know a thing about horses."

"But I'm guessing you know a great deal about beauty."

Minta made a gagging sound and put a hand to her mouth, and Lily whirled on her. "Dear Araminta! I knew you shouldn't have come, when you are so lately recovered from croup."

"What croup?" demanded her sister, as Lily hustled her back into the carriage, slinging the door shut behind her. "Don't worry, Mr. Wright. She is no longer infectious."

"I am glad you were spared her illness then, Miss Ellsworth. Will you be attending the Race Ball at the assembly room?"

"Yes, with my stepmother."

"Then, if I am not premature, may I claim you for two dances? Perhaps the first and...the supper dance?"

Glowing with satisfaction, Lily curtseyed her agreement, the grumbling of the other men in earshot only adding to her pleasure. Mr. Wright then assisted her back into the carriage, this time with an infinitesimally longer press of his hand on her own. He gave one more bow and led Slapbang away, both horse and owner the undisputed conquerors of the day.

Ah, but that was not the last sweet moment, for no sooner were they gone than the other gentlemen complained and clamored, insisting she promise them dances as well, and so good was Lily's mood that she graciously granted them right and left: to flaxen Mr. Caxton, to well-trussed Mr. Trimp, to ancient Sir Basil, and to several others. Even dull Mr. Dailey received his share.

When it was finally over, Tyrone had finished a full chapter of his book, and Minta was groaning with impatience. Mr. Ellsworth distributed some final smiles and waves worthy of King George before ordering the coachman to take them home, and he patted his daughter's knee with a pleased sigh. "I think the true winner of the races today was you, my dear Lily."

Remembering all, all this, Lily in her cushioned church pew could not help but smile again, lifting her shining eyes to the nearest window where an insipid St. Eadburh sang at her father's behest to the crowded banquet. Just as the saint enchanted throngs of Wintonians with her warbling, so would Lily enchant throngs more with her beauty and her dancing. Oh, she could not wait for the Race Ball! Who knew how many more gentlemen would be there to enchant and vanquish? And she would save her sweetest smiles for Mr. Gilbert Wright of Meadowsweep, owner of Slapbang, winner of the King's One Hundred Guineas Plate!

Here, however, another sort of bang roused her from her glorious reverie. Mr. Pennyworth's Book of Common Prayer pitched off the pulpit to land loudly on the stone floor below him. The wandering attention of the congregation returned at once to its shepherd, only to see the curate himself sputter, hand still lifted in emphasis. "'O my father, my father,'" quoth Mr. Pennyworth, "'the chariot of Israel, and the horsemen thereof!'" Then he crumpled to his feet and rolled down the four pulpit steps.

"Good heavens!" breathed Mrs. Ellsworth. "I believe he has fainted. William, you had better see to him."

At his wife's behest, Mr. Ellsworth rose, holding up his hands in his most patriarchal fashion to calm his fellow parishioners, but everyone was too alarmed to pay him any attention, and it was Mr. Harvey the sexton who reached the curate first, taking up the old man's hand to feel for a pulse and then laying his head to the clergyman's chest.

"He's dead! Mr. Pennyworth has died!" he cried, to collective gasping and shrieking and fainting. Anyone who did not faint, or who was not needed to tend to someone who had, then rushed or clambered or scrambled forward to see for himself.

"Make way for Mr. Beckford the doctor," bellowed Mrs. Pease, the wife of one of Hollowgate's tenants. "And give the poor man some air."

Mrs. Pease, having both an imposing person and a loud voice, was instantly obeyed, and Mr. Beckford permitted to come forward without hindrance.

It was no use.

After some minutes in which his every movement and effort and frown was observed and catalogued, Mr. Beckford rose to his feet again and announced, "It is true, I'm afraid. Mr. Pennyworth is no more."

The drama of the moment more than made up for the earlier dullness of the sermon, and that day would be long remembered in the annals of St. Eadburh's.

It was probably the best fate which could have overtaken Mr. Pennyworth's legacy, for his soporific sermons were immediately forgotten, and he was thereafter deemed by one and all a very good sort of parson who was taken from them far too soon.

As St. Eadburh's had only lost its rector Mr. Gregory a few months before, he having removed to the eastern side of Winchester to serve at St. John in the Soke, losing another clergyman so soon felt like a malediction, and soon enough the eyes of the congregation turned to Mrs. Ellsworth. Being the sister of Mr. Gregory, it seemed natural that she assume his authority in this situation.

And despite being a quiet woman of uncertain age who generally attracted little attention, Mrs. William Ellsworth drew herself up on this occasion, a spot of flattering colour appearing on either cheek.

"Have no fear," she said in her clear, warm voice. "I will speak to my brother the rector. A new curate for St. Eadburh's will have to be found."

Chapter Two

He is blown up with Compliments, as a Foot-ball is with Wind, and...like the Leathern Bauble, he deserves soundly to be Kick'd.
— E. Ward, *London Terræfilius* No. 1. 27 (1707)

Enclosed by high walls, the Winchester deanery was a large and handsome stone residence within the cathedral close. Parts of the home dated back to a medieval priory, including the thirteenth-century porch with its pointed arches, a favorite subject for sketchers and painters. Other portions were more recent, such as the brick building fondly called "Nell Gwynn" because Dean Clarke had thrown it up to house Charles II's mistress. That king and Mrs. Gwynn further enjoyed the addition of the long gallery, with its Perpendicular window and promenade leading to the garden. And once out in the grounds, the eye naturally rose to the home's clasped purlin roof and the cathedral behind.

Admired in equal measure to the historic building was the incumbent himself, for Dean Fellowes and his wife had occupied the deanery as long as most residents of Winchester could remember. Being in their seventies, the Felloweses had raised two daughters long before, the elder married to a rector in possession of three prosperous livings and the younger equally successful, having married the squire of the nearby estate Meadowsweep. Both daughters soon produced children of their own, and the dean and his wife now boasted three granddaughters and two grandsons.

The dean's wife Mrs. Fellowes did not believe in playing favorites, but everyone in the family knew nonetheless that her darling grandchild was Simon Kenner, her elder daughter's son, perhaps because he had followed in his father's and grandfather's footsteps and become a clergyman, serving as curate at his father's parish in Eastleigh.

This stubborn preference mystified her other grandson Gilbert Wright, eldest of the Meadowsweep cousins, and he had once taken his mother to task about it: "What is it about Simon that Granny likes so much? He doesn't ride, he doesn't shoot, he doesn't box."

"Nor is he as handsome as you," said his fond mother with some resentment.

"And he's a mere curate!" Wright scoffed. "Uncle John will leave him a generous inheritance, to be sure, but nothing like mine. Nothing like Meadowsweep."

"Not a bit like."

"And he always speaks in that—sly fashion, so one can never tell if he is joking or not."

"A sad flaw in my nephew's character," agreed Mrs. Wright, "but frankness and sweetness of temper like yours are rarely met with, my love."

Wright's sweetness of temper was put to the test, however, the very next time he rode into town after the races, for his cousin Sophie met him at the deanery porch, crying, "Gilbert! What do you think? Mr. Pennyworth has gone and died, and Grandpapa says Simon will have the curacy!"

"I haven't the faintest notion who Mr. Pennyworth is," he grumbled, dismounting and handing the reins to a groom who scurried out, "and Simon already has a curacy." This was exactly it: what was a pitiful curacy in comparison to the King's Plate? Should she not begin with congratulations on Slapbang's triumph?

Truth be told, on the best of days he found Sophie Kenner trying. She was a short, pert little thing with round brown eyes and glossy brown hair and a sprinkling of freckles across her snub nose, and she had loved him since she was six. She was now nineteen and had not grown on him one jot. Especially when he had seen the heavenly Miss Ellsworth the day before. Moreover, where Miss Ellsworth was queenly and alluring and made a man feel like a prince when she so much as glanced at him, Sophie was an eager puppy, always underfoot and yearning for a pat.

"Simon is going to give up Eastleigh," she continued breathlessly, "because St. Eadburh's—Mr. Pennyworth was the curate at St. Eadburh's—is much closer to Winchester and is a little larger, and

Granny says a rising young man like Simon must be closer to the seat of power. The bishop, you know."

'Rising' young man, indeed! Wright slapped his gloves against his thigh. What was the fuss in a country curate going from one curacy to the next? If the bishop ever noticed Simon, it would be because of their grandfather the dean, not because of whichever mouldering little church chose to pay him £50 per annum.

But, being sweet of temper, he only said, "Is the future Right Reverend to be found within today?" When Sophie looked blankly at him, he pulled a face. "Simon. Is Simon here?"

"Oh, yes. He's meeting with Grandpapa and Mr. Gregory, the rector of St. Eadburh's." Taking his arm (which he hadn't offered), she lowered her voice conspiratorially. "Mr. Gregory used to do the duties of St. Eadburh's himself, you know, until Miss Ellsworth of Hollowgate jilted him."

Wright stopped as if he had run into a wall. "Miss Ellsworth? Miss Ellsworth was engaged to the man?"

Delighted to have astonished him, Sophie nodded. "Miss Ellsworth who then married the attorney from Darby and West and became Mrs. Robert Fairchild. All quite shocking because everyone thought she was as respectable as her father was scandalous. And then she turned out to be as changeable as he!"

But he had already relaxed and was in motion again. "Oh, *that* Miss Ellsworth. The *former* Miss Ellsworth."

"Yes, but you mustn't mention any of the Ellsworths, Gil, because Mr. Gregory's sister went off and married old Mr. Ellsworth—became his fourth wife, if you can believe it!—and altogether the Ellsworths are a touchy subject for the rector."

He very much wanted to mention the Ellsworths—or at least he wanted to mention Miss Lily Ellsworth—but he could keep his counsel until the rector was gone. Sophie accompanied him as far as the entrance hall, where she then made an apologetic face and slipped away. She had gone out of doors in the first place to escape such a gathering. And indeed, Wright thought the clergymen in their black frock coats resembled crows come to roost in the deanery parlor. Mr. Gregory at least was a big and burly man who looked like he could hold his own in a boxing ring, but Wright's cousin Simon took after his grandfather the dean: both were fair and lean as rakes, though Wright knew from past experience that Simon's wiry frame belied unexpected agility and strength.

"Gil!" cried Kenner now, rising to thump him between the shoulder blades. "You look a hundred guineas richer than the last time we met."

A typical Simon-ish greeting, somewhere between sincere and mocking. In response, Wright merely gave a grunt.

"Did Sophie tell you?" his cousin went on. "While you and Slapbang were riding roughshod over the world, Providence did throw me a sop. We're going to be nearer neighbors now. Mr. Gregory, allow me to introduce my cousin Mr. Gilbert Wright of Meadowsweep."

"Mr. Kenner has agreed to become my new curate at St. Eadburh's," announced Mr. Gregory, rising to make his bow. His voice was loud, as if he were delivering a sermon in the cathedral and not simply speaking to someone three feet away.

"That's splendid," Wright bellowed in return, to pretend enthusiasm. "When will this take place?"

"As soon as I can hire removers," answered Kenner. "Grandfather already has several young men in mind to replace me at Eastleigh. I was just going to ride over now and have a look at the rectory, if you care to join me. Unfortunately Mr. Gregory can't be spared for the task this afternoon."

The stocky rector shuddered. "No, no. No time. In fact, I had better be on my way. Diocesan business. Dean Fellowes, Mr. Kenner, Mr. Wright." He bowed to each in turn, his massive chest making him look like a rooster bobbing its way across a barnyard.

"I'll go with you, Simon," said Wright with alacrity. "Hollowgate is in St. Eadburh's parish, is it not?"

At the word "Hollowgate," the rector froze—turned crimson—and too late Wright remembered he wasn't supposed to mention the Ellsworths. Well—he hadn't! And if the old parson couldn't stand to hear even anything *related* to the Ellsworths, he'd do better to flee Winchester entirely.

The stocky Mr. Gregory fled the deanery, at any rate, and Dean Fellowes sighed, shaking his head. "Poor, poor man. He still takes it hard, his broken engagement to Mrs. Fairchild."

"And his own sister's defection, I suppose," said Kenner. "You said after she married Ellsworth, he had to hire someone to keep house for him."

"You'll need a housekeeper yourself, Simon," Wright pointed out. "If you'll no longer be living with my aunt and uncle Kenner."

Kenner grinned, clapping Wright's arm. "Brace yourself, Gil. Because Sophie wants to do it. For a little while, at least, to set me on my feet. I think she has visions of me neglecting my new duties to escort her to social events. And she just may have hopes of seeing more of you."

His cousin grimaced. "I neither know nor care what Sophie expects of me, for I have other plans."

"Have you, Gilbert?" asked his grandfather. "More horse racing?"

There was not the least note of disapprobation in the dean's voice, but the spot was already sore, and Wright replied curtly, "As a matter of fact, sir, I received a generous offer for Slapbang after he won the Plate."

"Good for you," said the old man, giving his forearm a squeeze. "But I wouldn't be too quick to part with good horseflesh like that. You have a chance to make Meadowsweep a center in the racing world."

"I hope so, sir," Wright said, mollified. He couldn't resist a sidewise glance at his cousin. "After the race I did receive many congratulations and met some prominent people in the county, including—er—Mr. William Ellsworth of Hollowgate and—some of his children. That's why I mentioned the place."

Dean Fellowes gave a slow nod. "As a matter of fact, Simon and I were discussing the Ellsworths before Gregory came. If Simon is to take St. Eadburh's, he had better become familiar with the more prominent members of his congregation. The man and his family have an interesting history, as you might be aware. Not only in relation to poor Gregory. The current Mrs. Ellsworth—Gregory's sister—is the fourth to hold that post, and she is stepmother to Ellsworth's five children by three previous wives."

"That's a precious lot of wives. Though Ellsworth seemed harmless enough," muttered Wright, frowning.

"And so I believe he is, as long as whomever he is married to manages to remain above ground." The dean clicked his tongue regretfully. "He's had some bad luck there, to be bereaved three times. But he was faithful to the living. Ellsworth's amours have ever been in sequence, rather than in parallel."

A little silence fell, and then Wright began again, unwillingly. "And certainly the father's...activities cannot be held against the children." But then he remembered how the eldest Miss Ellsworth had jilted the rector, and his countenance flushed.

The dean raised a thoughtful brow. "My dear Gilbert, you are very solicitous for these new acquaintances of yours. If it is not the old widower who has captured your attention, I daresay it is his beautiful daughter, Miss Lily Ellsworth."

Wright swallowed, wanting to whack his cousin when he saw him grin. "Sir," he said.

"Ah," Kenner drawled, "hence your eagerness to accompany me to the rectory. I was surprised, I confess, that my domestic arrangements held such allure for you. Allure for Sophie, yes. You, no."

But Wright had changed his mind. The temptation to explore the neighborhood of the fascinating Miss Ellsworth was strong, but there was no guarantee he would see the young lady herself—why would she be standing outside Hollowgate beside the road, after all? Not to mention, a whole afternoon of Simon's superiority, paired with Sophie's adoration, would be insupportable. No, no. He would just have to see Miss Ellsworth at the ball in a few days.

"On second thought," said Wright, "think I'll go for a ride instead. Fine day for a good, hard ride. And I'll see about having a plaque made up to hang outside Slapbang's stall."

Kenner shrugged. "Just so. Sophie and I will be off, then, but I suspect we will see plenty of each other in the coming days, sweet my coz."

"Suppose so," said Wright. He wanted to say something to the effect that Simon had better not get any ideas about making up to Miss Ellsworth himself, but such an admonition was just as likely to make Simon do it, so he grudgingly kept his mouth shut. But he was glad when his grandfather brought the matter up himself.

"You and Gilbert are of the age and the means to think of taking wives," sighed the dean, remembering them as playful boys careering on the deanery lawn and darting about the close. "You especially, Simon. It is fitting for a man in ministry to have a helpmeet."

Kenner grinned. "Not you, too, Grandfather. Granny has given me a version of this speech every year since I took orders and has trotted every possible lady before me as a candidate."

"More to the point," Dean Fellowes continued, ignoring his raillery, "an unmarried curate is a worry to any parish. You were not troubled by this at Eastleigh because the congregation was so elderly, but at St. Eadburh's..."

"At St. Eadburh's I must marry or be viewed as a fox among the hens?"

"Nonsense. I know you are no predator, Simon, but your singleness will be a distraction. You are a good-looking lad, and I would not be surprised if you cause some heartaches."

Kenner grinned even harder to see how his grandfather's remark drew an exasperated muttering from his cousin. "Sir, what would you advise then, if I wish to choose a bride? Would it be better to plunge in at once, snatching up the first young lady who catches my eye, or would it make my flock easier if I left it entirely to them and married whomever they nominated?"

"Dear boy, I am in earnest."

"Pardon me, then, sir," apologized his grandson, his mouth twisting ruefully. "But I hope you understand it is a highly private matter. I would please you and Granny and the good folk of St. Eadburh's if I could, but I can hardly be expected to marry on command or be glad to have it discussed widely."

This drew a fond pat. "All right, all right. Well said, young man, and true enough."

Each grandson clasped his hand in turn, and then the three parted ways.

Chapter Three

Gather ye rosebuds while ye may,
Old Time is still a-flying;
And this same flower that smiles today
Tomorrow will be dying.
— Robert Herrick, "To the Virgins, to Make Much of Time" (1648)

For pity's sake, hold that basket straight, Bea," urged Lily. "If the flowers slide out they'll be spoiled."

"But I'm afraid someone will catch us, Lily," her youngest sister whispered, straightening the basket nevertheless. "Catch us cutting Mr. Pennyworth's flowers."

"They aren't Mr. Pennyworth's flowers any longer," Lily reasoned. "Mr. Pennyworth is dead. If they're anyone's flowers, they're Miss Greg—Mama's, rather, because she planted them when she lived here. And Papa's, in a fashion, because Hollowgate accounts for a generous portion of Mr. Gregory's tithes."

"But I wish we would cut flowers from Florence's garden," persisted Beatrice. "She has so many of them."

"So she does, but Flossie planted *her* favorite flowers, and, as it is our stepmother's birthday, I think she would prefer a bouquet of *her* favorite flowers. Besides, if we don't cut some of these heavy cabbage roses, the plants might fall over! Mm...and these damask roses smell heavenly! I want some for my room. Don't you? I'm going to cut them all, I think. If I don't, they'll just be wasted, you know. What is that poem about 'full many a flower...'?"

But Beatrice had no interest in poetry, and Lily gave up trying to wheedle her into tranquility. Honestly—if she could take a whisker of Araminta's recklessness and stuff it into Beatrice, nobody would lose by it.

"The basket is getting heavy," ventured Beatrice, several minutes onward. "And it's terribly hot out. Isn't your head beginning to ache, Lily?"

Knowing how easily the seven-year-old could dissolve in tears, Lily suppressed a snappish retort and straightened. "Very well, very well, my tender little poppet. We'll return home and see if Wilcomb has any lemonade for you. Here—give me the basket and I'll carry it."

Looping it over her arm, she took Beatrice by the hand to lead her around to the rectory gate—only to halt with a little scream. Beatrice screamed in sympathy. Down bounced the basket, spilling its precious contents over the garden gravel.

The gentleman leaning against the corner of the house watched the proceedings calmly. He was lean as a rake, the black of his clergyman's frock coat accentuating both his length and the fairness of his colouring. His pale eyes, somewhere between grey and blue, flicked to each Ellsworth sister in turn, down to the scattering of roses across the path, and then back to Lily's face. Lily's blushing face. She was always a rosy girl, but now she was positively scarlet.

"Did you not want the flowers after all?" he asked mildly, before Lily could decide whether defiance, groveling, or flirtation would serve her best.

She lifted her chin, opting for brisk self-assurance. "I do, as a matter of fact. Thank you." With a nod at her sister, the two of them bent to gather their booty.

The next thing they knew, the young man was stooping beside them, the hem of his coat dragging in the dust. "Careful of the thorns," he murmured. "Though some might consider a prick or two simply...poetic justice for denuding my rosebushes."

"*Your* rosebushes?" echoed Lily over Beatrice's gasp.

"Just so."

The three of them stood. And though Lily found the top of her bonnet reached no farther than his nose, she could not let herself be cowed. Clearly, audacity must carry her through a *faux pas* of this magnitude. "Thank you for your assistance, sir. I was not aware someone had filled the place of curate of St. Eadburh's."

"I've not yet been read in, to be sure," he replied. "Nor taken up residence in the rectory."

"I see. Well, then. In that case, the rosebushes I have 'denuded' still belong to my stepmother's brother." Lily did not dare glance at Beatrice, who was pressed against her, because she could already feel her little body trembling and just *knew* Bea would crumble, given any encouragement.

"Then your stepmother must be Mrs. Ellsworth, *née* Miss Gregory, sister to Mr. Clifford Gregory."

"She is."

"And that would make you *Miss* Ellsworth." With a nod in Beatrice's direction, he added, "Accompanied by a younger sister."

"Yes. This is Miss Beatrice." Lily hoped the man wouldn't address Bea directly because the girl's trembling was reaching violent proportions, threatening to vibrate the roses right out of the basket again. If that happened, Lily thought, she would abandon them. They would go home and raid Flossie's garden, as Beatrice had preferred all along.

The man gave an exaggerated bow. "What a pleasure to make your acquaintance," he said, a note in his voice Lily suspected was suppressed laughter.

Therefore she curtsied in return (also a touch too precisely), but the effect was ruined when Beatrice tried to imitate her, only to collapse on her unsteady legs. With little enough ceremony and a grimace of impatience which she hoped her bonnet brim hid, Lily hauled her sister to her feet. "Poor, tired Bea," she said brightly. "It's hot out, and it's rather knocked her up."

"Kn-knocked me up," gasped Beatrice.

The gentleman turned to her, his expression softening. "I'm sorry to hear it, Miss Beatrice. If I had a stick of furniture or a thimble of currant juice within, you would be welcome to them. But alas."

In return the little girl gave him a timid smile.

Then his gaze returned to Lily, and the mocking gleam reappeared. "Sofa and drink have I none, but such as I have I give thee—oh—I mean—such as I have you have already helped yourself to. But please do tell Mrs. Ellsworth that, if she would like any more of the rectory flowers in the future, she need not be afraid to ask, despite my coming. I suppose she feels proprietary toward them, after so many years."

"Hmm," was the indeterminate sound Lily made in response.

"Indeed," he continued blithely. "I am relieved to hear you had her permission to take every last rose from the garden. It sheds a different light altogether, you understand, than if you had decided on your own to cut them all. Because that—well—some might view *that* as...stealing."

Her face flamed again, and there was a mutinous flash in her blue eyes before she lowered them. But when she spoke, her voice was deceptively sweet. "Ah. Too right. Spoken like a true clergyman. And one not even installed yet! Which makes them *not* your flowers—yet—as I mentioned. And hence, not your concern."

"No, I did catch that, Miss Ellsworth. You explained that you consider them your—ahem—how exactly would one describe the relation? You consider the flowers still the property of your...step-uncle...would it be?"

She was unable to repress a shudder at the thought of calling Mr. Gregory her "step-uncle"—the man who had very nearly been her brother-in-law—but tried to pass it off by twitching a leaf from her skirts. "Possibly. Possibly."

"In any event," he went on serenely, "How glad I am it *wasn't* stealing. And that nothing happened here today to endanger the good opinion I hope to enjoy of all my flock."

But Lily would have none of this condescension, even if she suspected he was trying to rile her. "I share your gladness," she replied. "For different reasons. Because, while St. Eadburh's remains officially *between* curates, and I am not yet required to court anyone's good opinion, we Ellsworths like to remain on pleasant terms with the subordinates of our near connections the Gregorys."

Beatrice made a croaking sound, pinching Lily's hand between the folds of her skirt.

Before Lily could pinch her back, one of the rectory windows flew up, and a young lady with brown hair and a snub nose poked her head out. "It's so dreadfully stifling in here, Simon, and the paper and paint so old-fashioned! Oh! We have visitors. Already. Shall I come out?"

"We won't trouble you," Lily put in quickly, seizing on the opportunity the interruption afforded. Tugging on Bea's hand, she began to retreat. "Another time, perhaps."

"When I'm 'official'?" asked the curate dryly.

But Lily pretended not to hear. "Good afternoon," she said to his left shoulder. And then, hitching the rose basket to the side farther from the window, she called back to the young lady: "Good afternoon."

By the time Miss Kenner found a means of egress to the garden, the visitors were gone. "Oh," she drooped in disappointment. "I would have liked to meet that girl. She was very, very pretty. Did she say what her name was, Simon?"

"She admitted to being Miss Ellsworth of Hollowgate."

Sophie frowned at her brother. "What do you mean, 'admitted'? Oh, Simon, I hope you weren't strange and off-putting. Especially if she will be one of your parishioners."

"'Strange and off-putting'? I should hope not. Whatever would make you say such a thing?"

"Because Gilbert sometimes calls you an eccentric quiz, and I would hate for you to give such an impression to others."

At this, her brother looked thoughtful, remembering his cousin's interest in Hollowgate and its denizens. He could see how a person of Miss Ellsworth's attractions had turned Gil's head, but Kenner could hardly imagine Gilbert Wright matching wits with the young lady.

No—if Gil were so fortunate as to "win" the lovely Miss Ellsworth, she would lead him a merry dance.

In looking about her, Sophie soon forgot her anxiety for her brother. Her little frown deepened. "Why—it isn't much of a garden, is it? Those rosebushes look healthy enough, and yet they haven't managed to produce a single blossom!"

To her surprise, he chuckled. "They did their best, Sophie. But I fear they were overmatched."

Chapter Four

The customs of England do not exclude the clergyman from any species of amusement; the popular preacher is to be seen at the theatre, and at the horse-race, bearing his part at the concert and the ball.

— Robert Southey, *Letters from England by Don Manuel Alvarez Espriella* (1807)

The assembly room at St. John's House in the Causeway was spacious and splendid, glowing in candlelight, its dark rose walls ornamented with elegant plasterwork, the white stucco medallions and garlands seeming extensions of the lace hairbands and embroidery of the women's gowns. Lely's full-length portrait of Charles II stared down upon the attenders, quite casting in the shade other, smaller pictures of past benefactors. And in this glorious setting, tucked in one of the window alcoves beneath the likeness of the Earl of Wiltshire, Lily and her stepmother admired it all.

"At last," breathed Lily. "It's like a dream!"

Lily and her older sister Florence had planned on attending the Race Ball and other festivities the previous years, only to be prevented first by the poor health of their last stepmother and secondly by the woman's death, which plunged the Ellsworths into mourning. Or, at least, into mourning clothes.

Now, a year after the demise of the third Mrs. Ellsworth, Florence was married, but Lily had arrived at last, the fourth Mrs. Ellsworth by her side.

"I'm so delighted to have you with me, Miss Greg—I mean, Mama," she said, pressing her stepmother's hand.

"I don't suppose I'll be with you for much of the evening," returned Mrs. Ellsworth with her gentle smile. "Considering all the gentlemen who asked in advance to partner you and those whom you will meet tonight, I may not have you by my side ten minutes together!"

"It's too bad Papa doesn't like this sort of thing, so he could keep you company."

"Never mind me, Lily. I see the dean's wife Mrs. Fellowes across the way, and I would be happy to sit with her while you're dancing. But first I think we will be swamped with introductions."

She was not wrong. It was a repeat of the scene at the racecourse, only this time those hoping to meet her stepdaughter traded on their clerical connections. Mrs. Ellsworth being the sister and daughter and granddaughter of Winchester clergymen, any young man seeking to meet Miss Lily Ellsworth had only to seize the nearest cleric of his acquaintance to effect an introduction.

"Dear me," murmured Mrs. Ellsworth as she saw them approach. "Who knew so many clergymen attended the Race Ball? I believe we are in danger of being trampled by every last unmarried rector, vicar, curate, prebendary, chaplain, and precentor in the diocese."

Perhaps. But there was one who kept his distance.

Lily spied the lanky new curate of St. Eadburh's almost upon entering the room, even though he wore a black tailcoat with buff breeches and white-gold waistcoat on this occasion. "Not the least bit clerical," she muttered. "If I had not recognized him, I might have tried to catch him in my net."

She knew enough about him now, however, to know *that* would not do at all. When Beatrice told their stepmother all about the encounter in the rectory garden, Mrs. Ellsworth promptly dispatched a note to her brother Mr. Gregory. "His name is Mr. Simon Kenner," Mrs. Ellsworth reported, after reading the rector's response. "And he is a grandson of Dean Fellowes and a cousin of the Mr. Wright whom you met at the races. And the young woman you saw was *not* his wife, but rather his sister Miss Sophie Kenner, who comes to keep house for him."

Lily shrugged upon receiving this information. Married or unmarried, she had no particular interest in clergymen as suitors (only see how that had turned out for her sister Florence!), even if Mr. Kenner had not first repelled her with his superior attitude.

Clergymen must serve as dance partners, however, and she turned from the sight of Mr. Kenner to favor the approaching gentlemen with her brightest look. Nor was she saddened to learn they weren't *all* clergymen. Everyone paid respectful attention to Mrs. Ellsworth, some even asking after her brother Mr. Gregory, but all the while they stole glances at dark-haired Lily, admiring her rosy colour and pleasing shape, shown to advantage in blue silk embroidered with silver. A matching silver ribbon wound through her intricate curls, all the product of an iron, since her hair was naturally straight.

"Mr. Frayne. Mr. Gosworth. Mr. Willett." With each introduction, Lily curtseyed and gave a demure smile, and Mrs. Ellsworth later told her husband, "With some of them I could almost *hear* them—thump!—fall right over in love with her."

The men ranged in age from older than Sir Basil to as young as Lily herself. Tall ones, short ones, stocky ones, bony ones, hairy ones, bald ones, rich ones, poor ones. Ones with beautiful manners and ones with leers. Ones with titles and youngest sons of nobodies. Well-tailored ones and threadbare ones. Attractive ones and ones with—unfortunate disadvantages.

"How did you enjoy the races, Miss Ellsworth?"

"I loved them. I wish I could watch horses race every day."

"Is this your first time at St. John's House?"

"Yes, but I hope it will not be my last. It's perfectly beautiful here."

"Would you honor me with the first dance, Miss Ellsworth?"

"Oh, I'm terribly sorry, but I have promised it to Mr. Wright." (She had to say this several times, being asked more than once.)

Even the appearance of Mr. Dailey could not dampen her mood, though when he heard Lily agree with Mr. Frayne that, yes, the portrait of Charles II was very fine, he had to tell them all there was to know of the picture's history and provenance. How it came to be there, the monarch bestowing it in acceptance of the freedom of the city in 1682, etc. etc. Nor did Mr. Dailey neglect to mention who painted it, who accepted it on the city's behalf, and what precisely was meant by the "freedom of the city."

"Mr. Wright!" cried Lily in great relief, upon the approach of that gentleman. She gave a low curtsey in response to his bow. "I thought you forgot your promise to dance with me."

"Never." He was thinking she was even lovelier than he remembered, and he gloried in the scowls the rest of her admirers threw him as he led her away. "If I had somehow forgotten, your dress would have reminded me."

"Indeed? How so?"

"You're wearing the Meadowsweep colors: blue and silver. Like Slapbang's silks."

Lily clicked her tongue and gave him a coy look. "Dear me—I hope you won't think it was on purpose."

It had been, of course, not that she would own it. It was too bad the prize horse wasn't there in the flesh because Lily was thinking with her usual clarity that Mr. Wright was less magnificent than she recalled, without the radiance lent by Slapbang—if only he could carry the triumphant beast everywhere with him! But he was well enough and better-looking than every other gentleman present save Mr. Dailey. Mr. Wright's fine tailoring showed to advantage in a ballroom, and she suspected the application of pomade, for his middling brown hair now gleamed in the candlelight. Likely he would grow as bald as her father and her uncle Charles, but, as she studied the shape of his head, she concluded that the consequences would not be so dire for Mr. Wright as for her father.

They took their place in the set, and she glanced up and down the lines, calculating that the dance was sure to last twenty minutes, given the number of couples. Her sister Florence had once chided Lily that standing up for two dances with a gentleman was no way to determine if the man would make a compatible husband, and while Lily agreed in principle, she thought it provided useful data nonetheless.

For example, she learned that Mr. Wright expected her to begin the conversation, or else was at a loss to begin it himself. She cast about in her mind, thinking again that it was too bad winning racehorses were not considered acceptable ballroom accoutrements, before deciding they could *talk* about Slapbang, in any case.

"What does a racehorse do, Mr. Wright, when it is not racing?"

"Train for the next race, naturally. Eat, sleep, train, and race. That pretty much sums up Slapbang's life."

"I see. I hope he likes it, then." She thought about asking for further details on how a horse trained but then decided she didn't care. "Will you enter him in other races this season?"

"Yes, several. This will be a busy, busy season. Stockbridge, Fareham, Salisbury. Then on to Canterbury, Sussex and Lichfield, if he holds up."

"How exciting! Suppose Slapbang should win them all! You would be rich as Croesus by the autumn."

"That doesn't happen very often, Miss Ellsworth, one horse winning them all. But I hope he will continue to do me credit."

He took her hand for the promenade, and Lily gave a shiver of pleasure. Not for the contact between them but because she saw people observing them and whispering to each other. She had expected to delight in the attention of the gentlemen, but now she discovered she equally enjoyed the wistfulness of the young ladies. Why—they envied her her partner! It invested Mr. Wright with more fascination in Lily's eyes, and she favored him with a brilliant smile. Perhaps she would ask about the horse-training after all.

Nor was Gilbert Wright indifferent to the pleasure of provoking jealousy. The family's fuss over his cousin's new curacy and their relative unconcern for the conquering Slapbang had injured his complacency, but in the sunshine of Miss Ellsworth's attention this offense was forgotten, and his cup once more brimmed full. Only see how she smiled at him, the beautiful creature!

As nonchalantly as he could manage, Wright's gaze drifted to where his cousin Simon stood beside their grandmother Mrs. Fellowes. Kenner wasn't looking, but Wright had the undeniable feeling that he *had been* looking, just an instant earlier. Oh, hurrah! *Victoria!* And why shouldn't Simon look? For Gilbert was dancing with the prettiest girl present, while Simon was trapped making conversation with a seventy-year-old woman.

Mr. Wright returned Lily's brilliant smile.

When they reached the bottom of the set, they had to wait for one iteration of the pattern before they joined again. Lily cocked her head and regarded him.

"Mr. Wright, don't look now, but someone is staring at you. Someone behind you."

He grinned. "Is it a blond someone, rail-thin, black coat, talking to an old woman?"

Her blue eyes widened. "Can you mean your cousin Mr. Kenner? Does he often stare at you in assembly rooms? No, indeed, sir. This is a *female* someone: brown hair and rather adorable. And perhaps ador*ing*."

"Oh." He shrugged. "I suspect it's my cousin Sophie."

Ah-ha, thought Lily. *That* was why she looked familiar. It was the young lady who called out of the window at the rectory. Very interesting. So she admired her cousin Gilbert Wright, did she? Well, she couldn't have him! That is, not unless Lily decided she didn't want him, and that wasn't likely. At present Gilbert Wright pleased her very much indeed.

Despite warning Mr. Wright against peeking at his admirer, Lily stole another glance and found the girl still looking at them.

No, this Miss Kenner could not have Mr. Wright, but perhaps she would not be too resentful about it because it did not sound from his tone that Mr. Wright had ever given her any encouragement. Lily could not then be blamed for winning him, if Miss Kenner were inclined to be reasonable about it. And Lily thought it would be nice to have a new friend nearby—with Florence off and married. Lily's stepmother was agreeable enough, but girls rarely considered stepmothers in the category of *friends*; nor could Lily imagine her harum-scarum younger sister Araminta supplying Florence's place. But Miss Kenner might do very well indeed.

"Perhaps you might introduce me later?" she asked Mr. Wright. "If Miss Kenner is your cousin, then she will soon be my neighbor."

His brow darkened, but he was spared answering right away as they entered the figures again. He did not know if he liked the idea of Miss Ellsworth and Sophie getting acquainted. Suppose they liked each other, and Miss Ellsworth was then frequently at the rectory? Simon might begin to get ideas about her. Miss Ellsworth was a catch, after all, and Simon, for all his failings, was not stupid. Moreover, their grandfather's repeated advice might stir action. But though he racked his brain, Wright did not know how an acquaintance could be escaped. He could hardly ask a girl to avoid the company of her new parish priest!

He chose the next best alternative when the dance brought them together. "I can introduce you. But Sophie isn't like you, Miss Ellsworth."

"No? How is she *un*like, sir?"

"She's not clever or elegant or—or subtle like you." *Nor half as good-looking*, he added in his head.

"Not clever or elegant or subtle?" she smiled. "You mean to say, then, that Miss Kenner is—let me see—dim and...uncouth and...simple?"

He stared, wondering, and Lily had to stifle a laugh. But she couldn't resist rallying him further. "But Mr. Wright, perhaps I like to befriend such persons. That I might shine in comparison."

"Well, you don't need Sophie's help to do that."

"What lovely compliments you pay, Mr. Wright. Still, I will cling to my strategy. It never hurts to surround myself with nincompoops."

He did not answer for a moment because the dance required some tricky hops, but when they were got through and they took hands again, Wright said decisively, "I will introduce you, then."

Then Lily did laugh. "For shame! That is not very gallant of you, sir, to let me apply such disgraceful terms to your cousin."

"There you wrong me," he protested, still confused but glad to see her laugh. "I only wanted to avoid contradicting a lady."

"Very well, then," Lily answered solemnly. "I understand. I will withdraw my criticism of you, in that case. But then I insist: if Miss Kenner is not the hopeless lump you led me to believe she was, I would certainly like to meet her."

Lily would have got her way all the same because, when the dance ended and Mr. Wright returned her to her stepmother's side, Mrs. Ellsworth was speaking to the dean's wife while both Miss Kenner and Mr. Kenner stood by.

"Miss Ellsworth," said Mrs. Fellowes, not in the warmest tone. She had once been fond of Lily's sister Florence, before Florence jilted Mr. Gregory, but she had never been especially enamored of Lily. Lily's stepmother, too, had plummeted in Mrs. Fellowes' estimation, having left her brother's house to marry William Ellsworth. Poor Mr. Gregory! was Mrs. Fellowes opinion. Such a double abandonment was striking a man when he was down.

"Mrs. Fellowes," chirped Lily.

"Miss Ellsworth," began Mr. Wright, "may I present to you my cousins, Mr. and Miss Kenner? Simon, Sophie, this is Miss Ellsworth."

"I so wanted to meet you, Miss Ellsworth, when you and your little sister were in the rectory garden," Miss Kenner began eagerly. "It was your little sister, was it not?"

"Yes. Beatrice."

"Do you often walk there? I mean, in the rectory garden? If you do, we hope you will continue your habit even after we have come. We wouldn't mind at all, would we Simon?"

He merely bowed, but Lily was quick to say, "It isn't a habit. We wouldn't think of invading your privacy and would not have come even on that day, had we known we would disturb you there."

Miss Kenner's face fell a little. "But that is just what I mean to say! It would not be a disturbance. I hope you will come all the time, Miss Ellsworth."

Politeness dictated that Mr. Kenner second this opinion, whether he agreed with it or not, but he said nothing. Instead, he merely regarded Lily with the same composure he showed when he caught her stripping his rosebushes bare, and Lily thought it would serve him right if she replied, *If it were only a matter of invading* your *privacy, Miss Kenner, I would not stand on ceremony...*

As if she had spoken the words aloud, the very corner of his mouth twitched. Then he said easily, "What a pleasure to watch you dancing with my cousin, Miss Ellsworth. What was the name of that particular one...All in a Garden Green? Or was it Under the Rose?"

Lily gave him a hard look, but his face was all innocence. It was his sister who rapped him with her fan. "Simon, you goose. It wasn't either one, which you would know, if you danced more."

"Do you like to dance, Miss Kenner?" Lily asked her, deciding to ignore the provoking brother. If it would not have required turning her back on the entire party, she would have shown him her shoulder, as she did Mr. Dailey when he displeased her.

"I do! I love to dance." Miss Kenner ventured a peep at her cousin Mr. Wright, whereupon he took a sudden interest in his sleeve cuff. None of this was lost on Lily, and whether or not she intended to keep Mr. Wright for herself, she thought it discourteous of him not to ask his cousin.

"Here comes Mr. Frayne for you, Lily," said her stepmother.

"Dancing with Frayne, are you?" It was Mr. Wright's turn to scowl. But it had its good effect, for he turned curtly to his cousin and said, "What do you say, Sophie? Take a turn with me?"

"Oh, yes, please!"

Thus it was that both young couples sallied forth again, with varying degrees of satisfaction.

Mr. Frayne yielded to Mr. Caxton, who yielded in his turn to Mr. Willett, who gave way to the tightly-trussed Mr. Trimp, who then bowed Lily to the ancient (in Lily's eyes) Sir Basil, before she had time to think. But what she thought then was, if so many Winchester clergyman were inclined to dance, and if so many Winchester gentlemen of *all* sorts were eager to dance with *her,* specifically, was it or was it not discourteous of the odious Mr. Kenner, that he did not attempt to join their number?

It should not have bothered her—the evening being such an unqualified triumph—but it did. Niggle at her. The only balm to her offended vanity was that nor did he attempt to dance with anyone else.

But she wondered all the same.

Chapter Five

That he did in the general bosom reign
Of young, of old; and sexes both enchanted,
To dwell with him in thoughts, or to remain
In personal duty, following where he haunted.
— Shakespeare, "A Lover's Complaint" (c.1609)

The reading in of a new clergyman was a day marked in red letters on the calendar of any parish church, and Mr. Simon Kenner's ceremony at St. Eadburh's was no different. Not only was the congregation present in unusual entirety, but it was joined by the rector Mr. Gregory and a number of Mr. Kenner's distinguished family members, including the dean and his wife.

Lily's feelings that morning were a mixture of anticipation and dread. Some days earlier, her stepmother had said to Mr. Ellsworth after dinner, "My dear, you know my brother's new curate is to be read in this Sunday."

"Yes, my love, I am aware," her husband smiled upon her. "What a good thing for Mr. Gregory, after the sad and premature loss of Mr. Pennyworth."

"Indeed," agreed Mrs. Ellsworth. "And what would you say, William, to a little celebratory luncheon afterward? Just some cold sandwiches and tea and such. We had Mr. Pennyworth on the same occasion, if you recall, though poor Mr. Pennyworth had no additional friends and relations to be hosted."

"Certainly, certainly," he answered beneficently. "As the foremost family of the parish, we must be expected to welcome the new curate and whoever pertains to him."

The younger Ellsworths had each their own response to the proposed invitation: Lily continued to sew but wondered if Mr. Wright would come to his cousin's installation (though he had not mentioned it at the Race Ball); Araminta groaned aloud and went so far as to ask to be excused, a request which was denied; her twin Tyrone wisely understood that then neither would he be excused and returned his attention to his book; and Beatrice, who was sitting beside the family terrier Snap on his ugly embroidered cushion, tugged the dog onto her lap and said, "Poor Snappy! He will have to be locked up in Minta's room the whole time, for he is certain to dislike at least one of the visitors."

On Sunday Lily dressed with particular care, choosing a blue gown that matched her eyes and a chip bonnet trimmed with silk cornflowers. Her appearance caused Minta to raise an eyebrow. "My word. Setting your cap for the new curate, are you?"

"Not at all. Whatever would I want with a curate? But you never know who else might be there. And for heaven's sake, Minta, how are you already all awry? You look like you were dressed in the dark by a blind person."

Her younger sister shrugged. "If I were dressed by a blind person, it wouldn't matter if the room was dark, would it? But you can't blame me—I had to lock Snap up, and to lock him up I had to catch him, and to catch him I had to chase him the whole length of the gallery because he was in a mischievous mood, and he wedged himself behind the plinth of the bust of Great-Great-Great Grandpapa."

By the time the Ellsworths entered the church, however, everyone was trim and tidy, Mr. Ellsworth with his wife on his arm, trailed by his assorted offspring. They filled their pew nicely, though Beatrice especially wished Florence were still with them. Her other siblings were not willing to cuddle with her, and Beatrice was too shy as yet to burrow against her stepmother's side. Lily had succeeded to Florence's place at the end of the pew, and from there she was able to look about discreetly.

To her disappointment, she did not see Mr. Wright, though any number of Mr. Kenner's presumed family members occupied the pew normally designated for the forever-absent Whisp family. There was the dean and Mrs. Fellowes. There was Miss Kenner. There was some other man and his wife with them, who Lily guessed were Mr. Kenner's parents.

Well, drat, she thought. *I should have asked Mr. Wright point blank if he intended on coming.* Somehow, at the supper dance of the Race Ball, they had ended in talking about Slapbang again, and Mr. Wright had said he would take the horse next to the Stockbridge races. Perhaps he was still there? Though surely there was no horse-racing on a Sunday. She could not help being miffed—how taken with her could Mr. Wright have possibly been, if he had let so many days go by without calling or sending any word?

A general shuffling of feet and clearing of throats followed, and then the long, lean figure of Mr. Kenner rose from the bench on the chancel.

In a black frock coat and surplice like that, the man ought *to look like a bat in an apron*, Lily complained to herself. *Mr. Pennyworth always did. And Mr. Gregory would have as well, except he was so burly and enormous.*

But for whatever disobliging reason, Mr. Simon Kenner did not look a thing like a bat in an apron. To Lily's dismay, he looked...impressive. With his height and his fair, curling hair and his solemnity and his long hands which held a leathern portfolio.

A murmur broke out in the congregation, and Lily caught the churchwarden's wife Mrs. Pittman saying, "Why, he's a handsome one! Not in the ordinary sense, mind you, but there's something—something—*commanding* about him. Masterly, even."

And there was. Lily did not know why. She supposed he could not be older than his middle or later twenties, and she knew this curacy was a more prestigious one than his last, both because of its proximity to the cathedral and because important men like her father were present, yet Mr. Kenner did not look daunted. True, his colour was higher than when she met him in the rectory garden and again at the Race Ball, but otherwise she would have thought him hardly aware of how every eye was fixed upon him.

Utter silence fell when he stood at the reading desk and opened his portfolio.

Never had the Thirty-Nine Articles held everyone so spellbound.

In a clear tenor voice that carried without strain, he read. And he read very, very well. To her astonishment, Lily felt a lump grow in her throat when he came to the bit about "one Christ, very God, and very Man; who truly suffered, was crucified, dead, and buried, to reconcile his Father to us, and to be a sacrifice," and she was not the only one, for she heard a sniffle or two behind her.

"He ought to be on the stage!" muttered someone, only to be hushed.

And—mercy!—when Mr. Kenner reached "the lust of the flesh, called in Greek, φρονημα σαρκος, (which some do expound the wisdom, some sensuality, some the affection, some the desire, of the flesh)," a whirlwind of fan-fluttering broke out, and Lily felt her own face heat. She lowered her gaze. Not that he was looking at her. He was not looking at her. And yet she felt *seen*.

Heavens. She had cut all this man's roses and spoken to him impertinently? What was it about him that so struck her today? Was it, she wondered, that he was like a stage player? One man when he stood before the church, robed in his official vestments, and another when he went about the rest of his life? Frowning, she gave a little shake of her head. No, that was not it. That implied hypocrisy, as if Mr. Kenner had something to hide, and she did not suspect him of smiling and smiling in the pulpit—not that he did smile—while being a villain elsewhere. It was that in this setting, the authority in which his position clothed him lent him a fascination, a gravity Lily could not help but respond to.

Though no sooner did she admit as much, than she rebelled against it. How insufferable such a man would be, to have on hand all the time! Lily was not of a naturally worshipful nature and admired few people beyond her sister Florence and perhaps her aunt Jeanne—and even they came in for their share of criticism from her—so to be presented with one who seemed to command respect, if not a little awe...Lily did not like it one particle. And how highly he must think of himself, to be able to preach sermons without blushing, to people he did not even know, many of whom were a great deal older and more experienced in life. Why, she should stand up herself and treat him to a sermon on humility!

Caught by the notion, she set at once to compose her imaginary work in her head, disregarding the actual sermon Mr. Kenner began to deliver after he made his Declaration of Assent.

She would take as her text the passage in the gospel (Lily didn't remember precisely where it was found), where the self-satisfied guest came to the luncheon or supper or party or whatever it was and chose the best seat, only to have the host approach (Lily pictured him bearded, sheepish and apologetic, yet gleeful) to tell Mr. Smug he had to sit lower down because a worthier guest had arrived. Ah! Such a crushing blow to the self-satisfied guest, who, in his lanky, fair, surplice-draped person bore a suspicious resemblance to Mr.

Kenner. The mortified guest crept lower, as he was bidden, and did not dare open his mouth again for the remainder of the meal, not that anyone noticed because no one was speaking to him anyway. In utter disgrace, he gnashed his teeth when he saw the host then bid a humbler guest (in blue, with a chip bonnet ornamented by silk cornflowers) to come higher, please! She must not efface herself thus, the host insisted. Not when she was the guest of honor, and all were anxious to pay her tribute.

Lily gave a delighted sigh, a smile spreading across her face, much to the puzzlement of Mr. Kenner, who was at that very moment speaking of the Israelites in mourning by the rivers of Babylon. In his surprise, there was a hitch in his delivery. Did he have something stuck between his teeth, that she should smile? Or had he by chance said something inappropriate? But no—a quick survey of the rest of the congregation showed them all still solemn and attentive.

He swallowed, annoyed, but then forged ahead, wholly unaware that his auditors liked him the better for his stumble because it made him more sympathetic. Thus they favored him with attention never given in the past to Mr. Pennyworth and only to the first five or ten minutes of Mr. Gregory's homilies.

"That went as well as it might possibly have gone," Dean Fellowes declared, when the congregants had finally all been dismissed, after having been introduced, greeted, and their good wishes received. Kenner thought he would never remember all the names, though the flock was only a few heads larger than the one he had shepherded at Eastleigh. Only the Ellsworths seemed to be sticking in his memory, though they had merely bowed and taken their leave, knowing they would see him shortly at Hollowgate.

"Very sound," agreed his grandmother, her arm looped through that of her elder daughter. "Marina, how proud you must be."

"I have heard him preach before," his mother demurred, but Kenner could see from the way she pursed her lips together that she was indeed proud.

"You lost your train of thought when you got to the part about singing the Lord's song in a strange land," his father pointed out, "but it was not without its effect."

"Mm," said Kenner, remembering Miss Ellsworth's delighted smile.

"I don't know what effect you can mean, John," objected his wife, spurred by this mild criticism. "They hung on every word. They were *entranced*."

Kenner had been a curate long enough to recognize when he had or had not a congregation's attention, and he only teased, "Careful, madam, or you will blow me up with compliments." But he thought again of Miss Ellsworth. If *that* young lady had been entranced, it had not been by his sermon, he warranted. She listened as attentively as the rest at first—he had been conscious of those bright blue eyes fixed on him—but then away she went. And her abstraction should not have ruffled him (one could not be in his profession long, if inattentive parishioners made one heartsore), but it had.

"I am so looking forward to seeing Hollowgate," spoke up Sophie at his elbow, with a little bounce. "They say it's a fine Jacobean house, but comfortable and renovated. Not shabby or old-fashioned within."

"Yes, and we had better be on our way for the luncheon," her grandmother answered.

The short walk was spent in Sophie peppering her grandmother with questions about the Ellsworths (Mr. Gregory keeping his distance and speaking doggedly with the dean).

"My dear girl," replied Mrs. Fellowes, "do lower your voice. They have indeed a spotty history, the Ellsworths. Though, to be fair, the first Mrs. Ellsworth was Miss Baldric of Hollowgate, a respectable and lovely heiress whom Mr. Ellsworth succeeded in enchanting, penniless as he was. The marrying-the-governess business came afterward, with the second and third wives. Not that the current Mrs. Ellsworth—the incumbent, so to speak—was one. As you know, she is Mr. Gregory's sister, and she kept house at the rectory for him, much as you will do for Simon."

"With any luck, Sophie, you might make the fifth Mrs. Ellsworth," put in Kenner.

"Oh, very amusing," she returned, giving him a little push. But then she turned back to her grandmother. "I like the looks of Miss Ellsworth—Miss Lily Ellsworth—very much, Grandmama. How pretty she is!"

"Hm. Handsome is as handsome does, Sophie."

"Of course, madam! But do you mean to say that Miss Ellsworth does not *do* handsomely? I want very much to be friends with her."

Despite her native distrust of so beautiful and popular a girl as Lily Ellsworth, Mrs. Fellowes was at heart a just woman, and she gave a grudging but honest answer. "I know no actual harm of her, other than that she looks something pert and self-satisfied."

"I would look self-satisfied, too," sighed Sophie, "if I were half as pretty. When I danced with Gilbert at the Race Ball, he could hardly look away from her."

The dean's wife grimaced. Trust Gilbert to be taken in by a pretty face! The boy was all about flash and dash, in life and—apparently—in love. No sense at all in him. Not like his cousin Simon.

They were walking up the drive to the house by this point, and Miss Kenner was not the only one who felt her pulse quicken. Mr. Gregory had avoided Hollowgate since his former betrothed jilted him, only attending his sister's wedding breakfast because it could not be escaped. And though Mr. Simon Kenner ought to have been chiefly concerned with how the important Mr. Ellsworth would receive him, it was the daughter—the pert, self-satisfied, but admittedly beautiful daughter—who had him straightening his cuffs and removing his hat to pass a hand through his fair hair.

When the footman swung open the great front door, it was to reveal all the Ellsworths gathered in the entry hall, admiring a lavish basket laden with hothouse and summer fruit, little Beatrice pleading with her stepmother, "May we have the pineapple? May we?"

"Ah, welcome," Mrs. Ellsworth greeted the guests. "You catch us having just received a most generous gift."

"I don't know what you mean by 'us,'" said Araminta, snatching up an orange to toss, "because the note was addressed to Lily from Mr. Slapbang."

"From Gilbert?" asked Dean Fellowes, his eyebrows lifting as he glanced at his wife. "It's too long since we visited the Meadowsweep hothouses, my dear, if they produce such...abundance."

Lily blushed with self-consciousness, Mr. Wright's note still in her hand. It read: "Dear Miss Ellsworth. I am stuck in Stockbridge with horse problems, but I asked Samuelson the head gardener to make you up a basket of Meadowsweep goods because I thank you for the dances at the Race Ball. –G. W." Not Shakespeare, precisely, but manly and to the point.

"Of course the note is to me," she replied, tucking it back in the basket. "To thank me for the dances at the Race Ball."

"*I* danced with him too," muttered Miss Kenner, but her tone was more chagrined than indignant.

Lily impulsively took Miss Kenner's arm. "And why need Mr. Wright send you a basket of fruit, when you may visit Meadowsweep at any time and raid their hothouses to your heart's content? We have only our kitchen garden at Hollowgate, and a pineapple is such a treat."

This soothed Miss Kenner, only to have vexing Mr. Kenner say, "If Gil sent every one of his partners save my sister such a thank-you, there would be nothing left for you to raid at Meadowsweep, Soph."

"Mr. Kenner," interposed Mrs. Ellsworth, seeing Lily's eyes narrow. "May I be the first to say how very glad we are you have come to St. Eadburh's. Your sermon this morning was first rate."

"Just so," pronounced her husband. "I congratulate you, sir. Quite invigorating, after Pennyworth. Excellent Pennyworth. And

Mr. Gregory—" he gave another bow, "delighted to welcome you to Hollowgate once more."

While the rector did not look equally delighted to find himself in the bosom of their family again, he bobbed his massive chest in a bow of acknowledgement, and the company followed the Ellsworths into the drawing room.

Chapter Six

I am glad, though you have ta'en a special stand to strike at me, that your arrow hath glanced.
— Shakespeare, *The Merry Wives of Windsor*, V.v.2801 (c.1597)

As Mrs. Ellsworth had assured her husband, the luncheon for the new curate was an informal thing. Bobbins the footman and Boots the maid brought in trays of sandwiches and fruit (a selection of Mr. Wright's offerings superadded), while Lily made the tea.

They must all pay plenty of attention to Mr. Kenner, naturally, with the exception of the younger children, whom Mrs. Ellsworth had succeeded in persuading her husband might be excused. Lily found herself seated beside her stepmother on a sofa, directly across from the new curate, and because she was not expected to say anything, she had leisure to scrutinize him beneath her lashes.

It was as she had judged: he was not as handsome as Mr. Wright, who in turn was not as handsome as the classical-featured Mr. Dailey, but there was something about Mr. Kenner's face and person that arrested one's gaze. It might be the lines of him. Or the angles of his nose and jaw, softened by his curling fair hair and darker swooping brows. Or it was his thin, flexible mouth, the corners of which curved and lifted as he spoke or smiled or hid a smile. Because he was so lean, he gave the impression of someone even taller than he was, but he did not strike Lily as wanting in grace or strength. And his hands—he must be a musician, she decided, or those long, sensitive fingers would be altogether wasted.

"Have you and Miss Kenner arranged the rectory to your liking?" Mrs. Ellsworth was asking.

There went the corners of his mouth, lifting in a surprisingly gentle smile. "I would be a hard man to please if we had not," he answered. "Sophie manages admirably. It was a pleasant home to begin with. I believe you and Mr. Gregory grew up in the rectory, Mrs. Ellsworth?"

"We did." She threw her brother an uneasy glance, knowing he had never dreamed of leaving his lifelong home until the pain of his broken engagement with Florence Ellsworth.

Mr. Gregory's chest swelled with a doleful sigh, and Lily, who had never wanted Florence to marry him, felt pity stir. Pity not unmixed with amusement. Which probably ought not to be called pity, then. In any event, she intervened in the conversation for the first time.

"What do you say, Miss Kenner—is your brother a hard man to please?"

"Oh," Miss Kenner gave a little deprecating hunch of her shoulders. "Simon can be *very* hard to please, but not in matters of housekeeping, I suppose. He is not the type to fuss over wallpapers or how I choose to place the furnishings."

"What does he fuss over, then?"

"Lily," murmured her stepmother.

Instead of being abashed, Lily gave a roguish grin. "You are right, Mama—it is rude to speak of Mr. Kenner as if he were not present. Mr. Kenner, then—what do you fuss over?"

His blue-grey eyes met hers, and there again was the tiny twist at the corner of his mouth. "What man will admit his failings to those whose respect he hopes to win, and over whom he hopes to wield a modicum of spiritual authority?"

"Only a modicum? You are too modest in your ambitions, sir."

"Call it modesty, if you like," he replied. "I would call it realism."

"If you will not confess to any failings yourself, I will be forced to apply to your sister for information," persisted Lily.

"Ah, but then your picture of me would be skewed in the opposite direction, Miss Ellsworth. For who, of any of us, would shine brightly in a description supplied by our intimates?"

"Too true!" struck in Mrs. Fellowes, disliking the raillery between her favorite grandson and the likes of this pert girl. What was Miranda about, letting her stepdaughter carry on so? "Though I will say you are as near faultless as it is humanly possible to be, Simon."

He grinned. "I should have made an exception for descriptions supplied by overfond grandmothers. But forbear, madam. Much as I would love to agree with you, I only an hour ago stood before the good folk of St. Eadburh's and assented to Article 9: 'whereby man is very far gone from original righteousness, and is of his own nature inclined to evil.' What would the Ellsworths think of me now, were I to oscillate?"

Mrs. Fellowes was a sensible woman but not a witty one, and unable to think of a rejoinder to his teasing, she sat back and chose another sandwich.

Lily understood as clearly as if it were written that she had displeased the older woman, and, having no wish to make trouble for her stepmother, she too resumed her silence.

That left the gentlemen to carry on the conversation, and talk turned to diocesan matters, the weather, the state of the crops, the Siege of Cairo, and so forth, until the clock struck and the dean said to his wife, "We had better be going, my dear."

Mr. Gregory was quick to spring up as well, thanking his host and hostess in his loud way and bowing his burly self in various directions. Lily expected the Kenners to participate in the general exodus, but when she found Miss Kenner by her side, smiling shyly at her, she said at once, "Miss Kenner, are you in a rush? Perhaps we might go for a walk? The grounds of Hollowgate are very pleasant this time of year, and I can force my sister Minta to accompany us, when it is time to see you home."

Her face lit up. "Oh, Miss Ellsworth, I would like that very much, though I don't want to inconvenience your sister. Simon can come back for me."

"But then we will inconvenience Mr. Kenner," Lily pointed out. With a quick peek to ensure Mr. Gregory was out of earshot she lowered her voice, adding, "The need for chaperonage in this instance is silly, in any case, for you saw how short the walk is. Florence—my older sister—made it all the time by herself when she—when she was engaged to the rector." (This last in a whisper.)

"Are you already whispering on so short an acquaintance?" came a dry voice behind her. "A conspiracy born of an hour in each other's company bodes ill for the rest of us."

Lily whipped around, her brows drawing together. "As does a habit of eavesdropping, sir."

"Habit?" asked Mr. Kenner mildly.

"Or it might be more accurately described as a tendency to skulk about," amended Lily. "First in the rectory garden, and now here."

Mr. Kenner held up his long hands in mock surrender. "In the garden—*my* garden—I confess, I heard voices and came to investigate. And if it were allowable to correct a lady, I would point out that 'skulking' implies I crept through the shrubbery to do so. But let that rest. I will only address *this* occasion, when I drew near thinking to fetch my sister. Everyone is leaving, you know, Sophie."

"I'm not," declared Miss Kenner, as Lily pressed her lips together to hold in a retort. "Simon, Miss Ellsworth and I are going for a walk. And she and her sister Miss Araminta will take me home afterward."

In answer to this he only bowed, though his eyes flicked up to Lily's, unreadable. "Very well. I will see you when you return." With a nod at Lily, Mr. Kenner turned away to speak with her parents.

Lily led Miss Kenner through the gallery (where various portraits and busts had to be identified and enlarged upon, at Miss Kenner's request) out to the walled garden. The garden which used to be Florence Ellsworth's especial domain. And if the girls had not been conspiratorial when Mr. Kenner accused them of it, they soon became so, for Lily was chatty by nature and Miss Kenner—or Sophie, as she insisted on being called—determined to admire her.

"How charming this place is!" cried Sophie, when she had been shown Florence's beds of flowers and the many fruit trees. "I would spend all day out here whenever it was fine."

"Florence often did. Or much of the day. I don't like to garden myself, but she did, and so did my mother and grandmother Baldric. Now I'm afraid our gardener Barney has it all to do."

"Where will your sister and her husband live, then, when they return from Brighton?"

"Flossie says they have secured a little home in Kingsgate Street," replied Lily, offering Sophie one of the damson plums. "Papa wanted them to live at Hollowgate because he always likes his family about him, and he was used to thinking of her only so far away as the rectory—if she married Mr. Gregory, I mean."

Taking a bite, Sophie dabbed the damson juice from her lips with her handkerchief. "Is—Mr. Ellsworth sorry she did not choose to marry Mr. Gregory, then?"

Lily hesitated, the urge to tell all the delicious details warring with how she knew her sister and stepmother would prefer she stay mum. And because she was one-and-twenty now, discretion eked out the victory. "I think we are all content with her decision," she answered. She plucked another damson from the tree and rolled it between her hands. "What of you? Are you sorry to leave Eastleigh?"

"Eastleigh is not so far. And I am so excited to live away from home for the first time! There is so much more to do and see in Winchester than at home—" she broke off, her colour rising, and Lily guessed Sophie was thinking of her cousin Mr. Wright. "I have made Simon promise to take me to every ball and assembly I wish."

"Did he not protest?" asked Lily. "Being a clergyman and all? I noticed he did not dance at the Race Ball."

"Oh, no. Simon is not strait-laced like that. He likes balls and dancing, generally. And he said he will dance at the next assembly. I'm glad of it, too, for then there will be one set at least where I don't have to stand stupidly and hope someone asks me."

"Come now. I know you danced at least with your cousin Mr. Wright, for I saw him ask you," said Lily daringly.

Sophie turned a bright crimson. "I suppose he could not help but ask me." Biting her lip, she made a venture of her own. "You must have—quite caught his eye, Miss Ellsworth, for him to send such a glorious basket. Ordinarily, when he is caught up in racing season he can think of little else. I know that if I ever hope for Gil to notice me, I almost have to throw myself in the roadway for him to stumble over. And then he would probably only stop for fear of injuring his horse."

Lily laughed at this picture and thought she did indeed like Sophie Kenner, and more than ever she did not want the girl to dislike her as a rival. Therefore she wound an arm through hers. "Well, never mind Mr. Wright, if he cannot be made to appreciate so charming a cousin. And don't forget you agreed to call me Lily. In any event, did you dance with Mr. Frayne or Mr. Caxton or Mr. Willett?"

"Hmm. With Mr. Caxton, the very pale one, and Mr. Frayne, yes. And with Mr. Dailey who talks so much."

"That he does," groaned Lily. "He's like a very handsome encyclopedia which will not stay shut."

"He admires you, I think. In fact, all the gentlemen admire you very much, Miss Ellsworth."

"Lily. *Lily.*" But she could not suppress a wriggle of delight. "You are too kind, Sophie, but I hope you're right. I cannot help it! It's been my ambition to make a stir. And if *you* had had to wait through a stepmother's illness, followed by months of mourning, you would understand why I have been longing to have some fun. I would dearly love to have a whole host of suitors and to dance my way from gentleman to gentleman!"

Sophie sighed longingly over such a vision, though she could not picture herself doing anything similar. "But what about marriage, Miss Ell—Lily, rather? Do you not also want to have someone in particular, eventually, and a house of your own, and all that? I certainly do."

"Of course, of course. Eventually. It sounds a *trifle* dull, however. And what house of my own would be half so spacious or pleasant as home? Look at my sister Florence, leaving Hollowgate for some confined little cottage!" Laughing, she gave a little twirl and plumped down on the marble bench beside them. "No—I want to draw out this period of my life. Not that I don't want all the gentlemen to propose to me—I *do*—but I don't want to have to accept any of them anytime soon. I only fear that, if one refuses them, they might give up and go away."

Sophie's eyes were very wide. "I wouldn't know about that. No one has ever proposed to me." When Lily patted the bench, Sophie sat down next to her. "Have *you* received a proposal, Miss—Lily?"

"No," confessed Lily with a sigh. "Not yet."

That was a relief to Miss Kenner. They were still even there, though she supposed it would not be long before she was left behind.

"What sort of gentleman do you prefer?" was Sophie's next venture. She traced a line with her slipper in the gravel and strove to sound offhand. "Myself, I like the active, sporting sort. Self-assured. Dashing, even."

The Mr.-Gilbert-Wright sort, Lily interpreted this. She wondered if she should come right out and tell her new friend that she planned on marrying Mr. Wright in the end. It would sound presumptuous, considering he had made no offer. But it wasn't *dreadfully* presumptuous because Lily knew with a certainty that he would. Why else would he dance with her twice and send her such a lavish present?

If Sophie Kenner were not already learning, she would soon, that Lily Ellsworth was a straightforward sort of person. Lily turned to her now, that she might look right into Sophie's round brown eyes.

"I would have to say, Sophie, that I like that sort as well. In fact, out of all the gentlemen I have met so far, I consider your cousin Mr. Wright head and shoulders above the rest. So I would say I prefer *him,* if I prefer anybody. But you mustn't say a word of this to anyone, of course."

Sophie went limp as a flag on a windless day. "Oh. I see. I was afraid of that. Of course you think Gil is wonderful. I do too. I always have. And—you are so pretty—and he likes you already." Some of the freckles on her nose disappeared as she wrinkled it in dismay, and her eyes filled.

Lily watched this surrender in some amazement. Having grown up in a family of five children, four of them sisters, she was unused to instant capitulation. Why, even Beatrice managed better than this! "Come now, Sophie!" Lily clicked her tongue reprovingly. "If you like him yourself, where's your spirit? Don't you at least want to challenge me to fisticuffs? Or tear my hair and say I can't have him? Your brother Mr. Kenner must not have been very unkind to you, growing up, or you would be better able to defend yourself. No, indeed. He has not done his duty there."

Sophie was all confusion at this playful turnabout in her companion. "But—I—Simon—teases me often, but he has never, never pulled my hair nor struck me!"

"How very odd. I begin to think Mrs. Fellowes spoke the truth, in calling him as 'near faultless as it is humanly possible to be.' But then there is the evidence of my own eyes. And my own eyes tell me the man has a decided streak of wickedness."

"Wickedness!" echoed Sophie, her own woes forgotten. She half rose. "Miss Ellsworth, Simon isn't wicked at all!"

"Well, if you object to the word, we will call it mischief," conceded Lily, rising herself. "And you mustn't take on so. If I call your brother wicked or mischievous, I almost mean it as a compliment. I think angelic people are very tiresome. Much as I love my sister Florence, I love her *least* when she is being angelic."

But Sophie Kenner hardly knew what to make of such unusual opinions, and she said unhappily, "I had better be going. There is still a great deal to be done at the rectory."

Lily saw at once that she had overstepped, and she frowned. She still wanted to be friends with the girl, but it would be tedious always to have to explain when she was joking! (Or, at least, *half* joking.) Mr. Simon Kenner may have neglected to beat his sister, but if Sophie admitted that he had teased her, should she not therefore be more practiced in recognizing when someone else did so?

Botheration.

"Oh, dear," sighed Lily. "Well, if you must go, you must. Let us look for Araminta." Leading the way to the half-door, she unlatched it and let them out. It being no use seeking Minta within doors, Lily skirted the outside of the house along the length of the gallery, listening for the hollering or general boisterousness which usually accompanied her sister.

Soon enough she caught, "Excellent! Excellent! Well done, sir!" and followed this to the lawn which stretched to the west of Hollowgate. When she and Miss Kenner came around the corner of the house, Lily saw a bundle of tightly packed straw set on end,

Minta and her friend Aggie leaping up and down gleefully beside it, pointing to where an arrow had pierced the red scarf pinned to it.

It was a moment's work to trace the probable trajectory of the arrow back toward its shooter, and there stood the curate Simon Kenner, nocking a second one.

"Oh, look," said Miss Kenner. "You will not need to walk me home after all. Simon is still here. He is a marvel at archery. My cousin Gilbert says archery is hardly worth the name of sport, but Simon says that is only because Gilbert could not hit the side of a cathedral at ten paces."

Lily had never given much thought to the activity herself, beyond finding it a nuisance whenever Minta hit something or someone she was not supposed to hit, but she had to admit to herself that Mr. Kenner made a fine figure, drawing the bowstring smoothly back along his jaw, his shoulders settling as he released his breath. She wanted to call out to Minta and Aggie to move farther away from the target, for pity's sake, and not to be idiots, but somehow she thought it would distract and annoy Mr. Kenner, and surely *he* would tell them to back away—?

He did not.

The arrow flew. Lily held her breath, but it pierced neither her sister nor Aggie and landed just below the previous shot. Araminta and her friend whooped and applauded again. In her bouncing, Minta caught sight of Lily and called, "Lily! Come and see! Mr. Kenner is a crack bowman, and I have bet him he cannot hit the target three times in succession. He has to retreat five paces each time, and he's already backed up once!"

As bidden, Lily directed her gaze toward the crack-bowman curate, who had withdrawn the requisite distance once more and turned to face them. If he was aware of her scrutiny, he gave no indication, merely setting himself as he had before, loading the bow and drawing it.

"Come here, Minta, Aggie," hissed Lily.

Aggie obeyed from politeness (everyone but Araminta obeyed Lily implicitly), but Araminta only retreated after an expressive roll of her eyes and audible sigh. In the event, the wisdom of her choice was borne out, for Mr. Kenner's third arrow soared wide of the target, landing with a thud in the grass, not five feet from where Minta had been standing.

"A miss!" declared Minta, eyeing the arrow indignantly before rounding on her sister. "That was your fault, Lily. I'm sure our movement distracted him."

"Nonsense," returned Lily. "Suppose he were aiming at a deer in the wood, and another deer appeared beside it—should he not be able to put such things out of his mind? If he cannot abide a little distraction, you should not have been standing anywhere near where he aimed!"

"We *weren't* anywhere near where he aimed," insisted Araminta. "If you had seen him shooting earlier..."

But Lily wasn't listening. Still indignant, she whirled on the approaching curate, calling, "What are you thinking, sir, shooting at my sister and Aggie? You might have killed them."

"I certainly might have," he replied, his long strides closing the distance rapidly, "had I aimed for them."

"Aim? You call that aim? You missed the target by a good ten feet."

"When they moved, I was no longer aiming for the target."

"Simon is an excellent archer," interposed Miss Kenner, but neither her brother nor Miss Ellsworth acknowledged this.

"Then where, precisely, were you aiming?" demanded Lily. Just imagine if Florence came back from her honeymoon, and Lily had to report that she let the new curate shoot their younger sister!

"I was aiming nowhere. At nothing. It was a wasted shot."

Lily could not prevent a scoffing sound, and she threw off Araminta's cautionary hand. "Oh? Is it so very hard to admit yourself in the wrong? Or do you truly fancy yourself the sort of archer who could shoot an apple off my head at a hundred paces?"

"Miss Ellsworth," he returned swiftly, "the true feat would lie in resisting the temptation to shoot off your head altogether."

A shocked silence greeted this remark, Miss Kenner even clapping her hands to her mouth, presumably because she could not clap them to her brother's. Araminta's and Aggie's eyes were round as buttons, and Lily suspected hers were much the same.

As for Mr. Kenner, his mouth popped open for an instant and then snapped shut. He shut his eyes. Then stared up at the blue sky and down at the grass.

Slowly, he released a long breath.

Then—at last—he said, "I beg your pardon."

"Mm," managed Lily. She knew she ought to say more than that. It was only polite that she demur and say she should not have provoked him, but for once she had no more words at her command than if he had indeed shot her head off.

It was Miss Kenner who rescued them. Seizing her brother's arm, she tugged on him. "We had better be going. Thank you so much for the visit, Miss Ellsworth. And do say again to Mrs. Ellsworth that we are so grateful for the luncheon. Good-bye. Good-bye, Miss Araminta, Miss Agatha. Good-bye."

The Ellsworth sisters and Aggie wordlessly watched them go, until they reached the drive and were then lost from view. Then, and only then, did Araminta say, "I think you made him lose his temper, Lily." Aggie gave a concurring nod and a low whistle.

"It seems the man does have flaws," muttered Lily.

"Wait until Flossie hears how you've *alienated* the new curate on his very first day!"

"Don't be ridiculous. And don't tell Flossie."

"I would have been angry myself," went on Minta, to her sister's annoyance, "if I could shoot like Mr. Kenner and had to suffer the slings and arrows of an archery ignoramus like yourself."

"He really was quite fine," spoke up Aggie, brushing her white-blonde hair from her forehead. "Before you came, Lily, he was hitting everything we asked him to: trees, *leaves*—everything!"

"You shouldn't have been standing so close to where he was aiming," Lily insisted stubbornly.

"But that's just it, Lily," Minta retorted. "If you had seen him shooting earlier, you would have known we were *nowhere near* where he was aiming because he was so accurate. I think you ought to apologize to him."

"Apologize?" Lily nearly squeaked. "Was *I* the one who said I wanted to shoot his head off?"

"He only said he was *tempted* to shoot your head off," replied the unlikely peacemaker, "and one can hardly blame him. We all are tempted, from time to time."

Sputtering into silence, Lily spun on her heels and left them without another word.

Araminta nudged her friend, and they went to collect the arrows.

"Do you think she'll apologize?" Aggie asked, some minutes later.

"Oh, yes," said Minta, letting the arrows rattle down into the quiver again and taking up her bow. "She may not have said anything, but that was me winning the argument."

Chapter Seven

And I will place within them as a guide
My Umpire Conscience.
— Milton, *Paradise Lost,* III.195 (1667)

Simon Kenner read the same column of the newspaper for the third time, only to find his mind refusing to absorb any more of its contents than it had on the previous two attempts. In disgust, he folded the paper and slapped it on the table, taking up his coffee.

"Another cup, sir?" asked the waiter. He wanted to tell the young clerical gentleman that there were other patrons waiting for the *Chronicle* if he was finished with it, but something surly in the man's expression stopped him.

Kenner shook his head and dug in the pocket of his frock coat for a coin. Letting it clink in the dish, he rose and pushed his way out of the coffee-house into the High Street.

It promised to be a warm day, and the thoroughfare bustled with marketgoers and tourists, the Stockbridge Races having concluded and those at Fareham not yet begun. Another ball would be held the next evening, this time at Burchar's Assembly Room, and he wondered if Miss Ellsworth would be there.

Miss Ellsworth.

Kenner gave an inward groan as he strode toward the West Gate, hearing himself say yet again how he would be tempted to shoot off her head. What had he been thinking? How could he have so forgotten himself as to blurt such a thing to a member of the most prominent family in his new flock, no matter the provocation? It had been years—*years*—since he had yielded so disastrously to impulse, and he hoped it would be years more before he did so again.

While he was not the sort of man to torture himself with rehearsing his worst moments over and over, that was exactly what he had been doing the last two days, and he had walked into town to clear his mind, having made no progress on his correspondence or the week's sermon.

He would have to apologize.

Again.

With more evident sincerity.

There was no alternative, if he was to live and work in peace among his new congregants. Miss Ellsworth did not look like a gossip, and Sophie would keep her mouth shut from sheer mortification over her brother's conduct, but Kenner did not see how it could *not* get about. *Have you heard what the new curate of St. Eadburh's said to Miss Ellsworth of Hollowgate? Not only was the man* shooting arrows *at Miss Araminta, but when Miss Ellsworth justifiably took exception to this, he declared she had better take care too, lest he shoot* her *head off next!*

Sophie said nothing of the matter to him either, confining herself to chewing her lower lip and watching him with anguished looks when she thought he wouldn't notice, but the actions did not escape him any more than the fact that she had not called again at Hollowgate. Of course, neither had Miss Ellsworth called at the rectory, but Kenner had not expected her to.

He would go this afternoon, he decided. With or without Sophie—he did not know yet which would be better—but he would go. And if Miss Ellsworth were not at home, she would know by the gesture alone what he meant to do, and that would be a beginning.

The rectory hove into sight along Cock Lane, the maid-of-all-work Vickery out sweeping the step. Pausing, she bobbed him a curtsy, her protuberant blue eyes fixed on him. "More callers, Mr. Kenner, sir."

These visitors were not the first. It might even be said that the rectory had been *inundated* since his reading-in, with every member of the parish feeling called upon to do his duty by the new curate. But with the Miss-Ellsworth calamity on his mind, Kenner's heart stalled. Had she anticipated him?

She had not.

When he entered the parlor, it was to find two families crowded there: the Weekses, from which Miss Araminta Ellsworth's friend Aggie sprang, and the Termans. The bald and bearded Mr. Weeks and his pale wife had three daughters, ranging from the eldest Miss Weeks (dark gold hair) to honey-gold Miss Frederica, to white-blonde Aggie. The Termans, however, had only the one daughter Miss Terman. Kenner could see from Sophie's trembling smile that she had been at some pains to ensure everyone had a chair to sit upon and, when the greetings had been accomplished, he hastened to help her serve out the teacups before removing her workbasket from a little wooden stool, that he might perch upon it.

He twitched with impatience in giving the more important guests their due because the person he most wanted to speak to was Aggie. That is, he wanted to determine what was known in the larger world of the shoot-her-head-off incident. And it was only after what seemed an interminable discussion of his reading-in, how the Kenners were settling in, and what fine weather they were having, that he could turn to Aggie and say, "The weather must be a delight to you as well, Miss Agatha. Have you and Miss Araminta been enjoying more sport out of doors?"

The two elder Miss Weekses stared at this direct address to their oft-disheveled, awkward maypole of a younger sister, and were even more taken aback when Aggie answered him boldly enough, "We have, sir."

Miss Weeks gave a conciliating cough. "Aggie has been much indulged by us, Mr. Kenner. Always out of doors engaging in various unseemly activities..."

"More...archery, say?" said Kenner, after a hesitation.

Not lacking in sympathy, Aggie caught his look and gave one, barely perceptible shake of her head. "No more archery."

His shoulders eased, and he was able to return to the general conversation with more patience.

He had met the Weekses and the Termans briefly at his reading-in, and the rector Mr. Gregory had shared backgrounds on all the congregation. Kenner knew, for instance, that the Weekses were a rising family, their vast fortune made in silk manufacturing compensating for what they lacked in pedigree. Mr. Weeks had purchased an estate neighboring Hollowgate and gave conspicuously to all causes, letting it be known that he would not object to being made a magistrate. As for the Termans, genteel and impoverished, Kenner knew they shifted as best they could on money left to Mrs. Terman by an aunt. Mr. Terman had never worked, having had great expectations of an inheritance once, which ultimately failed to materialize. Both the older Miss Weekses and Miss Terman had attended the same town school where Miss Araminta and Miss Agatha still went, and Kenner guessed they must be near in age to Miss Ellsworth. Not friends with Miss Ellsworth, however, he supposed, as the oldest Miss Ellsworths had famously been educated by the governesses who later became their stepmothers. In any event, they seemed harmless enough, the older Miss Weekses and Miss Terman. Polite, docile, ladylike. He wondered how any one of these young ladies would respond to their priest telling them he would like to shoot their heads off.

Not many more minutes passed, however, before he found himself thinking he might say whatever he liked to the gathered company with no harm done. For it was soon clear that they came determined to be pleased by him, and Kenner was abruptly reminded of his grandfather's warning: an unmarried clergyman was a distraction.

"Will you be at Burchar's tomorrow evening, Mr. Kenner, Miss Kenner?" asked Miss Frederica, the boldest of the three. She had a peculiar habit of pressing her lips together and chuckling after most speeches: *hm-hm-hmmm.*

"Yes, Sophie and I will be at the assembly," he answered, "and I have promised her I will not merely hold up the wall this time."

This was greeted as a delightful witticism, eliciting Miss Frederica's odd hmm-ing, the appearance of Miss Weeks' two upper front teeth in a laugh (it did not require much to make such prominent features reveal themselves), and a measured smile from Miss Terman, who in truth had not been elated to find her family's call coinciding with that of the Weekses.

But it was when Kenner chanced to say, "Yes, I expect we will like Winchester very much, as it has three circulating libraries, where Eastleigh had only one," and the chuckle was heard and the two incisors appeared and Miss Terman's measured smile stretched another fraction of an inch, that he realized he was in danger.

That is, he realized he was considered by those present as an eligible party. Even had his grandfather not warned him, Kenner would not have been able to avoid this startling conclusion.

It was not that he was unaware of his eligibility, or that he had made any unreasonable vows against marriage to himself—though, unlike at St. Eadburh's, the wages his former curacy paid would not have supported a family. It was that he was an ambitious young man and had, to this point, given more thought to his profession than his domestic situation. If he had thought of a wife, she appeared only as a vague, indistinct figure, someone of good clerical connections, good sense, good education. A younger version of his grandmother Fellowes, he supposed, to be met with at some distant date.

Certainly no possible matches presented themselves in the East-leigh church, with its modest collection of the elderly and the humble. But St. Eadburh's was another matter altogether, it appeared. In his new church he clearly would have to be careful—careful not to bestow particular attentions on any one young lady, lest he find his name unavoidably linked with hers.

As if determined to outlast each other, neither the Weeks nor the Terman families showed any signs of departing after fifteen minutes. Nor after a half hour. Kenner had enough time for his thoughts to move from cautious dismay to consideration.

After all, why not? Why not choose a good woman and marry her? He might not be a wealthy man, but he could well afford a family now. The curacy paid decently, and his grandfather spoke of further possible emoluments, now that he was in Winchester and could add various duties at the cathedral if opportunities arose. As the dean observed, if Simon Kenner married, he might both remove the distraction to his congregation and strengthen his standing in the community.

Very well, then. A good, well-connected, sensible woman. Reasonably attractive, if possible.

By those standards either of the Miss Weekses or Miss Terman would do, and he would have to get to know them better. He wished he had not remarked Miss Weeks' prominent front teeth or

Miss Frederica's *hm-hm-hmmm,* but perhaps their giggling would subside when they were more comfortable with him. And too bad as well about Miss Terman's abject poverty, but if she proved satisfactory in every other respect, poverty need not stop him. But he could not help thinking that, if feelings did not enter into the matter, and if she had been five years older, he might have liked Aggie best of the bunch because her silence on the archery incident demonstrated admirable discretion. A clergyman's wife should be wise and discreet. Ready to listen. Slow to judge. And slower still to speak.

Not hasty and irascible. Nor provoking, as some young ladies were—young ladies who might be beautiful and rich but whose temperament made them unsuitable. That is, clergymen's wives should not be wasp-tongued young ladies who goaded one into saying things one later regretted.

As soon as the visitors finally took their leave he was reaching for his hat.

"Where are you going, Simon?" asked Sophie.

"Hollowgate."

"Oh! Should—I come?"

"I am going to apologize to Miss Ellsworth. You may accompany me, if you like."

"I *would* like," she said simply, taking a deep breath of relief. Finally! She had been wringing her hands these past two days, fretting over the possible rift between Hollowgate and the rectory, and what it might mean for Simon's curacy and her own incipient friendship with Miss Ellsworth. At last, at last, Simon would set things to rights.

When the footman admitted the Kenners to the parlor across from the main drawing room, they found the unexpected conjunction of Mrs. Ellsworth seated on the sofa, her hands full of needlework, and, standing at the window playing tug-of-war with the terrier Snap, their cousin Gilbert Wright.

"Why, Gil!" cried Sophie, blushing with awareness, before she remembered herself and made the appropriate greeting and curtsey. To her relief, the little dog masked her embarrassment by setting up a loud barking and dashing around her in circles.

"Stop, Snap! Shhh—stop that at once!" reproved Mrs. Ellsworth, taking hold of the dog's collar to settle him. "You see that Mr. Wright has followed up his generous basket with a visit," she explained. "I have been trying to entertain him until the others return from visiting their relations in town. You are likely not acquainted with the Charles Ellsworths, Mr. and Miss Kenner. They do not belong to our parish. I was telling Mr. Wright that Charles is my husband's younger brother. He and his wife Jeanne have two sons between the ages of Lily and Araminta."

"We look forward to meeting them, madam," said Kenner politely. He ought to say something in explanation of their own call, but he was as distracted as Sophie by Gil's presence. How could he hope to beg Miss Ellsworth's pardon with his cousin by?

When Sophie made a great show of picking Snap up, taking a seat on the sofa beside Mrs. Ellsworth and admiring her embroidery, Kenner was left to join his cousin at the window. He wondered idly if his own colour was as heightened as Gil's.

"How did Stockbridge go, then?" he asked after a pause.

Wright shrugged. “Not like Winchester but all right. What are you doing here?”

“Calling on my congregants,” he replied. “You? That was quite the basket you sent. We saw it when they invited us for luncheon after my reading-in.”

His cousin’s brow knit. “Yes, well—if you must know, I’m waiting for Miss Ellsworth.” With a thrust of his chin he lowered his voice and added, “There’s a ball tomorrow, and I’m going to ask her for the first two dances.”

“Splendid,” answered Kenner lightly. He was aware of a prick of irritation that he could not account for, and it was an irritation all the more irritating because he sensed the difficulty of apologizing with his cousin present was not its sole cause.

“Is that why you’re here too?” demanded Wright. “To ask her to dance?”

As always in Gilbert’s presence, the temptation to nettle him was irresistible. But this time the urge was magnified by that mysterious irritation. “Not a bit of it. It had not occurred to me. But then, when I do get around to courting someone, Miss Ellsworth is not at all what I would have in mind.”

As expected, Gil swung immediately from belligerence to indignation. Throwing a glance at Mrs. Ellsworth and finding the good woman showing Sophie a pattern from her workbasket, he muttered, “Then you’re blind, Simon. Or a fool. Because Miss Ellsworth is the most beautiful girl in the county, and rich, to boot. You’d be lucky if she so much as looked your way.”

"Well, I'm not certain what good a look from her would do," Kenner answered pleasantly, "except to freeze and intimidate me. I'm a mere curate, you know—not the man of fame and fortune you are. Therefore I had better leave the beauties to you."

Wright scowled in suspicion. But it was easier to resent the slight to Miss Ellsworth than to fathom Kenner's speeches. "I don't know what you mean about her freezing and intimidating you. She is the sweetest creature living!"

"Is she?" Kenner's mouth twisted in his maddening grin. "You might know best about that. Though I daresay—living creatures aren't all that sweet, are they? Original sin, you know, and so on and so forth."

Gilbert Wright was no theologian, however, and before he could settle on an appropriate response, Sophie gave a squeal of surprise. The terrier had leaped from her lap to scratch and jump at the door, and this was immediately followed by sudden noise and bustle as the three Miss Ellsworths and their brother swept in, smelling of sunshine and summer and all in a clamor about their uncle Charles and aunt Jeanne and cousins Benjamin and Austin—a clamor which cut off with the swiftness of a guillotine blade dropping when they saw their guests.

Miss Ellsworth (whom both gentlemen were watching) went a flattering pink, but neither Wright nor Kenner could guess its cause. Wright hoped it was from the pleasure of seeing him, but Kenner suspected she was chagrined to be cornered by the curate in her own parlor.

"Goodness me," she murmured. "We are overrun. But what an unexpected pleasure! Sophie—" Going first to the curate's sister, she took her by the hands. "How delightful. I thought to myself that if I did not see you today, I surely would at the ball tomorrow evening. Will you be there?"

"We will," breathed Sophie, with a glance at her brother. He was being his most remote, still standing at the window, with his arms crossed over his chest, but their cousin came forward, all dash and affability.

"As will I, Miss Ellsworth," declared Gilbert Wright, "and I hope I will have the pleasure of dancing with you again."

In response to this she dropped a playful curtsey. "Even if I did not wish to dance with you, sir, I could hardly object, when you sent us such a beautiful pineapple."

Two spots of colour appearing on his cheeks, he said, "I am glad you liked it. Does that mean then that—you *would* like to dance?"

"For such a pineapple, sir, we would *all* like to dance with you," was Lily's incorrigible reply. But when she saw uncertainty still marring his countenance, she relented. "It would be an honor, Mr. Wright. Which dance would you like to claim?"

"Well, then," he smiled, more confident now. Rocking on his heels, he took hold of his lapels. "What would you say to the two first?"

"Thank you, sir. And now, tell me—how did Slapbang fare at Stockbridge? Did he breeze to the finish? Was there much heart-break among his competitors? I mean among the other jockeys and owners, of course, for who can tell what a heartbroken horse looks like? Or indeed, what would break a horse's heart?"

The young man's eagerness faded again. "The judge was worthless," he complained. "He could only place the first three, though anyone with eyes to see could have done better, and Slapbang wasn't among them."

"Oh, too bad," Lily shook her head, not really understanding and thinking Mr. Wright was not nearly as handsome when he was disgusted.

"He'll do better at Fareham," said Wright. "It's a better course. More to his strengths."

"Mm-hm. I'm sure you're right." The next thing she knew, Mr. Wright had drawn up the chair beside hers and was going on about his horse with all the attention to detail she usually attributed to Mr. Dailey. Lily must hear of Slapbang's diet and sleep and the jockey's diet and sleep and the trainer's new theories. She must learn of the bets laid, the weather, the course conditions. Every inch of the Stockbridge races must be accounted for, as well as where Slapbang stood in relation to the field at each point.

Lily took up her sewing and stitched away, glad she did not have to do more than nod or murmur or ask, "Oh? What then?" from time to time. In contrast, Sophie Kenner drank up every word with sincere interest, but she might have been the carpet, for all the notice he took of her. But when Sophie asked a question that *must* be answered, Lily took advantage of Mr. Wright's distraction to see if everyone else was having more fun.

In short, they were. For the rest of them were gathered around Mr. Kenner while Minta told some rollicking tale about their cousins, with Tyrone putting in a word now and then and Beatrice bouncing on her toes in excitement. Mr. Kenner made some low, dry remark, raising his long fingers as if he were touching his hat brim to someone, and provoked a wave of laughter. But even as he did so, his gaze met hers, and Lily felt as she had one time as a girl, when she pressed her eye to the crack of the door and saw one of the footmen kissing one of the maids.

Her face heating, she lowered her own gaze once more to her sewing, glad that Mr. Wright was not the observant sort. *Not like Mr. Kenner.*

Her heart had sped the moment she entered the room because she had spent the previous two days debating whether or not she owed the new curate an apology. Minta thought she did, and Lily thought she did not, but it was so unusual for Minta to insist on a moral point that Lily's resistance eroded in the face of it.

"You were a perfect *shrew,*" Minta accused. "You came roaring in without even knowing what had gone before. Like a fishwife. Like a scold. Like a *virago*—"

"All right, all right. I understand how you feel about the matter."

And now here was Mr. Kenner, but here was Miss Kenner and Mr. Wright as well, and there was no opportunity! She could not very well tell Mr. Wright to excuse her; nor could she ask Mr. Kenner to remain behind. It was all too frustrating. She did not even *want* to beg his pardon, but now that she had decided she would—or she thought she had decided she would—most *likely* she would—now the obstacles preventing her getting the nasty business over with made her want to scream.

It was only when everyone was taking leave and Lily had abandoned all hope—when Mr. Wright had pressed her hand and reminded her of her promised dances, and Sophie had pressed her hand and said she looked forward to the ball, and Mr. Kenner had *not* pressed her hand nor hardly looked at her, and Lily had slumped back on the sofa in disgust—only then did things take a turn.

Mr. Kenner popped his head back in.

"Miss Araminta, I forgot to take that sheet music you told me of."

Minta sprang up to fetch it, while the curate entered the room again as far as the slumped Lily.

"Do you play the pianoforte too, Mr. Kenner?" she asked, struggling upright.

"Fiddle. Miss Araminta and I are going to work on a duet."

"What great friends you are becoming."

"'If it be possible, as much as lieth in you, live peaceably with all men,'" he quoted softly.

Lily sat up even straighter. Was he hinting that she should apologize? If he was, it made her contrarily not want to satisfy him. But that was childish. She had been waiting to do it the past hour, for mercy's sake. Pressing her lips together, she had a final tussle with herself, but before anything could emerge, he said, "I wonder if I might claim a dance of my own at the ball tomorrow, Miss Ellsworth? Say, the third, if Gil has taken the first two?"

Nonplussed, her lips parted. But she managed a nod before Minta came skipping over, waving the sheet music. "Here it is, Mr. Kenner! And mind you don't fudge the hard parts!"

"Never," he agreed.

He made them another bow, and then he was gone.

Chapter Eight

There is that speaketh like the piercings of a sword: but the tongue of the wise is health.
— Proverbs 12:18, *The Authorized Version* (1611)

Burchar's Assembly Room was not so elegant as St. John's House, having neither painted plasterwork nor royal portraits, but it was large and serviceable and glittering with candles, and it would live in Lily's memory because, before Mr. Wright even came to claim her for the first dance, she nearly received her first proposal of marriage. The would-be proposer was Mr. Dailey, but a girl must start somewhere.

"Mrs. Ellsworth. Miss Ellsworth."

The Almost-First-Proposal began with Lily's heart sinking to her slippers when she heard Mr. Dailey's voice, but she made her curtsey and told herself that at least the man was handsome. If only he could keep silent and let his looks do the talking—he would have a thousand young ladies vying for his attentions.

Giving him an absent smile, she ruthlessly left her stepmother to do all the nodding and hmming and ah-ing and you-don't-say-ing, only to have Mrs. Ellsworth called away the next minute by an acquaintance!

"Miss Ellsworth!" cried Mr. Dailey, seizing his chance. "I understand what you must think of me—for not calling after the Race Ball, when I gave every indication of wanting to call. But you understand vital estate business summoned me back to Crossdown. One of the tenants has an overseer subject to fits of drunkenness—not that I would trouble a lady with such matters—and when the two came to have words, Fleming—the overseer I refer to—made some difficulties. Matters escalated. As master of Crossdown I was called upon to intervene. It is one of the consequences of consequence, I fear. Your father could explain to you, if he were here, he also being a man on whom many depend. In any event, I succeeded in arbitrating between them, though if Fleming had not thrown up his place he likely would have lost it anyway. Such are the fruits of drunkenness and disorder—and—again—forgive me for mentioning such things, but I did so want to assure you that I otherwise would not have let a day go by without—"

"How dreadful, Mr. Dailey! Such difficulties," Lily cut in, seeing he was about to begin again from the beginning. Across the room she noted Mr. Wright's arrival and the female flutter which accompanied it. He was too far away to save her yet, but perhaps she could catch Mr. Caxton's or Mr. Frayne's eye. "I am glad you were there to assist them in coming to a resolution."

"Thank you, Miss Ellsworth. I knew I could rely on your understanding. As Hollowgate is as large an estate as Crossdown, I have no doubt your father treats with many similar issues, tenants and the—poorer rabble—being what they are."

"Yes, indeed," said Lily, who, in truth, paid no attention whatsoever to the management of Hollowgate or the tenants and rabble—richer or poorer—who populated it.

"I was of course trained in management affairs by my late father, who himself learned it at the knee of my grandfather. Crossdown has been in the Dailey family for a hundred years, and I do not intend that it will do otherwise than flourish under my supervision—and it *is* flourishing, you understand, Miss Ellsworth. But while I am cognizant of the honor of my responsibilities and authority, I have oftentimes lamented the lack of family to share my joys and woes—"

"Have you no family, then?" murmured Lily. Although the Kenners had just appeared at the musicians' end of the hall, she tore her eyes from them, her attention snapping back as she sensed Mr. Dailey was working up to something important.

"Sadly, no. The Daileys have a long and storied history—at some point I will tell you those stories—but I was the only one of four children to survive into adulthood. My mother I never knew, and my father I lost some eighteen months ago. Therefore, apart from one elderly uncle in Portsmouth and his daughter, a spinster—who is my heir, though she is some years older—and who would certainly prefer I survive her, as I make her a generous allowance, and she has no interest in running an estate—Portia, that is. There was a time when we thought Portia would marry, but the young man was lost to fever in the Indies—"

"Very sad," Lily interrupted again, crossing her fingers behind her back. She hoped to be spared a windy digression on Cousin Portia's misfortunes. "About your lack of family. Sad indeed. I have a large family, as you know. In fact, in the area of mothers, some might say I have had more than my fair share."

"Ah, but I consider your large family one of your many charms, Miss Ellsworth!" he declared, putting a hand to his manly chest. "Indeed, I would be hard pressed to name all your manifold charms, they are so... manifold, which is why I was dismayed not to be able to call, as, indeed, I already said. I know you must be fairly harassed with the attentions of various gentlemen, but I flatter myself that few can offer you what I propose to lay at your feet, should you—"

He was coming to the point! Lily thought, wanting to clap her gloved hands together. She would refuse, of course, but it would be her first practice in refusing in such a way that he would go away still thinking highly of her. She hoped. She did feel rather sorry for him, after his pitiable story, but not sorry enough to endure a lifetime of such monologues.

"—Should you choose to consider my suit. I mean to say, Miss Ellsworth, that I am on tenterhooks, and you must forgive this work of the moment, of impulse—only not 'impulse' because I have given it much thought. Indeed, I have thought of little else since I met you at the races. But 'impulse' in that I did not mean to speak now—here—where we might be interrupted at any moment—"

Cruelly, this was precisely Mr. Dailey's fate because he had nattered on too long, and Mr. Gilbert Wright materialized at Lily's elbow to claim his dance.

"Evening, Dailey," was his terse greeting, after he bowed to them. "Sorry to break up whatever little tale you were telling, but Miss Ellsworth has promised me this dance."

Mr. Dailey's handsome face crumpled at this blow (and even Lily was disappointed because another minute would have done the trick), but soon his square jaw reasserted itself and he retorted, "No matter. Miss Ellsworth, if I might have the next...?"

"She's promised me that one, too," was Mr. Wright's pitiless reply.

"The one after, then," persisted Mr. Dailey as they began to walk away, clenching his perfect, straight teeth.

"Oh, dear. I promised that one to Mr. Kenner," Lily called back with genuine regret, before Mr. Wright took hold of her elbow and steered her into the line. She allowed herself a little sigh: even if Mr. Dailey secured a dance later, he could hardly renew his addresses as they went through the figures. Her first proposal would have to wait.

Mr. Wright danced as he lived: accurately, athletically, and with a bluff confidence that made an adequate substitute for grace. He certainly never trod on his partners' toes or wandered in the wrong direction or made a girl otherwise embarrassed to stand up with him, and Lily was, on the contrary, filled with pride. What he lacked in subtlety she provided, and she knew they made a handsome couple. It only remained to be seen how long Mr. Wright would take to come to the point. She did not expect Mr. Dailey's speed from so deliberate a man as Gilbert Wright, but then—nor had she expected it from Mr. Dailey.

"I suppose you like a fellow like Dailey," was her partner's initial venture, when some minutes had passed.

"Certainly."

"Bit of a bore."

Lily said nothing.

"When did you promise Simon a dance?"

"When he asked," she answered lightly. "When you both were at Hollowgate yesterday."

Wright made a scornful sound, remembering how Kenner had said Miss Ellsworth was not the sort of young lady he would court. So much for that. "I think he means to marry this year. Simon."

"That would not surprise me. A clergyman of his age and situation."

He gave a grunt as he circled left with her. "Do you think him a pleasant fellow?"

One of her eyebrows rose. "Mr. Wright, do you intend to ask my opinion of every gentleman of our acquaintance? If you do, I will regret agreeing to *two* dances."

He coloured as he took the woman's hand diagonal from him in a bone-crushing squeeze which made her squeak.

"If a lady were to pose such questions," Lily continued when they returned to their positions, "about this or that other young lady, she would surely be accused of fishing for compliments. And as I have already complimented you on your pineapple, sir, I feel I have more than done my duty by you in that regard." She knew, even as she said it, that her playful talk would puzzle him, but he was so plain-spoken himself that she could hardly help it.

As she guessed, he wrestled with this a minute, eventually responding, "I will send you another, then, since you like them so well."

It was as she was amusing herself at Mr. Wright's expense that she looked down the line and saw Mr. Kenner dancing with his sister. Sophie, predictably, was watching Lily and Mr. Wright and gave Lily a tentative smile, but Mr. Kenner did not so much as turn his head. When he took the hand of the woman diagonal to him, the young lady smiled and simpered, and his own flexible mouth moved in return, and Lily was surprised to see the woman lower her lashes and send him a sidewise peep. Why, Mr. Kenner might make his first conquest before Lily's very eyes! Well—and why not? In a cathedral town like Winchester, there were probably more young ladies who dreamed of marrying clergymen than otherwise.

Lily was soon directing her own covert peeks at the curate and making further discoveries. Including—Mr. Kenner's grace. His long lines and spare frame lent him something of the panther in his movements, something smooth and feline. It was a wrench to look away. And another wrench to compare it with Mr. Wright's deliberate, methodical style of dancing. *As if he were stumping around on wooden legs. Legs as wooden as he is.*

She frowned at the thought. That was not altogether true. Nor was it fair. Mr. Wright was not wooden through and through. He was not wooden-*headed,* for instance. Well—not wooden-headed about everything. He was clearly an admired and respected sportsman and landowner in their world. It was only Lily's repartee that could fluster him, but could she truly object to that? It would make him easier to manage as a husband if she were a touch cleverer than he. And Lily would much prefer a manageable husband. Only look at her father William Ellsworth! All Lily's life he had done exactly as he pleased, no matter how difficult or painful or awkward his decisions made life for his children. When Lily married, she wanted to be the one making the decisions. And if that required marrying a man slightly dimmer than she, then so be it.

Having reminded herself of her own good sense, Lily made an effort to be pleasant, refraining thereafter from teasing Mr. Wright or bewildering him, and when he deposited her by her stepmother's side he could be forgiven for thinking had had put his best foot foremost.

"You danced beautifully, Lily," said her stepmother. "And do you know who else I observed who is a pleasure to watch? You will never guess, so I will tell you: our new curate."

Even as she spoke, the new curate approached, his sister on his arm, and Mrs. Ellsworth gave a little "oh!" when they stopped before them. And then he was bowing to Lily, and she was laying light, gloved fingers on his forearm—a forearm every bit as firm as Mr. Wright's—that he might lead them to the floor. Another longways dance had been called, and, as it was the third dance of the ball, the number of couples was at its maximum. They would, Lily calculated, be dancing a very long time.

I will apologize to him, she thought, the dither of the last few days coming upon her again. Then—*I will* not *apologize to him. It is ancient history now. It would be peculiar to refer to it again.*

"Mr. Kenner—"

"Miss Ellsworth—"

With a quirk of his flexible mouth, he nodded to her. "Ladies first, please."

Very well. She took a deep breath. "Mr. Kenner, about the other day—"

But at that, without any hesitation in the movements of the dance, he held up a finger. "Pardon me. I must withdraw my offer to let you speak first, if that is the subject."

"Hardly courteous of you," Lily replied stiffly.

"I am only cruel to be kind, Miss Ellsworth. You see, I have been intending to offer you another apology—a proper apology—for what I said to you several days ago. I refer, of course, to the bit about being tempted to make an archery target of your lovely head."

She swallowed, wondering if this was how Mr. Wright felt in speaking with her—uncertain what was meant in earnest and what in jest. Did Mr. Kenner really think she was lovely, or was that just a sop to her vanity?

Say something in any case, Lily urged herself.

In the pause, he went on. "It was inexcusable. For multiple reasons."

"Mr. Kenner—it is I who should beg your pardon. My sister Araminta tells me I was in the wrong to—fly at you in such a manner. That—had I been present throughout, I would have realized she and Aggie were in no danger. But as I did *not* realize—"

"But as you did *not* realize, you said and did what was justifiable," he finished for her. "I fear you have only succeeded in excusing yourself and casting the blame once more upon me, Miss Ellsworth."

"I have not!" cried Lily. "And it's discourteous of you to misconstrue my words—" Abruptly she broke off, for she had caught the corner of his mouth twitching. Why—he was rallying her, just as she had rallied his cousin about the pineapple, and Lily had taken him as literally as Mr. Wright ever took her.

Her eyes sparked. "Very well then, Mr. Kenner. If both you and I seem to believe you were more at fault, you *must* have been. We can't both be wrong."

To this he only bowed, though his grin could no longer be suppressed, and his good humor robbed her barb of its satisfying sting. At least, if this was how he was going to be about it, she need no longer feel guilty. In fact, she might speak her mind freely!

"Certainly the rector Mr. Gregory never said anything so shocking to me," Lily went on. "Nor did the former curate, the poor Mr. Pennyworth. I suppose you have not been a member of your profession long, Mr. Kenner, but you can hardly hope to go far if you cannot better control your tongue."

"True, true," he agreed amiably. "But I have suppositions of my own, Miss Ellsworth. And one of them is that *no one* has been much in the habit of saying such things to you, reprehensible though they might be."

"I should say not! Of course no one has said such things to me because no one has ever *wanted* to shoot my head off before!"

He raised innocent eyebrows. "Oh—no? But—well—to be sure, you would be the best judge of that."

Lily's bosom swelled, and if she had happened to have Minta's bow and arrow to hand just then, Mr. Kenner might have been a corpse littering the ballroom floor. The gall of the man! Why, he might ask any man present this evening, and every last one of them would declare her an angel! Beginning with his own cousin.

"You, of course, are entitled to your own opinion," she said, her tone as lofty as she could manage, "and how fortunate it is that manners dictate we keep such opinions of others to ourselves, else we might all of us learn more than we would like." *Beginning with* you, *sir.*

As if she had said the latter aloud, he gave a sage nod. "You must be quite the philosopher, Miss Ellsworth, and I need not tell you that, 'A word fitly spoken is like apples of gold in pictures of silver.'"

"And I need not tell you," she retorted, "that, 'Even a fool, when he holdeth his peace, is counted wise.'"

The shaft fell wide again because Mr. Kenner actually *laughed* when she said this. Laughed and gave her an extra twirl which would have made her stumble, had his other hand not flown out to steady her waist. Lily startled, as if that hand were a brand fresh from the fire, and her cheeks went scarlet.

Her partner's colour rose in turn, and he muttered, "Excuse me."

They danced in silence for some minutes, until the awkwardness of *not* speaking grew too much for her to bear.

"How—do you and Miss Kenner like the rectory?" she ventured, when they had reached the bottom of the set.

"It's a lovely home."

She half expected another gibe about all the flowers she had cut, but it was not forthcoming.

"It's quieter. When I was curate for St. Botolph's in Eastleigh, I lived in my childhood home and rode over to carry out my duties. And, living at home, I found that not only is a prophet without honor 'in his own country, and among his own kin,' but his own kin tend to be loud and to involve themselves in the prophet's business."

A reluctant smile played on her lips. "So does Miss Kenner mind her own business? It must make it easier to write your sermons."

"Indeed. This week it was not Sophie who disturbed me." He frowned in thought, and Lily would have liked to ask what distracted him but did not dare. The frown passed, however, and his voice was light again. "Not that it matters so much to congregants such as yourself, Miss Ellsworth, but a new curate does like to do his best by the sermon."

"Why would it not matter to congregants like me?" she asked warily, sure he intended another insult.

"Because, if I am not mistaken, you were not paying a great deal of attention when I delivered my maiden sermon in the pulpit of St. Eadburh's."

"I—"

But she was not in the habit of being anything but candid, so no easy falsehood sprang to her lips. Instead she said, "I had much on my mind. I will pay as much attention as you like to your next sermon."

"Yes. I'm sure you'll be rapt."

Her chin rose. "You might think me a flatterer for saying so, Mr. Kenner, but I think your efforts will be well-received in general. Mr. Pennyworth was not so apt to shine as a preacher."

"You preferred Mr. Gregory, then?"

Lily considered. "I listened to at least ten minutes of each of Mr. Gregory's sermons, so that must mean I did."

"Then I will aspire to interest you for *eleven* minutes."

She shrugged this away. "But sermons will not be your only duty, you know. You must marry and bury and baptize. Visit the poor and sick. Wait upon the bishop and curry favor."

"You seem familiar with the responsibilities required."

"Oh, my sister was going to marry Mr. Gregory, at one point, as I'm certain you're aware, and she knew all about that sort of thing and didn't mind it."

"She only minded Mr. Gregory, then?"

Lily stifled a giggle and saw an answering gleam in her partner's eye. "She has married an attorney," Lily answered, avoiding the question. "So I imagine her chosen life will require listening to him talk of papers and proceedings, instead. Settlements and such, wills and...won'ts."

"Are you capable of reducing all professions to such distillations of tedium, Miss Ellsworth, or only those you are most familiar with?"

"I daresay you gentlemen find your work interesting, and that is the important point."

"Yes, I suppose, as such work falls to our lot," he conceded. "If you were a man, what career would you choose, then?"

Her eyes lit up, and a genuine smile spread across her face. "I think—yes—I would be a highwayman. That is, if I could not be a king."

"I think I might safely say you would be neither. Highwaymen's careers are often cut short by their own hangings, and there aren't many kings in all the world. Moreover, what sort of answer is that? That is like saying you would be a wolf, if you could not be a lion. Or a thief, if you could not be the householder. Suppose you confine yourself to what is possible? Butcher, baker, candlestick-maker?"

"Ah, I don't think I could choose then," she sighed. "In that case, I would prefer to remain Lily Ellsworth."

The music was drawing to its close, and Mr. Kenner made his bow before offering her his arm.

"You will not find many to agree with you there," he murmured, barely audible over the hum of talk which rose as the dancers broke up. "For I could point you to a host of gentlemen who are even now hoping to change your name."

Her breath caught at the compliment. It *was* a compliment, was it not? That he had noticed she was desired and popular? He did not say *he* hoped to change her name, but neither did he exclude himself.

However, before she could preen herself on another possible conquest—*the supercilious Mr. Kenner!*—he burst her swelling self-importance with one prick of his lance. Adding more to himself than to her: "And that must be what is meant by 'for better or for worse.'"

Chapter Nine

I bear a charmed life, which must not yield,
To one of woman born.
— Shakespeare, *Macbeth,* V.viii.2485 (1606)

The church was as full as it had been for his reading-in, and Kenner was gratified to find them just as attentive. Or mostly he was gratified. Between Miss Ellsworth seated on the aisle in the foremost lefthand pew, and the Miss Weekses two rows behind, and Miss Terman staring at him unblinkingly from her seat on the right, he hardly knew where to look as he read. He had danced only once with each of the young ladies at Burchar's, holding to his plan to indicate the general harmlessness of his intentions by dividing his attentions with mathematical precision, and he had not called on a single one of them the following day. But he wondered now if, in his deliberate detachment, he only played a gentleman's version of Miss

Ellsworth's game. Where Miss Ellsworth seemed intent on collecting as many hearts as she could for her own amusement, Kenner wanted to excite as little interest as possible until he determined whom to pursue.

Miss Ellsworth had danced every dance and, apart from the first two sets with his cousin Gil, she did not grant any other partner such favor. Mr. Caxton had won her for the supper dance, but it was a hollow victory, for Sophie and Gil sat on her other side, and she spoke to them as much as she did to him, if not more. Poor Mr. Caxton had made the unfortunate choice of a light buff coat and waistcoat which, coupled with his fair, fair colouring and the blond wainscoting of Burchar's supper room, concealed him from view as effectively as if he had hidden under the table. Or so it appeared from where Kenner sat with his partner Miss Scott—or was it Miss Scotch? A stocky, jolly young lady who—like every other young lady he met, apart from Miss Ellsworth—laughed at his feeblest joke and smiled upon him as if he were a marvel she could scarcely credit. Miss Scott or Scotch had been unique in her frankness, though, telling him plainly that her mother told her it was time to marry. "And since my governess declares I speak French like a Spanish cow, and my music master wishes he might stop his ears when I play the pianoforte, it's very good for me that I have three thousand pounds."

Three thousand pounds was indeed nothing for a curate to sneeze at, but Kenner still had not recovered from the crassness of her mentioning it. Why not simply hang a sign around her neck? He was spared her presence this morning, at least, as she told him frankly that she belonged to a different parish but wished she might hear him preach at St. Eadburh's.

No, the ball at Burchar's had not resulted in warmer feelings toward any of the available young Winchester ladies, but he supposed these things took time. There was no need to rush into anything, as his cousin Gil was doing with Miss Ellsworth. Had it not been for the circuit of horseraces in every corner of the country which called him away, Kenner guessed Gil would have offered for her already. As it was, he left her open to every comer in town.

While Kenner had not called at Hollowgate on Saturday (or anywhere else but at an ailing parishioner's), Sophie had. "Simon, I do believe every young man in Winchester made his appearance while I was there!" she reported back. "Mr. Dailey—who looked quite put out to find the drawing room full—Mr. Willett, Sir Basil, Mr. Frayne..." Sophie told off each gentleman on her fingers. "...Mr. Gosworth, Mr. Trimp, Mr. Caxton...and even two officers whose names I can't remember. In short, I think only Gil was missing because he went off to Fareham, you know."

"Oh?"

"Simon, do put down your pen a moment," urged his sister, drawer her chair nearer his desk. She then folded her hands in her lap, hoping to appear calm. "I—think our cousin is—very fond of Miss Ellsworth, don't you?"

He hesitated. "I think he is as—fond—of her as I have ever seen him of anyone."

Her freckled little nose wrinkled at this blow, but it was no more than she expected. "Then—do you suppose we ought to warn him?"

Her brother grinned. "Warn him off Miss Ellsworth?"

"No, indeed! What do you mean, 'warn him off'?" she cried. "No—I mean warn him that he might lose her to someone more attentive, if he is not careful."

He shrugged. "Would it be so great a loss?"

"Simon! How can you—? I do not think for an instant you are half so blind to Miss Ellsworth's charms as you pretend. How could you be? You, alone, of every young man for miles around?"

Some unreadable shadow flitted across his features, but Sophie knew well that, if her brother did not choose to share his thoughts, she would never guess them.

"I am *not* blind to Miss Ellsworth's charms," he answered after another moment, carefully tapping the pages of his sermon on the desk to straighten them. "I see very well that she is a beautiful girl."

Sophie sighed. "Beautiful and rich and clever and charming. I don't suppose Gil could do any better."

"On the contrary, Gil could do *much* better. Oh, don't gasp at me, Soph. For one thing, Miss Ellsworth may be beautiful, but she is well aware of the fact. For another, she may be rich, but Gil hasn't any need of money. For a third, what would he do with a clever wife? Miss Ellsworth would eat him for breakfast. And, as for her charm, since she chooses to exercise it on all and sundry, its very commonness cheapens it."

"Simon!"

"But most importantly of all," he went on inexorably, "I do not think she cares for him. Not any more than she does for Caxton or Dailey or Gosworth or the other dozen you mentioned. Therefore, if

Gil were to 'lose' her, he might find it in the end not so unendurable a loss."

Shaking her head in amazement, Sophie could only stare at her brother. Six years younger than he, she was long in the habit of adopting his opinions over her own, but in this instance unfamiliar doubt assailed her. *Would* Gilbert truly be better off without Miss Ellsworth? *Might* he be better matched with someone less...showy? Someone *less* remarkable? Someone, perhaps, like his cousin Sophie Kenner?

If she had not been so preoccupied with what Simon's thunderclap meant to her specifically, she might have speculated on what her brother's opinion revealed about himself, in addition to the light it cast on Miss Ellsworth. But Sophie was too caught up in wondering if she might, after all, have a chance with her dashing cousin, when matters played out.

"If...you truly think all this, Simon," she hazarded, her voice trembling only a little, "*ought* you to warn him off?"

Kenner grimaced. He knew exactly where that would lead, if he were to caution Gil. His cousin would accuse him of wanting Miss Ellsworth himself. Or call him a dog in the manger. And any repudiation of such charges would go unheard, sincere though it might be.

And it would be sincere, would it not? Kenner surely did not covet Miss Ellsworth for himself, and she might marry anyone she pleased. It was their lookout.

"Our cousin is a grown man," he replied at last. "Not only would such advice be deemed officious, but it might make him even more set on her. He must see to himself, sink or swim."

Sophie sagged in disappointment. "Oh. Very well. Perhaps—perhaps Miss Ellsworth might refuse *him*, in the end."

She might, he thought. And then again, she might not.

Kenner consulted his watch on the corner of the pulpit. Eleven minutes. The exact amount of time Miss Ellsworth had promised she would listen to him, when she teased him at the ball. Almost without volition, his gaze drifted in her direction, just in time to see her gloved fingers rise to her lips to hide a yawn.

He bored her, did he? How might that be, when every other person in the church was wide awake—even her father Mr. Ellsworth—and silent with attention? There was not even the shuffling of feet or muffled coughs or the creak of the pews as restless people shifted their weight.

"...The—er--the continued seeking of the Lord while in exile," he fumbled, losing his place in his notes as he set his watch back down, "leads to—leads to—" His own momentary distraction was enough to distract his listeners, and it led to an outbreak of the very noises he had just congratulated himself on not exciting: shuffling, coughing, creaking. A hymnal even tumbled to the stone floor with a *slap* and was scrambled after.

Miss Ellsworth's bonnet ducked down, and when she straightened, her eyes met his exasperated ones. She was smiling.

Ah. She had done it on purpose, then. Yawned. And he had pitched headlong into her trap like Joseph into the pit dug by his brothers. A faint line appeared between his brows. Why should she affect him at all? Was he no wiser, then, than his cousin Gil or any of the myriad young men swarming to her like flies to a honeypot? It was one thing to live on good terms with his flock—he was not sorry he and Miss Ellsworth had resolved their difference—but quite another to make a fool of himself. He had no intention of making a fool of himself. None at all. If anything, he intended for the whole world to believe as his sister believed, that he alone was unmoved by her charms. Because he was precisely that—unmoved.

"Mr. Kenner, we are having a little card party this week..."

"Mr. Kenner, I would like to fill some vases with flowers and make wreaths for the church..."

"Mr. Kenner, my grandmother was so grateful for your visit, and would it be terribly much to ask that you come again? She has been so poorly for weeks..."

"Mr. Kenner, the hinge on our pew door is so stiff that I fear it will break if pushed too hard. Might Mr. Harvey inspect it...?"

Even as he stood at the door after the service, replying to each of these addresses, he was aware of the Ellsworths' approach and braced himself unconsciously. It was the patriarch William Ellsworth who addressed him, smiling graciously. (Truth be told, since the St. Eadburh living was largely supported by Hollowgate tithes, Mr. Ellsworth felt the new curate's success and popularity reflected glory upon him, however little he had to do with his selection.)

"Excellent, excellent, Mr. Kenner. I commend you. A very good sermon indeed."

"Thank you, sir."

"My daughter Araminta tells me your talents extend beyond the pulpit."

"Miss Araminta?" echoed Kenner, glancing over Ellsworth's shoulder. Miss Ellsworth was speaking with Sophie, but he saw Miss Araminta bouncing on her toes behind her stepmother, and when she caught his eye, she squeezed forward, popping up under her father's arm and then having to straighten her bonnet.

"Minta praises your archery," Mr. Ellsworth went on, "and claims you play the fiddle as well."

The pun escaped Kenner before he could stop it: "I play the fiddle as well, yes, but not as well."

Ellsworth blinked in puzzlement, but Miss Araminta gave a delighted, if unladylike, snort. "See, Papa? Can't we have the Kenners to supper and music?"

"Certainly, if they are willing."

Seeing no alternative, as inadvisable as Kenner thought it to spend an evening in company with Miss Ellsworth, he bowed. "Of course. We would be glad of it."

"When shall it be?" Ellsworth turned and asked his wife. "And should we invite any others? Too bad Flossie and her Robert are not yet returned. Some of Lily's friends, perhaps?"

"Oh, Papa! Please—none of her blockheads!" pleaded Miss Araminta. "It is bad enough they come every morning. If we invited some of them to supper, we would have to endure their company the *entire day*."

"None of them?" he teased. "And you must beg Mr. Kenner's pardon, Minta, as his cousin Mr. Wright has been among the callers more than once."

At her rueful look, Kenner hastened to say, "It's all right, Miss Araminta. I've been known to call him worse than a blockhead, and he me. The joys of family."

"What would you and Miss Kenner say to Wednesday or Thursday sennight?" Mrs. Ellsworth asked.

Miss Kenner must be consulted, of course, and her conversation with Miss Ellsworth interrupted. When the invitation was repeated, Sophie's eyes flew to her brother's face, but finding it impassive she replied, "Perhaps Thursday sennight, then? That will give Simon and Miss Araminta the most time to practice their instruments. Will you play for us too, Lily?"

"Mm. I don't know. I suspect Mr. Kenner has a critical ear, which makes me timid to put myself forward."

"You, Miss Ellsworth? Timid? How refreshing."

"And you, Mr. Kenner—critical? How comfortable."

"Thursday sennight it is, then," Mrs. Ellsworth said quickly. "How lovely to look forward to. We will wish you a good day."

The Ellsworths gave way to the Termans at the church door, and Kenner heard himself saying and doing all that was expected of him, but his mind was far away. Supper at Hollowgate! Playing his fiddle while Miss Ellsworth looked on...

Why could he not speak to Miss Ellsworth as he did every other young lady of his acquaintance? Why could he not resist the urge to engage with her? If Sophie doubted he could be blind to Miss Ellsworth's charms, her skepticism now threatened to infect him.

One thing was certain: if he must spend a Thursday evening in her company, he would utterly avoid her until then. See her only at church the next Sunday but nowhere else. That, at least, he could manage.

Chapter Ten

There be three things which are too wonderful for me,
yea, four which I know not:
the way of an eagle in the air;
the way of a serpent upon a rock;
the way of a ship in the midst of the sea;
and the way of a man with a maid.
— Proverbs 30:18-19, *The Authorized Version* (1611)

Lily began to think Mr. Dailey had given up on proposing to her when several days passed after the ball. He came to Hollowgate at last, however, only to be thwarted by the presence of several other gentlemen callers whom he could not succeed in outlasting. He came again the very next afternoon, but then he found the drawing room full of Lily's stepmother and youngest sister and Miss Sophie

Kenner, all working on vases of flowers for the church, while Master Tyrone perched in the window seat, reading. But while Mr. Dailey could not propose, he could yet bore, and he treated whoever could be brought to listen to further detailed accounts of the difficulties in managing so vast and prosperous an estate as Crossdown. Mr. Frayne and Mr. Trimp were told of the inflamed hoof afflicting one of Crossdown's prized horses. Mrs. Ellsworth must hear of the linens the housekeeper reported missing. Tyrone received a thorough analysis of recent poaching incidents and who the gamekeeper thought responsible. And poor Sophie, who was too polite and too aware of her role as a clergyman's sister—Sophie bore the brunt of the Tale of the Drunken Overseer.

"I told Rickford—one of my longest-standing tenants, you know—that the man had an evil reputation—Fleming, that is—and that he—Rickford—was too soft in overlooking the man's frequent debauches—if one might mention such things in present company—"

Sophie made a deprecating sound and threw Lily a helpless look, but Lily mercilessly pretended not to see and rammed another delphinium in her vase.

"One must take a firm hand, I advised Rickford," Mr. Dailey forged ahead. "Rarely is drunkenness a singular indulgence, and habitual drunkards lose much time to purported illness. Therefore I advised Fleming's instant dismissal, for which the man bears me a grudge. I have no doubt he slanders me in every public house and byway from here to Southampton."

"Dear me," said Sophie. "How unfortunate. Can nothing be done to help the man?"

Lily later told her that asking Mr. Dailey a *question* was Sophie's downfall, for his response to this well-meant interrogatory took all of seven minutes to deliver, though at heart it might have been distilled to, "In my opinion, no."

But on Mr. Dailey's third visit he met with better luck, for it was on that occasion he found Miss Ellsworth walking the grounds, in view of her sister Miss Araminta and Miss Araminta's friend Miss Agatha, but essentially alone. To be frank, Lily had decided her suitor must be given his chance and had contrived her relative solitude, but a confusing mixture of anticipation (her first proposal!) and dread (this might take hours) flooded her nevertheless.

"Why, good morning, Mr. Dailey."

"Miss Ellsworth." He removed his hat, bowed, replaced his hat. "May I—take a turn with you?"

She nodded her permission. A light summer rain had fallen the previous evening, and therefore she indicated the gravel drive for their walk. For all Mr. Dailey cared, she might have pointed to the edge of a cliff, for, once the moment was upon him, the blood rushed through his veins and pounded in his head and chest. He removed his hat again, turning it round and round in his hands as he walked, before finally seeking relief in words.

"Miss Ellsworth. What a pleasure to have this moment with you. On such a pleasant day. Warm. Warmer than I expected, after the rain last night." He swung his arms in an effort at nonchalance, but it only sent his hat rolling away and himself in pursuit. Once it was recovered, he crammed it down on his waving locks. Cleared his throat. "This is quite a well-maintained drive. Excellent. I commend your father's groundskeepers. The drive at Crossdown is somewhat narrower and more winding than this but is otherwise much like. The whiteness of the gravel, you understand."

"I see."

She did not phrase it as a question, but that did not deter him. A discourse on gravel followed, ranging from its sources to its uses, to which Lily had little to add.

When the wonders of this subject were exhausted, Mr. Dailey cast about, finding himself no nearer his goal. Then, in a fit of inspiration, he bent and ripped up a handful of lady's bedstraw to present to Lily. "Miss Ellsworth—these bright blossoms bring you to mind."

"Because they are commonplace?" She tilted her chin, pretending to consider. "Or because they are weedy, perhaps?"

Such a rejoinder would have nonplussed Mr. Wright but was no bar to Mr. Dailey. "Not a whit!" he avowed, even placing a fist to his chest. "I mean you are bright, Miss Ellsworth. Bright and summery and beautiful. Sweet as honey." He took a deep sniff of the bouquet she held to make his point.

At least he had not compared her to the gravel.

"Thank you, Mr. Dailey. Our cook Wilcomb has used lady's bedstraw to curdle milk for cheese, when she cannot get rennet."

But Mr. Dailey would have none of this, and he had already dropped to one knee. Seizing Lily's hand (and causing the flowers to spill to the ground), he cried, "Miss Ellsworth, I must take what opportunity is afforded me—"

Her rosy face blushing rosier, Lily made a half-hearted attempt to withdraw her hand. "Mr. Dailey—we might be seen!"

"Let the world see! Miss Ellsworth, from the very moment I met you at Worthy Down, you have charmed me. You have entranced me. You have bewitched me. I have never seen your equal for beauty or grace. If you would do me the honor of becoming Mrs. Dailey, I would account myself the most fortunate man in England."

"Mr. Dailey." She pulled on her hand again, and he reluctantly released it. "While I am deeply, deeply flattered and honored by your offer, I feel we hardly know each other."

"What do you not know? What am I not willing to share with you? You may ask me anything."

Lily didn't doubt that, but she had no desire to stand there until sundown learning all there was to know about Mr. Dailey. She held once again the inward debate which had occupied her since the ball at Burchar's—should she tell him there was absolutely no hope?

Yes.

Absolutely she ought. Because there wasn't any.

But—!

But she was only one-and-twenty and could not help thinking that handsome Mr. Dailey was a feather in her cap. For most other girls would accept his offer. Why, either of the elder Miss Weekses would, Lily was certain. As would Miss Terman. In her poverty, Miss Terman would fall on her knees, fasting, for such a catch as Mr. Dailey—!

(Perhaps the more important question she could have asked herself at this juncture was why, when she thought of other young ladies who would rejoice to accept Mr. Dailey, she should think first of those seen dancing with Mr. Simon Kenner. Mr. Kenner, who had nothing to do with the matter. But Lily did not ask herself this.)

To give herself a moment, she bent to retrieve the scattered flora and tidied the stems into a smaller nosegay, already wilting. Her sister Florence had often collected lady's bedstraw, drying it with other flowers to make fragrant *pot-pourri*. And wouldn't it be lovely to dry some for her, since the Fairchilds would return soon? Lily could stuff it into a cushion for her new home in Kingsgate Street. Yes!

But the thought of Florence gave Lily pause. Only imagine what Flossie might have to say, if she learned that Lily had allowed a gentleman to hope, where he had no business hoping. It would not be very pleasant to listen to the lecture that would surely follow and be unable to mount any proper defense.

With this sobering thought, Lily straightened.

There was relief in making a decision, at any rate.

"Mr. Dailey," Lily said firmly, her natural frankness coming to the fore, now that she no longer tried to restrain it, "I regret that I must say this, but I fear it will be little use in us getting to know each other better. While you have much to recommend you, I fear we would not ultimately suit."

"Don't say that, Miss Ellsworth!" he begged. "I have rushed you. I have compelled an answer from you, when, as you say, you feel you hardly know me. I understand why you believe it necessary to refuse, under those circumstances."

"That is not it at all," answered Lily, with a hint of impatience. Once she had made up her mind, she did not enjoy having to argue the point. Marching onward along the gravel drive, she forced him to hurry after her until she halted at the brick-and-iron arch marking the entrance to the estate. "I would not want to mislead you, sir. Therefore I think it best if you take my answer as final." She threw back her chin as if she expected him to march right off into oblivion.

"But—*why*?" he persisted, not marching anywhere. He held up his palms helplessly. He would be a particularly obtuse young man not to be aware of his own eligibility, and perhaps he, too, thought of the many young women who would welcome his addresses.

Lily grimaced at the gatepost so that her bonnet brim would shield her from Mr. Dailey's view, her eye falling to a brown jug tipped on the grass. *Pah!* Why could people not carry their rubbish away with them? But living so near the barracks, the Ellsworths were no strangers to evidence of the sometimes disorderly soldiers. There had been jugs before, besides the occasional cigar stub.

"Why?" repeated Mr. Dailey, when she did not respond. Then, before she could, he made a lunge and took hold of her hand again. "If you cannot give me the answer I long for today, let us go on as we were before and pretend I never spoke—only don't dismiss me out of hand, Miss Ellsworth."

Vexed now, she tried to tug free, but she might as well have tried to tug down the gatepost, and no sooner did she slacken this effort then he gave a pull of his own, drawing her tumbling against his chest.

"Mr. Dai—!" was as much as she managed to say before Mr. Dailey's perfectly-cut mouth descended to cover her own, and Lily in her downright astonishment went limp as day-old lady's bedstraw. Her first proposal was accompanied by her first *kiss*? And this, after she had unequivocally given her first *refusal*?

When he released her, she stumbled backward against the gatepost, her ankle bone striking the overturned jug and her hand flying to her lips.

His handsome eyes were dark. "You will reconsider...?"

Her own glittered with fury. "I will not," she hissed. "And don't you ever, *ever* take such a liberty again, sir. I—I am most displeased. Most. Good—good day to you."

She spun on her heel, not pausing even when he uttered, "But—I rode here."

What was it to her if he rode, or flew, or crawled from the earth?

Without turning back, she said quietly over her shoulder, "I will have one of our grooms bring you your horse. Please do not follow me."

Dailey stood some minutes at the end of the drive, watching her go, frowning as he tried to work out to what degree Miss Ellsworth was genuinely offended. She had not resisted him, nor slapped him, after all. Nor had she threatened to tell her father or to set the dogs on him. Therefore, was it merely a show of maidenly modesty? And, if it was, should he for his part now send a note of apology? How long would she think it necessary to freeze him?

Removing his hat, he ran thoughtful fingers through his hair. He might know a lot about many things, but the ways of women remained mysterious. It was even possible that Miss Ellsworth now considered herself engaged to him. In which case, he ought to ask to speak with her father.

For the present, he thought it best not to follow her. He would wait for the groom to come with his horse. He leaned to pick up one of the discarded flowers, pinching off a sprig of blossoms to tuck in a buttonhole, which was when he heard tentative footfalls behind him.

Turning, he saw two young ladies, one with dark gold hair and one with tresses of honey gold. They looked familiar, though he did not know them, so he touched his hat politely. This caused some giggles, and they crowded closer to each other.

"Good afternoon." He bowed courteously. "Calling at Hollowgate?"

"No—no," said the one with the darker hair. "The rectory." She bit her lip with her prominent front teeth and clutched her companion's arm more tightly as they edged past (as if he might bite them), and Mr. Dailey wondered how much they had witnessed. Possibly nothing, he assured himself. In his experience, young ladies were frequently timid and giggly around him. It was one of the things he admired in Miss Ellsworth—her confidence.

If only it were permissible to ask these two whether they thought Miss Ellsworth was truly angry! If they saw the kiss, they saw her response. Surely they could interpret it for him. Was she angry, or had she tacitly consented to an engagement? Angry or engaged? Engaged or angry?

But the young ladies only continued on their way toward the Cock Lane gate, giving one final glance at him before they passed through, and before they were out of earshot he caught another burst of smothered giggles.

With a sigh, Mr. Dailey gave it up. Only time would tell.

Chapter Eleven

O Charity, divinely wise,
Thou meek-ey'd Daughter of the skies!
— Hannah More, *Search after Happiness* (1773)

Whatever Mr. Dailey's uncertainty about the matter, Lily suffered no doubts. Indeed, her only regret was that nothing had prepared her to meet with such effrontery. She should have struck him, or kicked him, or pushed him, or *something*! She should have told him he must answer to her father for his conduct! But instead she had let the shock paralyze her. She had not even railed at him properly, though she thought of a thousand things she might have said, after it was too late to say even one of them.

"Well, I have learned one lesson, at least," she muttered to herself as she hammered on the pianoforte keys. "Should I ever, ever find myself in such a situation again, I will be prepared. Prepared to fight, with both words and blows."

Her fingers hit a jarring discord, which made her stepmother put her hands to her temples and say faintly, "Lily..."

"I am sorry, Miss Gr—Mama, rather," she said at once. "I won't play anymore, if you have a headache." She scowled at the sheet music, still seeing Mr. Dailey's maddening handsome face, but when she finally glanced at Mrs. Ellsworth, the latter's pallor made her forget her own troubles. "Dear me—Mama—are you unwell? Perhaps you should go and lie down."

"I will be fine," answered Mrs. Ellsworth with a wavering smile. She ran a listless hand over Snap's belly, as the terrier sprawled beside her. "It will pass. But if you could ring—? A little tea and a biscuit might help."

Lily's eyes grew round. "Tea and a biscuit? But—wouldn't you rather—" A new thought struck her, and she gave a soft gasp of recognition. It had not been so very long since—that is, Lily well remembered her second stepmother's discomforts when—

"Mama, are you—*in the family way*?"

Her stepmother's cheeks pinkened, and Lily had her answer before she even spoke.

Stunned, Lily stared without seeing at the keys of the instrument. *Another* Ellsworth to add to the Assortment? Great heavens. Of course it was nothing she had not expected—she had even told Florence it would be likely, but it was one thing to speculate on another brother or sister and quite another to give to airy nothing a local habitation and a name.

"When?" whispered Lily.

"Mr. Beckford says in the early spring."

"Does Papa know?"

"Oh, yes." Mrs. Ellsworth folded a crease into the shirt she was mending and then smoothed it out again. "And we were going to tell you all very soon. I would not have said anything today, only—"

"Only I was so loud and jangling on the pianoforte," finished Lily. Rising from the bench, she came to sit beside her stepmother, shoving Snap away. She removed the sewing from Mrs. Ellsworth's hands to take them in her own. "I can be very quiet now, Mama. I feel this strongly. How I wish Flossie were home again. She would know what to do."

"There is nothing to do," replied Mrs. Ellsworth calmly.

"But I might—help with the housekeeping. Or—or—or help you teach Beatrice. To lighten your cares." As soon as she said it, the two of them laughed. Lily was not known for her housekeeping skills or her patience.

"Never mind all that for now, Lily. Only—there is perhaps one favor you might do for me..."

"Anything."

"I was going to call on old Mrs. Hambly and her niece this afternoon and bring them a basket. She's been very poorly of late. Could you go for me? You might take Minta or Beatrice or even one of the maids with you..."

If Lily had not just promised, and if she had not sincerely wanted to help her stepmother, she would have made some excuse. She had a healthy young person's dread of the poor and old and sickly and had only ever gone with Florence when her older sister had no one else to accompany her. Mrs. Hambly and her niece! Oh! But she put a brave face on it and spoke of a visit to the Hamblys as if it had been her especial wish for ever so long.

Minta, of course, begged off, swearing she and Aggie had plans, and Beatrice said, "Oh, Lily, Mrs. Hambly is so frightening! She looks like a heap of rags, and she smells oddly. Please don't make me go."

It was Tyrone who surprised her. "I'll come, if I only have to wait outside for you." For which willingness Lily nearly hugged him.

After Wilcomb the cook filled a basket with a crock of soup, a pie, a cheese, and some ripe fruit, draping a clean cloth over all, Tyrone shouldered this burden, whistling cheerfully as they walked the graveled drive.

"Aren't you concerned, Lily, that you'll miss your troop of admirers if you go out now?" he asked. "Or is this a ploy to make them think you're a Lady Bountiful?"

Lily made a face. "I do not think even Lady Bountiful could honestly say she enjoys calling on the Hamblys. And as for my so-called troop of admirers, they will have to do without me for one day. What about you? Aren't you concerned you will lose an afternoon's reading?"

He shrugged. "It's only *The Midnight Bell* again, and it's too pleasant a day to spend with Alphonsus and his melancholy."

"By all means, then, let us spend it with the Hamblys and *their* melancholy."

The unfortunate Hamblys lived on the first floor of a neat but dilapidated cottage off the footpath from Weeke. There was a pig rooting in the shrubbery and a hen pecking at something beside the walkway, but Lily did not think it was the Hamblys' pig or hen, for neither old Mrs. Hambly nor slightly-less-old Miss Hambly were the active, livestock-rearing sort. The animals must belong to the ground-floor occupants. With a sigh she took the basket from her brother, who then helped her unstick the door to the gloomy, close staircase.

"Off you go, Lady B," he grinned, as he plopped down upon the step to wait and flick a pebble or two at the hen.

The staircase had no rail, but Lily supposed the enclosing walls with their chipped plaster served the same purpose, as she bounced from one to the other, maneuvering herself and the heavy, awkward basket up the creaking steps without spilling herself or the soup.

Her first knock was too tentative, betraying her unwillingness to be there, but then she took herself in hand and gave the door a proper rap. This raised a murmur of voices within, followed by surprisingly firm footsteps for ladies so frail as the Hamblys, and then the door was thrown open.

To reveal Mr. Simon Kenner.

The fair-haired curate, he of the wiry strength and panther grace.

"Mr. Kenner!" breathed Lily.

"Miss Ellsworth!" For an instant she read alarm in his pale eyes, usually so unrevealing.

"I—did not expect to see you here."

"I confess my imagination was equally limited." He held out his arms for the basket. "May I...?"

Gratefully she gave it to him, and he retreated to allow her to enter. Not that the confined space allowed him to retreat far, and Lily repressed a shiver as she squeezed past, her skirts brushing against his breeches. He was warm. Or it was a warm day. Or warm in the cottage.

A little panicked, she turned her back to him. The Hamblys' sitting room was as stifling and gloomy as the staircase, and Beatrice was right—it did not smell very delightful within—but Lily pasted a smile on her face as she greeted wizened little Miss Hambly and the heap of rags which resolved itself into old Mrs. Hambly (Lily mentally applauding Beatrice for the accuracy of her description).

"Mrs. Hambly. Miss Hambly. What a—what a pleasure," she began, taking the chair Miss Hambly indicated. It was warm, and Lily suspected Mr. Kenner had lately occupied it. "My stepmother Mrs. Ellsworth sends her regrets that she has a headache and could not come today, but she hopes you will feel better soon, Mrs. Hambly, and that you both might enjoy some—some treats from Hollowgate."

"How too, too, too kind of you, Miss Ellsworth," squeaked Miss Hambly, admiring the basket's contents. "Too, too kind."

"It was—my stepmother's idea," admitted Lily, all too, too aware of Mr. Kenner looking on while she was showered with all these "toos."

"Ah, but it was you, Miss Ellsworth, who have borne the burden and the heat of the day," the unsettling man observed blandly from his post by the door. "How too, too kind of you."

Lily threw him a dark look, but he only blinked at her, his eyes once more inscrutable, and she must perforce return her gaze to the two withered women, determined not to peer at the clock face over Miss Hambly's shoulder which would tell her how soon she might be released.

For his part, Kenner was dismayed by the tumult Miss Ellsworth's appearance provoked in him. When he opened the door to find her blue eyes glowing up at him in the dimness, his breath stalled, and once he had relieved her of the basket, he took care to stand as far from her as the small room allowed. How was it she looked so vivid and pure—like a bright star piercing a clouded night sky? Like an angel of mercy? Only a minute earlier, he would have scoffed at using such words to describe her, but then—only a minute earlier, he had been thinking of her as quite the opposite of an angel.

For the day before, the two Miss Weekses had called at the rectory, bursting in upon Sophie where she sat embroidering the hem of the altar cloth for Transfiguration Sunday. Kenner himself had been working in his library and not in the parlor, but as the doors to both rooms stood ajar and the rectory was compact, he heard every word that was spoken.

"Oh, Miss Kenner! Miss Kenner! You will not believe—" they panted as soon as Vickery admitted them and withdrew again.

"Let me tell it, Frederica," insisted Miss Weeks, "because I was the first to see them—"

"Yes, and you would have walked right into them, if I had not stopped you," retorted her sister.

"Walked into whom?" asked Sophie.

The two sisters talked over each other again in their eagerness. "We didn't know, at first—"

"That's not true—I knew straight off—"

"You didn't, until he released her!"

"I did—I have admired the ribbons on her bonnet before because they were the very ones I thought to purchase in June—"

"They weren't. You wanted the darker ones."

"No, I wanted *those* ones."

"Please, Miss Weeks, Miss Frederica," pleaded Sophie. "Of whom are you speaking?"

"Miss Ellsworth!" crowed Miss Weeks, taking up the thread again. "We saw Miss Ellsworth just now!"

"Miss Ellsworth and a gentleman who was at the ball the other day. A very handsome gentleman. *Very* handsome."

"They were standing at the archway that leads to Hollowgate."

"Well," said Sophie reasonably, "what is so extraordinary about that? Miss Ellsworth *lives* at Hollowgate, after all, and every gentleman near and far calls there. To be sure, she has so many admirers." This last was said on a wistful note.

"Would we make such a fuss if they were merely standing there?" demanded Miss Weeks. "No, Miss Kenner—she was—he was—they were—they were—kissing!"

"Kissing?" cried Sophie, and she jumped to her feet so hard the sofa slid back. (The scrape of it conveniently drowned out the sound of a bottle of ink being knocked over in the library, and Kenner had to scramble in silence to right it and to blot the dark puddle spreading across his sermon.)

"I don't believe you!" declared Sophie. "And it's—wrong of you to spread such falsehoods."

"Why would we invent such a story?" Miss Frederica said, her voice rising in indignation. "It was Miss Ellsworth and some gentleman from the ball, standing nearly in the lane and *kissing*."

"Then—then—then it's very clear he either took an unwanted liberty with her or—or—or they're engaged," pronounced the loyal Sophie.

"Well, they must be engaged, then," Miss Weeks answered airily. "Because she didn't struggle at all. Not one bit. Nor did she give any sign of distress. When they left off, they only whispered to each other, and then she was gone, and he stood looking after her."

"It was rather...delicious," sighed Miss Frederica.

"You mean to say, it was rather scandalous," corrected her sister.

"That, too. But deliciously scandalous."

"Well," said Sophie, at a complete loss. "Well."

After another minute, in which Kenner did not move so much as a muscle, he was listening so hard, Sophie seemed to collect herself because she asked, "What did this man look like, besides being handsome? More than one gentleman could be described so."

"Tall. Youthful, with a fine person," Miss Weeks said at once.

"Brown hair with a wave to it," added Miss Frederica. "And a manly voice."

Had it been Gil? Kenner wondered. Had Gil proposed? Gil's hair did not wave, and Kenner thought he was still at Fareham, but perhaps he had come galloping back in such haste it rumpled his hair, sensing that he might lose ground to all his rivals. Describing Gil as 'very handsome' was a stretch, moreover, but tastes differed, Kenner supposed. Certainly the words would better fit Dailey—could it have been him? Brown hair meant it was not Caxton. And 'youthful' ruled out Sir Basil.

Kenner tapped his fingers soundlessly on the desk. Likely even differing tastes would not ascribe a 'fine person' to Trimp, so that eliminated *him*. And as for Frayne and Willett, one was very short and the other alarmingly tall, either trait distinctive enough that Kenner thought the Miss Weekses would have remarked it.

So it was either Gil or Dailey who embraced Miss Ellsworth in full view of the road and any passersby. Not that it should matter who it was, or that it had happened at all. And the fact that it did matter troubled him.

Deeply.

Had he been a different sort of clergyman, Kenner might have deluded himself into thinking his disquiet stemmed from seeing a member of his flock go astray, but he knew that, had the Miss Weekses come upon, say, Miss Hambly being kissed out of her senses by a handsome man in the road, he would have been more likely to grin than to grit his teeth.

Damnation.

She had turned his head, then, and he might as well admit it. At least—to himself. Not that any other person need be told (least of all

Miss Ellsworth). Especially now that she was engaged. And Kenner did not doubt she was engaged. For, whatever he might think of her, she was a gentlewoman, and unengaged gentlewomen were hardly given to embracing strange men in full view of the public.

And now here she was, on a most uncharacteristic mission of mercy, ambushing him in the incommodious space of the Hamblys' home before any resolutions he formed had time enough to harden. He blamed this lack of preparation for what he said next: "It is indeed kind of you, Miss Ellsworth, to take time away from your many...engagements."

Before he spoke, Miss Hambly had been in the middle of cataloguing each symptom of her aunt's decline and remarking on whether the severity of that particular symptom had increased or lessened from the preceding day, and she fumbled to a halt at his interruption.

Lily's head whipped up. "To what engagements do you refer, sir? I am not aware of having any more engagements than fall to other young ladies in my position." (That Lily could retort so swiftly to the curate showed that she likely had not been giving Miss Hambly her full attention.)

"Perhaps I was mistaken in referring to 'engagements' in the plural," he returned. "When a young lady comes to achieve the chief 'engagement' for which her life has trained her, I imagine it eclipses the rest."

There was no mistaking the genuineness of Lily's baffled stare. Poor Miss Hambly peered from one to the other of her guests, unwilling to thrust herself into an argument she knew nothing about, and her aunt Mrs. Hambly only caught a word or two of it in any case and was more concerned with the draft she felt creeping under her shawl.

Kenner cursed inwardly. Why the devil did Miss Ellsworth not know what he was referring to? She was by no means so blockish that she could not follow a play upon words.

And she was not. Her puzzlement gradually gave way to a glare, and when she spoke again, her voice was brittle. "Even if I were engaged to be married, sir, if that is what you are hinting at, I assure you that it is not a state toward which my whole life has been directed. I have many interests and abilities which I have cultivated solely for my own pleasure and that of my family." (Had any of her siblings been present, they might have laughed at this and dared her to name which ability she had cultivated for *their* pleasure, but fortunately for Lily, even Tyrone was out of earshot.)

"You are…not…engaged, then?" Kenner asked slowly.

"To be married? Indeed not! Whatever gave you such an idea?"

"I—" There was no possible answer to this. He could not say, *You* must *be engaged because the two Miss Weekses saw you kissing somebody in the street and then came to the rectory to blab your misdeeds.* Had they somehow been mistaken in their witness? But how on earth could they be? They knew Miss Ellsworth—had been members of St. Eadburh's their entire lives, as had she—knew their younger sisters were bosom friends—

Lily was reaching her own conclusions. "Sir, did someone *tell* you I was engaged to be married?" As difficult as she found to credit it, had Mr. Dailey been saying it was so? Who else could it possibly be? Why, she would *murder* the man when she saw him again! But—but—was Mr. Dailey even acquainted with Mr. Kenner?

Kenner's mind was racing. If Miss Ellsworth was not engaged, then she was free. And if she was free, then he—if he were fool enough to try—

But no sooner did this realization send the blood rushing to his face than he remembered there was still the kiss to account for. If Miss Ellsworth was *not* engaged, what was she doing kissing strange men?

It might have been her brother, he guessed. But, no, the Miss Weekses would have recognized Tyrone Ellsworth. *One of her cousins, then, whatever their names were. They belong to a different parish, and the Miss Weekses might not be acquainted with them.* But what sister kissed her brother or her younger cousin like a lover? Perhaps it had been a peck on the cheek. But would that be deemed "deliciously scandalous"?

You are catching at straws, he reproved himself.

Stop.

Short of asking Miss Ellsworth if she had stood in the Romsey Road yesterday and received a man's embraces, Kenner did not know what could be done to shed light on the matter. And even if such a question were not utterly *outré*, it did not guarantee him an honest answer.

All these thoughts flew through his mind in the space of an instant, but he could see by Miss Ellsworth's raised eyebrow that she felt she had waited long enough for his answer.

"No one told me you were engaged," he said, thankful to hear how steady he sounded. "It was—a shot at venture—nothing more—considering how many offers you will be certain to receive in future."

Instead of appearing flattered, her blue eyes narrowed further and her mouth worked. Then, with a visible effort, she replied, "Ah. Will you permit me in that case, Mr. Kenner, to observe you are a far more accurate archer with a literal bow and arrow, and if you would please to confine your 'shots at venture' to bales of hay, I, for one, would thank you."

He said nothing, only giving a stiff bow. After a few minutes of stilted, distracted conversation with the Hamblys, he promised to call again and made his departure like a man reprieved at the eleventh hour.

Emerging from the dimness of the staircase, Kenner nearly tripped over Tyrone on the step.

"Whoa there, Mr. Kenner! Didn't know you were here. Did Lily make it up all right with that basket?"

"She did."

"She'll be envying you your escape, I imagine." He grinned at the curate. "In strictest confidence, paying these sorts of visits are more in my sister Flossie's way. But, to give credit where credit is due, some part of Lily must have wanted to come because she rarely does anything she doesn't want to."

Given Miss Ellsworth's recent activities, Kenner hardly found this comforting. But he gave the lad the approximation of a smile and went on his way.

Chapter Twelve

...You shall chance to whip your Information,
And beate the Messenger, who bids beware
Of what is to be dreaded.
— Shakespeare, *Coriolanus,* IV.vi.56 (c.1616)

It was Aggie who shed light on Mr. Kenner's odd remarks.

Lily and Tyrone returned from the Hamblys to find Minta and her friend playing at bowls on the lawn while Beatrice looked on.

"This was why you were too busy to come with me?" asked Lily dryly.

"I couldn't very well go," said Minta, "when Aggie was expecting to find me here."

"And I had to escape my house," Aggie added, sending her ball rolling right up to click against Minta's. "Because my sisters can talk of nothing else all day long but finding husbands. Which man of their acquaintance would make the best husband? And is so-and-so more eligible than thus-and-such? They say they must choose from whomever you reject, so they are quite anxious to know whom you will choose."

"Who says I will choose anyone?"

Minta and Aggie shared a significant look. Then Aggie nudged Minta and Minta rolled her eyes. "Fine," she sighed. "But you mustn't shoot the messenger, Lily, when I ask this. Is it true that you were really kissing somebody yesterday in the road? Because that was what Aggie's sisters told her."

"Was I *what?*"

"My sisters said they saw you," squeaked Aggie, hunching up her shoulders as if she thought Lily might hit her. "And you didn't see them. And I'm afraid there has been some talk."

Aggie was right to cringe because Lily looked in danger of combusting. "Talk? Who is talking, if not them? Who have they been talking to?" She drew a sudden sharp breath, her mouth falling open, and her fists clenching. "They called at the rectory, didn't they? That's why he—why he said—"

Breaking off, she clutched her arms around herself, making an almighty effort, as if she would keep herself from spinning apart.

"Why who said?" prompted Bea. "And whom did you kiss, Lily?"

"I did not kiss anyone!" shouted Lily, heedless of who heard her. "*He* kissed *me*! And caught me so off guard that I could not respond properly. It was that confounded Mr. Dailey! And it is *your sisters*

I must thank, Aggie, for Mr. Kenner asking me today if I was engaged!"

"Are you?" persisted Minta.

"NO! Mr. Dailey asked me, and I said No. Definitively. Conclusively."

"How conclusive could it have been, if he kissed you?" was Tyrone's mild question.

Lily whirled on him. "What sort of brother are you? I've been insulted! You should be threatening to call him out."

Tyrone looked appalled. "I'm fifteen, and you want me to call him out? I've never fired a pistol in my life! I think it far more likely Flossie's Robert will feel obliged to challenge Mr. Dailey."

"Flossie's Robert? Oh, no! Then—shhhh!" Lily held up her hands, distressed. "None of you must say anything about it to Mr. Fairchild—to Robert, rather. Not a word! Because—suppose he were to be killed by Mr. Dailey and Florence made a widow?"

Beatrice burst into tears, Flossie's new husband being quite a favorite with her.

"Wait—and you don't care if *I'm* killed?" demanded her brother.

"Of course I care." With a groan, Lily dropped to sit in the grass. "I've lost my mind. I don't know what I'm saying. And *do* stop crying, Bea."

"I've only just started," whimpered Beatrice, "so you needn't make it sound like I've been at it all morning. I—I don't want R-Robert to die!"

"He isn't going to die, you goose. I was exaggerating. I suppose he might only assault Mr. Dailey and get beaten himself and then arrested and thrown in the Gaol."

This drew another wail—a prolonged one—from the little girl.

"Hush—do hush, Bea." Lily patted her impatiently and not very soothingly. "Listen to me: Robert isn't going to die or get beaten or arrested or sent to the Gaol because he isn't going to call Mr. Dailey out. And he isn't going to call Mr. Dailey out because he isn't going to know a thing about it."

"He'll hear the gossip," Minta could not help pointing out.

Lily scowled. "Oh, yes. I forgot the gossip. Dash it all." She ripped out blades of grass as she sat there, thinking, and the others waited in silence, Minta only passing her wooden ball from hand to hand but not bowling it.

"All right," Lily said at last. "See here. This is going to be the story, as near the truth as I can make it: Mr. Dailey took me by surprise and kissed me without my permission. I then told him it would never do, and we had better not marry, and we came to an understanding. He will never try it again, and I have forgiven him; therefore no one is to make any sort of fuss about it because it wouldn't be Christian."

"*Have* you forgiven him?" sniffled Beatrice.

"No, of course not. I mean—I will—eventually, so let us just imagine I already have, for the sake of argument. Or for the sake of peace, rather." Lily eyed Aggie beadily. "Is that clear, Aggie? Can you say as much to your sisters?"

Aggie bobbed her towhead eagerly.

Which is how it soon got about in Winchester that Miss Lily Ellsworth was in the habit of kissing young men for amusement.

The Fareham races being ended, Mr. Gilbert Wright would have gone directly from the stables at Meadowsweep to Hollowgate, except that it was his grandmother's birthday. And the beginning of August always meant a birthday dinner *en famille* at the deanery in honor of Mrs. Fellowes. There was no way around it, but he told himself he would call at Hollowgate the very next day, come what might.

He was the last to arrive, finding the largest parlor stuffed with Wrights and Kenners, the windows open to the summer warmth and lemonade being passed by one of the maids.

"Many happy returns, Granny," said Wright, bending to kiss her cheek.

"Dear boy," she murmured. "How glad I am you've come."

"Any luck with Slapbang at Fareham?" his grandfather asked. "I saw nothing in the *Chronicle.*"

"You must check again next Monday because Slapbang won the very last race of the day, the Fareham Plate. Not quite the King's Plate, but not bad. Kingdom Come tried to make another go of it, but Slapbang put him in his place again, by nearly a distance."

"Hurrah! Hurrah! Will you enter Slapbang at Salisbury?" clamored his younger sisters.

"Most likely."

"Surely the beast isn't wearing down, if he won again," Dean Fellowes observed.

"He is in prime condition," his grandson assured him. "I have even received several requests that I put him into breeding service in the spring."

"Excellent! Strike while the iron is hot, my lad."

"Indeed, yes," Wright answered, his colour rising. "I intend to make arrangements with them. But first, in the meantime, I may have other, more pressing business."

At that, it seemed to him every member of his extended family gave some other member of his extended family a Significant Look. His younger sister Amelia even stifled a gasp, bouncing up, only to be silenced and stilled by a thinning of the lips and a shake of the head from their mother.

"What?" he frowned. "What is it?"

"My dears," said his grandmother, rising to her feet and compelling the gentlemen to theirs. "Let us enjoy our dinner and leave serious talk for later."

"Serious talk? What can you mean, Granny?"

When she didn't answer, Wright attempted to catch first his father's eye, then his mother's, then his grandfather's, but at the deanery Mrs. Fellowes ruled with a benevolent hand, and he knew he had no choice but to wait and wonder.

It was only after fish soup, fricasseed chicken, ragout of onions, snow and cream, a salad, a raspberry tart, and several toasts to Mrs. Fellowes' health and happiness, that the dean's wife signaled the ladies' withdrawal. "We will have music, my dears, so do not be long."

Although the conversation during the meal kept to farming and horseracing and diocesan matters, Wright had not once forgotten that there was a Topic the family was avoiding, even if he were not reminded of it by his sisters' furtive glances (not to mention his cousin Sophie's—though he took care not to look her way). Had he not been so absorbed in his own concerns, he might have remarked that Simon was unusually silent as well, and it was to Kenner that his father and uncle and grandfather deferred, after a mere ten minutes over their port.

"We will leave you to it," said the dean quietly, sliding back his chair and nodding for his two sons-in-law to follow.

When the door shut behind them, Wright pushed his half-empty glass away. "All right, then. Out with it, Simon. What is it? What is this subject which concerns me, which you all have been determined to dodge?"

His cousin released a slow breath. It was not as if he had looked forward to this conversation either, and he had known it was coming longer than Gilbert. Kenner had been nominated by his grandmother as the most appropriate person to address the issue, but if she had been able to see some ways into his heart, he suspected it would have changed her mind altogether. But, if not him, who?

Bulls were best taken by the horns, as the saying went.

Kenner pushed his own glass aside. "It's about Miss Ellsworth."

"Miss Ellsworth?" Wright's voice rose in pitch and cracked, to his embarrassment. He cleared his throat. "Is she unwell?"

"She is...perfectly well, I believe. But there have been...rumors about her recently."

"What—sort—of—rumors?" Without his glass to clutch, he found himself digging his fingernails into the tablecloth. "What do you mean? And why are you the one to tell me of them?"

Kenner grimaced. "Granny thought, because Miss Ellsworth belongs to my congregation—and because I know some of the parties involved—I should be the one to brave your wrath."

Then Wright was on his feet. "What wrath?" he asked wrathfully. "Why should there be any danger of my wrath? Tell me it all at once, Simon, or by G—"

"Exactly," said Kenner. "Look, Gil. In a nutshell, the matter is this: Miss Ellsworth was seen—embracing the man Dailey—or he her—or both mutually—in full view of anyone who cared to witness it."

"It's a lie!" roared his cousin, striking the table. There was a brief pause in the music drifting in from the parlor, and, with difficulty, Wright lowered his voice. "It's a lie, and I'll smash anyone who claims otherwise."

Carefully, Kenner slid back his own chair and rose, thinking it best to put space between himself and his grandmother's china, glassware and cutlery. "Then I'm afraid you'll have to take on the whole county, Gil, including Miss Ellsworth herself, who has freely admitted to the incident."

"Damn you!"

His eyes wild, Wright lunged for Kenner, hurling him backward into the buffet. The vase of flowers thereon toppled over, spilling stems and water across the surface and splashing the wallpaper, while a silver platter clattered to the floor. The music from the parlor halted again, but Kenner was not aware of it, too busy wrestling his hot-brained, hare-brained cousin off him. "Gil—stop—*whoof!* Stop, you idiot!"

"Take it back! Take it back, you bastard!" cried Wright, fists flying. Kenner's own were not slow to respond, especially when one of his cousin's blows connected with his lip and drew blood, and he felt his own anger surge. *Did the fool think he* liked *being the bearer of such news?*

Kenner was not in the habit of engaging in physical brawls—but he and his cousin had spent much of their boyhood settling matters thus. Or Gil had liked to settle matters thus, until Kenner grew too tall and strong to be effectively subdued in that manner. It had been years, though, since any of this had been necessary, Gil having not only matured but also having grown to respect his cousin's wiry strength. On this occasion, however, they were more evenly matched because Wright was so distraught, and what would ordinarily have been a bout of perhaps a minute stretched into two. Long enough that Mrs. Fellowes made a movement toward the drawing room door, only to have the dean say, "No, no, Katy, you had better let them sort it out."

"But my china!" she protested.

"What if Simon hurts Gil?" whispered Sophie.

"Nonsense," retorted her mother. "But let us hope Gil doesn't black his eye—otherwise how can Simon stand in the pulpit on Sunday?"

Another thirty seconds passed, and then—at last—all the thumping and grunting and knocking about gave way to silence.

"Thank the Lord," said the dean.

And— "That's that," said his son-in-law Mr. John Kenner. "I'm glad *I* wasn't chosen to play messenger."

The dean's other son-in-law Mr. Thomas Wright flapped his newspaper open again and said dryly to his older daughter, "Well, Anna? Let us have the rest of your concerto now. If they're not both dead, they'll be in soon enough."

They were not both dead, though they were both winded and Kenner had a knee to his cousin's back. "Do you yield?" he asked thickly, ferreting out his handkerchief to press to his lip.

Wright muttered something profane but in the affirmative, and Kenner pushed off him to sit with his back propped against the wall.

"Tell me everything," muttered Wright, through his own thick lip.

Kenner complied, beginning with the Miss Weekses rushing to the rectory to share what they had seen in the Romsey Road and ending with the Miss Weekses rushing to the rectory to report what their sister Aggie said that Miss Ellsworth said on the matter. In between—it could not be avoided—he mentioned seeing Miss Ellsworth himself at the Hamblys, where she confirmed that she was not engaged.

"It all fits together, unfortunately," Kenner concluded. "And Granny thought you should know. You *were* planning on offering for her, were you not?"

"What do you mean, 'were'?"

"What do you mean, what do I mean?"

"Who says I will *not* offer for her?" Wright insisted.

"Excuse me, Gil—excuse us all—if we assumed you might not want to marry a woman who..."

"Who *what*?" he prompted ominously, his fists balling again.

"Oh, for heaven's sake, man," groaned Kenner. "Use your head, Gil."

"What? You all decided to take what two gossipy, jealous girls had to say for gospel? Instead of—instead of defending an innocent girl's honor, you—you all—"

"The so-called innocent girl was the first to claim her honor did not need defending!" Kenner snapped. "She told Miss Agatha Weeks—a young lady *not* given to gossip, mind you, and certainly *not* jealous—that she had forgiven all, and one can only suppose she did not find the offense so very offensive."

"You don't know her!" Wright bellowed, pounding a fist on the carpet. "You don't know what an innocent—what an *angel* she is!"

Kenner had a flash of memory: opening the Hamblys' door to find Miss Ellsworth on the stairs, her eyes aglow in the dim light.

"She looks like an angel, I'll grant you," he said quietly.

"She *is* an angel!" insisted his cousin, not appeased by this grudging concession. "And I am still going to marry her, if she'll have me."

Kenner threw up his hands. "Gil—think this through. Even if everything I told you today had not happened, do you truly believe you could make each other happy?"

"What do you mean?" Gil growled.

"I mean, the mere fact that you think Miss Ellsworth is an angel. Wait—wait—hear me out! Gil, no woman—no *person* is an angel. I've said this before: each of us has his fatal flaws, and some flaws are made the more fatal for being brought together."

"What are you saying? That Miss Ellsworth and I would not be a good match?"

Kenner had no particular desire to be set upon or punched in the face again, so he chose his words with care. "I think, Gil, that...Miss Ellsworth is accustomed to having her own way and to...finding herself cleverer than those around her."

"What of it? I should be glad to indulge her, and—and what man would want a stupid wife, when he could have a clever one?"

Kenner ran troubled fingers through his hair. "I don't know, Gil—a stupider wife might be less trouble to you in the long run. A sweet little, adoring, obedient, stupid wife."

"You all just want me to marry Sophie."

"I don't care a straw if you marry Sophie. And I probably ought to object to you calling my sister stupid. She's really only stupid about you, Gil."

"I won't marry her, in any event."

"Fine," returned Kenner with an impatient wave. "But must you therefore marry Miss Ellsworth?"

A gleam of suspicion dawned in his cousin's eyes, and his brows drew together. "Say, Simon—are you certain you aren't trying to persuade me against Miss Ellsworth so that you may have her yourself?"

Kenner had prepared himself for this question (and had, in fact, posed it to himself), so he was able to respond lightly, without any telltale hesitation or blush. "Don't be ridiculous. You know I plan to be bishop one day—what sort of bishop's wife would Miss Ellsworth make? I can't turn around to find her kissing every deacon and dean she can lay hold of."

This very Simon-like response did nothing to allay Gil's fears, but he knew it was no use wishing for a serious answer if Simon chose not to give one. Very well. There was one certain way to make sure Simon didn't get Miss Ellsworth for himself, and that was to marry her first.

Pushing himself to his feet, he thrust a hand toward his cousin to help him up.

"Well, Simon, you can tell Granny and everyone else that you did your duty, but that I insisted on going my own way."

Kenner brushed himself off and tucked his soiled handkerchief back in his pocket, tentatively touching his broken lip with the tip of his tongue.

"Indeed, Gil. You took the words right out of my mouth."

Chapter Thirteen

Wouldst thou have a serpent sting thee twice?
— Shakespeare, *The Merchant of Venice,* IV.i.68 (1600)

Lily, would you do me the kindness of explaining this?" asked her father at the breakfast table. He held up a folded note in his hand, and Lily must perforce leave off buttering her toast to come and fetch it.

Crossdown, Hants.

5 August 1801

My dear Mr. Ellsworth,
I had the pleasure of making your acquaintance at Worthy Down some weeks ago, whilst we watched sev-

eral races, and have since called numerous times upon your family at Hollowgate, though without the specific good fortune of encountering you again. (Your wife Mrs. Ellsworth and children explain you are much occupied with estate business, which could not be more comprehensible to me, as I too am the sole master of an extensive estate, I believe approaching, if not equaling, the proportions of Hollowgate. But more on that shortly.)

Again, as I say, though my pleasure in our introduction has not yet been repeated, I have nevertheless greatly enjoyed and benefited from increasing friendship with the rest of the Ellsworths in general and with Miss Ellsworth in particular. To wit, my admiration for Miss Ellsworth has grown beyond the bounds of mere friendship—

From the style and loquacity alone Lily did not need to read every word of the crammed epistle to guess its author, and her horrified eye skipped to the bottom of the sheet, which was signed, indeed, "'Yours etc., Walter Dailey.'" Not only that, but the sentence directly above read, "'...as I am certain Miss Ellsworth has told you of my intentions, my wish to speak apart with you will come as no surprise. With your leave, please expect me at eleven o'clock.'"

Her appetite vanished, she looked at her father. "It's not possible."

"Ah, now—what can you mean, 'not possible'? Not possible that our Lily has captured a rich young man's heart?" Mr. Ellsworth's mood—always benign and cheerful, since he did his best to ignore anything upsetting in life—had been especially serene since the announcement of their new sibling's looked-for arrival in the spring. "I have been expecting such requests, Lily, since that day at Worthy Down. My question for you is, how have you not warned me that you had such an understanding with Mr. Dailey?"

Her younger siblings gasped (Beatrice) and smothered snickers (Minta and Tyrone), and her stepmother turned amazed eyes on her, but Lily was recovering. "I did not warn you, Papa, because there was nothing to tell. There is no understanding with Mr. Dailey. He did—propose to me—a couple of days ago, but I refused him. I cannot think why he should come again. I was very clear."

Her father sighed, clicking his tongue regretfully. "He seems an amiable young man, my dear, in addition to being quite eligible."

"He may be amiable, Papa, but he is also proving most thick-headed. And, first and foremost, he talks entirely too much."

"Well, well. You are particular in your tastes. So be it."

"Can you not send him a reply, Papa," she coaxed, "and tell him not to come at all?"

"I'm afraid not, my love. For one thing, the note might miss him, and for another it is best to keep on good terms with one's peers."

"Well, I won't see him again," Lily declared. "I simply can't bear to. The man could talk the hind leg off a donkey! I will walk the grounds until someone tells me he is gone."

"You could hide in Flossie's garden," suggested Araminta.

"I don't need to *hide*," she replied testily. "There is a difference between wanting to avoid seeing someone who has no business coming in the first place and *hiding*. Hiding implies I think I have done something wrong, and I haven't."

Therefore, whatever Lily was doing an hour later, keeping to a path through the copse that paralleled the drive, she was not hiding. And to prove this, she offered to take Snap with her for a very long walk, a duty usually passed among her siblings or to Mrs. Ellsworth or an under-footman.

Snap the terrier, like all dogs, adored his walks. But he especially enjoyed those rare instances when Lily accompanied him because her mind always wandered, and she let him go where he pleased and do whatever he pleased, which usually involved sniffing everything he could and leaving an appropriate calling card. Therefore her behavior on this occasion frustrated him. Firstly, she kept the line tight in her hands, so that he could not range as far as he liked, and secondly, she tugged him away from the gravel drive where he was wont to run. How could he pay each tree a visit and discover who or what had been by?

Like the clever pup he was, he bided his time until she should be distracted into loosening her hold. And his moment came when she finally heard the crunch of horse hoofs on gravel (Snap having caught the sound a full ten seconds earlier, when the horse was still in the Romsey Road). With a muffled gasp, she dropped his line altogether and darted behind the nearest tree. He was free!

The terrier gave a joyous string of barks, launching himself with abandon at the red squirrel which had maddened him with its taunting and scampering.

"Snap!" hissed Lily, torn between chasing him and staying out of sight.

But the rider, seeing the dog streak across his path, drew rein with a crunching spray of gravel. Then, turning his mount in a slow circle, he made to survey his surroundings.

Cursing the dog under her breath, Lily emerged from the copse, beckoning the terrier with fierce gestures which he wisely ignored.

"Why, Miss Ellsworth!" cried the rider, and, at the sound of his most un-Mr.-Dailey-like voice, her gaze snapped to meet his.

"Mr. Wright!" she breathed.

Eagerly the dashing young man swung himself down and reached to catch at Snap's line. "Good morning to you, Miss Ellsworth. I didn't expect to find you out here."

"Nor I you." Lily threw an uneasy glance back toward the end of the drive. Oh, dear. How could she simultaneously invite Mr. Wright to the house while also preventing Mr. Dailey seeing her?

"I was just coming to call," he said, "and how glad I am to catch you here, though I would have waited for your return if I had not found you within. I've been sorry even to be gone the last few days—at Fareham, you know, where Slapbang—"

"Mr. Wright," she interrupted hastily, snatching Snap's line from his grasp, "I too am glad to see you. But—as you see, I am engaged in walking the dog. Would—it be possible for you to return later? Perhaps in an hour?"

"But—er—what if I just joined you as you walked?"

"Oh—that wouldn't do. Because—what about your horse, sir?"

"Thunder won't go anywhere without me," he assured her, a little uncertain at her reception. "I can hand him off to a groom when we reach the house."

"Oh—but—but—Snap here doesn't like it when I don't give him my full attention. He is quite a demanding little beast."

Mr. Wright looked dubiously at the demanding little beast, who was lifting a leg beside the nearest tree. "Well, if you think it better, Miss Ellsworth..."

"Absolutely," she answered crisply, giving a jerk on the line. "Enjoy your ride on this beautiful day, and we will see you in an hour. Come, Snap."

But just then the mischievous, tormenting red squirrel chose to chitter at his enemy from a safe post halfway up the neighboring lime tree. With a volley of enraged barks, Snap hurled himself toward the adversary, taking Lily with him into the shrubbery, where she stumbled and tumbled into a heap among the twigs and branches and leaves, her skirts flying halfway to her knees.

"Miss Ellsworth!" gasped Mr. Wright, rushing to her rescue while trying his best not to steal a second look at her shapely limbs.

To the din of chitters and squeaks and bow-wows were added Lily's shrieks and a great rustling and flapping as her knight floundered in the bushes, all while Snap darted back and forth and round and round, tangling them all together.

Which is how Mr. Dailey came upon them when he trotted up the drive the next minute.

"Oh! Do be careful," Lily was chiding. "Your button is caught on my lace, and if you pull that way you will tear it. Oh! Don't pull that either—the line is wound around my ankle."

"What the devil?" demanded a shocked Mr. Dailey, his mount rearing as he sawed at the reins. "Madam, is this man assaulting you?"

"What's that?" spluttered Mr. Wright, twisting to face this impudent interlocutor (and tearing Lily's lace in the process). "How dare you! 'Assault,' indeed. I am trying to help Miss Ellsworth!"

When Lily herself sat up, harassed and unkempt, her skirts now *above* her knees, Mr. Dailey nearly lost his seat. For once, he was utterly at a loss for words, and she took advantage of it. "I was tangled in Snap's line, and Mr. Wright was so chivalrous as to come to my aid," she explained, whipping her skirts down, even as she untangled her ankles and tucked her torn lace back in her bodice. That blasted dog! She would grind him into sausages for this, she would!

Mr. Dailey could not speak, but he could dismount and tower over them with magnificent disapproval. Ignoring Mr. Wright, who was struggling to come upright, Mr. Dailey extended an imperious hand to Lily, which she ignored with an attempt at matching disdain. Her effort was not nearly as successful, however, considering her crooked bonnet and the hank of her dark hair which hung down untidily.

"Miss Ellsworth," Mr. Dailey intoned, "are you injured?"

"Only in my dignity," she said shortly. Plucking out a hairpin, she twisted her loose hair and skewered it back in place. "These accidents will happen. I was walking Snap here and—" with a vague wave she indicated the resulting mayhem.

"I was coming to see your father."

When Lily said nothing to this, Mr. Dailey fixed his eye on Mr. Wright. "Did you hear me, sir? I was coming to *see her father*."

"And I was coming to see Miss Ellsworth," retorted Mr. Wright. "But, as it is, I am not sorry to encounter you here, Dailey, because disturbing rumors have reached my ears. Rumors about you taking liberties with Miss Ellsworth."

At once Lily forgot her embarrassment at being found scuffling in the hedge with a gentleman, her legs on display for all the world. "To what rumors do you refer, Mr. Wright?" she challenged, her eyes blazing violet. "Who has been gossiping to you about me?"

Could he possibly have called upon the Miss Weekses? Did he even know them?

"I would rather not say, Miss Ellsworth," he hedged. "Suffice to say, there is a general consensus that Dailey here did not treat you with the respect due a gentlewoman."

"I say," protested Mr. Dailey, "you do us a grave injustice, sir, both in believing such nonsense and in repeating it—"

"There is no 'us' here," Lily interrupted, spinning on him next, her finger upraised. "Please do not refer to 'us.' *You* did insult me, sir, but *I* have chosen to forgive you for it."

"I knew it!" cried Mr. Wright, thrusting himself in Mr. Dailey's face. "You insulted this faultless young lady, injuring her reputation, and you will answer to me for it!"

"You dare accuse me of misconduct toward her, Wright, when I discover you assailing her in the bushes?"

"Assailing? *Assailing?* Say that to my face again, sir!"

In other circumstances, Lily would have appreciated Mr. Wright's determination to defend her, but she was too vexed by the gossip he referred to to welcome it now. Groaning therefore, she thrust her own arm between the two men and forced them apart. "I hardly know which of you to berate first, sirs, but I had better begin with you, Mr. Wright."

"With me?" he echoed in incredulity.

"With you, if you are going to take up arms for me, which you haven't the least right to do. I have a father and an uncle and a brother and two cousins and a brother-in-law who can do so, if I call upon them. Which I am not. Because, as I just said—no matter what anyone has told you—I have forgiven Mr. Dailey." Lily whipped around, as if withdrawing her blade from one opponent in order to stick it through the next. "And, as for you, Mr. Dailey, I have no idea why you would be calling on my father today, when I was abundantly clear with you that there was *no hope*."

"But—are you certain? You can't mean that!" said Mr. Dailey.

"Of course I can mean that! Why can't I mean that?"

"Oh, Miss Ellsworth—if you only knew how I have reproached myself. Because I was too forceful, too sudden on the other occasion. I am a straightforward man—some might even call me brash—but I should have taken into account a lady's delicate sensibilities. You are a fragile flower, which I handled too roughly in my eagerness—"

"'Handled'?" shouted Mr. Wright.

"Mr. Dailey, do stop. I beg of you."

"But Miss Ellsworth, if you have truly forgiven me as you say you have, why would you now tell me there is no hope?"

"Because, sir, there wasn't any hope even before you made yourself odious!" she said sharply, goaded into rudeness.

"You heard the lady," Mr. Wright chorused behind her.

Lily shut her eyes briefly, lest she roar at Mr. Wright for his continued, unnecessary interference. Did he think she could not handle the situation by herself?

When she had counted to ten, she turned to give him a sweet smile that would never have fooled a wiser man.

"How gallant you are, Mr. Wright. But I do hope you will understand that I feel well able to manage this in my own way. Moreover, Mr. Dailey might feel better if you were not party to our conversation, as I am certain you must understand. Therefore, if you would so kindly wait here while I have a word with him..."

With no choice but to yield, he gave a grudging nod. Favoring Dailey with a parting glare, he then bent to take Snap's line.

"Please, Mr. Dailey, if you will accompany me," Lily requested, beginning to walk back down the drive toward the gate.

He slumped, defeat already pressing upon his fine figure, but he caught at the reins of his horse and obeyed.

When the two of them stood once more beneath the brick-and-iron arch at the end of the drive, she crossed her arms over her breast and said, "What I want to say is this: Mr. Dailey, I wish you every happiness in the future, sir, but I pray you will oblige me and take my answer as final. We will not suit, and I will not make you happy. I am sorry to cause you any pain. And—I will tell my father that we spoke, and he will understand why you do not keep your appointment today."

With that she held out a hand to shake. He regarded it for a moment, likely debating whether he should give voice to the many speeches bubbling up inside him, but there was no wavering in her implacable gaze. Therefore, with a muted sigh, he took her proffered hand gently in his own and carried it to his lips, a touching gesture that made her feel more warmly toward him than she had since first they met—that is, than she had before he ever opened his mouth. As a result, she smiled kindly upon him before turning on her heel to go.

And though she did not see it, Mr. Dailey in a fit of sentiment kissed his hand to her retreating form before slowly mounting his horse once more to ride away.

Mr. Wright had used his few minutes of solitude to deliver himself of both the little terrier and Thunder his horse, forcing the two creatures on a passing gardener and pretending not to notice the man's reluctance.

Then he dusted himself off, straightened his waistcoat and neckcloth, brought order to his hair, and experimented with several stances with which he might greet his beloved when she returned. One leg forward and a hand at his hip? Too aggressive, perhaps. He did not want to alarm her with the force of his affections, as Dailey had. What about leaning with his back against a tree, one knee bent, with his foot upon the trunk? No, no—too unconcerned. She might think he took his success for granted. Perhaps—pacing back and forth?

"Blast it all," he muttered. "This must be why men get down on one knee. It solves the problem of what to do with oneself." He wished he had kept the confounded dog. It would have given them both something to look at or talk about.

And then she reappeared, and he panicked. As if spasms seized him, he assumed first one of the rejected poses and then the next, before abandoning both and pacing the width of the avenue twice. He removed his hat to tug on his hair, undoing his earlier effort to smooth it.

"Mr. Wright—are you unwell?"

For one dreadful instant he thought he might burst into tears or throw up. She was so perfect he was almost afraid of her. Perfectly beautiful. Perfectly sweet. Perfectly angelic! Only witness her divine dismissal of Dailey, who—he admitted in his extremity—had full as much to offer Miss Ellsworth as he did himself—with the exception of prize-winning Slapbang, of course.

"Oh, Miss Ellsworth," he croaked, falling to one knee in the time-honored manner, if only because he did not know how much longer he could stay on his feet without collapsing. Words would not come, but he clasped his hands together and held them to his chest in mute appeal.

Lily could not account for herself. She honestly could not.

Because here, as she anticipated, was her moment of triumph. The man she had chosen as her eventual life partner was (literally) at her feet. She didn't want to marry him *now*, but she certainly wanted to keep him around to marry *later*. So she ought to be beside herself with joy.

And yet.

And yet she was aware of a flash of exasperation. For—must he choose this moment, after such a trial as she just had gone through? As if Snap and the bushes and the tangled line and Mr. Dailey's obtuseness were not more than enough excitement for one day?

Not that she would have been any better pleased if Mr. Wright had taken himself off without speaking.

Because there was just no pleasing her, was there?

Even the adoration on his face vexed her in her current mood. She had much preferred how he looked at other times: parading with victorious Slapbang at Worthy Down, or descending on the posse of jealous gentlemen to claim her for a dance. Or even threatening Mr. Dailey, as he had minutes earlier. At present he looked like she might be sweet to him or stomp on him, just as she pleased, and he would make no protest. Hadn't he any more spirit than that? Did he not realize how much more winning he was when he showed a little self-assurance?

But something must be done. Clearly he wasn't going to stand up again until the situation was dealt with. But she could hardly accept an implied proposal, could she? Well—she supposed she could. She had only to drop to her own knees and return a melting glance and the deed would be done.

But I can't do it, thought Lily. *I simply can't. First Mr. Dailey does all the talking and all the assuming, and now Mr. Wright wants* me *to do all the talking and all the assuming!*

Maybe she would reject him after all. Send him away with a flea in his ear as she had Mr. Dailey. Because there would be some other promising gentleman at some point, would there not? In her mind's eye she caught the shadow of a lean figure, lounging against the wall, pale eyes regarding her with something like wry judgment. The very picture made anger at herself flare—what was promising about *that* one?

Maybe she would never marry at all.

Something of her thoughts must have shown in her angelic eyes because Mr. Wright began to sputter and gulp, like cold coals being jabbed back to life by a scullery maid.

"M-Miss Ellsworth! D-Dearest Miss Ell—Ellsworth!"

"Yes?" she prompted absently.

The crisis upon him, Mr. Wright dug down deep within his soul. Called upon his manhood and his lineage. Remembered it was his horse which had won the King's Plate and none other.

Clambering to his feet again he made his stand, wobbly but upright, and threw himself once more into the fray. "Miss Ellsworth, you know I would do anything for you."

It was the right note to strike, for she looked at him again, having to tilt her chin a little because he was taller than she.

"As you saw," he forged onward, gathering courage, "I would defend your honor and your privileges—"

Lily wondered if he had been reading Spenser's *The Faerie Queene* and imagined himself the Redcrosse Knight. But she held her tongue, determined to hear him out.

"Not only from such as Dailey, but from—the whole world! The *whole world.* Because I adore you, Miss Ellsworth. Yes. And I would brave anything for you. Anything at all, if you would only consent to be my wife." He thought about seizing her hand at this point, but something about the calm way she stood, not even appearing fluttered, made him rule against it.

Onward.

"Even without your promise, I am willing to defy gossip—"

"Gossip?" repeated Lily ominously.

But with the gathered momentum of a massive boulder crashing down a slope, Mr. Wright was unstoppable, and equally deaf to any subtleties of tone. "It doesn't matter to me what Rumor might say about you kissing Dailey," he avowed. "Nor does it matter to me that my own family tried to warn me away from you! Why, I even attacked Simon for repeating such rubbish, such falsehoods—"

Her hand flew up, whether to silence him or to ward something off Mr. Wright could not tell. "Mr. Kenner? What has Mr. Kenner to do with this?" she demanded, her eyes glittering as if she might spring at him herself. "Tell me! If he was talking of me, he had no business to do so! He had no right."

Startled by her sudden vehemence, Mr. Wright lost his train of chivalric thought. "What? Oh—er—I think Granny put him up to it. But he—er—just told me the bit about Dailey kissing you and the Miss Weekses witnessing it, and you saying it was—er—nothing."

"I did *not* say it was 'nothing,'" Lily fumed. "I said I had *forgiven* Mr. Dailey his impudence! Why is that so difficult for everyone to comprehend? And Mr. Kenner had no business—no business at all—to be repeating such hearsay and making such conjectures! He should be *ashamed* of himself. Our own clergyman! He should—rot in a pit of shame. He should be—be burnt at the stake for saying anything of the kind of a member of his flock, whether it was true or not!"

Mr. Wright's eyebrows had been creeping up his forehead throughout this speech, likely having never imagined such words—so violent! so vivid!—issuing from the rosy lips of his angel.

"You are beside yourself," he said inadequately.

She was. She could not deny it. How did Mr. Kenner dare? It was not enough that he was *listening* to gossip about her (whether the gossip was true or untrue), but he credited it? Credited it and *repeated* it, thus magnifying the damage? And then he sought to interfere with his cousin's intentions toward her?

Well, though she could not burn Mr. Kenner at the stake for his crimes against her, she could relieve her feelings on his unfortunate cousin. "If you are so eager to come to my defense, sir, why did you not punish your cousin for saying such things about me?"

"But I did," insisted Mr. Wright. "I *did!* I just said so. I attacked him for it, Miss Ellsworth, at my own granny's birthday dinner. Split his lip, even!"

"Did you?" breathed Lily, a brilliant, genuine smile illumining her features. "Did you really?"

Her mood shifted so rapidly it made him dizzy. Like a snake swaying to the notes and movement of its charmer, Mr. Wright leaned toward her. "I did."

"And did his lip really bleed?" she asked eagerly.

"It did. Do you believe me now, Miss Ellsworth, that I would back you against all comers?"

"I begin to."

"And will you let me do it, your whole life long? Will you be mine?"

She never would have agreed to it so soon, she thought later, if Mr. Kenner had not entered into it.

The confounded, interfering Mr. Kenner.

But he *had* entered into it.

And therefore, Lily spoke the words she had never intended on speaking for some time yet, if ever.

"Yes, Mr. Wright. Yes. I will be yours."

Chapter Fourteen

The mirth and fun grew fast and furious.
— Robert Burns, *Tam o' Shanter,* II.561 (1790)

Almost as soon as she gave her promise, Lily wished she could snatch it back.

For Mr. Wright capered in the drive. Tossed his hat in the air. Hallooed like a fool. Seized her by the waist and swung her around. And then he planted one firm hand on either side of her face, knocking her bonnet off, and kissed her.

That makes two times, she thought, when he finished crushing her mouth and resumed his capering. *Two kisses I didn't ask for and did not particularly enjoy*. She supposed Mr. Wright's kiss was preferable to Mr. Dailey's, since he had a right to it and went about it with a direct, manly vigor. Still, if that was kissing, Lily was not terribly eager for more.

"Name the date!" he cried, taking her hands in his own. "Name it, and do not make me wait too long, my dearest angel."

"I—couldn't possibly right now," she said, feebly. "This is all so very—sudden."

He grabbed her and kissed her again, harder, and she tried not to stiffen. "Mr. Wright—someone might see us." At least she was not standing in the Romsey Road this time.

"Gilbert," he murmured against her hair. "Call me Gilbert."

"Mr. Wright," Lily said again, recovering some of her usual spirit when she found herself crossed. She pushed against him, and he reluctantly released her. "I think you'd better go now."

"But—shouldn't I speak with your father?"

"Not yet—please! Let me—talk to him first. Just this morning he was preparing to hear Mr. Dailey's suit, and if *you* now turned up instead—!"

He frowned and nodded. "I see. Yes. All right. That makes sense, I suppose. Yes. Well, then. If you would like to explain to him first. I will write to him later. Tomorrow, perhaps."

She shook her head, pleading. "No—no. Nothing. Don't do anything until I tell you—please."

"But—then I can't tell my own family yet?"

"Of course not! How could you tell your family if I haven't told my family? And how could you possibly tell them so soon, when you say they talked about me—*warned* you against me? They will not congratulate you, sir."

"They will love you, Miss Ellsworth. I swear it. They will adore you, as I do."

She wished she shared his conviction. Lily retrieved her fallen bonnet and clamped it back on her head. "Please, sir—it may be a few days. Or longer. I—have to wait for the proper moment."

"A few days?" he echoed, dismayed. "But I will be gone to Salisbury for more races."

"Gone to Salisbury? Perfect," said Lily. "I think we had better not see each other again until you return."

His jaw dropped. "—Miss Ellsworth—that might be a week or more altogether."

"So long as that? Hmm." She gave him an encouraging and not very lover-like pat on the arm. "You go race your wonderful Slapbang and conquer the world, and I will see what I manage here at home. And then—and then come back whenever the races are over, and we will decide what to do. Perfect."

Mr. Wright looked neither pleased nor persuaded by this plan, but Lily was so desperate to be alone that she gave him a peck on the cheek and another shove and hurried away, calling over her shoulder just as she had to Mr. Dailey, "I will have them bring you your horse! Good-bye!"

Lily did not return at once to the house, even after finding a groom to send Mr. Wright and Thunder on their way. How could she, when there was so much she must decide?

In the first place, now that she was engaged to the man she had planned to win, did she want him after all? It had all happened so quickly! Far more quickly than she ever intended.

Once our engagement is known, all the other gentlemen will vanish, she mourned, as she skirted the lawn, keeping an eye and an ear out for Minta and Aggie. All the fun would be over. The fun of people fighting to dance with her and the fun of them all crowding the parlor at Hollowgate, saying admiring things to her while they scowled at each other. The fun of exciting the jealousy of other young ladies. *The fun of Mr. Kenner seeing how everyone likes me, even if he doesn't.*

Lily halted, though she had not spoken the words aloud. Heavens! What was wrong with her? That man was the whole reason she was in this mess! If she had not been so furious to learn of his interference, she never would have acted so impulsively.

Yes. It was entirely Mr. Kenner's fault everything must now be given up, months and months before she had wanted!

Unless—Lily grasped herself by the elbows. Unless she were to turn right around and jilt Mr. Wright.

I could write a note to him. He and I would be the only ones who ever knew there was any engagement to be broken. And if I do it at once, could an agreement of an hour's duration even be called an engagement, really? Mr. Wright would never tell anyone. He would never proclaim me a jilt because that would mean he *was the one jilted. Only look at Mr. Gregory, who still creeps around as if Flossie's rejection were stamped on his forehead!*

She resumed her feverish pacing, her hands balled in fists.

On the other hand, if she jilted him now, Mr. Wright had more pride than Mr. Gregory. Mr. Wright would not creep around, and he would not ever, ever ask her again to be his bride. In fact, Lily likely would never see him again. So if she ended it, she must be absolutely certain she wanted him gone forever. And did she?

No—she liked him well enough and better than most.

And if she did not marry Mr. Wright, she would have to gamble on someone else equally eligible and likeable appearing one day. It could happen. Only look how Florence's husband sprang up from nowhere to steal her heart! Not that Robert Fairchild was anywhere near as eligible as Gilbert Wright. He was handsomer, to be sure, but he had no fortune of his own to speak of and came from a comparatively humble family. No—Flossie had married below herself—not that she seemed to mind.

With a sigh, Lily sat on the straw haystack that served as Minta's archery target. No, she had better keep Mr. Wright. She could go much further and fare far worse. And, for a young unmarried woman, there was always the danger of stretching one's fun too long—of losing one's bloom and ending up unmatched. It would be better to marry prematurely and spend the rest of her life as mistress of Meadowsweep, than to eke out every last ballroom flirtation before either marrying someone less desirable or surrendering to old-maidhood.

Another sigh emerged, and she tilted her head back to stare at the sky, dotted by only a few clouds.

Her decision was made.

Nevertheless, that being so, Lily had no intention of rushing things. Extracting two pieces of hay from the bale with her fingernails, she began to knot them together. She had one whole week now before the secret need be revealed. Mr. Wright would be gone to Salisbury, and in his absence she might do whatever she pleased. Coquette to her heart's content. Enjoy herself as much as she possibly could in seven days. And then, when he returned, that was soon enough to deal with matters. And even then there was no reason to set an early wedding date, after all. Why not be engaged as long as she could?

Her spirits lifting a little, she rose and shook out her skirts. It was no mean achievement, winning the most eligible man of her acquaintance, but who could blame her for wanting both to have her cake and also to eat it?

Lily's plan to do as she pleased for at least a week received an immediate fillip when she returned to the house and found her stepmother seated in the larger drawing room, sewing and dutifully conversing with three of her stepdaughter's admirers. The incongruous gathering made Lily want to laugh: short Mr. Frayne was seated on a low divan, while giraffe-tall Mr. Willett towered by the mantel, and flaxen Mr. Caxton blended into the ivory wainscoting. (Honestly—if she were ever to marry Mr. Caxton, she would forbid him to wear ivory or buff. He looked all of one shade, like when Wilcomb rolled out pie crusts.)

"What a delight to find you here, sirs!" Lily beamed, her sincerity plain. When her curtsey was made, she flipped open the lid of her workbasket and nipped out the silk case she was sewing for Florence's cushion.

"We were talking of music," Mrs. Ellsworth supplied.

"Yes, Miss Ellsworth," Mr. Willett said eagerly, creaking and bowing from his post at the mantel like a crane erected for chimney repairs. "I was just telling Mrs. Ellsworth that you and she simply must come to the Haydn performance on Monday. It is his new

'Emperor' string quartet. Very fine, I hear. It would be my pleasure to escort you. Treat you, that is."

"Why, that sounds lovely," said Lily. "What would you say, Mama? If your—head—is feeling well enough."

A little chorus of concern over Mrs. Ellsworth's head erupted, which the woman dismissed. "I am perfectly well. But—if I do feel a touch of the headache, perhaps Araminta could accompany you, or your aunt Jeanne."

"Or both!" cried Mr. Willett, not wanting to see his good fortune snatched away before he could enjoy it. "I will purchase five tickets, for whichever of your family members choose to come."

Then Mr. Frayne must get his revenge by inviting Lily and all her younger siblings to the Magdalen Hill Fair, which she also accepted, for Tuesday. One of those younger siblings—Araminta—flung into the room at that point, accompanied by Aggie, and when the invitation was repeated to Minta, she grew so excited and Aggie so openly envious that Mr. Frayne could do no other than to include Miss Agatha in the blanket invitation.

Poor Mr. Caxton was in despair that he would not gain a share of the largesse being distributed, but when the two younger girls thumped down at the pianoforte to hammer out a triumphal march, he leaped to his feet in a fit of daring. "Miss Araminta—Miss Agatha—might I prevail on you to play a little dance music?"

Minta and Aggie smiled uncertainly at each other, embarrassed for the young man, but it was merciful Mrs. Ellsworth who answered, rising. "No, girls, allow me. For unless Mr. Caxton desires to dance a jig all by himself, he will need a partner, and you two may form another couple for the square."

Laughing then, the girls helped pushed back the other furnishings and roll up the carpet before Mrs. Ellsworth launched into Rufty Tufty. Then it was Mr. Frayne and Mr. Willett left to gnash their teeth, as the two couples took hands, Lily and Mr. Caxton, Minta and Aggie, circling and arming and skipping. Lily could not have enjoyed herself more, her premature engagement completely forgotten in the fun.

But on the fourth time through the figures, when Mr. Caxton took her hand to lead her up again, the drawing room door flew open in their faces, and there stood Bobbins the footman, poised to admit a handful of guests. Namely, the dean's wife Mrs. Fellowes and her grandchildren Simon and Sophie Kenner.

"Oop!" said Mr. Caxton, stumbling over his own feet. Though Lily managed not to be pulled over by his misstep, she could only gawp for a moment. But as she registered the new visitors' shocked expressions, it was not long before her initial embarrassment was overtaken by a different emotion. Oh—were the gossipers in Mr. Wright's disapproving family here to collect more tales about her? Well, then. Let them try! There was nothing reprehensible about dancing in one's own drawing room in the middle of the afternoon while one's stepmother looked on.

In the meantime, the music had broken off. "Mrs. Fellowes! Mr. and Miss Kenner! What a pleasure," breathed Mrs. Ellsworth, her pale cheeks warming as they always did when she saw the dean's wife. "Bobbins, won't you bring some tea?"

"Good afternoon, Miranda," replied Mrs. Fellowes, her lips thin as her hostess performed the introductions to the several gentlemen. "I was calling at the rectory and thought it had been some time since I was at Hollowgate."

"How glad I am you thought of us. Won't you be seated?"

"Are you certain you wouldn't rather continue dancing?" asked Mr. Kenner is his mildest voice. "If you would, might I ask Miss Araminta and Miss Agatha for the two next? I daresay Miss Ellsworth is already claimed."

"She is!" Mr. Frayne and Mr. Willett chorused.

"Well, we aren't going to dance anymore," Lily interjected briskly, already in motion to replace the chairs. She would *not* let Mr. Kenner rile her. Or she would not let him rile her *again.* She had already been riled into an engagement, and that seemed like quite enough to be going on about. "Dancing was just a whim. I'm certain you must be thinking, sir, that this is neither the time nor the place for it."

"Why would I think that? After all, 'to every thing there is a season,'" he noted. "But I'm sorry if this is no longer a time to dance—that must mean you now think it a time to mourn."

She gave a cool laugh as she kicked the carpet to unroll it again. "Is that how the verse goes? It has been very long since I read it."

"Oh, yes. It is worth re-reading. All of those beautiful juxtapositions. Though I'll admit some of them are rather odd: 'a time to cast away stones, and a time to gather stones together,' for example. And then, of course, there's 'a time to embrace, and a time to refrain from embracing.'"

For a second she held very, very still. Because he could not be referring to any *particular* embracing, could he? Even a habitual disturber like himself could not be referring—in her own drawing room!—to her embrace of Mr. Dailey?

She could not know—she could not guess—that Kenner was vexed with himself as soon as he spoke. Why should he allude to what he knew, as if it occupied him? It would take no keen mind to realize that, if it occupied him, it troubled him. But somehow the telltale gibe had emerged of its own accord, provoked perhaps by the sight of her frolicking with still three *more* gentlemen.

With an effort, Lily took up her sewing again, smoothing the silk in her hands. "So informative. How convenient to have always the right word, the right verse, at the tip of your tongue. More of your 'apples of gold,' I suppose." Then, before he could respond, she turned abruptly away to address his sister. "How have you been, Sophie? I was going to send a note, to ask if you wanted assistance filling flower vases for Transfiguration Sunday."

Sophie flushed guiltily. "Oh, thank you, Miss Ells—I mean—Lily. Miss Agatha's sisters were kind enough to—drop by, and the vases are all done."

Turning the silk cushion case inside-out, Lily stitched furiously. So the Miss Weekses not only spied on their neighbors and spread gossip, but they also hoped to insert themselves between Sophie Kenner and herself? Well, they could have her! If Sophie was not going to defend Lily from ill fame—if she was going to believe whatever the Miss Weekses put about and then propagate it to her whole extended family—Lily no longer wanted her friendship. She didn't need her! (It must be said that Lily could be unjust in her anger, but since so few people are wise when they are angry, and since they too often assume the worst before everything can be made clear, this failing hardly requires excuse or explanation.) Her silver needle glinting as she whipped it through the fabric, she continued to seethe. The Miss Weekses were welcome to both Kenners, as a matter of fact! Let them all get together and discuss Lily Ellsworth's flaws for sport. Let the Miss Weekses befriend Sophie and enchant Mr. Kenner and win Mrs. Fellowes' approval. Lily was in no mood to speak to any of them or their faction.

And they will all have to eat their words, won't they, when they learn Mr. Wright and I are engaged, in spite of their opinions.

"Is it a pillow you're working on, Miss Ellsworth?" asked Mr. Caxton, drawing his chair nearer hers.

"It is."

"How lovely that colour will look, when you rest your dark hair against it," declared Mr. Willett boldly.

Under ordinary circumstances, Lily would have frozen him for this unseemly remark, but in her current mood she gave him a coy look and clicked her tongue. "This cushion is for my sister Mrs. Fairchild, and though her hair is the same colour as mine, I suspect her husband would not appreciate you talking of it."

"When do Mr. and Mrs. Fairchild return?" asked Mrs. Fellowes, favoring both Lily and Mr. Willett with a stern look.

"Her last letter said perhaps later in the month and certainly before my brother returns to school," Lily replied, affecting not to see the look. "There is still work being done on their new home in Kingsgate Street."

"Will they attend St. Swithin's-upon-Kingsgate or St. Michael's?"

"I believe St. Michael's," answered Mrs. Ellsworth. "If Mr. Fairchild does not wish to continue at St. Thomas's, where he attended when he lodged in St. Thomas Street."

"St. Thomas's would be a walk on a cold morning from Kingsgate Street," the dean's wife observed, "and I always hold with staying in one's own parish."

"It isn't so long a walk," Lily countered. "Even should Florence want to come all the way back to St. Eadburh's from Kingsgate Street, I daresay it wouldn't take more than fifteen minutes. Tyrone boasts that he has run from the College gateway to Hollowgate's arch on the Romsey Road in seven."

At this speech, Sophie gave a gulp and Mrs. Fellowes's eyebrows floated up. There was a little pause, and Lily felt her own throat tighten in dismay. How could she have been so careless? It was one thing to resent them talking about her (and to suspect the wretched Mr. Kenner of teasing her about it), but quite another to *remind* them of where the scandalous kiss had taken place! Mrs. Fellowes would see it as evidence of Lily's shamelessness about the matter, she was certain. Thank God her stepmother knew nothing of it—Mrs. Ellsworth continued to stitch in ignorant peace. And a furtive glance discovered no particular awareness on the part of Lily's three would-be suitors. *Bless Mr. Dailey,* she thought, *for not trumpeting his exploits.* It meant all the gossip traceable to the elder Miss Weekses had swirled only through Winchester's clerical reaches, then. Or through them and the Weekses' circle.

Rescue came unexpectedly from Mr. Kenner. "That doesn't surprise me—seven minutes. I would wager Master Tyrone would win many a foot race, if he ever grew as fond of running as he is of books."

In her relief, she sat back and gave him a wavering smile. Their eyes held, each trying to read the other.

It was Lily's gaze which dropped first. Dropped to his long fingers tapping silently on the cushion of his chair. The tightness in her throat eased, only to be replaced by a puzzling inward flutter.

Was he friend or foe? Why nettle her one moment only to help her, the next? Why patch over an awkward moment now, when he had not hesitated to create one earlier? And more significantly, what did he care if she was uncomfortable, when he had already shown himself willing to injure her in his cousin's esteem? Mr. Wright had exposed Mr. Kenner's true self. Her brow creased. Perhaps he regretted his earlier provocation and could not help wanting to smooth things in company, preferring to save his dagger thrusts for private conversations.

As for Kenner, he wouldn't have minded knocking his head against the wall in frustration. Because which was the worst part? Finding Miss Ellsworth three-deep in men? Or having a fling at her earlier and earning her vexation instead of a smile? Or was it not being able to tell if Gil had proposed yet? *Had* he? Gil was not a patient person, and soon he would head off to Salisbury for more races. Mystery within mystery. The proposal would happen sooner or later, however. And when it did, would she accept his cousin? And what would Kenner do if she did not?

"Mr. Kenner," Araminta roused him from his brown study, "have you been practicing for Thursday evening?" She played a teasing trill on the pianoforte.

"What happens Thursday?" asked Mrs. Fellowes.

"Simon and I are coming to supper," explained Sophie. "And he and Miss Minta are going to play music for us."

"How delightful," said their grandmother. "It has been too long, Simon, since I have had the pleasure of hearing you play."

Please don't invite her. Please don't invite her. Lily tried to send her stepmother the silent message, and it must have worked, for Mrs. Ellsworth said nothing and continued to sew.

But Mrs. Fellowes was not the only one to envy the exclusive supper. Mr. Willett felt it necessary to say, "What a musical week it will be for you then, Mrs. Ellsworth and Miss Ellsworth. Haydn with me on Monday and then a musical supper. What will you play on Thursday, Miss Araminta?"

"Not Haydn," replied Minta. "But I can't say. The program is a surprise."

Mr. Kenner looked surprised himself. "Are you great enthusiasts for Haydn?" he asked Mrs. Ellsworth.

"I'm afraid I don't know enough to say either way," she replied. "What about you, Lily?"

"I know nothing of his string quartets," she murmured. "I imagine Monday's concert will be as much a surprise as what Minta and Mr. Kenner play Thursday."

And while Lily had no reputation as a prophetess, her prediction in this instance proved altogether true.

Chapter Fifteen

Really, aunt, I don't know what you mean.
— Isaac Bickerstaff, *Love in a Village,* III.ix.72 (1763)

Transfiguration Sunday passed quietly. Mr. Kenner preached. Lily grudgingly admired the vases of flowers in the church and grudgingly acknowledged the curate's continued hold on his congregation's attention (including her own). After the service, while her father and stepmother spoke with neighbors and tenants and she stood with her family in the churchyard, her gaze drifted to where Aggie's older sisters talked with Sophie, throwing glances in Mr. Kenner's direction all the while. They were not his only observers. Impoverished Miss Terman watched as well, and Mr. Beckford's niece Miss Beckford. Lily could see the attraction—she could, she admitted. She had grown used to the clerical gown and surplice Sunday required and the black he usually wore other days, with the exception of his attire at Burchar's. She could see he was a graceful man—not at all giraffe-like, though he and Mr. Willett were equally lean—and that he had rather nice hair and hands and that wry mouth which drew one. She admitted his preaching voice was moving and effective—even captivating. And his family connections were very good. No—she understood the interest he raised among hopeful young women and their parents.

But was she really, truly the only person who found him as unsettling as he was attractive? The only one who did not know what to make of his pale eyes and unreadable demeanor? And the things he said! Could she be the only person who thought the man velvet one moment and barbed the next? For instance, would Mr. Kenner ever tell Miss Weeks or Miss Frederica or Miss Terman or Miss Beckford that she had a "lovely head," while, in the same breath, confessing that he would like to shoot it off? And that was only what he said to Lily's face! Who knew what emerged in the privacy of family, except that, whatever it had been, it was enough to make Mr. Wright attack him.

"...Opinion on Mrs. Hambly's condition?" Mrs. Ellsworth was asking the doctor Mr. Beckford. "When Lily called on her and her niece..."

Lily shifted from one foot to the other, not wanting to revisit the Hamblys even in memory, though she and Tyrone shared a grin. Beatrice gave her hand a tug. "Look, Lily, what I found." She held up a brown jug. "It was on Osbaldiston Baldric's gravestone. Isn't he the portrait at the end of the gallery? The one we call Baldy Baldric?"

Minta snatched the jug and gave it a shake. "Empty. I hope Baldy enjoyed it."

Beatrice's eyes grew round. "Can ghosts drink?"

"Don't be ridiculous," said Lily, quick to nip the idea in the bud, lest Beatrice develop a fear of the gallery. "Minta didn't mean it, and there aren't any ghosts. This was left here by one of the soldiers from the barracks, I'll warrant. I found another jug just like it beside our gate when—the other day. And the next time I dance with an officer, I will certainly tell him what I think of his men strewing the neighborhood with their debris."

"Isn't it Mr. Harvey's job to keep the graves tidy?" asked Beatrice.

"Yes. The churchyard and the church itself."

The siblings surveyed the weeds and general slovenliness of the churchyard doubtfully.

"If it is, he's done better in times past," Minta said. "It never looked like this when Mr. Gregory was here."

"I daresay Mr. Harvey slacked his labor when Mr. Gregory left, and Mr. Pennyworth was not the man to take him to task." Lily shrugged. "Well, Mr. Kenner will have to speak with him, if he doesn't want his church falling to pieces."

As she made this remark, it coincided with one of those little pauses in all the conversations taking place around them and resulted in her voice carrying further than she intended. "Oh, dear," she whispered, blushing in confusion. The twins muffled a snort, glancing (as indeed everyone in the churchyard did) toward Mr. Kenner.

Lily fully expected the barbed version of the curate to make reply, and she was not disappointed, though he hid the barb within the velvet. With a little bow across the distance, Mr. Kenner said, "Thank you, Miss Ellsworth. Indeed, St. Eadburh's falling into ruin is a consummation devoutly to be avoided. And a concerned young lady like yourself, so eagle-eyed and...crammed with excellencies, shall we say, is a boon to any parish."

His admiring congregants all but applauded such a lofty-sounding speech (the other young ladies even frowning in envy), but Lily saw the fleeting quirk of his lip and the gleam in his eye before he turned away, and she did not need her bookish brother saying on the walk home, "That Mr. Kenner must like his Shakespeare, Lily. But I'm not certain he meant it as a compliment to say you were 'crammed with excellencies' like Malvolio."

"Indeed. You may set your mind at rest," was her dry reply. "He most certainly did *not* mean it as a compliment."

Mr. Willett insisted on picking up Lily and Mrs. Ellsworth in his barouche for the Haydn concert, followed by Lily's aunt from St. Thomas Street, though they all might as easily have walked. But it was a pleasure to arrive with bustle and importance at the concert room in the High Street.

Lily's aunt Jeanne raised wondering brows when she noted Mr. Willett's great height. "If you choose this one, *ma petite chérie*," she whispered when he was assisting Mrs. Ellsworth from the carriage, "you will break your neck trying to look at him all your life."

"There is no chance of me marrying him," Lily whispered back. "So *ne t'en fais pas*."

The concert room was entered by a large lobby in which fires were lit at either end, in addition to the blaze of candles in the chandelier. These, combined with the gathering crowd, made things quite warm, but Mr. Willett officiously craned his lengthy neck and, with many a polite bow and please-pardon-us, herded them through to the cooler concert room, where only a few people had yet taken their seats. "Will these chairs do? Let me fetch programs."

"*Qu'il est grand comme une girafe!*" marveled Aunt Jeanne when he was gone. "I think you are only a little taller than the buttons of his waistcoat, my Lily. But he looks at you with admiration."

"All of Lily's suitors look at her so," Mrs. Ellsworth chuckled. "And she has another one in her collection who is as short as Mr. Willett is tall."

"*En effet?* But you must describe to me all Lily's suitors, Miranda. No—let us play a game: you name one, Lily, and Miranda will supply the adjective."

"Only one adjective?" Lily asked.

"Jeanne, I think it hardly fair or charitable to reduce a person to one adjective," protested Mrs. Ellsworth.

"One," insisted her sister-in-law solemnly. "You must do it. And why do you assume your one word must be... *désobligeant*? You may praise them all, if you like."

Mrs. Ellsworth smiled. "All right, then. Let me see...you have met Mr. Willett, and I've told you how short Mr. Frayne is—"

Jeanne Ellsworth shook her head and held up a finger: "*One* word. You must hurry, Lily. The *girafe* will return any minute."

"Fine. Er—Mr. Trimp."

"—Tight."

Lily collapsed in giggles, and her stepmother pressed her lips together to stifle her own, but Jeanne cried, "Another, another!"

"Mr. Dailey."

"Handsome."

"She *is* being charitable," Lily said wryly to her aunt.

"Is he not handsome, after all?"

"No, no—he's handsome all right. Let me see...Sir Basil."

Mrs. Ellsworth looked pained. "Older."

"Mr. Caxton?"

"Pale. That one was easy."

"Mr. Gosworth."

"Oh—dear me. 'Nondescript.'"

Lily hesitated then. "And...I suppose, Mr. Wright."

Her stepmother hesitated in return, but seeing Mr. Willett approaching, she murmured, "Victorious."

"Ah..." Jeanne nodded wisely. "That is one I must hear more about."

"I met some of your acquaintances in the lobby," he announced as he handed each of the ladies a program, "and could not avoid inviting them to sit with us, but the young man demurred."

"Which young man?" asked Jeanne promptly. "I know all of them. Was he tight or older or handsome or pale?"

Mr. Willett held up his palms. "I must beg to be excused from descriptions. And though I could not recall his name, unfortunately, you see him over there, with the young lady."

His three companions accordingly looked, and Mrs. Ellsworth said, "Why, it's the Kenners."

"Who are the Kenners?" Jeanne asked.

"Mr. Kenner is our new curate."

Jeanne turned to her niece. "But his wife is charming! She has a—how do you say—*nez retroussé.* And she looks about your age, Lily."

"Snub nose. And she is his sister, not his wife," replied Lily, subdued. "And, yes, she is about my age."

"Shall we greet them?" her aunt persisted.

"Perhaps during the interval. Everyone is taking his seat now."

"Oh! She is nodding at you, Lily."

Mrs. Ellsworth returned the gesture, but Sophie continued to look their way, waiting for Lily to see her. Mr. Kenner had taken the seat on the farther side of his sister, but when Sophie tapped him with her fan, he too turned and gave one general nod. Lily saw he was wearing the handsome white-gold waistcoat from the ball at Burchar's.

"Ah..." said Lily's aunt again, in a way that meant she had many questions to ask later. But for now the bustle of people taking their seats prevented this, and soon the Kenners were lost to view.

Lily had questions herself. Mr. Kenner knew they would be attending this concert—Mr. Willett had told him as much on Saturday. So had he then gone and purchased tickets, or were they already in his possession? It had to be the latter. Mr. Kenner did not behave in the least as if he wished to be numbered with Lily Ellsworth's suitors—even her healthy vanity could detect no evidence of this.

Therefore he must be here as a music lover. He did play the violin, after all. Why should he not be interested in Mr. Haydn's new work?

Unless—

Unless he were here as a spy, of sorts. Could it be possible that Mr. Wright asked his cousin to keep an eye on Miss Ellsworth in his absence?

Oblivious to the opening strains of the music, Lily tapped her closed fan against her other hand, thinking, thinking, thinking. *Don't be ridiculous,* she scolded herself. *Mr. Wright has nothing sly or subtle or underhand about him. He would never think to spy upon me.*

Mr. Kenner, on the other hand...Mr. Kenner was the very embodiment of slyness and subtlety. Lily didn't know if she would go so far as to call him "underhand," but nor could she rule out the possibility. Mr. Kenner had already tried to turn his cousin against her; he might very well have taken it upon himself to gather further evidence of her unsuitability.

Well! Apart from the mere fact of her attending a concert with Mr. Willett—and that in the presence of her stepmother and aunt—he would find little enough to accuse her of this evening! After her experience with Mr. Dailey, Lily had no intention of giving any other gentleman overmuch encouragement. She did not mind being *just friendly enough* to give everyone a little hope, but that was all. Harmless. Utterly harmless.

But though she did not think herself at all in the wrong, the thought of Mr. Kenner spying on her—if he was indeed doing so—made her grind her teeth.

It must be said that Lily did not pay a great deal of attention to the concert. She was aware of the music and found it pleasant, but not being particularly musical nor inclined to sit still for long periods of time, she rather wished she had her workbasket with her. Without sewing to occupy her, she was thrown back on observing her fellow concertgoers, from Mr. Willett, who would loom over her like a tree swaying in a windstorm to point out something in the program or a neat little passage by one of the musicians; to her aunt, who hummed along without knowing the melody; to her stepmother, rapt, with a single tear threatening to slide down her cheek. As for the Kenners, Lily could only see part of the back of Mr. Kenner's head and a sliver of his left hand, and yet the sliver of his hand drew her eye more than once. His long fingers tapped out the rhythm on his leg or occasionally gestured to the flow of the music, and Lily found herself watching them as much as the musicians.

He has very nice hands, I admit. (Who knew there were so many admissions to be made about him?) It occurred to her that, when the Kenners came for supper and music on Thursday, she would be able to watch him as he played his violin. Would he bend and sway as he played, as these musicians did? Would he, like they, close his eyes during certain passages, carried away to someplace in his mind?

At the interval, the audience rose to walk about the room, and Lily's aunt gave her hand a squeeze before tucking it in her arm. "You must introduce me to these Kenners."

An excuse was forming on Lily's lips, but before she could voice it she saw Sophie Kenner already making her way toward them and beckoning her brother to follow.

"Good evening! Mrs. Ellsworth, Lily, Mr. Willett. Isn't this lovely? Simon had bought tickets as a surprise for me."

"Good evening, Miss Kenner," Mrs. Ellsworth replied. "What a thoughtful surprise on his part. Would you allow me to present my sister-in-law Mrs. Charles Ellsworth? Jeanne, this is Miss Kenner and her brother, the curate of St. Eadburh's, Mr. Kenner."

Lily was proud of her pretty aunt, with her curling, silver-streaked black hair and her faint accent, but Jeanne Ellsworth was as forthright as she was pretty, and she delighted in matchmaking, so Lily dreaded what she might say if she took an interest in Mr. Kenner.

"When you last called on us, Lily, you did not say your new curate was a young man," was her aunt's first remark. "I assumed he was elderly like Mr. Pennyforth."

"Pennyworth, Aunt Jeanne."

"Pennyforth, Pennyworth, *ce n'est pas grave*. The age is more interesting to me."

"Why so, madam?" was Mr. Kenner's light question.

"To be sure, because I am old now, and my young family members interest me, as you must interest your older relations."

"In fact, Mr. and Miss Kenner are grandchildren of the Felloweses, Jeanne," explained Mrs. Ellsworth. "That is, the dean and his wife."

"Ah...I see. And you grand-dean-children are music lovers as well?"

"My brother plays the fiddle," Sophie volunteered. "He has been looking forward to this concert ever since he saw the advertisement for it in the paper."

Lily felt a little weight lift off her—so he was not spying on her, then!—and a resulting smile lit her face. "What do you think, then, Mr. Kenner? Has it met your expectations?"

"It has exceeded them," he answered quietly, his colour rising at both her smile and her address. "Both the music itself and the performance of it."

"Well, sir, if you are *connoisseur* enough to look forward to this night, my expectations for your own performance at Hollowgate rise very high indeed," Lily teased. She gave her aunt's hand a swing. "Minta has invited the Kenners to supper, Aunt Jeanne, and enlisted Mr. Kenner to play a duet with her. Neither one will say more about it. It is a great secret."

Jeanne chuckled. "But if it is Minta's idea, I can guess. Is there any piece called The Celebrated Bowler or The Harmonious Batter?"

"If there were, my part in it would be exceedingly small," Mr. Kenner answered, "for I'm wretched at cricket."

"Well, by the same token, it can't be The Accurate Archer or anything like that," Lily remarked, "or how then could Minta accompany *you*?"

"Touché," said Mr. Kenner. "A hit, a most palpable hit."

Lily regarded him archly. "You do know, Mr. Kenner, that you are not the only person in Winchester who reads Shakespeare?"

He affected surprise. "Am I not?"

But Lily was grinning. "My brother Tyrone reads him too, and he is quick to recognize and share with others a quote, or even a *veiled insult*."

His grin matched hers. "A perceptive lad, your brother. I will keep that in mind."

Mr. Willett cleared his throat, anxious to remind them all of his presence, and Lily dutifully turned to him. "And how are you enjoying the music, Mr. Willett?"

"Very fine. A pleasure only added to by the pleasure of your company." He attempted to apply this heavy compliment to both Lily and the Misses Ellsworths by looming over them all in turn, before ending with a grimace in Mr. Kenner's direction. "And now we had better return to our seats."

"May I call on you tomorrow, Lily?" blurted Sophie.

"I would like that," said Lily sincerely, "except Mr. Frayne is taking my siblings and me to the Magdalen Hill Fair. Wednesday, perhaps?"

"My mother is coming to shop with me on Wednesday."

"Even better, then," answered Lily. "Because then, when I see you on Thursday, you can tell me all about what you bought."

The groups parted at that point, and this time Lily's aunt arranged it so that Mr. Willett sat between Mrs. Ellsworth and Lily, leaving her to whisper in her niece's ear undetected.

Not a great deal of whispering, but enough to disturb, because the first thing she said was, "I do believe *la girafe* was not friendly to Mr. Kenner."

When Lily made no reply, Jeanne said, "First I wonder why that is. But then, I too am 'perceptive.' And I ask myself, Why has my Lily not considered adding this curate to her collection of admirers?

He is not handsome, and yet he is. But better yet, he is...interesting. He is *drôle*. Not all men can carry on *la plaisanterie*, you know."

"Very often his '*plaisanterie*' comes at my expense," hissed back her niece, fanning herself. "And I don't know where you get such ideas. We hardly spoke to him."

"I can tell," said Jeanne ominously. "I do not need a hundred words spoken. I can tell."

"Maybe I don't want to collect clergymen."

"Then it is unfortunate you live in Winchester, *pauvre chou.*"

"Well, in any event, he is not in my collection, nor does he have any desire to be."

"My beautiful Lily, he would have the desire if you wanted him to have the desire. I can see with my eyes. You have only to lift your little finger. Why do you not lift it, then, *ma petite chérie,* and see what happens?"

Chapter Sixteen

The crow that is so black, my dear,
Shall change his colour white;
And if ever I prove false to thee,
The day shall turn to night, my dear,
The day shall turn to night.
— *Roxburghe Ballads*, "The True Lover's Farewell" (1710)

Her aunt's words stuck with Lily. She found herself thinking of them as she prepared for bed. She found herself thinking of them still when she woke the next morning. Could Mr. Kenner's heart really be collected like any other? It would be a fitting revenge for his attempt to malign her to his cousin. And yet, it was not revenge Lily thought of.

No. She thought of what it would be like, to see those pale eyes warm with love for her. Or to note hesitation in his movements which were always so certain. Or to hear doubt in that arresting voice. It would be...delicious. Rolling over onto her breast, she fingered the tassel of the bedcurtain, the dark hair which had loosened from its braid tumbling over her shoulder and the coverlet tangled beneath her.

But it would also be dangerous, collecting Mr. Kenner. Because somehow she did not think he was a man she could command, as she could the others—Mr. Wright, Mr. Willett, all of them. Even Mr. Dailey, who had caused her such trouble, only disobeyed out of dimness, rather than willful rebellion.

Mr. Kenner would be different, however. He would never submit to her will from any desire to please her, not if it did not also please himself. And therefore his behavior could not be predicted.

Her braid slipped down now, brushing the carpet, and, with a sigh, she rolled onto her back again, staring up at the plaster rose on her ceiling with its swags of plaster ribbon.

Moreover, Aunt Jeanne had no idea—no one did—that Lily was engaged to Mr. Wright. Not only would it be wrong under the circumstances to lure Mr. Kenner into her train, but it would also be terribly disloyal to Mr. Wright and might even cause a permanent family conflict. (Which reminded her, she thought with a grimace, she really ought to tell her father soon about her engagement. Suppose Mr. Wright returned, and she had not yet done it?)

But these reasons, numerous and weighty as they were, were not all. Mr. Kenner would be dangerous not only for having his own mind, and he would be dangerous not only because he was her intended's cousin, but perhaps the most dangerous part of his dangerousness was that—and here Lily groaned and put a pillow over her face—was that there might be the narrowest, slightest, most *infinitesimal* possibility that, if she tried to collect Mr. Kenner's heart, her own heart might be collected in return. And then what would become of her?

As soon as she allowed herself the thought, she sat up and thrust the pillow away. Even stuffed it under the coverlet, as if that would make her wayward notion vanish accordingly.

"It is all nonsense," said Lily aloud. "Utter flim-flam. Firstly: Mr. Kenner is not at all the sort of man I could love. He is a clergyman, and I do not want to be a clergyman's wife. And he is fair, and I think I prefer dark-haired gentlemen." Of course, many men of her acquaintance lost their hair altogether, no matter the colour they were originally blessed with, so this might take care of itself in time. Nevertheless.

"Secondly," she persevered, slapping at the buried pillow, "I suspect I am not the sort of young lady *he* prefers." She frowned. To be precise, this did not count as a reason for *her* to reject *him*. Which meant it wasn't really a second reason. She kicked her legs beneath the blankets. This was no time to split hairs! Any reason must be a reason. Therefore—she was not the sort of young lady Mr. Kenner would prefer.

Throwing off the covers, Lily could almost hear her aunt Jeanne say, "*Et alors?* What sort of young lady does the young man like?"

Lily didn't know. Perhaps someone like her sister Florence: serious, earnest, kind, steady? Florence would have made an admirable clergyman's wife. But if that were where Mr. Kenner's preferences lay, Florence was already married, and neither Lily nor the Miss Weekses nor Miss Terman nor Miss Beckford were anything like Florence. But perhaps one of those young ladies would be willing to be Florence-like.

No matter. What every other girl in Winchester chose to do was not Lily's concern. And in the meantime, she had reached her conclusion: it would not be advisable to add Mr. Kenner to her collection, even if it were possible. None of the supplementary reasons need be given, once the fact of her engagement became known. Aunt Jeanne would understand soon enough.

Everyone would.

At least the day at Magdalen Hill Fair confirmed that Mr. Kenner had not been spying on her at the Haydn concert because he was not to be found among the milling crowds. As it was, Lily and her siblings lost sight of tiny Mr. Frayne several times, until Minta suggested they all buy bright red feathers for their hats. Mr. Frayne declared this a capital idea, sliding the quill through his hatband and proving so good-humored throughout the day with them that he came away a great favorite.

"Mama, he let us choose which booths and tents we would visit," Beatrice reported at the supper table, "and which foods we would taste."

"You must have chosen quite a few," Mrs. Ellsworth smiled, "because you all have little enough appetite now."

"And he won us a pie," said Araminta, "by hitting a target with a ball. Several gentlemen tried before Mr. Frayne, but they didn't throw hard enough. And then little Mr. Frayne stepped right up while they sniggered behind their hands, and he *launched* the ball like—like—a—"

"Like a trebuchet," suggested Tyrone.

"Yes!" Minta struck her fist on the table. "Like a trebuchet—*bang!*—right in the center of the target." Sighing with the memory of it, she declared, "The pie wasn't very good, but that didn't matter. I have decided Mr. Frayne is my favorite of Lily's beaux. After Mr. Wright, I suppose, because Mr. Wright still does have Slapbang."

"I like him too," agreed Tyrone. "Frayne, that is. He didn't fall asleep when we listened to the players recite."

"Dear me, what an impossible standard you all set," Lily returned wryly. "Let me see: your own way at the fair—delightful; ball-throwing abilities—*indispensable*!; remaining conscious for twenty minutes together..."

"I think he is my favorite, too," put in Beatrice.

"Sadly," replied Lily, "I feel like Mr. Willett when I stand next to Mr. Frayne, all of twenty feet tall."

Her siblings laughed, but Mrs. Ellsworth said, "Poor Mr. Frayne. He cannot help his stature."

"You needn't pity him, Mama," remonstrated Lily, "because I freely admit I like him very much as well. He improves on acquaintance, and I am certain he will have no trouble finding a wife. Only she will not be me."

This would have been the perfect opportunity, Lily thought later, to announce that she was already engaged, in any event, and to Araminta's second favorite, Mr. Wright. But—for whatever reason—she hesitated, and the supper conversation moved on. And then it would have been odd to drag it back to herself. At least, that is what Lily told herself.

Wednesday brought another round of calls from her suitors, some overlapping, and Lily suspected Mr. Willett would be the next to propose, but she spent the day sewing and finishing her letter to Florence. And then Thursday came, with Araminta shut in the drawing room to practice on the pianoforte, and Mrs. Ellsworth busy with Wilcomb in the kitchen, and Lily left to hear Beatrice's lessons. Not that she heard much. Her mind was too preoccupied.

She would tell her family about the engagement the very next day, she decided. They were too busy today, and she didn't want them discussing it with the Kenners. Friday would be soon enough. And it would have to be Friday, because who knew when Mr. Wright would reappear? Yes, Friday.

Or Saturday, at the very latest.

Promptly at seven, Bobbins opened the drawing room door and announced to the gathered Ellsworths, "The Kenners, if you please."

Having prepared herself, Lily's gaze floated right past Mr. Kenner to his sister, who appeared both eager and nervous.

"How lovely you look, Lily!" Sophie said, rising from her curtsey to take Lily's outstretched hands. "Like a queen of the fairies, with that ribbon and those beads in your hair."

"You are lovely yourself. I like you in green."

"Do you? My cousin Gil says that green makes me look like a pea pod in spring."

"And what is wrong with pea pods?" Lily retorted. "I'm glad you were brave enough to defy his opinion."

Sophie smiled ruefully. "Oh—I'm not, really. It's just that I love this dress, and I—I knew Gil wouldn't be here. I made Simon forgo his black tonight, that he might complement me. See? What do you think of him in a fawn-colour waistcoat?"

Thus called upon, Lily was forced to consider the man. Mr. Kenner was turned half away, speaking with her parents, and yet, by a certain stillness of his shoulder, she thought he might be aware of her regard. He had a rather striking profile, finely cut like a cameo. *He is not handsome*, Lily reminded herself. But he more and more gave the impression of a handsome man, and she did not know what to do about it.

Aloud she said lightly, "Fawn-colour complements you well. But then, you know, I prefer nearly any colour to black."

Kenner could have ignored this comment, but Minta heard it and jeered, "Silly Lily! Whoever heard of a clergyman who wore colours?"

"I did not say he should wear colours," Lily rounded on her. "I was merely expressing my personal preference for fawn-colour over black."

"Well, then, you'd better not marry a clergyman," her sister persisted. "For they're forever in black."

"Were you always this clever, or did they teach you that at school?" Lily said shortly. "And for mercy's sake, take your hands out of your pockets and stand like a lady. You'll be whistling, next."

"Don't be so hard on her, Miss Ellsworth," drawled Mr. Kenner, having turned to face them. "It would be good for Miss Araminta to keep her hands warm and limber, that she might play the better after supper."

"See, Lily?" taunted Minta. "I'm keeping my hands warm and limber. Nobody cares how cold *your* claws get, but *I* must think of my duty to others." And then, rocking on her heels, she did whistle a scrap of a tune.

Lily knew it was no use hoping her father would reprimand Minta (and indeed, Mr. Ellsworth smiled benignly and bent to pat Snap). Nor would her stepmother, whose authority over them was of such recent date that she tried to avoid its exercise whenever possible.

It was Mr. Kenner who intervened, now coming to join their little circle. "I admire your pockets, Miss Araminta. Not frequently found in a lady's gown. The pockets in my clerical robes I find equally convenient, both for warmth in a chilly church and for carrying items. In fact," he mused, "I would go so far as to say the pockets are what I love best about my robes—apart, of course, from their enchanting blackness."

Minta gave a burst of laughter at this, and Lily would have been on the defensive, had she not seen the teasing glint in his eye. "Oh?" she rallied. "And I suppose, as a clergyman, black is your favorite colour?"

"Second favorite," he answered promptly. "Giving place, perhaps, only to a particular shade of violet blue. Indigo."

As Lily was wearing that evening an indigo silk gown, she blushed and drew back slightly. With any other gentleman, she would have deemed that remark flirtatious. But with Mr. Kenner, classifying it as such felt presumptuous. Maybe indigo blue truly was his favorite colour. She was glad she hadn't known it beforehand, then, so he could not suspect her of wearing it to please him, and she certainly would avoid the colour in future on any occasion where he might be present, lest he draw such a conclusion.

The party proceeded to supper, Mrs. Ellsworth on Mr. Kenner's arm and Mr. Ellsworth escorting Sophie. They were a small enough group that, though Lily sat to her father's right and Mr. Kenner at the other end to Mrs. Ellsworth's right, they could all converse together. The younger Ellsworths had much to say about the fair, and Mr. Frayne's exploits were rehearsed again. Then Mr. Ellsworth wanted to hear the Kenners' opinion of the Haydn concert, and Lily asked after Sophie's shopping expedition with her mother. But eventually talk turned to St. Eadburh's.

"Mr. Kenner," said Mrs. Ellsworth, "I know I speak for my brother Mr. Gregory as well when I say we are very pleased with how the church is faring under your curacy."

"Thank you, madam," he answered, with a bow of acknowledgement.

"Excellent preaching!" declared Mr. Ellsworth from his end of the table.

"Yes, Mr. Kenner," added little Beatrice. "Minta and I have not been at all tempted to play ball during the service, and last Sunday Tyrone did not even bother to bring a book."

Another bow, this one accompanied by a grin. "Shameless flattery. Why, if not for Miss Ellsworth's dissenting opinion, my head would be quite blown up."

"My dissenting opinion?" echoed Lily, putting down her fork with the bite still on it. "Mr. Kenner, difficult as it is to credit, are you fishing for a compliment?"

"Good heavens—in the 'unclean fishpond of your displeasure'? I should hope not. I was only referring—teasingly—to your warning this past Sunday that the church was 'falling to pieces.'"

She sat up the straighter for his raillery. "Mr. Kenner, I was referring to the physical church, its building and grounds. Nothing of a more...metaphorical nature. I was thinking that you might want to speak with the sexton Mr. Harvey because the church and yard are not so neat as they used to be."

"This dear girl of mine," smiled her father. "So generous with her opinions."

"I didn't intend," she continued, "for anyone but my siblings to hear me that day, sir."

"But having been heard," Mr. Kenner resumed, "I would like to defend myself and say I am aware of Mr. Harvey's...neglect and paid him a visit. I'm afraid he is not feeling quite the thing."

"Oh, no," breathed Mrs. Ellsworth as the others chorused in dismay. "I will go to see him."

"I—did not realize," Lily said, abashed and now feeling guilty for criticizing the poor old man. "Obviously. Or I would not have said—" she broke off. But then she swallowed and added in a rush, "But—Mama—I will come with you when you pay your visit." When her sisters and brother stared in most unflattering surprise, she wished she had not spoken at all. Nor did she know if it was better or worse that her father raised his hands to declare, "Our little angel of mercy." Worse, probably. What if Mr. Kenner thought she was trying to win his approval with good deeds?

Lily's discomfiture was short-lived, however, for soon enough the ladies left the gentlemen to their port, Minta rushing ahead to the drawing room so she could pound away at her music one final time.

"How kind of you, dear Lily," her stepmother murmured, taking up a seat beside her, "to offer to visit Mr. Harvey. I know the Hamblys were so grateful for your attentions because they told me so repeatedly when next I went."

"Hm," said Lily. The cushion case for Florence was nearly finished. Tomorrow or the day after she would stuff it with the lady's bedstraw drying in the scullery.

"When will Flossie and Robert return?" asked Beatrice for the hundredth time. She had taken up her own embroidery hoop and was working on a cloth punctuated with perfectly awful knots and lumps that were supposed to be violets.

"I am eager to meet them," spoke up Sophie Kenner. With no sewing to occupy her, she stood beside the pianoforte, ready to turn Minta's music.

"I hope my gift will be done in time," Bea fretted.

"As I told you after her last letter, Flossie said they will be back in less than a fortnight," answered Lily. "But I can finish your edges for you, if you're not finished by then."

This offer drew more stares from her family, and irritation fluttered her. "What?"

"Why the sudden burst of saintliness?" asked Tyrone evenly. "First with old Mr. Harvey and now with Bea."

She bent to rummage in her workbasket, though she didn't need anything. "What a selfish little imp you must think me, from the way you all are acting. But—I suppose—with Florence gone, I must grow up a little."

"That makes sense," peaceable Sophie agreed. "I find I have much more responsibility keeping house for Simon than I ever did at home."

"But Lily, are you being kinder now because you want Mr. Kenner to like you better?" asked the artless Beatrice.

It was Sophie's turn to stare. Flushing, Lily gasped, half in outrage, half in mortification, and she nearly burst out with, "I'll have you know, I'm already engaged!" But she managed to clamp her mouth shut before this flew out, only favoring her youngest sister with a glare that could have blistered paint.

At once Beatrice shrunk back, lip trembling and eyes filling, though she did put out her tongue after a moment—in a hesitant way, so she could claim she was only licking her lip if Lily roared at her. Mrs. Ellsworth intervened, reaching to draw the young girl to her. "Now, Bea," she murmured, "it isn't done, to ask such things. Mr. Kenner already likes Lily very well."

"Indeed," seconded Sophie, faintly. Her expression was thoughtful as she continued to regard Lily.

"No, but I mean, does she want him to fall in love with her, like the other gentlemen have," sniffled Bea, only making matters worse.

Mrs. Ellsworth gave a tiny shake of her head, and no more was said. Beatrice's awkward question hung over the drawing room another minute, but then they roused themselves. Minta hammered through her piece once more; Sophie put up the next sheets; Tyrone opened his book; the rest of them resumed their sewing. Lily's mind was racing, however. Bea was so vexing! Perhaps especially because there was a grain of uncomfortable truth in her words. Lily *did* want Mr. Kenner to like her, it seemed. Not that she had changed her mind about "collecting" him or thought she could make him like her in the way the other men did, but she discovered she wanted him to like her as a person. He was so clever and well-respected and well-liked that his opinion meant something. And, unlike every other gentleman of her acquaintance, he was so difficult to please. She wanted him to admit to his cousin Mr. Wright that Lily Ellsworth was a fine person who would make a fine wife. That was all. It wasn't so very much.

When Mr. Ellsworth and Mr. Kenner rejoined them, the patriarch's bosom swelled with satisfaction as he took in the outwardly peaceful scene. Ah, he was proud of his beautiful family and only wished it were allowable to draw attention to Mrs. Ellsworth's delicate condition.

A rearrangement took place: Lily vacated the sofa for a chair so that her father might sit beside her stepmother; Minta leaped up to bring Mr. Kenner his violin case; Beatrice gave Lily one last pouting look before putting away her work and taking Snap upon her lap; and Tyrone shut his book.

Mr. Kenner took up his instrument and tuned it briefly. Then he smiled at Minta. "Ready? Ladies first."

The content of the program was no longer any great surprise to anyone in the family, as Minta had been practicing diligently the last few days, but Lily was not prepared for how their performance would affect her. That is, she had supposed Mr. Kenner would play well, and he did; and she had likewise guessed correctly that his long, artistic fingers would show to advantage as he drew the bow back and forth. But the entrancing nature of his play caught her completely off guard. To her alarm, she could scarcely remove her eyes from him, from the grace and long lines of his person—for he stood while performing—and Minta might not even have existed, for all Lily looked at her.

And Minta had succeeded in keeping one secret: she had not revealed that she and Mr. Kenner intended also to sing. For all her boisterousness, Araminta Ellsworth had the finest voice in the family, and, as Lily would have imagined from his preaching, Mr. Kenner's held its own. Among other pieces they sang "Abroad as I was Walking" and "Hares on the Mountains" in turns and "Sweet is the Budding Spring of Love." And Lily could not decide if she liked Mr. Kenner's fiddling better than his singing or his singing better than his fiddling, though she feared she could have listened to either for an eternity. *Oh dear, oh dear. What can it mean?* How could a Haydn string concerto performed by strangers leave her unmoved and make her wish for her workbasket, whereas these simple songs performed by Mr. Kenner held her spell-bound?

Applause met the end of the performance, accompanied by excited barks from Snap at the noise, and Lily roused herself to join in. Minta hopped up to give a droll curtsey as Mr. Kenner bowed, and Mrs. Ellsworth nodded toward the servants hovering in the doorway to bring in the tea.

Because Lily had been making the tea since Florence's departure, no one commented on her moving over to do so now, and the other Ellsworths rose to gather at the pianoforte.

"This is one of my family's favorites," Minta told Mr. Kenner, sitting down again to dash through the opening bars of "True Lover's Farewell." "Do you know it?"

"I don't," he admitted, "but would love to hear it."

"I can play it!" announced Beatrice. "Let me play, Minta, and you all sing."

"Very well, but do play it as fast as you can," Minta urged. "It's a ballad, not a dirge."

The song had only five verses, but Beatrice did indeed play very slowly, in her desire to be accurate, often halting mid-bar to say, "Oh, no, that wasn't right—let me start again."

From her seat beside the tea urn, Lily tried to sing along with the limping accompaniment, but she hushed abruptly when Mr. Kenner left the group to take a cup from her.

"Please, don't let me stop you," he said, dropping into the chair beside her and reaching for the sugar tongs. "Especially when that must be a favorite verse: 'The crow that is so black, my dear, shall change his colour white.' Though perhaps you would rather sing 'shall change his colour fawn.'"

"I did not say fawn-colour was my favorite," she replied promptly. "Only that I preferred it to black."

"What is your favorite colour then, Miss Ellsworth?"

"Bl—" she broke off in confusion. For heaven's sake, if she told him her favorite shade was blue, he would be certain to think she was making up to him!

She might as well have said it aloud, for a smile tugged at the corner of his lips. "We share that, then. Blue is our favorite. I ought to have that sentence engraved and hung upon the wall, Miss Ellsworth, for it just might be the very first thing you and I have agreed on."

"I was not aware we had *dis*agreed on many things," she answered warily.

He clicked his tongue in mock regret. "Oh, dear. That puts me in the embarrassing position of disagreeing with your opinion that we have not disagreed."

Apart from an arch look, Lily made no response. She knew the one, chief area where they did not see eye to eye—her suitability as a wife for Gilbert Wright—but she could hardly bring it up.

Casting about, she lit on a new subject. "You play the fiddle and sing very nicely."

"Thank you. You did not find your mind wandering after eleven minutes?"

"Now, Mr. Kenner," she replied in her sweetest tone, "I hope you have not been dwelling on that remark of mine. I'm sure I only said it out of a mischievous desire to annoy you."

"Things like that do sometimes stick in my gizzard, to put it indelicately. It's a great comfort to hear you say you were only being mischievous. Though, on the other hand, our Lord did say that 'of the abundance of the heart the mouth speaketh.'"

"Oh?" was her indistinct response, and the tea things rattled against each other as she set down one cup too hard.

She tried again. "And—anyone who can encourage Minta to pursue her music or, indeed, any other activity within doors, must be considered a friend of the family. We all wonder what will become of her. Sometimes I try to picture who Minta might marry, but I always give it up."

Lightly he said, "How very odd. I confess I have caught myself wondering the same thing about *you*, Miss Ellsworth, with much the same result."

This touched a tender spot, and her eyes flashed. "I'm certain it is none of your concern whom I marry, Mr. Kenner, and, in fact, I am inclined to view your pondering the matter as something of an impertinence."

Sighing, he leaned back in his chair and crossed his ankles, letting his gaze follow the painted plaster cornices adorning the ceiling. "Not to disagree with you *again*, Miss Ellsworth, but I imagine most everyone's innermost thoughts would qualify as impertinences, if others could only know them. My mistake was in speaking it aloud. But I assure you, I meant my impertinence in the most harmless manner possible. As your parish priest, you know, I would likely be the one marrying you."

"You mean—performing the ceremony."

"Yes, of course that's what I mean." He gave a chuckle, sitting up straight once more. "Heavens! I hope you did not interpret that as a proposal. You belles are inclined to hear a proposal in a man's most innocent remarks."

If her eyes had flashed earlier, they now blazed. "I did not misunderstand you, sir, nor am I prone to. You may rest easy, Mr. Kenner. Though I would advise you to be more guarded in your phrasing when speaking to other young ladies in your flock."

"Ah, but they aren't belles." He gave an ironic little bow that only made her angrier, but thankfully Beatrice's halting play came to an end, and the others came to take their tea.

They shared no more conversation, and Lily refused even to look in his direction the rest of the evening, her spirit still roiled.

But when her hair was braided and the maid gone and the candle blown out, Lily lay on her back, her hands clutched over her breast and sleep very, very far away. Because how could she tell her family of her engagement to Mr. Wright, when her thoughts were more and more full of his maddening, mocking, masterful cousin Mr. Kenner?

Chapter Seventeen

Love is Lord of all.

— *Dryden,* translator, *The works of Virgil* (1697)

There being no direct coach to Salisbury, Kenner had to pass through Romsey, but he was not sorry for the delay. He needed as much time to think as possible before meeting Gil. If he could find Gil.

The Winchester to Romsey coach took him, predictably, out of town along the Romsey Road. Which meant it passed Hollowgate, and Kenner in his outside seat could not help turning his head in case there was a glimpse of indigo blue.

It had come to this, then.

Ignominious defeat.

Where he once prided himself on being cleverer than the ordinary sort, making up in sense and detachment what he might lack in conventional handsomeness or dash, making up in ambition what he might lack in wealth—here he was, as common as the rest of the herd. As hackneyed, and as pathetic.

Because in less than two months he had gone from indifference to taking a wife, to thinking his grandfather was right—that he ought to, and sooner, rather than later. And he had gone from thinking he would apply his considerable intelligence to the process, selecting the best candidate and methodically winning her, to losing his head like the greenest swain for the young lady who besotted every unmarried man in a five-mile radius of Winchester.

What a fool he was, Kenner thought.

Because he could not ignore her. Not for the life of him. If she was near, he must look at her. If opportunity afforded, he must speak with her. If he spoke with her, he must try to evoke a response. And when she responded—when she looked at him or spoke to him—every fiber of him responded too. Crossing swords with Miss Ellsworth was pure stimulation. Excitement. Danger.

He said too much around her. He pushed too far. When her eyes fired up, he wanted to feed the flames. To throw himself into the furnace, though it scorch him.

There had been little sleep the night before. He had spent it wrestling—wrestling his pride into submission. Until, when he finally yielded in the early hours, admitting at last that he was no better than anyone else around him and as helpless as they to resist her, his overthrow led not to depression, as he expected, but to an elation he had never before experienced.

For he loved Lily Ellsworth.

He loved Lily Ellsworth!

Her high spirits and her sharp tongue. Her beauty and her wicked streak. Her refusal to be daunted by him. She was her own person, wholly irrespective of him, and Kenner could not resist it.

Too soon, however, reality dampened his brief and intense mood. To wit, how could he pursue Miss Ellsworth, when his cousin Gilbert Wright had made it very plain that he intended to offer for her? Not that Kenner had any intention of doing the noble thing—stepping aside to gnaw his own heart in unrequited love because Gil had aspired to her first. On the contrary, he persisted in thinking Gil and Lily Ellsworth would be a mismatch, but that did not mean he, Kenner, could woo her from under his cousin's nose without fair warning.

Thus, the trip to Salisbury on the spur of the moment. He must speak with Gil before Gil had a chance to propose, though his rash cousin might run him through for it. But, if Kenner lived to tell the tale, he could then turn his attention to sorting out the next—and likely greater—problem: how he might persuade Miss Ellsworth to return his affections. She was not indifferent to him—her hasty temper showed that. But "not indifferent" was a far cry from love. A far cry from how he himself felt.

At the White Horse in Romsey he had an ale and a sandwich while he waited for the Salisbury coach, climbing into it an hour later and joined by an elderly widow and her companion. The ride inside was stifling, especially as the ladies requested the windows be closed and the leather curtain lowered, but Kenner finally dozed from sheer exhaustion, not coming to until the coach turned down Catherine

Street in the afternoon and rumbled to a halt before the Antelope, a sizeable inn whose stables extended all the way to Brown Street. If Gil weren't staying at the Antelope, a good number of the racing crowd certainly would be, and someone would surely know where to find him.

But luck (whether good or bad, time would tell) was with Kenner, for when he descended from the coach and made his way inside, he found the vast tap room well-crammed and Gilbert Wright himself holding court at the bar, his tankard raised and voice loud.

"Simon!" Wright bellowed, catching sight of him. "Behold my cousin, Simon Kenner! My man, let us have some ale for my cousin!" He hammered on the bar as a whoop went up.

"Drunk as a piper," muttered Kenner as helpful hands shoved him forward. In this setting he was glad he had not worn clerical garb.

"Slapbang took the City Plate!" roared Wright, when his cousin reached him. "That's thirty more guineas in my pocket."

"Keep shouting about it, Gil, and they won't be there for long."

"The City Plate, man!" the proud owner crowed.

Kenner took him by both shoulders. "I hear you, and I congratulate you."

"I'm going to buy *you know whom* something with the winnings," he declared. "A great big ring. Or earrings. What would you say, Simon? Ring or earrings? And should they be sapphires? Pearls? Sapphires for her eyes or pearls for her fair complexion?"

"I would say keep your voice down."

"Voice down," repeated Wright in a carrying whisper. "That's good. Keep my voice down. Did I say her name aloud? I hope I didn't say her name."

"Lord."

"Oh ho! What's that?" Wright shook an admonitory finger in his cousin's face. "Clergymen. Priests. That is to say, men of the cloth. Should not take the Lord's name in vain."

"In point of fact, Gil, I believe the command is more generally applied. But never mind *that* 'Lord,' for you're as drunk as one of the more ordinary sort."

Wright nodded sagely at this. "Ah. You may be right about that." With an effort he placed his tankard precisely on the bar. "What—brings you to Sabserry—Slawsbeserry—S-Salisbury? Have they m-made you dean of the cathedral?"

"Come and stick your head under the pump, and I'll tell you."

"Is it—she, then? Is *she* well?" Wright demanded suddenly, straightening and swaying.

"If she weren't, why would I be the one sent to tell you?" Kenner returned with a grimace of impatience. "Come."

A few splashes under the pump had his cousin sputtering and sobering and blaspheming. "Stop—stop, Simon," Wright gasped, collapsing against the nearby trough. "That'll do. Lord." He slapped at his various pockets until Kenner took pity on him and handed him his own clean handkerchief.

"Better?"

"Better," grunted Wright.

"What would you say to a cup of coffee, Gil? Have you found a good coffee house here?" While Kenner could have asked to retire to his cousin's room at the inn, he predicted Wright would be less likely to lunge at him in public.

"Milford Street," sighed Wright, still mopping his brow.

Even in the coffee house Gilbert Wright received congratulations on his good fortune and claps on the back from departing patrons, as well as a coffee cup raised in toast from a man seated at the counter, under which treatment he began to revive, and by the time they secured a more private table toward the back, Wright had recovered his colour.

"Well, Simon?" he prodded, when they had given the waiter their order. "What brings you to Salisbury in pursuit of me? I suppose I ought to have asked if Grandfather and Granny are all right."

"Perfectly well, as far as I know," answered Kenner. His own confidence seemed to dwindle as his cousin improved, and he was struggling to maintain his composure.

The waiter reappeared, with their coffee on a tray. "Compliments of Haskins and Company."

"Who?"

The waiter gestured toward the man seated at the counter, who touched his hat.

Wright looked around. "Well-wishers," he muttered. Looking pleased, he touched his own hat and nodded in response. "I haven't paid for a thing in Salisbury since Slapbang won."

Kenner wasn't attending. He gripped his own cup, glad to have something for his hands to do.

"What is it, then?" His cousin prompted, grimacing at him. "Is it you? You're dying and you want to extract a deathbed promise from me?" Wondering at the unusual constraint in his so-superior cousin, it added to his good humor, since the man so frequently made him feel at a disadvantage. But something was definitely odd about Simon today—was that even perspiration forming on his lip?

It was. Kenner wished he had not given away his handkerchief. *Good heavens, you fool! Steady. Spit it out, man.* Just witness what Miss Ellsworth had done to him—his habitual self-possession was nowhere to be found.

He took a sip of his drink, tasting nothing. Then, like a criminal facing a firing party who had been asked if he had any last words, he blurted, "Look, Gil—it's this. I've come to ask you if you've offered for Miss Ellsworth yet."

For a minute his cousin could do no more than stare in surprise, but then Wright groaned, setting down his cup with such force that it spilled over. "Not this again, Simon! Did I not make myself perfectly plain the last time? I want you and everyone else in the family to mind his own business. I'll marry who I want to marry, and that's all I'm going to say about it."

"The family didn't put me up to it this time," admitted Kenner in a low voice.

"What? No?"

"No."

"But—who then?"

"Just tell me: you still intend to ask her, I'm guessing."

Wright got a funny look on his face. Discomfiture? Indecision?

Kenner waited, watching.

At last his cousin made a dismissive motion with his hand, as if waving away a fly. "Er—yes. That is, I still intend to ask her. And I—I am—confident of her reply."

Kenner sat back in his chair, one leg of which was shorter than the others. It needed a wad of paper set under it. When he sat forward again, again it rocked. "You're…confident, you say?"

Wright's lower lip protruded. "Yes."

"Because…?"

"Look here, Simon. What are you getting at? I don't have to give my reasons. I don't have to explain myself at all. But—yes—I'm confident. Miss Ellsworth and I have—have—" his ale-induced ruddiness deepened as he tried to think what might be said, when he had given her his promise not to make any announcements. "We have…talked *around* the matter, and she—did not discourage me."

Kenner's mouth gave that wry twist that made his cousin want to push his chair over. "And why would she discourage you? The girl's a flirt, Gil. She hasn't discouraged *anyone*, unless you count Dailey, and that was only because he got her in a corner, figuratively speaking, and forced an explicit answer out of her."

"How dare you speak of her thus!" cried Wright, taking hold of the corners of the table. "I resent you saying anything about her of that nature, you hound. She's an ang—"

"—An angel, yes, I know," Kenner interrupted. "And for God's sake, keep your voice down." He let out a slow breath, gathering himself. His cousin wasn't the only one in danger of running away with this. "Let me make this quick before we do end up grappling together. You remember weeks and weeks ago at the deanery? Slap-bang had just won the Winchester King's Plate."

"Of course I remember."

"And Grandfather told me that, if I was going to be the curate of St. Eadburh's, I ought to get married."

Comprehension dawned on his cousin's face, and a relieved laugh escaped him. "Damn you, Simon, is that what this is about? Did you chase me down to tell me you're going to court one of those Miss Weekses, and you can't decide which one?"

"No. I chased you down to tell you that I would like to court Miss Ellsworth."

If he had clubbed his cousin over the head, Gil would not have looked any more stupefied.

I probably look the same myself, Kenner thought ruefully, *and have, ever since I realized my feelings for her.*

"You're—you're joking me," Wright croaked after a minute.

"No."

"Then you're saying that because you want a rise out of me."

"Gil, to be frank, that's about the last thing I want."

"Have you—said anything to her?"

"I have not. I wanted to do you the courtesy of informing you, first."

"Informing me. Not asking me."

Kenner held his gaze steadily. "Informing you. Not asking you."

Wright's face reddened and his breathing grew rough. "Well, that's villainous of you. You knew from the start that I was pursuing Miss—pursuing *her*, and now you want in, just to rankle me."

"I know this will be hard to credit, Gil, but you have nothing to do with it. If you were to light on any other young lady in Christendom, you would do so with my blessing."

"Yes—and same to you! If it isn't to vex me, why should you choose the one girl I already chose and who I told you I chose? That alone should have been enough to make you look elsewhere, if you had any honor to you."

Kenner grimaced and ran a hand through his hair, unused to finding himself on the low ground of the argument. "I'm not proud of myself, Gil. If it's any defense, I'm hardly alone in choosing her. You're pretty much up against the whole county. No—I never meant to like her."

"Well, just *un*like her, then! You say you haven't said anything, so don't! Give it up and go away."

"It's too late for that," Kenner retorted through gritted teeth. "I didn't mean to like her, but now I do, and I don't intend to 'go away' simply because you saw her first. I am saying we must each take our chances. You may try to win her, and so may I. And whoever succeeds—well—he succeeds."

Wright's jaw set like iron. "Then I have news for you, Simon," he bit out, shoving away his coffee cup. "Because I've already succeeded. What do you say to that? It hasn't been announced yet, and I wouldn't have said anything now, if you had not driven me to it, but—"

The colour was draining from his cousin's countenance. "But—what?"

"But I have already proposed to Miss Ellsworth and been accepted!" thundered Wright, slamming an open hand on the table top.

He had the satisfaction of seeing Kenner look positively ill. Grey-faced. Hollow. But his satisfaction was mixed with temper at the man's presumption.

"But you just said—I mean—that can't be," Kenner managed.

"Of course it can. And is. What would you know about it? Ask Miss Ellsworth herself, if you doubt me."

"But—why did you not say so at first?"

"Because I told you it wasn't announced. She asked for more time before we did so. A little mess to mop up, after Dailey, you know."

"But she—" Kenner broke off.

"But she *what*?" prompted his cousin severely.

Elbows on the table, Kenner rubbed at his temples. *But she does not behave like a woman engaged*, he could not say. He had no intention of repeating the scene at the deanery, and, in the moment, he hardly cared for his cousin's feelings. He was too consumed with his own.

Miss Ellsworth, engaged? But how could it be? It simply *couldn't* be.

It wasn't that she had said nothing about it. It wasn't that her family had said nothing of it either. Presumably they didn't know. It wasn't that she went to the Haydn concert with Willett or the Magdalen Hill Fair with Frayne or danced in the drawing room with Caxton.

It was that—it was that she gave no sign of her heart being touched. If she had accepted Gil—and Kenner couldn't imagine Gil would lie about such a thing—she did not do so from love. She did so because Gil was rich. Gil was attractive. Flashy. Sporting. He had a prizewinning horse and was heir to a vast estate.

And those things were enough, apparently. Those things were all that mattered to her. She flirted for fun and married for dash and wealth.

She has no heart, Kenner thought in bitterness of spirit. *She doesn't love him. She has no heart, and I am a fool.*

"You had better not be about to tell me such a tale as you did at the deanery," growled Wright, when Kenner showed no sign of finishing his thought. "Because I just might murder you this time."

"I will refrain, then," said Kenner, with a shadow of his usual dryness. He was taking himself in hand. There was no alternative. Straightening in the unstable chair, he picked up his coffee again and took a calm, measured sip. It had gone cool.

Wright eyed him warily. "You will refrain because you have no such story to tell, or you will refrain because you don't want to be murdered?"

"Both. Neither. What you will. I was merely surprised by your news. And disappointed, naturally. Your announcement has certainly blown up any plans of mine and left me little save a desire to don sackcloth and ashes, go out in the midst of Salisbury, and cry with a loud and bitter cry."

Wright's frown deepened. It was hard to triumph when he was not certain how in earnest his cousin was. "Then—you won't try to court Miss Ellsworth after all?"

"How can I, when she is already engaged?" Kenner slipped his watch from his pocket and consulted it. "If I go now, I can catch the return coach via Stockbridge."

"Well, then. Well, then. But—say, Simon—you won't mention our conversation, I hope? She wanted to choose the time to tell both her family and everyone else, and I'm afraid I've told you somewhat prematurely. Driven to it, and all."

"I'll be silent as the grave." Digging a coin from another pocket, Kenner let it ring in the dish.

"I would be especially grateful if you feigned ignorance with Miss Ellsworth," Wright added with a nervous smile. "You know—look surprised when she tells you about it. Certainly don't bring it up beforehand if you talk to her."

Kenner was already rising.

"Have no fear, sweet my coz. The lady in question and I may never speak again."

CHAPTER EIGHTEEN

Whatsoever ye have spoken in darkness shall be heard in the light; and that which ye have spoken in the ear in closets shall be proclaimed upon the housetops.
— Luke 12:3, *The Authorized Version* (1611)

No sooner did he see his cousin off on the Stockbridge coach than Gilbert Wright's conscience smote him. Not for swearing Kenner to secrecy—no—nor for planting a figurative dagger in his heart (Wright had no idea he had done so), but because he did not like to begin his engagement to Miss Ellsworth with a deception.

He could not do it. He *should* not do it, he decided. It was an action unworthy of his angelic betrothed, and, of equal weight, he was not confident he could keep the secret from her. Wright did not imagine Kenner would betray him—no, his fear lay with himself. Miss Ellsworth might be angelic, but she was also, as Kenner pointed out, fiendishly clever. One blurt, one misstep, and Miss Ellsworth would discover all. No—better by far to confess his act and beg forgiveness.

Therefore Lily received a wheel of Wiltshire Loaf cheese accompanied by a note.

The Antelope
Salisbury, Wilts.

14 August 1801

My dear Miss Ellsworth,
I hope to follow this cheese to Hollowgate shortly and see all the Ellsworths in person, particularly you and your father. Slapbang won again, taking the City Plate by a length and a half, putting me thirty guineas ahead.

My cousin Simon Kenner paid a visit, and I'm afraid I mentioned our understanding to him in the excitement of the race's aftermath. I hope you will pardon my enthusiasm, especially as we are now so soon to see each other again and make all plain. I must first wind up affairs here and then take care of some business at Meadowsweep with the horse but will call Sunday and accompany your family to church, if that is convenient.

Yours most sincerely,

Gilbert Wright

The wheel of cheese thumped to the floor, and Lily very nearly followed it. Groping her way to the brocaded bench, she crumpled onto it. "Mentioned their understanding to him"? No, no—go back further than that—what on earth was Mr. Kenner doing in Salisbury in the first place? Well—cousins were allowed to visit each other. It was not so very odd.

But—but—

No. The more important thing was that Mr. Kenner *knew* now.

Knew she was engaged. Knew—worse—that she had been engaged the entire time Mr. Wright had been absent from Winchester. What must he think of her?

"Well?" she murmured. "What of it? I haven't done anything wrong." She reviewed the past week. Why, even if she was engaged to someone else, a girl could spend her time as Lily had—dancing with gentlemen callers in her own drawing room and going to a concert with one and to the fair with another, all with family members present.

Yet even as she made these arguments to herself, Lily was aware she would certainly take it amiss if she heard Mr. Wright had gallanted a different young lady every day he had been in Salisbury. More than likely she would have made quick work of their "understanding" and sent him on his way!

Then there was the additional mental knot to be picked at: if Mr. Kenner had told his cousin of Lily's questionable activities—and he must have, having not hesitated to inform on Lily before—why did Mr. Wright not mention them? Not throw them in her face? Quite the opposite. He sounded as if nothing at all had occurred, and they would proceed according to their agreed-upon plan.

Therefore, had Mr. Kenner *not* mentioned what Lily had been up to? And if not, why not? And again, if not, why go to Salisbury at all? *What* must he think of her?

It was all so puzzling, so mystifying.

The maids Monk and Boots were heard at the end of the screens passage, and Lily scrambled to her feet, replacing the cheese on the marquetry table by the entrance and whisking Mr. Wright's note into her bosom. "Here's a cheese," she called, already hurrying away. "Please let Wilcomb know."

Dashing into the parlor where her writing desk stood, Lily flung herself down and seized a sheet of paper. Time must be wasted mending the pen and finding more ink to replace the nearly-empty stand, but she composed her message in her head, even while she fussed with such tasks, so that the writing of it came fast.

Hollowgate
Winchester, Hants.

15 August 1801

Dear Mr. Wright,
Thank you for the Wiltshire loaf and hearty congratulations on Slapbang's victory. I hope this reply reaches you quickly.

It was most unfortunate that you shared the news of our conversation with your cousin because I have not yet informed my father, or indeed anyone, *about the circumstances. In fact, Mr. Wright, it pains me to say that I have reconsidered. Your offer was a great honor to me, and you will always have my esteem and gratitude. But I am afraid I cannot marry you after all. The fault lies entirely with me. I am not yet ready to marry and may never do so.*

Please forgive my broken promise—we have both been guilty of not living up to our word, I'm afraid! I am confident your cousin Mr. Kenner will not have shared your news with anyone, and therefore no one but he need ever know what took place between us. I wish you every joy in future.

Your very obliged and—

But then Lily was forced to whisk her sheet away, unfinished and unblotted, when Bobbins the footman entered, intoning, "Miss Kenner and Mr. Frayne." And then, directly on the guests' heels, Lily's younger siblings and Aggie and Snap tumbled in. Lily's heart stopped an instant when she saw Miss Kenner, only to start again when her curate brother did not appear.

"What was that monstrous cheese Wilcomb was carrying?" demanded Araminta.

"A gift someone sent," muttered Lily. But this quelling answer would not satisfy, and she soon had to admit the name of the sender.

Minta barked with laughter. "Mr. Wright certainly thinks you eat a great deal, doesn't he? I wish he would send cake next time. An enormous one with plenty of icing."

"Do stop, Minta. Mr. Wright only wanted to say that Slapbang won another race."

Her sister hurrahed for her favorite horse, but Sophie Kenner gave a little sigh. "That was...very kind of him to inform you."

"If I had a horse like his, I would want to publish its triumphs too," said Mr. Frayne generously, "though I never thought of using a cheese to do so."

Lily tried to appear unstudied as she moved away from the desk to join them all, though she was wishing with all her might that she could have had five more minutes to finish her letter. As it was now, the ink had likely smeared, and she would need to rewrite it before she could address and send it. Every minute mattered! Suppose Mr. Wright was already on his way to Meadowsweep? Oh, dear. Should she send her reply to the Antelope or risk sending it to Meadowsweep, where his parents and sisters would be sure to remark upon it? No, no—it must go to the Antelope, as soon as ever she could get rid of everyone. She must end this engagement while it was still only known to him, herself, and Mr. Kenner.

Sophie's evident unhappiness distracted her then, though Lily couldn't stifle the impatient thought that it would solve every problem, if only Gilbert Wright would fall in love with his Kenner cousin. "Did you already know about Slapbang winning the City Plate?"

Lily ventured. By which she really meant, *What did your brother tell you of his trip to Salisbury?*

Sophie received the question entirely otherwise, however, and she gave Lily a reproachful look from her sweet brown eyes. "I knew nothing of it. Gil didn't write to *me*."

Nor had Mr. Kenner shared anything, then, Lily guessed, reading her friend's innocent hurt. But how had he explained his absence to his sister the day before? A man without a horse could hardly jaunt over to Salisbury and back in an hour.

"Can we have the cheese with dinner?" asked Beatrice. "I know Snap would like some."

"I suppose," answered Lily absently.

"Or we could ring for some now, and we could toast it," suggested Minta.

"But then they'd have to build a fire, too," Tyrone pointed out.

"I can do it!" Minta cried, skipping up.

"Minta, you're sure to burn the house down," frowned Lily, roused from her distraction.

"Nonsense. Aggie and I have plenty of practice because we've helped the groundskeepers burn debris before." She gave a vigorous tug on the bell rope before kneeling beside the copper firewood bucket.

Caught in the excitement, Mr. Frayne joined her. "Have you any experience lighting the matches, Miss Araminta?"

"No...but I've seen the servants do it," she confessed, selecting a few promising pieces of wood.

"I would be happy to show you how." The little man's offer met with a chorus of eagerness, and Tyrone and Bea joined them beside the hearth.

"There aren't any spills, though," said Aggie, tipping the cup on the mantel to peer inside.

"Bea, get some scribbling paper from the desk," ordered Minta. "We'll tear it up."

Lily gave a little shriek, vaulting across the room to intercept her sister. "I'll do it. We don't want—we don't want Florence's letters or any important things torn up."

"I wouldn't have torn up Flossie's letters," said Bea crossly, but Lily ignored her, jerking open the desk drawers and slamming them shut in a flurry.

"There. Take those."

Her sisters shrugged, more interested in Mr. Frayne's operations with the tinderbox. Even Snap had thrust his head between the twins to observe. And once Lily was certain her letter to Mr. Wright would not be discovered (she folded it into the smallest compass she could and added it to his note in her bodice), she relaxed enough to smile upon the scene. Only Bobbins looked pained when he answered the summons, probably imagining the merrymaking's untidy aftermath.

Mrs. Ellsworth wore a similar expression when she entered the room, and Lily was quick to say, "Don't be distressed, Mama. I am right here to ensure we don't burn Hollowgate to the ground or leave such disaster behind that the servants all give notice."

"It isn't that, dearest," her stepmother replied quietly, coming to her side to speak. "It's that your father just received a most curious box, and he is coming even now to ask you about it. And if you will excuse her, Miss Kenner, I think it might be best to go meet him, Lily."

"Meet him?" echoed Lily, her eyes widening. Had Mr. Wright followed up his cheese with something even more peculiar? An animal, perhaps? But what animal could be sent in a box? Or was it worse than an animal—whatever that might be?

"Bravo!" shouted Araminta just then, leaping up. "Well done, Mr. Frayne. Give me a spill, Aggie, and we will light it with the match."

"May I strike the flint now?" asked Tyrone.

"Me! Me!" cried Beatrice.

Mrs. Ellsworth tugged on Lily's arm when the hubbub distracted Miss Kenner, but Lily had only risen to her feet, still puzzled, when the door opened again, and there were her father and Boots, the maid's arms heaped with a box of fabric samples and Mr. Ellsworth holding an open pattern book.

"Look what Mr. Haskins sent, my love," he addressed her cheerily, depositing the book in her arms and pointing for Boots to set the box down.

"Mr. Haskins?" Lily repeated blankly.

"The mercer in the Square. You know—Haskins and Company."

Lily dropped back down to her seat, shaking her head at the heavy book she held. "But—whyever should Mr. Haskins send anything? What is it for?"

Chuckling, her father took her rosy face between his thumb and forefinger and gave it a fond squeeze.

"'What is it for,' she says," he repeated, glancing around to see that he had everyone's attention. "Why, his card says that he hopes to be considered for all the needs of your trousseau and new household!"

"*What* trousseau and new household?" Lily almost shrilled.

"Heh heh heh. There is no need for further concealment, my love, because I wholeheartedly approve. I only ask, mournfully, must a father always be the last to know?"

Oh, no. *Oh, no!* Should she deny it utterly? Lie, and say the mercer must be mistaken? Or tell the truth, but say she had been on the point of ending it—whipping out her smeared letter as proof?

Slowly, shaking her head, Lily pushed the pattern book from her lap to the floor and rose unsteadily once more to her feet.

"Papa," she murmured, hardly audible.

But then she was enfolded in his arms, the very letter she thought of producing poking her uncomfortably, her face pressed to his shoulder and her hair kissed, and she heard, through the rumble of his chest, "Rejoice with me, you all! Lily and Mr. Wright are to be married!"

Reactions ranged from stunned silence (Sophie Kenner) to applause (Minta and Aggie) to gasps (Tyrone and Beatrice) to letting fall the match from his hand and setting the rug on fire (Mr. Frayne).

Shrieks and stamping and shouted advice and mortified apologies ensued, and, in all the fuss, it was left to poor Mrs. Ellsworth in her delicate condition to catch at Lily when she staggered, collapsing, to the sofa.

Chapter Nineteen

If any man among you seem to be religious, and bridleth not his tongue, but deceiveth his own heart, this man's religion is vain.

— James 1:26, *The Authorized Version* (1611)

Lily was soon surrounded by a circle of concerned faces as she got her breath back. No, not all the faces were concerned. Or not all concerned for *her.* Sophie looked like she was fighting tears, and Mr. Frayne's elfin countenance was greenish. Lily's first thought was, *Now the fat is in the fire*. Her second: *I will strangle Mr. Kenner with my bare hands.*

So much for his discretion.

"Are you quite all right, dear Lily?" asked her stepmother. "You were too sudden with her, William."

Affecting not to hear his wife, Mr. Ellsworth petted his daughter's hand, still amused. "Not turning missish on us, are you? No need to swoon in modesty—Mr. Wright is a husband to be proud of, young lady."

This additional twist of the knife made quick work of Mr. Frayne. He mumbled some excuse, fumbling a bow (not that anyone was paying attention to him, as they were too interested in Lily), and almost ran from the room.

"But the toasted cheese!" protested Araminta, when she saw he had gone.

Mr. Frayne's flight gave Sophie Kenner courage. "I—had better be going too. You will want to be—er—family time. Other calls—the Hamblys—Mr. Harvey—"

"Oh, Sophie." Lily lifted a hand toward her, but Sophie had already escaped.

So much for their friendship—if Lily was to marry Sophie's beloved and to hate Sophie's brother, it would be better to have as little to do with each other as possible. But she sighed nonetheless. Now, she supposed, the Miss Weekses would have Sophie all to themselves.

"Are you *really* engaged to Mr. Wright?" asked Beatrice.

But Lily took a leaf from her father's book and pretended not to hear. "Papa, tell me—how did the mercer know of my engagement? What did he write?"

Mr. Ellsworth retrieved the pattern book from the floor, nipping the notecard from where he had tucked it in the pages. "It's his trade card, my love. All the usual things on the front about silks and crapes and stuffs and damasks and so forth. And on the reverse he writes, 'With many felicitations on the occasion of your daughter's engagement to Mr. Wright. I have taken the liberty of sending our newest samples and patterns and would be delighted to be of service in fitting out Miss Ellsworth's trousseau. We also carry many fabrics suitable to the establishment of a new household. Yours etc.'"

"But how did he know?" Lily muttered. It had to be Mr. Kenner's doing because Mr. Wright had not shared his news with anyone else. If he had, he would have confessed that to her as well, wouldn't he have? In any event, Mr. Wright could have been more easily forgiven, it being *his* news to share, not—mere *gossip.*

"It's true, then?" Mrs. Ellsworth prompted. "You and Mr. Wright are engaged?"

While Lily could ignore her youngest sister, she could not avoid her stepmother's question. She thought of the letter tucked in her bodice. It could never be sent now, and the damage minimized. If the mercer in Winchester knew; everyone knew. And that meant she must either marry Mr. Wright or jilt him openly.

She swallowed and folded her hands together. "We...are. He asked me before he left for the Salisbury races, and I said yes, then, but I was not yet ready to make it known."

Mrs. Ellsworth's lips parted when she heard the qualifying "then," as if she meant to say more, but her husband just then held up his hands in what she recognized as his about-to-give-a-speech pose, and her mouth shut again.

"One thing is certain: your news is now common knowledge, Lily, and Mr. Haskins the mercer will not be the last to congratulate you on such a fine match. Rise. Receive your father's blessing. And, when you write to your lover, you must ask him to come and speak with me in the time-honored fashion."

"He will call tomorrow, I believe," said Lily, accepting her father's benedictory kiss with resignation. "Perhaps even attend church with us."

"Tomorrow it is," agreed her father, nodding for Bobbins and Monk to enter with the tea tray and the chunks of Wiltshire Loaf. "And now, though we have lost our other guests, let us mark the joyous occasion with a celebratory cup of tea and some toasted cheese."

Though circumstances had forced her hand, Lily's sanguine nature began to reassert itself by the following morning. Despite her troubles, she had slept well from sheer mental exhaustion. No helpful dream came to her in the night. No angel to point the way and declare, "Thou shalt marry Gilbert Wright" or, "Thou shalt jilt Gilbert Wright," and Lily decided she would just have to see how she felt about it when she saw him again.

But she was starting to see the humor in the situation. Because it *was* ridiculous, was it not? All summer she had intended on winning and marrying Mr. Wright, but when it came right down to it, she did not like anyone or anything making her mind up for her. How on earth had she come to be in this predicament? Was it all Mr. Dailey's fault, with his public embraces? Or was it Mr. Kenner's fault for not keeping his mouth shut? If Mr. Dailey had never kissed her, the Miss Weekses would never have spread gossip about it. And if they had never spread gossip about it, Mr. Kenner would never have told

Mr. Wright not to marry her. And if Mr. Kenner had never told Mr. Wright not to marry her, Lily would never have accepted Mr. Wright just to spite Mr. Kenner. What a muddle! Each step had led inevitably to the next, and now here she was.

But perhaps because she had already told Mr. Dailey a piece of her mind, she was inclined to lay the greater blame at Mr. Kenner's feet.

The terrible truth, Lily reproved herself as the Ellsworths walked to church (without Mr. Wright, thankfully), *is that I am a flirt. I am a flirt, and I am not yet tired of flirting. It was too easy to win Mr. Wright. He fell like overripe fruit. While I may have chosen him for my eventual husband, I didn't want to marry him* yet. *I don't want to marry* anybody *yet. And just when I've decided I would like to play with fire and see what can be done about the tiresome Mr. Kenner, the tiresome Mr. Kenner makes a wretched mull of everything and ties my hands!*

She was glad Mr. Wright had not appeared before church. For if the opportunity presented itself, Lily intended on letting Mr. Kenner know in no uncertain terms that she resented both his interference and his indiscretion. And she would begin by treating him with studied coolness. She would show him the "unclean fishpond of her displeasure," indeed. Pitch him in head foremost!

But Lily's plan received an unforeseen check.

For how could Mr. Kenner be hurled into said unclean fishpond, if he would not even approach its banks? And it seemed he would not.

If Lily meant to treat him with studied coolness, she found Mr. Kenner forestalled her with his own glacial indifference. He did not look at her once during the service, though she stared at him through narrowed eyes, yawned openly, fanned herself, whispered to Minta (and was hushed by the same), and even feigned dozing.

He must feel guilty, she assured herself. *As well he should.*

The congregation was no help at all, hanging on the curate's words with their usual rapt attention. Only one thing tore their notice from him, but as it caused Lily's heart to sink to the bottom of her slippers, she could hardly call it a victory: namely, right after the Eucharist, as Mr. Kenner began the Prayer of Thanksgiving, one of the church doors creaked open and in crept the tardy Mr. Gilbert Wright.

Heads unbowed; eyes popped open.

Hat in hand, he made his way up the aisle, his high colour betraying awareness of the attention he had attracted. His cousin's prayer suffered only the briefest hitch before it rolled onward, but it took the flock more time to recover as it watched Mr. Wright squeeze into the Ellsworth pew.

Lily's face burned. But with a mighty effort, she gave her betrothed a fleeting smile before lowering her bonnet brim. All around, a gentle buzz began to be audible. Nudges were given and received; throats cleared. When the praying Mr. Kenner got to the bit about "keep them that are engaged in matrimony firm to the faith," Mr. Wright even elbowed Lily, but she did not acknowledge it.

The minutes dragged. The Prayer of Thanksgiving ended, to be followed by a benediction which had never seemed longer. But at last the service concluded with the command to "depart in peace." At once, the muffled buzz swelled into a veritable wave of sound, from which “Ellsworth” and “engaged” and “that one” could be picked out.

Mr. Wright tapped the back of her gloved hand and grinned down at her. “Does this mean you have forgiven me? I take it I wasn’t the only one to spill the secret.”

“It is certainly spilled,” said Lily. His grin helped her mood. As did the flutter of the feminine half of St. Eadburh’s as they stared and murmured at Miss Lily Ellsworth’s piece of luck.

Before they could make their way from the pew, the family was ambushed by felicitations from those with whom they were on visiting terms and nods and smiles from the others. Lily allowed herself to be squeezed back when her father edged his way to stand at Mr. Wright’s side, the better to perform introductions.

Around her father’s shoulder, Lily saw Mr. Kenner make his way down the aisle, his surplice and robe billowing. Her heart sped and climbed somewhere up to the middle of her throat, but he sailed past them with only a nod at his cousin, to take his usual position at the door.

“Wretched man,” she whispered. “I’ll have my say, if it’s the last thing I do.”

But as determined as Lily was, Mr. Kenner matched her, and by the time the Ellsworths gained the church door, he had already replaced his surplice in the vestry and was striding away beside his sister.

It was Mr. Ellsworth who unwittingly salvaged the situation. “Mr. Kenner!” he called after the curate. “You have heard the news?”

Mr. Kenner turned slowly, and Lily saw his chest rise and fall as he took a deep breath. "I have, sir. And I do congratulate the happy couple."

"Well, then," said Mr. Ellsworth, oblivious to the curate's tepidness. He clapped his hands. "We are having a little dinner of celebration shortly. Will you and Miss Kenner not join us?"

"Er, sir—" began Mr. Wright, his hand lifting and then dropping back to his side. He did not want to stumble at the very threshold, so to speak, and cross his future father-in-law before he had even officially asked the man for his daughter's hand. Therefore he swallowed his objection to the Kenners' company and threw a false heartiness in his voice. "Yes, Gil, Sophie. Do say you will."

Lily saw Sophie's hand tighten on her brother's arm, but Kenner only gave a short bow.

"Two o'clock, say," declared Mr. Ellsworth. With a regal wave, he led his family away.

Mr. Wright duly closeted himself with Mr. Ellsworth when they returned to Hollowgate, and Lily found herself beckoned by her stepmother. "Do come with me, Lily, while I tell Wilcomb we will be nine at dinner. The day is so fine, I think we might set up a table on the terrace."

No sooner had Mrs. Ellsworth whisked her down the screens passage than she halted and took her by the elbows.

"Lily, darling, I hope you will forgive me and take this in the manner intended." As ever when she was uncomfortable, colour flooded Miranda Ellsworth's face, making her appear younger and rather pretty.

"That sounds daunting," Lily replied with lifted brows.

"I don't mean it to be. But without Florence here, I feel a responsibility to ask this question. Because—forgive me—if you have accepted Mr. Wright—if you are going to marry him—and a very pleasant and eligible young man he is, too—but—oh, Lily—can you assure me that you...love him?"

Going as scarlet as her stepmother, Lily replied too quickly, "I like him well enough." But the question made her squirm and breathed new life into her dreadful uncertainty: marry him or jilt him? Jilt him or marry him? What should she do, and when and why? She only knew that she was not prepared for this conversation, and it was even worse to have it in the screens passage, where a servant might pass at any moment.

"But is it enough, your liking?" persisted Mrs. Ellsworth. "I would hate to see you marry without love, Lily."

Perhaps it was Lily's unease that made her blurt what she later regretted: "Why? Because you did?"

Mrs. Ellsworth drew back, her hands releasing her stepdaughter and her face darkening. "I—I—"

"I'm sorry," Lily said at once. "That was impertinent, Mama. I'm sorry."

"I have learned to be fond of your father," Mrs. Ellsworth said, hardly above a whisper. "He is a good, generous man who loves his family and who has been nothing but kindness to me—"

"Please, you needn't—" Lily pleaded. "Justify yourself, I mean. It was wrong of me to say. Very wrong. Unforgiveable."

But her stepmother straightened, her chin lifting. "This is too important for me to take offense now and neglect to say what I ought to say. Lily, you are not in the position I was in. You are young and wealthy and beautiful, and in no danger of being forced from your home. You have not fallen to a brother's lot for shelter and support, as I had. Your father offered me so much when he asked me to marry him, and I was grateful. *Am* grateful. But Mr. Wright offers you nothing *you* don't already have, except himself. Therefore, I would rather see you marry for love. If you love him, I will rejoice. Only say so, dear Lily, and I will have done."

This assurance, however, was precisely what Lily could not give her, and the panic which flooded her as a result made her abrupt again. "I can't say yet. I don't know. And I wish you would not press me. I—had better go. When Papa and Mr. Wright come out, they will want to speak with me."

Mrs. Ellsworth's shoulders sagged, and she pressed her lips together before managing a nod, but Lily had already gone.

"I cannot say I am looking forward to this," Sophie Kenner confessed to her brother as they passed the gateposts and entered Hollowgate's drive. "It is not that I did not expect it—their engagement. Gil's admiration for Miss Ellsworth was obvious, even before you—tried to advise him at Granny's birthday. She is so lovely and vivacious."

Heartache is a selfish thing, and Kenner had been too absorbed in his own unhappiness to think of his sister, but he could not hear Sophie's despondence now without reaching out a hand to brace her arm. They were a sorry pair, he thought. The two of them each yearning for someone who did not reciprocate in the slightest. However, he could not help but wonder—was it better to be Sophie, blind to her beloved's faults, or to be like himself—all too aware of them?

In utter disregard of the feelings of some of those gathered, the day was indeed very fine. A blue sky, a bright but not oppressive sun, a soft breeze. The Hollowgate servants set a table on the terrace beneath the shade awning, heaping it with salads and bread and some roast fowl. Birds sang, and Minta snuck the terrier choice tidbits. Mr. Gilbert Wright, though he would rather not have had his cousins present, still considered it one of the most blessed days of his existence. He had been received by Mr. Ellsworth with all kindness, and the prize of prizes awarded to him.

Such was Mr. Wright's satisfaction that, before the meal was over, Kenner decided Sophie had the worse lot. After all, every doting glance Gil directed toward Miss Ellsworth, every endearment with which he addressed her, must be so many daggers through his sister's heart.

Miss Ellsworth, on the other hand, neither simpered nor murmured at Gil, and, in fact, treated him on the whole as any other person present, with the exception of Kenner himself. And Kenner was all too aware that he *was* the exception. For Miss Ellsworth spoke not one word to him, if she could avoid it. Nor did she look in his direction. Not that he had been sitting there like Snap, waiting for scraps. He had been equally determined neither to speak to her nor to look at her, so he supposed they must both be supremely satisfied with the result.

Had he schemed and planned, however, Kenner could not have lit on a more effective way to nettle Lily than to ignore her ignoring him. At her end of the table, she grew more and more desperate to nettle him right back. How dare he pretend she did not exist, after what he had done? How dare he disdain to acknowledge her, when he ought to be distraught with desire to beg her pardon?

One thing was clear: surrounded by family, there would be no opportunity for private conversation (or private castigation, as it were). If Lily wanted to have her say, she must create her own occasion.

"Have you—set a date for the wedding?" Sophie was asking. The dishes had been cleared, but the company was still at table, enjoying the weather, with the exceptions of Beatrice and Minta, who had excused themselves to toss a stick for Snap.

"No," said Lily, so shortly that the curate's sister blushed, and Mrs. Ellsworth took a deep breath.

"I am at her mercy," declared Mr. Wright, glancing around with a smile. His fond hand reached for hers across the table, but Lily pretended to misunderstand and intercepted it with the bowl of apricots.

"Yes, do have some more, Mr. Wright," she said. "They grow in my sister Florence's garden. In fact—the garden is at its height. Won't—won't you all come and see it? Barney and the groundskeepers have made it beautiful against Flossie's return."

It was when they were wandering in the walled garden, admiring the flowers and fruit and vines, that Lily snatched up a basket from beside the entrance and drifted with what stealth she could manage toward Mr. Kenner, who was peering into the branches of a tree.

"They're ready, these pears," she blurted. (Everything seemed to come out as a blurt today.)

Slowly, he turned to regard her, his carriage stiffening visibly. But he replied politely, "I see that. Are they Aldermaston pears?"

"Yes," said Lily recklessly, though in truth she had no idea. She thrust the basket at him. "You and Sophie should have some."

There was a glint in his eyes, and his mouth quirked reluctantly. "Miss Ellsworth, are you *still* feeling guilty over stealing our roses?"

"Obviously not," she sniffed, "for I never felt guilty in the first place. And if I did, I keep a short list of accounts." Snapping the nearest pear from its twig, she placed it in the basket.

There was a pause, and then he said, "Let me see, then. You have stricken the roses from your accompt-book—"

"They were never there."

"—And I trust my unfortunate archery comment is also squared—"

"Of course." Plucking two more pears, she handed them to him.

"So dare I ask if there is anything new on that list of yours? On which side of the ledger do I stand?"

After a sweeping glance to ensure no one else was listening, Lily hissed, "In truth, I have only one thing to accuse you of at present, sir, but it is a weighty one."

"Indeed? I had better hear it, then, the better to defend myself."

Lily tugged on another fruit, and it tumbled to the ground. She kicked it aside. "I would like to say, Mr. Kenner, that I—re-sent—your lack of discretion."

He stared, his brow puckering. "*What* lack of discretion?"

Her own brows flew together. "Do you deny it, then?"

"I would deny it vigorously, Miss Ellsworth, if only I knew what it was."

Hopping up for a pear just above her reach and missing it, she said through clenched teeth, "I refer to you telling all and sundry about my engagement to your cousin, when I am certain he must have told you it was not announced yet."

Extending his arm, Kenner's long fingers twisted and plucked the elusive pear. "Oh?" His eyes narrowed. "That is the accusation, is it? Oh, dear. A serious crime. Did it interfere with your fun?"

"Then you *did* do it!" she squeaked.

"On the contrary," he replied coolly. "I said nothing. For what motive would I have to rattle on about you or your concerns? To do so would imply I ever thought of you from one moment to the next."

Lily coloured, gulped. Began to speak, only to have nothing emerge. For one instant he thought (as did she) that she might actually tear up.

Confound me for a heartless bastard, he thought, keeping his hands to his sides with an effort. *Whatever my feelings for her, she is one of my flock and therefore has a claim on my care. I would never in a hundred years have said such a thing to anyone else in the parish, no matter how much they deserved it!* Why *can I not treat her like everybody else?*

"Miss Ellsworth." His voice was little more than a rasp. "Now—I'm afraid—I do owe you an apology. *Another* apology—"

"Are those for us?" asked Sophie, coming up beside him to take up the basket. "How delicious they look. Simon—may we go soon? I—have things at home I would see to." She gave his arm the lightest pressure, but he understood she had reached her limit.

"Of course." He swallowed, but it had no effect on the constriction of his throat. Miss Ellsworth wasn't looking at him. She was looking at the ground.

Damn everything.

"Good day, Lily," said Sophie.

"Yes," muttered Kenner. "Good day. Please excuse us, Miss Ellsworth. Excuse *me.*"

She nodded but said nothing, and then he must turn away to take leave of her parents.

Chapter Twenty

Her country beaux and city cousins,
Lovers no more; flew off by dozens.
— Oliver Goldsmith, *Essays* (1765)

When Lily's older sister had been engaged to Mr. Gregory the former rector, it had been a quiet matter. The Gregorys had no parents or other family living, and the Ellsworths at the time were in mourning following the death of the third Mrs. Ellsworth. Moreover, Florence Ellsworth was of a retiring disposition, unwilling to be the cynosure of all eyes and the name in every throat. And Lily had thought, whenever she were to become engaged, her experience would be as different from Florence's as night and day. Unlike Mr. Gregory, Lily's suitor would be young and dashing and would love her madly. Their engagement would be a whirlwind of gaiety, unfolding against the panorama of Winchester races and balls and such. And when the marriage finally did take place, Lily's husband would sweep her off to a smart townhouse or renovated castle or something of that sort, and she would lord it over him happily ever after.

Reality, as it unfolded, held some surprises. To be sure, Mr. Wright was young and dashing and rich and loved her as madly as he was capable. And certainly he enjoyed races and balls and gaiety as much as she did. And had Lily expressed her wish for a smart townhouse or renovated castle, he would have done what he could to purchase one. (As she said nothing about where she wanted to live in their married life, however, he settled for giving her a pair of very lovely sapphire earrings.) And he was certainly willing to let her rule over him. Lily had her way in everything. So why did she still ask herself, *Marry him or jilt him? Jilt him or marry him?* Marry him: surrender to a lifetime of exactly what she thought she had always wanted. Jilt him: run the gauntlet of public opprobrium—humiliating him and possibly damaging her own prospects irreparably.

Because she could not make up her mind, she stalled.

"Have you decided when, my love, you will make me the happiest of men?" Mr. Wright asked, on one of his every-other-day visits to Hollowgate.

"I think it had better be next spring, after my stepmother is safely delivered," answered Lily. That sounded far away enough.

"So distant a date?" he wondered.

"I couldn't leave now, Mr. Wright! When there is so much to be done. And besides, I need to learn more about housekeeping."

"But at Meadowsweep you needn't do anything you don't want to do," he pointed out. "My mother does everything of that sort."

"Yes, well—I don't know if I want to live at Meadowsweep."

"Not live at Meadowsweep!" Her intended was rendered speechless, and Lily guessed accurately that he was picturing the hour ride between town and his stable of prize horses.

"If we lived in Winchester, you could ride over there whenever you liked," she assured him, "just as you do now."

"Yes, I suppose," he conceded, though he had thought more than once that he looked forward to sparing himself the long rides when his courtship was ended. "Does this mean you would like to live in town? Have a nice cottage such as your sister and Mr. Fairchild will occupy? If so, we had better look into it."

"Oh, I don't know. I haven't decided. You mustn't press me."

So he sighed inwardly and did not press.

It was her father and stepmother who insisted on an engagement supper to include Mr. Wright's parents and sisters and his grandparents the dean and Mrs. Fellowes, to which Lily reluctantly agreed, but only because she would rather meet them all with her family behind her than venture alone into enemy territory. Moreover, one big, horrid supper would get it all over with.

"I suppose your family members have not yet changed their opinion of me, after my misadventures with Mr. Dailey," Lily said to her intended when the invitation was given.

He looked appropriately uncomfortable but insisted, "They have not spoken of it again. But there is no one who knows you, Miss

Ellsworth, who does not adore you. My family will be no different once they truly *know* you."

A valiant declaration, and one which said much for his fondness and loyalty, if not for his judgment. Lily was all too aware of *one* member of his family who knew her and failed to adore her. She had not seen Mr. Kenner since their last unfortunate conversation in the garden, and the manner in which they parted made her rather miserable. The momentary relief of expressing her displeasure that day had accomplished little, apart from whipping up Mr. Kenner's own displeasure, and now they were not friends again. Not only that, but, when she reviewed the scene in her mind, she suspected from his angry reaction that, indeed, he had not been the one to blab her engagement all over Winchester.

But what about his own cutting comment? Had *he* spoken from the overflow of his own heart? Did he really never, ever think of her at all, his indifference being so deep and impenetrable—or was that his anger talking? And why, *why* did she care so much?

I will send an apology, she vowed. But the days passed, and she didn't.

When her maid Monk brought her a note one morning, Lily's heart leapt. *He has apologized first—again!* She held it momentarily to her breast, imagining with what graciousness she would extend her pardon before asking his pardon in return.

But upon unfolding it, it proved not to be from Mr. Kenner, after all. In an irregular, untutored hand it read:

Miss Elswerth.

I take up pen to warn you that Walter Daily is an unwerthy man and you would do well to keep cleer of him.

An ononimuss well wisher.

"Who brought this?" demanded Lily.

Monk shrugged, still winding Lily's hair on the iron. "Binns found it on the doorstep and gave it to Bobbins who gave it to me."

"Well, it warns me against Mr. Dailey, which is ridiculous. Not only because I never see Mr. Dailey anymore, but also because he has only ever troubled me by his thick-headedness. This note almost accuses him of malice!" Lily might also have complained of the anonymous informant's spelling errors, but she suspected this criticism would be lost on Monk.

"Want me to toss it in the fire?" asked her maid.

Lily blew out her breath, considering. "I suppose not. If ever I do see Mr. Dailey again, I will tell him about his 'ononimuss' ill-wisher. I wonder who it could be."

She couldn't prevent a grin. If the note had warned her away from Mr. Gilbert Wright, there would have been any number of his family members who might have penned it, hoping to frighten her away—the problem would have been narrowing it down to just one suspect! But who would hate Mr. Dailey—?

The big, horrid supper was as awkward as she feared. While Mr. Wright's father Mr. Thomas Wright and Dean Fellowes seemed willing enough to acknowledge Lily's charms, the women of the family were more reserved, and the dean's wife decidedly cool. Miss Wright and Miss Anna, her intended's younger sisters, looked like they would have admired her if they dared, but being only fifteen and twelve, they did not dare. Lily was never more appreciative of her own family, especially for her stepmother's knack of drawing others out and keeping the talk flowing, Minta's general fearlessness, and even Tyrone's contributions when asked questions adults loved to pose, such as his opinions on possible reforms at Winchester College or whether he aspired to a New College fellowship. As at the supper with the Kenners, there was music afterward, but unlike the supper with the Kenners, everyone was heartily glad when the evening ended. Mr. Wright squeezed her hands in parting, whispering, "You see? They love you as I told you they would," and Lily could only hope he said it to be encouraging and not because he was blind.

When she lay her head on her pillow that night, her last thought before she drifted off was, *Jilt him, I think.* Because who could contemplate decades of such evenings?

How she would go about it remained to be seen, however, and Lily put it out of her mind in anticipation of the Thursday Assembly, which promised dancing and tea and cards at the rooms on Upper Brook and High Street. It would be her first assembly as an engaged woman, and she did not know what to expect. She supposed she would now have to discourage any gentlemen who persisted in clamoring about her, but she hoped this might be balanced by enjoyment of the general envy over her good fortune. One obscure corner of her mind wondered if Mr. Kenner and his sister would be there. Surely they would—Sophie had said Mr. Kenner promised her such things. And if he were there, could Lily possibly throw him a sympathetic glance? As a forerunner to an apology?

Her heart beating quickly as she and her stepmother entered the candlelit and garland-draped ballroom, Lily's sweeping glance caught on an altogether different sight. It was a swarm of her habitual suitors—or former suitors, she must call them now—gathered like honeybees around a fragrant new blossom. She recognized the flaxen Mr. Caxton, the giraffe-tall Mr. Willett, Mr. Gosworth, plump Mr. Trimp—even old Sir Basil Longworthy!—among others whose names escaped her. A few soldiers. A clump of clergymen. All gentlemen with whom Lily had danced and flirted.

And the blossom they hovered about?

"Miss Carlingford," spoke a voice at their side, and Lily and Mrs. Ellsworth turned to see Mrs. Fellowes. "The bishop's grandniece, visiting from Kent," she continued, after nodding at them. "A tidy fortune and, of course, impeccable connections. She will open the dancing and lead the set, I believe."

"Then Mrs. North the bishop's wife must be here?" asked Mrs. Ellsworth, looking around for the woman.

Lily didn't care about the bishop's wife. She was too intent on studying the bishop's grandniece. Younger—perhaps eighteen or nineteen? Pretty, with shining brown hair and an elegant figure, all set off by an ivory silk gown trimmed in gold-threaded lace. All the attention paid her put a smile on the girl's face and roses in her cheeks, and Lily knew exactly how delighted she must be.

Lily didn't *think* she sighed aloud, but she must have because her stepmother put a hand to the small of her back and said with enthusiasm, "Why here comes our dear Mr. Wright! How well he looks tonight. You must be proud of such a dashing grandson, Mrs. Fellowes."

"Certainly," said the dean's wife. "The dean and I are proud of *both* our grandsons. I don't mind telling you, Miranda, that, while Gilbert 'makes a splash,' as the young people say, in the secular arena, I don't doubt Simon will do likewise in the ecclesiastical. I tell the dean Simon will be a bishop one day. Or, at very least, an archdeacon."

A bishop! Lily shuddered. How dreadful that would be. That silly mitre on his head and even more clerical vestments to swoop around in. To be sure, the Ellsworths were rarely at the cathedral, and Lily had not seen Bishop North for some time, but she remembered a man dwarfed by the vast and soaring spaces, his voice reedy and thin. Well—Mr. Kenner's voice would be better in such a setting than Bishop North's, Lily conceded, and Mr. Kenner was taller and more impressive, but add a mitre to his head and he would be as giraffe-like as Mr. Willett!

"Miss Ellsworth," murmured Mr. Wright, bowing to her. "I believe this is one of my dances?"

"Yes." Lily curtsied in return.

"Shall we join the set? How beautiful you look." He could not have hit on anything more pleasing to say, downcast as she was by Miss Carlingford's ascendancy. Lily was so moved, to have him still prefer her to any other, that the smile she gave him then was genuine, radiant. The scales tipped once more in his favor. *Marry him.*

He stared at her glowing face. (Sadly, it must be admitted Lily did not often look at him like that.) Stared, and wondered if he could get her alone at some point in the evening to steal another kiss.

Mr. Wright was not the only one to remark that smile. Mrs. Ellsworth saw it with relief—surely Lily must be fond of her intended, then? He let Lily rule him like a tyrant, but it would be all right in the end if only she loved him.

Mrs. Fellowes, too, observed the smile, her own mouth thinning. *That girl! She has Gilbert wound around her little finger, the more fool he. Thank heavens Simon would never be taken in by such.*

But, unknown to his grandmother, Mr. Kenner also witnessed the smile, just as he was being introduced to the bishop's grandniece. Witnessed it and was aware of a surge of helpless anger. It set his jaw and flashed from his pale eyes, arresting young Miss Carlingford.

"Goodness. You're an intense one," she said gaily.

He roused himself to meet this, remembering his manners. Miss Carlingford was pretty enough. Her hair a few shades lighter than Miss Ellsworth's, and her eyes a fainter blue, as if she were a copy faded by the sun. "I beg your pardon," he said with a bow. "You have my full attention now."

She rapped him lightly with her fan. "I wonder if you dance as intently as you think, sir."

And then, because that left him little alternative, he gave the expected reply, "If you would do me the honor, you will judge for yourself."

Which was how Mr. Kenner stole Miss Carlingford from under every other gentlemen's nose and led her to the top of the room, just above Sophie Kenner and Mr. Frayne, who in turn were above Lily and Mr. Wright.

"All in a Garden Green," pronounced Miss Carlingford, when the master of ceremonies called for her request.

Lily's eyes flew to meet Kenner's when this dance was chosen. Neither one could help it, after the joke it had been between them. And then Lily could not say if it was this shared, fleeting glance or the thought of the dance itself which then made colour flood her face. One thing was certain: Miss Carlingford must be as accomplished a flirt as Lily, because All in a Garden Green was the most flirtatious of dances. For each three-couple set, it involved constant interaction among them, but, more importantly, the "kissing" of one's partner and the partner of the couple at the opposite corner. No one really kissed, of course, when the step was called out; they only brought their faces near each other, first to one side, and then the other, as if in greeting. But it was enough.

Lily could see from the light in Mr. Wright's eyes that he planned on calling on his privileges and kissing her in earnest at least once—perhaps on the final pass. So be it. It was the least of her worries. But what of Mr. Kenner?

She learned soon enough. The first time the figures brought them together, they joined their crossed hands. Suppressing a shiver, Lily barely inclined for the "kisses," but Mr. Kenner leaned in for them, saying under his breath, "1 Peter...5:14."

Lily had no notion what the verse referred to, and then they were rotating back to their partners.

On the second pass, she inclined a little nearer for the two "kisses" and heard, first in her right ear and then her left, "'Greet ye…one another…"

Again the figures separated them, Lily all a-flutter, both from anticipation of the rest of his meaning and from his soft warm breath, light as a real kiss, in either ear.

At the third iteration, her eyes locked with his as they joined their crossed hands. The caller commanded, "Kiss right, kiss left," and again they drew near each other—the closest they had yet been. And again, his breath brushing first one cheek and then the other: "…With a kiss…of charity."

Her eyes flew back to his before they were separated again. Was it his apology? Or an encouragement for her to apologize? In either case, Lily gave the slightest nod, and both of them smiled to themselves.

It was over too soon, and Mr. Wright did indeed plant a hearty kiss on either of her cheeks during the final pattern, but it was not the genuine kisses which elicited her blissful smile. It was that she was forgiven. Again. And she and Mr. Kenner were friends of sorts. Again.

Her intended returned her to her stepmother's side, asking if he might fetch her and Mrs. Ellsworth lemonade or orgeat, and Lily agreed because she wanted some time to look about her.

"I enjoyed watching you dance," her stepmother said.

"I am glad of it, but you won't have much more of that pleasure this evening," Lily replied. "Or, until Mr. Wright accompanies me again. For my suitors have all decamped to Miss Carlingford." Indeed, no sooner did Mr. Kenner escort the latter back to her great-aunt's side than the young lady was swallowed up again by Lily's defectors, and it was Sir Basil Longworthy who emerged triumphant to lead Miss Carlingford again to the floor.

Lily clutched her hands together. Her erstwhile admirers could be forgotten, if only Mr. Kenner would come her way, now that matters were mended—but he turned instead to the blasted Miss Weeks. *And I must stand by and watch, now that I am no longer wanted.*

But Heaven took pity on her, for just then diminutive Mr. Frayne approached to ask for the honor of dancing with her, and Lily accepted him as if he had been the king himself. If she hoped that at least one former suitor still pined for her, however, she was soon disappointed.

"Miss Ellsworth," he began, "I left Hollowgate very suddenly the other day, when your engagement was announced."

"We were sorry to see you go," she said politely.

"Yes, well—I admit to being somewhat overcome by the news. But now I would like to do the proper thing and wish you joy."

"Thank you, Mr. Frayne."

"My precipitousness did have an unexpected benefit, though," he ventured, boldness swelling his small frame an additional inch or two. "I—walked Miss Kenner back to the rectory. A very pleasant young lady, Miss Kenner."

Lily's eyes grew round. Then—he did not ask her to dance in order to vow undying love for her or to declare eternal enmity toward Gilbert Wright? No! He partnered her, rather, so he could assure her she was already forgotten! Replaced. Superseded.

Her normally graceful dancing gave way to something more mechanical as she absorbed this.

Well, then! So much for the devotion of men! Out of sight, out of mind, apparently. This conclusion was reinforced by seeing Mr. Kenner down the line of dancers, chatting with Miss Weeks, who hung on his words, while stupid Miss Carlingford called to them.

Lily's happiness leaked from her as rapidly as it had filled her, and she wondered if all men were so faithless. If she had refused to marry Gilbert Wright, would he even now be dancing attendance on Miss Carlingford? But, no—there he stood beside Mrs. Ellsworth, still holding Lily's glass of orgeat. When he saw her glance his way, he lifted his free hand and pointed to the glass, as if she had forgotten she asked for it.

He's a good man and loyal, Lily thought, waving back at him. Yes, she probably would marry him after all. Because even if she jilted him, she wouldn't deign now to receive the attentions of those who forgot her so quickly.

And Mr. Kenner doesn't want me, or why doesn't he ask me to dance? The thought slipped through before she knew to slam the gate, and it only made Lily unhappier.

Mr. Frayne returned her to Mr. Wright, and Lily sipped her orgeat. Over the course of the evening, other gentlemen asked to partner her, and Lily accepted, but with none of her former superiority. And though she was never without a partner the whole evening, nor was she required to refuse anyone. She danced two more times with Mr. Wright, but Mr. Kenner never approached.

Watching beneath her thick lashes as she circled and stepped, she observed the curate sometimes dancing, sometimes standing and talking. Apart from taking tea with Miss Carlingford during the break, the only young lady he partnered twice was his sister Sophie. But the tea with Miss Carlingford was enough, especially when tallied with her evident admiration for him, and Lily became aware of the ballroom murmurs gathering voice.

"What a *coup de maître* that would be for him, if he were to win the bishop's grandniece!"

"A wise move both for his pocketbook and for his clerical career."

"I've never thought him *handsome*, precisely—not like his cousin Wright—but there is undeniably something about him. He has an air..."

"Call it what you will, but I suspect Miss Carlingford has also remarked it."

"Ah, well, Dean Fellowes will be pleased, if it's his grandsons who carry off the prize young ladies of the year."

Everyone seemed terribly glad at the prospect. Everyone but Lily.

It was a dreadful evening, taken altogether. Not only must Lily learn of the fickleness of men, but there was the equally unpalatable lesson on the fleeting nature of popularity. Worse yet, she discovered something even worse than being a person whom people gossiped about: being a person whom *no one* gossiped about. And very worst of all, the pairing of Mr. Kenner's name with Miss Carlingford's opened a window to Lily's own heart, and, when she dared to peep through, she saw something most alarming.

I don't want just his friendship. (When this thought came, her glass of orgeat nearly slipped through her fingers.) *It isn't enough for me, a mere cessation of hostilities. No—Mr. Kenner might be content with a truce between us, but I—I want more. Oh, dear. Oh dear oh dear oh dear.*

A less practical girl might have decided then and there that the good and loyal Mr. Gilbert Wright must be jilted, but Lily understood that ending her engagement would not render Mr. Kenner suddenly in love with her. And, even supposing she were able to make Mr. Kenner forget their past differences, would a man in his profession not still prefer a Miss Carlingford, with her glorious ecclesiastical connections? Her connections and her spotless reputation? Miss Carlingford had not been observed kissing Mr. Walter Dailey in the Romsey Road. Miss Carlingford had not earned the disapproval of Mr. Kenner's extended family. Miss Carlingford had no history as a jilt. No, quite the opposite! Unblemished Miss Carlingford showed every sign of preferring Mr. Kenner from the outset, and what man could resist that?

"Hopeless," Lily whispered to herself, with one last glance at the man before she resolutely turned her back on him. "The sooner he is forgotten, the better."

If only it were that easy.

Chapter Twenty-One

O what a Gauntlet for any woman of delicacy to run!
— Fanny Burney, *Journals and Letters* (1788)

Mama," said Lily a few days later, as she and Mrs. Ellsworth sat sewing Tyrone's school clothing, "I thought I might come with you on some of your visits. You know—to the Hamblys and to Mr. Harvey."

Mrs. Ellsworth looked up from the robe she held, the hem of which must be let out. Her face was pale and tired. "Did you? That would be very, very welcome, Lily. I hoped to go this afternoon, but—"

"But you are feeling unwell again," Lily supplied. "I am sorry for it." She was vexed with herself for it, but she could not prevent her heart giving a little leap—if she went in her stepmother's stead, maybe she might see Mr. Kenner again!

"It's nothing," said Mrs. Ellsworth. "Only I think I am getting a late summer cold. I didn't sleep well, at any rate."

"You go lie down now, Mama!" Lily urged. "Monk and I have Tyrone's sewing well in hand, and I will get Tyrone or Bea or somebody to go with me. Does Wilcomb have baskets ready?"

On this occasion Tyrone excused himself from the mission of mercy, saying, "I don't know where the vacation went, but if I don't start reviewing my Latin, I'll for sure be croppled and put down low in the Classicus Paper."

"Heaven forbid," answered Lily, having no idea what he referred to.

Araminta was nowhere to be found, most likely off with Aggie somewhere, so that left little Beatrice. "You won't be any help carrying baskets," sighed Lily to her reluctant sister, "but at least your presence will satisfy propriety. Come on, then, and I don't want any of your complaints about people or places smelling funny. You can wait for me out on the doorstep, like Tyrone did."

Beatrice made little anxious sounds as she trotted beside her, occasionally darting a glance at Lily's sober face. "I don't know what's wrong with you, Lily," she said. "You haven't been cross and spiteful lately. You're just...sad."

Having her low spirits remarked on had the healthy effect of reviving Lily's crossness, and she scowled at her sister. "What nonsense."

"You know what I think is odd?" Bea asked, skipping a little away and out of arm's reach. "Remember how happy Flossie was when she was engaged to Robert, and how serious she was when she was engaged to Mr. Gregory?"

"What of it?"

"Well, you act as if you're engaged to Mr. Gregory—not glad at all."

"Oh, hush, and don't talk of matters you don't understand," snapped Lily. "And carry this crock of preserves, if a whole basket is too heavy for you. My arms are getting tired."

If Lily hoped she might see Mr. Kenner at the sexton's little cottage, she was disappointed. She did not even see Mr. Harvey, as it was. Only the maid-of-all-work met her at the door and whispered that Mr. Harvey was poorly that day and sleeping. She accepted the basket with a curtsey and promised that Mr. Harvey should have some of the broth as soon as he awoke, if she could get him to take it.

Lily rubbed her shoulder, glad to be rid of one of the baskets, at any rate. "Come on, Bea. It's off to the Hamblys next."

"I wish we didn't have to walk past the cemetery," whispered the girl.

"I told you there were no ghosts," grumbled her sister. "And if there were, we could hurl the Hamblys' broth at them."

"I'm going to come in with you at the Hamblys'."

"You are? But you said it smells funny or Mrs. Hambly smells funny or something of that sort."

"I don't want to wait on the step. I—thought I saw someone slipping through the trees when I was waiting for you outside Mr. Harvey's."

"Good gracious!" Lily felt the hairs on her arm rise. Beatrice's nervousness was infectious. This was just another reason why their stepmother had to teach Beatrice at home. The girl could never walk into town to school, as Araminta did with Aggie. Those two would be sure to run ahead, and Bea would then manage to scare herself to death.

They arrived without incident at the Hamblys' shabby dwelling off the Weeke footpath, however, to encounter the same pig and chickens and awkward stairs and confined sitting room that Lily remembered. This time there was no Mr. Kenner, however, and Lily heaved another sigh to herself. But it wasn't altogether true that he was not there because he was still *there,* she discovered, his memory greeting her at every turn. Where he stood and how she had been so aware of his nearness and the mocking words he addressed to her. Had they been friends then, before she realized she cared for him? They always seemed to teeter between friendship and enmity...

Only now that she had visited both Mr. Harvey and the Hamblys did she acknowledge her disappointment at not seeing him. What use were good deeds, if he didn't know she was doing them?

Miss Hambly showered praise on Lily again for coming, while Beatrice stared in dismay at the heap of rags that was old Mrs. Hambly. Lily could see from Bea's open mouth that her sister was avoiding breathing through her nose so that she would not have to smell anything, and as soon as the clock showed the passage of fifteen minutes, Lily said, "Such a nice visit, but I'm afraid we must be going."

"Oh, Miss Ellsworth, so, so kind of you and Miss Beatrice to come. I have a little something for your family." Miss Hambly sprang up, narrowly avoiding knocking over a vase of dried flowers. "When you brought your so-generous basket on the last occasion, I took the liberty of refilling one of the crocks with pickled cabbage and beets, which I prepared myself—"

"How—delightful," interrupted Lily loudly, to mask Beatrice's sudden gagging. "My stepmother and Wilcomb will be so pleased."

"Do you think?" asked Miss Hambly, dimpling. "I will put it in a net bag for you because I don't want it to slide around in the empty baskets, though I did seal it with suet on top, as a lid. As a lid under the actual lid, you understand."

"Yes. How clever. Thank you."

Five minutes later they were back on the footpath, Beatrice carrying the empty baskets and Lily the net bag with its crock of pickled vegetables.

"Couldn't we dig a hole and bury it?" asked Beatrice fretfully.

"Don't be ridiculous. You know Miss Hambly will ask Mama about it later, and then we would have to confess. Don't worry. No one will make you eat any. Or you can slip your portion under the table for Snap."

"Snap wouldn't touch it."

"You're probably right."

"Lily, maybe we could give the whole thing to Flossie and Robert as a present for their house-warming."

Lily laughed at this, and it pleased Beatrice so much that she had amused her disdainful sister, that she giggled too. Then Lily laughed harder, which made Beatrice laugh harder, and by the time they reached the base of the Weeke footpath, they were gasping and had to stop.

"It—isn't—*that*—funny," panted Beatrice, delighted nevertheless.

"Oh—it isn't just the wretched pickled cabbage," explained Lily, wiping away a tear and still snorting. "It's everything. Poor Mr. Harvey and the poor Hamblys and the pig in the shrubbery and your face when she gave us the vegetables—sometimes life is so dreadful that you have to laugh."

It was about to get more dreadful.

Because just then, when Beatrice picked up her baskets again and Lily the crock, the little girl gave an ear-splitting shriek, pointing past her sister.

Fully (and illogically) expecting a ghost, Lily whirled around.

It was not a ghost. But that was hardly a relief.

A man stood in Cock Lane: untidy, unshaven, unsteady on his feet. He gave forth an eye-watering smell of intoxicating liquors, and a jug, such as had been found at the entrance to Hollowgate and on Baldy Baldric's gravestone, dangled from his fingers.

Lily snatched at her little sister's trembling hand with her free one to pull her past the stranger, but he stepped heavily to block their path.

"Well, well, well," he drawled, none too distinctly. "What's this? The beloved one, all by herself?"

"Stand away, sir, and let us pass," Lily commanded with pretended bravado.

"Stand away? But I may not—get this chance again." He swayed a step nearer, cursing roughly, and Beatrice gave a moan.

"Get away from us," hissed Lily, "or we will scream!"

He raised heavy brows, considering, while swiveling to look first in one direction and then the other. "The little one already did scream. Which tells me there don't appear to be anyone about to hear ye."

There wasn't. The nearest home to where they stood was that of Mr. Beckford the doctor, and his house was not visible from the road. Lily darted her own glances about—this was Cock Lane! Where was everyone? The soldiers, the travelers between here and Romsey, the gatekeeper? One of the hundred farm wagons carrying the corn harvest, for heaven's sake? How came it to be so deserted?

The man lurched another step forward. "Demme...for Ged, he'll be sorry he crossed me."

Lily didn't stay to ask who. There was no time to reason with a drunk man. "Let's run, Bea!" she cried, giving an almighty jerk on her sister. But terror had turned little Beatrice to stone, and Lily's heave only caused the girl to lose her balance and drop the baskets, over which she then tripped. The next instant Lily felt the man seize her upper arm, and his hot breath enveloped her.

"Run, Bea!" Lily shouted again, flinging off her sister and booting her in the backside, even as she tried to writhe out of the man's grasp. "Run for Mr. Beckford!"

The kick in the hindquarters must have jarred something loose within her because Beatrice scrambled up and away, crying and gasping.

"Go!" roared Lily. And Bea went.

Now the man was pulling Lily toward him inexorably, and she was stamping her feet in blind panic, kicking and elbowing. One of her efforts caught him in the midsection, and he released her with a *whoof!* Doubling over, he coughed and gagged, and Lily didn't hesitate. She turned to flee, slipping and scrabbling in her fright, but she made it only a few yards before he hurled himself after her, catching her by the skirts, his own boot coming down sharply on her ankle.

Oblivious to the pain that lanced through her, Lily spun to face him. Dizziness made her head rock, and her vision began to narrow, but she fought it. She couldn't faint now. She couldn't. She *wouldn't.*

Somehow the net bag was still in her clenched fist—her only possible weapon. With every ounce of strength that remained to her, she took hold of the neck of the bag with both hands and swung it, as a blacksmith might his hammer, mouthing a prayer.

Now, a man who has not been drinking can easily dodge a crock of pickled cabbage and beets swung at him by a frightened, dazed young lady. But Lily's assailant had been imbibing rather freely that afternoon, as he did most days, and his faculties, both mental and physical, suffered as a result. Therefore the crock—the miraculous, marvelous crock—caught him squarely on the side of the head, a good solid clout, and he dropped like a felled oak: slowly, heavily, decisively.

Lily crumpled to a sitting position in the road, still conscious but breathless and stunned, as the sharp scent of Miss Hambly's pickle permeated the air, and the concoction of suet, cabbage leaves and sliced beets poured over the man's head like floodwaters over a boulder.

"I must have killed him," Lily muttered blankly, her vision darkening further, "for he doesn't open his eyes, and Miss Hambly's pickle is better than smelling salts."

Running feet were approaching. Too rapid and heavy to be Beatrice, but that was fine because Beatrice would be no use. Lily tried to get up, but her head and ankle protested this plan, and she fell back onto her bottom.

Now that she had time to notice, her ankle hurt rather badly.

"Miss Ellsworth!"—from a very great distance and as if through cotton wool—"Miss Ellsworth, are you injured?"

Now I know I'm delirious, thought Lily as the spinning in her head increased. *Because that sounds terribly like Mr. Kenner.*

When she opened her eyes, it *was* Mr. Kenner. He was sitting in the road, with Lily's head in his lap, regarding her steadily while Beatrice clung to her hand, crying.

She blinked up at him. "What—are you doing here?" Her fingers drifted toward his face and then fell back.

"I was at Mr. Beckford's, consulting him about Mr. Harvey."

"That man—" She tried to sit up, but Mr. Kenner pressed her back down.

"Easy, now."

"But did I—kill him?"

"Unfortunately, no," came Mr. Beckford's voice. Lily turned her head and saw the doctor kneeling beside her attacker, examining him while trying to stay clear of the cabbage. "You merely knocked him out. Well—you and all the spirits he drank knocked him out. Better help me drag him to the side of the road, Mr. Kenner, and we'll hail the next passing cart."

Mr. Kenner looked down at Lily. "Do you think you could sit up yet?" he asked gently.

She nodded, though she wasn't certain, but lying in the road was not particularly comfortable, even with her head in his lap. He and Beatrice assisted her, little Bea sniffling to a hiccupping halt.

"I think I can stand," said Lily after a moment. But when she tried and put weight on her ankle, her face went very white. Mr. Kenner threw out his hands, and she sagged against him, in too much pain to register or enjoy the novelty of the contact.

The same could not be said for Mr. Kenner. His expression was unreadable, but the telltale colour rose in his face. When she began to tremble, he told himself that was why he held her tighter for an instant.

"What is it?" he murmured. "What hurts?"

"My a-ankle," managed Lily, as Beatrice succumbed to a fresh wave of tears.

Scooping her up, he carried her to the side of the road, lowering her gently to sit upon the stone wall. Then, with reluctance, he released her. "Beckford, you'd better come and have a look at Miss Ellsworth's ankle."

The doctor obeyed, letting the unconscious man's head flop back down none too tenderly. "A little room, Miss Beatrice," he prompted, nudging Bea aside. He then proceeded to examine Lily's foot and ankle, removing her slipper and delicately pressing, bending, flexing, and asking questions, while Kenner with an effort averted his gaze.

"Nothing is broken," he announced after a minute. "But I fear you have a very bad sprain and will have some bruising. You will not be able to walk for some weeks, I imagine."

Her face falling, Lily gasped and Beatrice wailed anew. "Sh-h-h...it's all right, Bea. How many weeks, do you think, Mr. Beckford?"

"It depends. If you are careful in following my instructions, it might be as little as a month or so, but I should warn you it may also be as long as six before you can put all your weight on it and walk comfortably again."

At this pronouncement, Lily burst into tears herself, joining her little sister in a chorus of woe, leaving both gentlemen helplessly offering their handkerchiefs.

"I'm afraid you must stay off it, Miss Ellsworth," resumed the doctor. "I will bandage it tightly when we have you back to Hollowgate, and you must try to keep it elevated. Rest and compression and elevation. You are young and healthy. Perhaps only a month or six weeks."

Lily was nodding, trying to choke back her sobs and mopping her face with Mr. Kenner's handkerchief. A month! Possibly *six*! Attacked by a perfect stranger, not a five-minute walk from home, and this was the result? Not to dance or go anywhere or do anything for who knew how long? Did ever a girl have worse luck?

Her eyes welling again with self-pity and shock, Lily feared she would embarrass herself by having a fit of hysterics, and it was a great relief to her when they caught the creaking of an approaching cart.

"Stop! Stop!" called Mr. Beckford, springing up and waving his arms, though the driver had already seen the body lying in the road and was tugging on the reins.

The farmer Mr. Grayson and his son were tenants of Lily's father, taciturn men who listened to the explanations given and demands made upon them as if unconscious drunken assailants were strewn across their path every day. Retrieving a rope from under his seat, Mr. Grayson and the others contrived to bind the man's hands and feet and hoist him into the wagon bed, even as the man groaned and cracked his eyes open.

"No trouble out of you, now," Mr. Grayson soothed, as if Lily's attacker had been an unpredictable mule. "We're taking you to the constable. Expect you'll be confined a while." His calm gaze took in Lily, still shivering as she sat on the stone wall. "Did you want a lift, Miss Ellsworth? It'll save you a walk on that ankle."

But she shook her head, shuddering at the thought of sharing a wagon with the bound man. "No, thank you. I will find another way home, Mr. Grayson."

With a nod, the farmer clicked his tongue to his horses, and the cart creaked away with its human burden. Mr. Beckford and Mr. Kenner had a brief conversation, which ended in Mr. Beckford saying to her, "Miss Ellsworth, we have decided that I will ride over to Hollowgate and ask for a carriage to be sent for you. Mr. Kenner will remain here with you and Miss Beatrice."

"Thank you, Mr. Beckford."

Touching his hat, the old doctor strode away toward home and horse.

Beatrice was pressed against Lily's side as closely as she ever used to nestle against Florence, and Lily's arm encircled her. It was not a cold day, but they were both beginning to shake from the shock.

Mr. Kenner removed his hat, slapping it against his thigh and looking at them. He was a little unsteady himself. The sight and sound of little Beatrice Ellsworth—incoherent and panic-stricken—appearing on the doctor's doorstep—the tugging from her urgent hands—her sister's name emerging in chokes and sobs. Kenner had been running before he even knew what he was about—without even looking back to see if Beckford was following.

And the relief of seeing her sitting upright in the road—not dead, then? Not run down by a carriage?—before she collapsed. When he saw—and smelled—the man lying some feet from her, he hardly spared him a glance, too intent on checking her for blood or injury. Let the man be dead, for all he cared, so long as Miss Ellsworth was unharmed.

He took a long breath. "You've been very brave, Miss Ellsworth."

"No," said Lily simply.

He tried again, the hint of a grin lifting one corner of his mouth. "Are you fishing for compliments—wanting me to insist?"

But Lily was temporarily incapable of flirting or repartee. She turned her vivid gaze on him, earnest, troubled. "I wasn't brave. I was afraid. But Bea was with me, and I couldn't let anything happen to her—"

"And you didn't."

"—not when my sister will be back any minute," she went on, not heeding him. "With Flossie gone, I am responsible for them. Bea. Tyrone. Minta. It was—that was why I was upset with you for shooting an arrow at Minta weeks and weeks ago."

Then he did chuckle, taking a seat on the stone wall beside her. "Miss Ellsworth, because you have just been set upon by a drunken lout, in compassion I will forbear to remind you that I was *not* shooting at Miss Araminta."

She only shook her head, her hands worrying at her skirts. "Who do you suppose he was, Mr. Kenner? I think he was the one leaving the empty jugs around because he had another one with him just like those ones. And for some reason he called me 'the beloved one.'"

Kenner frowned. Was it more than a random encounter? But he strove for lightness, wanting to draw her out of her fear. "I can't say who he was. But, if there's anything to be learned, the constable will have it out of him."

"Yes." She shivered again.

"Would you like my coat?"

Lily looked at him like a disheveled angel, and then her eyes widened as she took him in for the first time. "Oh, Mr. Kenner! Your coat! You shouldn't have sat in the road."

That gleam in his eye again. "Probably not. But it wouldn't have been polite to stand over you when you were *lying* in the road."

Her survey moved to her own condition—dusty, wrinkled, stained—and, to their mutual dismay, her eyes filled again. "Oh," she breathed, plucking at a draggled ribbon hanging limply from her bonnet as she pulled it off her head. "Oh."

"Don't, Miss Ellsworth—" he urged, digging for his handkerchief before remembering he had already given it to her. "Don't cry." But she already was—weeping—to be joined again by her younger sister, though how Beatrice had any tears left was a marvel.

Feebly, Kenner patted each one's arm, but that only seemed to make matters worse, to judge by the shaking of their sobs. Surely he, as a clergyman, ought to be better at comforting the stricken?

With a silent curse, he slid from the stone wall and gathered both Ellsworth sisters in his arms, one to each shoulder, and held them for as long as it took to cry themselves out. He rocked them a little, murmuring comforting nonsense (and reminding himself sternly—for the love of all that was holy—*not* to kiss the top of Miss Ellsworth's head), until they began to regain their calm.

"I am so sorry," Lily gasped soon enough, drawing back to blow her nose. "So sorry, Mr. Kenner. Come, Bea, darling—we must stop crying. It—has been a difficult day. Difficult. When—when we are home p-perhaps we can ask Wilcomb for some chocolate and one of her—her—her biscuits."

Beatrice nodded, blowing her own nose in Mr. Beckford's capacious pocket-cloth. "I want to go home now."

"And you will," Mr. Kenner assured her, "it's but a minute's ride from the doctor's house to yours, and then they'll be back as fast as they can hitch up the gig." Both of them stared at him helplessly, and he found himself launching into a monologue of commonplaces as dull as anything Mr. Dailey ever came up with—his own opinion on chocolate and biscuits; his favorite biscuits; what Mr. Harvey had had for breakfast—*not* chocolate and biscuits—and Mr. Beckford's comments upon it; what he and Sophie preferred at breakfast and the effects of that on their constitutions; some prominent features of Mr. Beckford's horse; why he and Sophie kept no horse; where they would keep a horse if they did decide to keep one; and so on.

It worked like magic. Both Miss Ellsworth and Miss Beatrice hung on his words, taking comfort from these trivialities for their very triviality. And, as soon as he had promised, they saw the Ellsworth gig careering up Cock Lane at a harum-scarum pace, the head groom himself at the reins and Mr. Beckford on his little black mare behind.

After a few words with the groom, Kenner returned and tapped Beatrice. "You hop in first, so I can help your sister." Lily was attempting to rise on her one good foot, but he shook his head at her. "All you need to cap this day, Miss Ellsworth, is to tumble into the ditch. If you'll allow me..."

Aware of all the other eyes on them, he scooped her up once more in his most businesslike manner, each wishing he could carry her at least as far as Canterbury. But no.

He deposited her carefully in the gig and then backed up a step, only to have Lily impulsively extend a hand toward him, her eyes very bright. "Mr. Kenner—thank you. How can we thank you enough? You—you're a very good clergyman."

Not trusting himself to speak, he gave a brief nod and then backed away to give the carriage room to turn. And when it was out of sight, he gave a deep sigh before starting in the same direction, home to the rectory.

Chapter Twenty-Two

There she dwels in publique eye,
Shut up from none that list to see.
— Hadrian Dorrell, *Willobie his Auisa; or, The true picture of a modest maid, and of a chast and constant wife* (1594)

If Lily regretted no longer being popular enough for gossip, being attacked in the road restored her to general notice. In the days that followed, Mr. Wright flew to her side as soon as she remembered to send him a note. Her former suitors reappeared in their former numbers, if only for the sensation of it all. Every relation, neighbor, and acquaintance called to hear the story from her own lips. And yet she had little story to tell. Even of what she had, she held some back—there seemed no reason for her to mention her attacker referring to her as "the beloved one," for instance. Nor did she say anything of his growled, "He'll be sorry he crossed me," once she saw the martial light in Mr. Wright's eye.

"I don't know who he was," she said countless times from her sofa in the drawing room, the whole of which she occupied, in order to keep her snugly bandaged ankle elevated. Only Beatrice was allowed to cram herself onto the same piece of furniture—she and Lily holding hands. For Beatrice was the only one who knew what the wretched experience had been like and how terrified they both had been.

Well, Beatrice was almost the only one who knew. Mr. Kenner was the other, and he came too, one day with flowers which he passed to Mrs. Ellsworth and another day with a book for Beatrice. But he said almost nothing on these visits, only sitting too far away and listening to the talk.

"It's a miracle you weren't harmed!" declared their aunt Jeanne.

"There's talk of a watch being set," their uncle Charles added, "though the man is in custody until a trial can be held at the October assizes..."

"Do you think they'll hang him?" demanded the younger of Lily's cousins, red-haired young stripling Austin Ellsworth. "It's been ages since that's happened."

"A hanging!" cried Araminta, her eyes lighting. "You mean on Gallows Hill?"

"Where else would you suggest?" laughed their older cousin Benjamin. "If they had it in town outside the Gaol, it would be worse than Election Week for crowds."

Minta sighed. "Well, wherever it is, I don't suppose Papa would let me go."

"To a hanging? Most assuredly not," her stepmother put in quietly.

"Hanging is too good for the man!" declared Mr. Wright from his post behind Lily's sofa, striking it with his fist. "And if he were not held in the prison, I would see to him myself."

Lily didn't doubt it, after how he had behaved with Mr. Dailey. But she could only imagine how Mr. Wright's family would feel, if he took it upon himself to mete out "justice" for her! Heavens. They likely already blamed Lily for this new misadventure, though she had not invited the man to attack her any more than she had invited Mr. Dailey to kiss her on the previous occasion.

Venturing a glance at Sophie Kenner, she was relieved to see no fear or reproach there. On the contrary, Sophie gave her beloved cousin a rueful shake of the head, as if she regretted his impetuosity as much as Lily did. Could it be that Sophie was at last letting go of her girlhood adoration for her cousin? Was she accustoming herself to the idea of him marrying someone else? Lily hoped so, for it would mean they could be friends again. She could be friends with *both* the Kenners and see them as often as she liked. Unable to help herself, she peeked at Mr. Kenner, away over by the pianoforte. He had hold of some of the sheet music and was flipping through it absently, and Lily could not repress a little sigh.

At once Mrs. Ellsworth set down her sewing. "Lily must rest now," she announced, rising to her feet.

"Whatever for?" asked Minta. "She's just sitting there."

"These things take their invisible toll. Everyone, we do appreciate your concern and thank you all for calling. I beg you will all excuse my discourtesy—"

"*Je vous en prie, n'en parlons plus*," her sister-in-law Jeanne interrupted, on her feet at once and clapping her hands at her sons. "You heard your aunt. Lily must rest, and we must go."

Mr. Wright gave Lily a hopeful look, as if to ask if he might be spared the general banishment, but she merely settled back against the new cushion she had made Florence and affected a yawn.

"Very well," he said, as if she had spoken. "My dearest, I will return in a few days from Meadowsweep. There's the corn harvest, you know, and several people coming to see me about breeding Slapbang in the spring."

"I understand," Lily answered quickly, giving him her hand. "Mr. Falk my father's overseer is here, there, and everywhere this time of year. So busy. When you come again, my sister and her husband will have returned, and you can meet them. Go on, then."

He obeyed, as he always did, only giving her hand a fervent press and looking hard at her until she blushed and faltered, from awareness that he felt their parting so strongly.

She wished Mr. Kenner might hang back a moment in the general exodus—he called Minta aside and showed her something about the piece of music in his hand before he replaced it on the instrument—but then, with the briefest of bows toward her, he was gone. It was his sister who lingered behind until the room was nearly cleared, asking Mrs. Ellsworth if she might have just the shortest word with Lily..?

Lily felt her chest tighten. Please let Sophie not be hanging back to bewail Gilbert Wright after all!

Blushing, Sophie waited for the last Ellsworth to leave the room before pulling over a little footstool and perching on it beside Lily.

"Gracious, Sophie—what can be so secret?"

"Oh, Lily—it is no deep secret."

"Is it about Mr. Wright?"

"Gil? No!" declared Sophie, as if she had never thought about her cousin a day in her life. "It's about—that is, he said he—mentioned to you—"

Sudden enlightenment dawned on Lily. "Oh!" she breathed, both happy and relieved. Not Gilbert Wright at all, thank heavens. "I know what you want—it's Mr. Frayne you want to speak to me about, isn't it?"

Sophie blushed even rosier. "Yes."

"Good heavens—has he already spoken?" gasped Lily.

"No, no! Not yet. Not precisely. But I think he means to—soon. He hints—and, Lily, I know you have been much put upon lately and that Mr. Frayne was so recently an admirer of your own—but I wanted to ask if you would mind terribly—"

"No, I would not mind at all!" cried Lily, taking her hands in an affectionate clasp. "There is no need to beg my pardon, or anything of that nature. I am no dog in the manger. I confess, my vanity has taken many blows of late, but I gladly forgive Mr. Frayne his defection, if this may be the happy result. We Ellsworths think the world of Mr. Frayne!"

Sophie looked on the verge of tears with this unlooked-for praise. "Oh, Lily, I know he is no Gilbert Wright, but he is a very kind man."

Being engaged to Gilbert Wright, Lily could hardly say Mr. Frayne was worth ten of the former, though he was likely ten times kinder to Sophie Kenner than her cousin ever had been. No, she must content herself with embracing her friend and saying with unfeigned earnestness, "I think if Mr. Frayne does speak, you would do very well for yourself, Sophie, and I would be ever so happy for you."

Then Sophie did well up and laugh in apology and dab at her eyes and there was more hugging, and Lily must sit through a little enumeration of Mr. Frayne's sterling qualities, which she did with admirable patience, congratulating herself on being so good a listener. It made for a pleasant scene until Sophie said, "Of course, I would hate to leave Simon without someone to keep house for him, when he has just let me arrange everything to my liking, and I have not so much as hinted to him, but who knows? Simon might have been wishing me gone soon enough in any event—"

"Why—would Mr. Kenner ever wish you gone?" choked Lily, going as pale as Sophie was rosy.

"I mean—were he to marry," explained her friend. "Because any Mrs. Kenner he chooses would certainly want her way with the rectory, and in that event I would have had to return home to live with my parents again."

"But—is Mr. Kenner going to marry? That is—do you know if he has plans to—marry someone in particular?"

Sophie's snub nose wrinkled with a laugh. "You think Simon would tell me something like that? Of course I don't know. I can only say that I know of *several* young ladies who would be happy to accept. But you probably can guess them as well."

Lily's smile was less genuine now. "Of course I can. I have eyes. But—well—if you cannot guess whom *he* prefers, whom would *you* choose for him, Sophie?"

Sophie laughed, flipping her hand as if this were too easy a question to require much thought. "Oh, I suppose I would choose Miss Carlingford for him, though I don't know her very well yet. The Miss Weekses and Miss Terman and Miss Beckford are nice young ladies, to be sure, but if I could *choose* for him, it would have to be Miss Carlingford. Because Simon might then have any preferment he liked in the diocese, you know."

"As if being the dean's grandson weren't enough," Lily protested, striving for lightness. "You would have the bishop's grandniece for him, as well? Yes, yes. I imagine that would indeed answer. The only danger then might be that he would be positively *buried* under preferments. With the right wife, he might end as a bishop himself, with a silly mitre on his head. Whereas, if he married the wrong one..."

"With the wrong wife, he might well be a curate forever," Sophie finished. "Many clergymen do, you know—start and end as curates. Of course our grandfather the dean will do what he can, but a bishop's influence—! We have high hopes for Simon. And he has high hopes, too. He will never say so, but I know it." Her spirits still buoyed, Sophie bounded up from her stool. "But I mustn't tire you any longer, Lily. I will go now and come again another time. And I am so very, very glad you don't bear me any grudge about Mr. Frayne and that you approve of him..."

When Sophie was gone Lily reached for her workbasket. Pulling it onto her lap, she removed from it one of Tyrone's school robes, of which she was letting out the hem. He had grown full another two inches and was as tall as his father now, but they had wisely left plenty of fabric the previous summer for just this eventuality. For five whole minutes she stitched steadily, thinking only about what remained to be done before her brother returned to Winchester College.

Then she thought another three entire minutes about Florence and Robert returning and how soon she might see them and how Florence might feel about the imminent addition to the Ellsworth Assortment.

Then she wondered where Beatrice had got to.

But it was no use in the end.

The thoughts could not be kept longer at bay.

Even if I were not engaged to Mr. Wright, no one would want me as a wife to Mr. Kenner. Not even Sophie, who considers herself my friend. Why—his family already disapproves of me as a wife to Mr. Wright—how much more would they draw back in horror to imagine me with Mr. Kenner!

They think me a flirt. Frivolous. Scandal-plagued.

I would sink him.

He would be a curate forever. And while I would not care a jot about that, he *would care.*

Perhaps in time, as he saw himself passed over for those coveted preferments, he might come to regret his choice. He might grow bitter, discontented with his curacy and with living off his wife's fortune. He would see the wretched Miss Carlingford carried off by some wilier, wiser young clergyman with an eye to the main chance, leaving the curate of St. Eadburh's to gnaw his heart in silence as the more fortunate man climbed higher and higher.

Lily had her pride. She would not suffer herself to be thought any man's downfall—a millstone 'round the neck of his ambition!

She had her pride, but she had also her honesty.

And she knew now—had known since she opened her eyes in Cock Lane to find her head in Mr. Kenner's lap—that she loved him. Loved the kind, unkind, gentle, cruel, winning, maddening curate of St. Eadburh's. She loved him and, that being so, she could not marry his cousin. Even if Mr. Kenner married this Miss Carlingford and Lily never married at all, she could not marry Gilbert Wright.

This time her decision was final. She would end her engagement. When the furor of this attack on her passed, when everyone had forgotten about her, she would end it as quietly as she could manage.

And then what?

If she loved Mr. Kenner, she should be glad for him to have everything his family wanted for him and everything he wanted for himself.

There was no denying his talent. Only look how the congregation of St. Eadburh's admired him. If he were to spend his entire clerical life in their little church, would he not then fall into that bucket of all those flowers born to blush unseen, wasting their sweetness on the desert air? To be the curate of St. Eadburh's was not invisibility, per se, but it was little better.

Therefore, if this was the case—if she loved him and wanted for him what he wanted—she should be glad of Miss Carlingford.

But she wasn't.

I might be able to bear him marrying Miss Carlingford and becoming a bishop if I knew he only chose her out of ambition, Lily fretted. *Then I could think of him in that ridiculous mitre, sitting at the breakfast table in a bishop's palace across from her, and I would not feel so...miserable.*

But if he loved her—Miss Carlingford—Lily felt a sharp twist to her insides and knew she would hate it. If Mr. Kenner came to love Miss Carlingford, could all the bishop's mitres and palaces make her think it was for the better?

It was a good thing for Lily that her solitude was interrupted at this point by a commotion in the passage, complete with barking and hurried steps and joyous cries. It went on and on, getting louder and happier, until she impatiently slapped the sofa and thought about trying to hop to the door or calling out a pathetic, "What is it? Don't forget about me!"

But then the door burst open, and it was Florence flying in, trailed by her husband and the rest of the Ellsworths and Snap and a fair few servants, and Lily nearly did try to leap up in her excitement.

"Flossie! You're home! How well you look! We didn't expect you yet. Oh, how happy I am that you're back early!"

"No, no—don't try to get up—you mustn't move." Florence urged, crushing Lily to her. "Dearest, of course we're back. How could we not rush back, when we read the *Chronicle*?"

Lily stared over her sister's shoulder, astonished, and she wriggled free as soon as she could. "What do you mean? What did you read in the *Chronicle*?"

"About the attack on you—what else? Oh, heavens! We were stopping in Bognor Regis, and Robert returned from the reading room, and when he told me what he discovered, my heart stopped. We set out for home at once. I needed to see and hear for myself that you and Bea were truly all right."

"It's in the *newspaper*?" Lily all but screeched. "How—on—earth—did it come to be in the newspaper?" Craning her neck, she pinned her stepmother with an indignant eye. "Mama, did you know it was in the newspaper?"

It was Minta who braved the storm and spoke up. "Of course she did. We all did when it came out on Monday, but we decided not to tell you because we thought you might be cross about it."

"Cross? *Cross?*" Lily squeaked, her voice rising so high that soon only Snap would be able to hear her. "'Cross' does not begin to describe it! What business had anyone at the *Hampshire Chronicle* to write about it?"

Her new brother-in-law Robert cleared his throat, interposing calmly, "The incident did take place on a public road, and where public safety is concerned—"

Confound public safety!

"Am I—named?" gasped Lily.

The exchanged glances and silence told her enough.

In the newspaper, dear God. She was not just scandal-plagued; she was *notorious*. She was worse than her father had ever been, with his many marriages. Worse than Flossie had been, jilting Mr. Gregory. Well!—she supposed she could do whatever she liked now, because there was no deeper dye than pitch-black.

With a heartfelt groan, she sagged back against the sofa. Then she tugged from behind her the cushion she had made and pressed it to her face. "Here, Flossie. I made this for you," she mumbled into it.

There was one comfort: the return of the Fairchilds was exciting enough that, once Florence was convinced her younger sisters were not at death's door as her fearful imagination dreaded, the family was delighted to leave off talking about the attack for the hundredth time and to turn instead to discussing the couple's honeymoon and new home in Kingsgate Street.

But before the Fairchilds took their leave some hours later, Florence gave her sister another hug and murmured, "Don't think I've forgotten about your Mr. Wright. I want to hear much more about him and can hardly wait to meet him. And I hope you will be as happy with him as I am with my Robert."

"I doubt it," said Lily. "I'm only waiting to jilt him."

Too used to Lily's naughty tongue, however, Florence only laughed at this and kissed her. "I will come again soon. And we must devise a means to bring you to Kingsgate Street. Hire a sedan chair, perhaps? Because I want you and Aunt Jeanne to give your opinions on the furnishings. Speaking of furnishings—" she held up the cushion Lily had sewn and took a deep, delighted sniff. "Lady's bedstraw! I love it. This will make me homesick for Hollowgate, even if I am only a short walk away. However did you think of it?"

Lily shut her eyes and shook her head. "Some time I'll tell you, Flossie, but that is a story for another day."

Chapter Twenty-Three

One myshap fortuneth never alone.

— Alexander Barclay, *The shyp of folys of the worlde* (1509)

Even had Florence not let the cat out of the bag, the note Lily received from Mr. Wright two days later would have enlightened her that her story was now in print, and the *Chronicle* might not be the only trumpet blaring.

Meadowsweep

20 August 1801

My dear Miss Ellsworth,

Have no fear. I have seen the inflammatory hand-bill and will take care of the matter in the manner I deem fit. No man will by his repeated offenses cause you harm or dismay without answering for it. I plan this day to dispatch a letter to Dailey and will keep you apprised. It is perhaps fortunate that your injury prevents your being seen abroad at this juncture.

Yours most faithfully,
Gilbert Wright

"Hand-bill?" muttered Lily. "What on earth can he be referring to now? And what has Mr. Dailey to do with anything, that he should write to him?"

Urgently she rang the bell beside her sofa (which she tried to do as rarely as possible because it invariably threw Snap into a fever of barking and nipping at the nearest ankles), and when the footman hurriedly appeared, she said, "Bobbins, please—you must send someone to town directly. There is some sort of hand-bill being posted or distributed or something, and you must get me a copy."

"Oh—er—uh—" stammered the footman, so caught off guard that he did not even respond to Snap's taunting growls.

She sat up straighter, fixing him with a beady stare. "You already have seen it, haven't you," she accused. "This hand-bill."

When he only gulped and twitched, she thrust out an imperious hand, trying to keep her voice even. "Bring it to me immediately. At once. Please—I insist."

With a despairing bow, Bobbins vanished, returning after some minutes and handing Lily the rolled-up hand-bill as if it were a shameful record of his own crimes.

"Thank you. You may go."

> 1801 August 19. Winchester. The mayor, having learned with extreme regret of the recent assault on the Miss E—s in Cock Lane on 16 August, hereby assures all persons that the ruffian confesses to acting alone. Mr. Walter Dailey of Crossdown, Hants., has likewise come forward to say the attack was motivated by a private disagreement between himself and the accused. Therefore no further danger to the public is anticipated along the Romsey Road or Cock Lane. As a result of these disclosures, the special watch from the West Gate to Cock Lane Gate will be discontinued, although young ladies are always cautioned to be vigilant when walking alone.

Lily read and re-read the notice, alarmed and indignant, both by the assumptions behind it and by the conclusions her intended husband had drawn therefrom.

"For one thing," she growled through gritted teeth, "this makes it sound like I am in the habit of wandering Winchester all unaccompanied! For another, it does not explain what Mr. Dailey's private disagreement had to do with this man attacking *me*. No—it implies that my assailant accosted me in order to vex Mr. Dailey. At least that is what Mr. Wright interprets it to mean. And all that does is to link my name with Mr. Dailey's—again! Which means everyone either knows about Mr. Dailey kissing me or else they will ask their neighbor now and learn of it! Why—if not for my confounded ankle, I would find Mr. Dailey *and* the mayor *and* the printer and tell them all exactly what I think of them and their confessions and hand-bills and watches! But I—"

But she couldn't. Her ankle was her ankle.

Ooh—and Mr. Wright counted it lucky that she could not get about and defend herself? That she could not be seen abroad and show she had nothing to be ashamed of? Lily was ready to scream with provocation.

And there was more.

More cause for her to tear her hair and wring her hands and pound her fists against the upholstery. For while she wished she might effect her own vengeance, she dreaded to have Mr. Wright take it upon himself. He was sure to exacerbate matters. Sure to make her even more of a household name.

And there was more even than *that*, Lily realized, hurling her embroidery hoop across the room (an act she regretted straightaway because now she would have to hop or crawl over to retrieve it).

For if she was already beyond the pale of acceptable wives for rising young clergymen, what was this but an added nail to the coffin? *Oh,* she moaned inwardly, *I am so distraught I cannot even keep my metaphors straight.* But tangled metaphors or not, Lily did not see how Mr. Kenner could ever learn to view her with favor. Not that she had any hope of alluring him or was even trying to, but still—! With such mud flung upon her—and there seemed no end to it—how could he even continue to think of her as a friend? Supposing she never saw him again, except in church? And with her injured ankle, she would not be able even to go to church until after he had already married Miss Carlingford and gone off to be Archbishop of Canterbury. *Oh! It is all so unfair. Had I known I was going to prefer Mr. Kenner, I would have tried to win him in the first place and never mind all the others. And I would have been on my good behavior all along, and none of any of this would have happened.*

The house was quiet. Too quiet. Even Snap crawled under Lily's sofa as if to keep clear of her wrath.

"I am not going to sit here alone all day," she said aloud. "How is it that I can never find a quiet moment to myself in this house unless I don't want one?" She could picture them all: her father in his library; her stepmother and Beatrice having lessons in the schoolroom; Minta off with Aggie somewhere. Well, then, where was Tyrone? Couldn't he at least read in the drawing room, to keep her company? If she was going to sew his clothing, it was the least he could do. And shouldn't Florence come again, no matter how many new houses and furnishings she was arranging?

With a huff, Lily swung her legs to the floor and struggled up. After one fleeting attempt to put weight on her bad ankle—in case it had miraculously healed—a shot of pain encouraged her to abandon the idea.

It was a very long way to the drawing room door, and Lily studied the route. She could cling to the back of the sofa and hop along it, then hop without support over to her papa's favorite chair, and thence to the door. Or she could ring for Bobbins again and force him to assist her, as he and Monk did every morning and evening, to bring her downstairs and return her to her room, but she felt an unjust resentment toward him for having been the bearer of bad news.

She would manage herself, then.

It was in the hopping from Mr. Ellsworth's chair to the door that Lily met with disaster. Her hopping foot caught the very corner of the Wilton carpet, which promptly slid across the smooth boards, taking Lily's good foot with it and depositing the rest of her in a noisy heap on the floor.

The door opened, and Bobbins intoned to the space above her, "The Kenners, if you please."

"Gracious, Lily! Are you hurt?" asked Sophie, rushing to crouch beside her.

"No, no." Her face reddening, Lily sat up hastily and twitched her wayward skirts down to cover her legs. "I was—a little too eager to get about."

"It seems we are just in time, then," said Mr. Kenner. His voice was even, but he avoided her eyes, and Lily suspected he had caught a glimpse of her limbs. She could do nothing right around the man! Not one single, lone, solitary thing.

"Look what Simon found for you!" Sophie exclaimed with a gleeful bounce as her brother held them up: "Crutches!"

"Crutches," repeated Lily.

"They were at the Peases' farm," explained Sophie, "and we were calling on Mrs. Pease to thank her for the apples she sent us, and there they were, propped in the yard! And when Simon asked, she said they used to be for one of their hands who fell off a horse, but he was all better now, and of course we could borrow them." She bit her lip at the expression on Lily's face. "I mean—not that crutches are so very wonderful. They're not like pineapples from Meadowsweep, or anything, but we thought they might be useful—"

"They're the best!" cried Lily over the sudden obstruction in her throat. "Exactly what I need and better than any pineapples."

"Quite the compliment," Mr. Kenner said, "for we remember how strongly you felt about the fruit. Worth two dances, wasn't it?"

Amazed at his memory, Lily had no response to this, but she gestured toward the crutches. "Do let me try them." Rising to her knees, she tried not to shrink away when Mr. Kenner offered his hand to haul her upright. His grip was firm and impersonal and his jaw set, and Lily should not have gone crimson again, but that was precisely what she did. And if she were sensible, which she was not, there was no reason she should feel agitated when he helped her place the crutches—he touched her as calmly as if he were Mr. Beckford the doctor.

If I were a real *flirt,* she told herself, *I would be clumsy about this so I could collapse against him*. But the very idea paralyzed her. How did one flirt with Mr. Kenner? It was not possible. Or it was not possible *now.* He would turn those pale eyes on her, like a panther on his jungle prey, and that would be the end. He would see through her. He would read her thoughts and be horrified.

"Give them a try," he murmured. "Balance on your good ankle and swing them out. If they're too long for you, we can shave them down some."

She obeyed with little enough grace, being too conscious of him studying her and annoyed by Snap biting at these new wooden invaders, but soon enough the joy of being able to move at will and propel herself where she wanted to go overcame her embarrassment, and, after a circuit of the drawing room, she returned to the Kenners with her most radiant smile. "Oh, they're marvelous! They're wonderful! If you only knew how tiresome it has been these past few days, always to need assistance and to be marooned on that cursed sofa—how can I ever thank you enough for thinking of me?"

"Your joy is thanks enough," he replied, almost curtly. But when he saw his sister's brow knit, he added in a lighter tone, "Never let it be said I don't take care of my flock."

"No indeed," replied Lily, her smile fading. Perhaps he

thought her enthusiasm inappropriate. Embarrassing. Perhaps this was how the Miss Weekses or Miss Terman or Miss Beckford responded, whenever he paid the least little courtesy to them. And that was all it was—a courtesy. It could not even be exalted into proof of friendship, when he put it like that. It was merely a clergyman's thoughtfulness. All in a day's work. Miss Carlingford, with her exalted ecclesiastical connections would never have fawned on him for such a simple act of politeness.

"Thank you again," said Lily, muted this time. To give herself time to regain her composure, she propelled herself over to retrieve her embroidery hoop, only to drop one of the crutches with a clatter when she attempted to reach for it. Then Mr. Kenner was beside her again to provide another wretched clerical courtesy which Lily would as soon have done without. "Thank you," she muttered, crippling back to her confounded sofa to seat herself. Then, abruptly wanting to be alone, as vigorously as she had longed for company not ten minutes earlier, she added, "Have you many more of these visits to make today? Am I squeezed between the Hamblys and Mr. Harvey?"

"Oh, no," answered Sophie. "We saw the Hamblys yesterday, and Mr. Harvey is doing much better."

"I see you have seen the hand-bill," Mr. Kenner said quietly, picking up the paper from where it had fallen to the carpet.

"I have. I am not particularly happy about it."

"Nor is Gilbert," whispered Sophie with a grimace. She took a neighboring armchair and patted her lap so the terrier would join her. "In fact, he's in a perfect *rage.* Our family has talked of nothing else."

Lily could not repress a sigh at this.

"Has he—spoken with you?" prompted Mr. Kenner.

"He sent a note," she replied shortly. "Hinting that he was going to 'take care of the matter,' whatever that means. I would really rather it were all buried and forgotten."

"Perhaps you might tell him so, then."

"Oh, do, Lily," urged Sophie. "We are all a little anxious about him. You know Gil can be so headstrong and—impulsive at times."

Lily blinked at this. What was she supposed to do? Send a note saying, "Don't do anything foolish"?

"I think—whatever he plans on doing—it is too late for me to interfere. He said he was going to write to Mr. Dailey, but for what purpose I can't imagine."

Brother and sister exchanged a glance.

"He might listen to you in any event," Mr. Kenner persisted.

Lily remembered Mr. Wright and Mr. Dailey nearly coming to blows in the Hollowgate drive. Suppose Mr. Wright were to throw himself at Mr. Dailey again, and this time in some public space with everyone looking on eagerly? Lamed as she was, Lily could hardly come between them this time, and what a fuss there would be.

"Very well," she agreed. "I will send a note and ask to speak with him. I will try to persuade him not to act on my behalf."

"Oh, thank you!" cried Sophie, pushing Snap aside so she could fly to embrace Lily. "Gil thinks so much of you. How good you will be for him! We will leave you now, so you may write to him straight away."

"But—but—" Lily sputtered, dashed anew. It was bad enough to think the Kenners called on her out of clerical pity, but worse still to think they did so only to persuade her to rein their cousin in.

"But won't you stay to dinner? I think Papa said at two o'clock today because we hope my sister Florence and her husband may join us. It would be lovely to introduce you."

Genuine regret coloured Sophie's face, though Mr. Kenner's was impassive. "Dear me!" said Sophie, "how delightful that would be, but we must decline. Bishop and Mrs. North are holding a reception at St. John's House—it's Miss Carlingford's birthday, and they are making quite an occasion of it. It's really most inconvenient that they live in London most of the time, and we have no proper bishop's palace here in Winchester, for it would have been great fun to be invited to a palace."

"St. John's House is lovely as well," Lily replied, trying not to sound dismal. "I have not been introduced to Miss Carlingford, but I wish her many happy returns." She thought of that first Race Ball at St. John's House and how Mr. Kenner did not dance on that occasion. There they would all gather again, and this time without her. She supposed there was no dancing at an afternoon reception. What *did* one do at a reception hosted by a bishop? Pay homage to Miss Carlingford, presumably. That was to be expected. And then, if one were already married and not interested in courting her, there was always the great uncle to woo and flatter.

The Kenners did not stay much longer, and perhaps it would have comforted Lily, had she been able to follow them down the drive to listen to their conversation.

"I think she was mightily pleased with the crutches, wouldn't you say, Simon?"

"Yes."

A little sigh. "You know I am quite over Gilbert now," Sophie continued, "so you mustn't suspect me of anything when I say it is little wonder he loves her. When she smiles, she looks like an angel."

"Yes."

"I do hope he will answer her summons and be prevented from doing anything rash."

"Yes."

"Simon! Is that all you can say?"

He gave her a rueful sidelong glance. "What would you have me say?"

"Oh, I don't know." Sophie blew out a half-amused, half-exasperated breath. "You never say anything you don't want to. You are the precise opposite of Gilbert—everything is written all over his face and yours—is an inscrutable blank."

"Suppose I told you I too would like to bash Dailey over the head for his lack of discretion?"

"I would like you the better for it," Sophie answered stoutly. "Because, for all that Miss Ellsworth wore a brave face, I cannot imagine she is enjoying any of this. You know how people are talking—how they *have* been talking, ever since Mr. Dailey kissed her in the road. She needs friends, Simon. Therefore, I admire Gilbert the more for wanting to defend her, however ill-advised he might be in the way he goes about it, and I would admire you the more for wanting to champion her, even if only in your mind."

His mouth twisted in derision, whether at himself or at her she did not know. But he said, "Then admire away, Sophie. As far as that goes."

Chapter Twenty-Four

I call'd a Council, to know what

Course we should steer next.

— W. R. Chetwood, *The voyages and adventures of captain Robert Boyle* (1726)

Though Lily dutifully sent the requested note to Mr. Wright at Meadowsweep, he was not the first of his family to call on her the following day.

It being a beautiful morning, sunny and cloudless, Lily used her crutches to venture out of doors, making her laborious way to the bench in Florence's garden, where she and her stepmother proposed to work on Tyrone's school clothing while Beatrice read her lessons. Barney the gardener had set out additional chairs, as well as a table for Bea to write upon, and Lily was glad for their presence, distracting her from the thoughts which had occupied her since the Kenners' visit. While she ought to have been fretting over Mr. Wright and what he might do to Mr. Dailey, instead she found herself wondering and wondering what might have happened at Miss Carlingford's birthday reception. How she wished she might have had a spy there! If Florence had only married Mr. Gregory (the only time Lily ever wished for that particular outcome), she could have asked him as her brother, without raising any suspicions. But as it was, Lily was left to speculate.

"When Mr. Wright comes—if Mr. Wright comes," Lily told Mrs. Ellsworth, "I will need to speak to him alone, if you please. He is rather put out by Mr. Dailey speaking to whomever it was Mr. Dailey spoke to."

Her stepmother gave a pensive nod.

"It is an hour's ride from Meadowsweep," Lily went on, "so I do not suppose he will be here for a while yet."

Therefore, none of the Ellsworths were prepared for the appearance of Bobbins, not fifteen minutes later, peering over the half-door. "Mrs. Fellowes and Mrs. Wright to see you, Miss Ellsworth."

Lily stared. Mr. Wright's mother and grandmother? Surely not. Had her intended sent them in his place? Unthinkable. What was she to do with this embassy?

Mrs. Ellsworth recovered first. "Would you prefer to receive them here or in the drawing room, Lily? If here, we can ask Barney to bring more chairs out."

"Er—they requested to speak apart with Miss Ellsworth," uttered the footman.

"Oh!" said Lily and her stepmother at the same time, but then Mrs. Ellsworth rose hastily. "Come, Bea. We will finish in the schoolroom. Did you want us to help you return to the drawing room, Lily?"

Lily pictured herself struggling back within doors, arriving breathless and rumpled and red. She shook her head. "No, thank you. Bobbins, if you would bring them to the garden..." She hoped the parley would be brief. Perhaps they would ask what she wanted to say to Mr. Wright, as he was much occupied and apologized for not coming in person, etc. etc. She would request they tell him she did not wish him to take further steps with Mr. Dailey. They would thank her and take their leave. So, ten minutes altogether?

It did occur to Lily that Mrs. Fellowes and the dean had likely been at Miss Carlingford's reception—might there be some opening in which to broach that subject? Surely Mrs. Fellowes, as a fond grandmother, would welcome an opportunity to boast, if Simon Kenner had charmed the bishop's grandniece...

Of the two Fellowes daughters, Lily thought Mrs. Wright looked most like her mother. Both women were above average in height, solidly constructed, with stern but not unattractive features. When Bobbins ushered them into the walled garden, they might have been twins, with their furrowed brows and mouths pressed in troubled lines.

"Please don't get up," said the dean's wife, seeing Lily reach for her crutches. "And thank you for receiving us without notice, my dear."

Lily's eyebrows rose. She could not help it, to hear herself my-deared. She knew she had never been a favorite with Mrs. Fellowes, and even the engagement dinner had resulted in no more than polite nothings uttered among them. Lily was too aware of the family being arrayed against the match and Mrs. Fellowes too aware of Lily being—well—Lily. Mrs. Wright had been no warmer, doing neither more nor less than her mother. But on this occasion, she gave Lily a look not seen before—one might almost have called it *beseeching*.

When her visitors were seated (Mrs. Fellowes dragging her chair into the shade of a tree), Lily folded her hands in her lap and waited, saying only, "How kind of you to call."

Mrs. Fellowes looked at her daughter. Mrs. Wright looked at her mother.

"Miss Ellsworth—" they both began. Then Mrs. Fellowes bowed her head and yielded to her daughter.

"Miss Ellsworth," Mrs. Wright said again, "please allow us to say we are very sorry about this whole business. Sorry, of course, that you were accosted—"

"That my sister Beatrice and I were accosted," Lily interrupted. If hand-bills posted throughout Winchester were going to imply that she roamed the streets alone, she could not pass up an opportunity to correct this.

"Yes. Miss Beatrice and you," amended Mrs. Wright. "I am so sorry you both were accosted and greatly relieved that my nephew Simon's arrival was able to prevent—further harm."

Lily's bosom swelled, and she could not forbear saying, "Yes—*further* harm. I was frightened and my ankle—stepped upon—but no more. Before Mr. Kenner arrived on the scene, I had managed to knock out the assailant with—a crock I was carrying." She could not say what was wrong with her. Nothing Mrs. Wright said was not the truth, and yet it was not the whole truth. It could not be overstated that the man had not succeeded in beating her or—assaulting her virtue. And it was important to Lily to point out that she had not simply swooned away. She had *fought*.

"Commendable," said Mrs. Fellowes briskly. "Nevertheless—"

"Nevertheless, I was grateful for Mr. Kenner's assistance." This time she broke in for fear of sounding ungracious. Because it was also true that she was deeply thankful—more than thankful—Mr. Kenner had come. For what would she have done, had she woken up again in the road, still alone with her attacker? She would have crawled away, of course. But how far could she possibly have crawled before he regained consciousness?

At this point she pinched herself. *Stop talking. Just listen.*

The same thought must have crossed her visitors' minds because their mouths thinned further.

There was a little pause. In the distance, Lily could hear one of the groundskeepers whistling to himself.

"Pardon me," she said at last. "Please go on. I do thank you for your concern."

This yielding on her part was not without effect. Mrs. Wright's mouth even relaxed into a tentative smile, and she held up a hand as if she would have reached for Lily. "It has been a trying time for you,

Miss Ellsworth. We will be as brief as we can. The matter is this: you may be aware—Gilbert likely has told you—that he objects greatly to this Mr. Walter Dailey's interference in the matter."

She waited, and Lily gave a nod.

"And—you are likely also aware that, while my son is generally a sweet-tempered young man, he has his limits. When he feels—he has been wronged or someone he—cares for—has been wronged, he is quick to act." Mrs. Wright glanced at her mother when she said this, but Mrs. Fellowes' only response was to heave a sigh, and Lily suspected the two women had differing opinions on whether Mr. Wright's responses to his "limits" being surpassed were a good or bad thing.

This variance between them hinted at the first chink in their united front, and Lily naturally took a side, sympathizing with the mother over the grandmother.

"I have always thought Mr. Wright's loyalty and strength of feeling very admirable qualities," she volunteered therefore, even adding boldly, "though I know they have at least once placed him at odds with others. I know he and—Mr. Kenner—disagreed over whether Mr. Wright should offer for me, for instance." (With the narrowing of Mrs. Fellowes' eyes, it seemed safer to attribute the opposition to Mr. Kenner alone, rather than the entire clan.)

Mrs. Wright coloured, looking at once much younger than her mother. "Oh—Gilbert told you about that, then. Yes, so—er—you understand what I mean." Clearing her throat, she shifted on the little garden chair.

"Miss Ellsworth," the dean's wife struck in, "I imagine you think me a stern, strait-laced sort of person—no, please—let me say my piece. And your opinion might be shared by others in the diocese, but I would submit that those who know me best would call me affectionate and even overfond. If—if our family erred on the side of caution with our recommendations to Gilbert, it was done from that overfondness for him and not from spite toward you."

It was as close to an apology as Lily had ever heard from so august a person, and she bowed her head again in acknowledgement. Was this visit, then, to establish a new footing for Lily's relationship to the family? To admit they had opposed her in the past, but were now willing and indeed eager to invite her into the fold? Were they closing ranks around her in support, as a result of the trial she had undergone?

Just as Lily began to feel guilty for having decided to end her engagement to Gilbert Wright, and guilty for entertaining feelings toward her intended's cousin, and guilty for thinking ill of the rest of her intended's family, Mrs. Fellowes resumed.

"My daughter is beating about the bush, Miss Ellsworth, but I will do you the courtesy of coming to the point. The fact is, my grandson Gilbert has accused Mr. Walter Dailey of 'repeatedly' jeopardizing your good name. First by his attentions to you and now by this attack. The culprit—Fleming by name—claims he assaulted you in order to revenge himself on Mr. Dailey. Mr. Dailey had dismissed him from his position—"

"The Tale of the Drunken Overseer," whispered Lily to herself.

"—and, when Fleming witnessed the—er—the embrace between Mr. Dailey and you, he saw his opportunity to strike back."

Fleming had witnessed it too? Good gracious—had all the county been crouching in the shrubbery that day? Fleming must have just darted out of sight, she thought, remembering the empty jug by the gatepost.

"It's all, all Mr. Dailey's fault, then," marveled Lily. "If he had never forced that kiss upon me—or if I had not been so taken by surprise—if I had managed to *slap* the man—maybe this Fleming would have left me alone." And the Miss Weekses would have had nothing to gossip about.

"Well…" Mrs. Fellowes gave an expressive shrug. "Unfortunately neither was the case. He did force a kiss on you, and you did not, unfortunately, slap him. And now Gilbert has taken exception to Mr. Dailey's repeated involvement. He has challenged the man to a duel."

"A duel?" Lily gasped.

"He said nothing to you of this, then?"

"He said—he said only—I knew he was angry with Mr. Dailey—for heaven's sake, *I* was angry with Mr. Dailey—"

"Did you put Gilbert up to this?" Mrs. Wright pressed, sitting forward, only to draw back when Lily's eyes flashed at her.

"Put him up to it? How could I put him up to it when I did not know about it? No—Mr. Wright only told me he would 'take care of the matter,' but I assumed that meant he would—would perhaps give him a beating, as he tried to beat Mr. Kenner for speaking against me. I had no idea he would go to such lengths!"

Lily crumpled her sewing in her lap, wringing it in her agitation. "But how reckless of him! How—how foolhardy! Has Mr. Dailey responded?"

"He has," said Mrs. Fellowes stonily. "It is only because Gilbert's father was accidentally handed Mr. Dailey's response that this even came to light. My son-in-law Thomas confronted Gilbert and learned all these details, the whys and wherefores. And the hows: Gilbert and Mr. Dailey plan to meet at Worthy Down tomorrow at eight in the morning."

"Oh, no," moaned Lily, covering her face with her hands. She was conscious of a fierce ragout of feelings which she would prefer they not witness. A ragout in which concern for Mr. Wright, exasperation with him, and mortification for herself all combined.

Concern ought to be paramount, of course. There was a chance that he could be killed. But Lily thought he could probably acquit himself well with a pistol—only, if he did succeed in shooting Mr. Dailey without being killed himself, would he then be in danger of the law?

Yes, concern for Mr. Wright ought to be paramount, but exasperation insisted on making itself felt. Because what would a duel accomplish, except to make Lily even more infamous? Fighting a duel would only make the world believe that her honor had indeed been compromised, that he must go to such extremes. And if he objected to Mr. Dailey jeopardizing her good name, what was *he* doing but the same thing to the uttermost?

Hence, mortification. Was it not bad enough to be kissed against her will in public, but she must also be attacked, named in the newspapers and in hand-bills, and now have this ridiculous duel fought for her sake?

"I didn't ask for any of this!" Lily declared at last, throwing aside her sewing, her countenance scarlet. "Not any of it! I could challenge Mr. Dailey to a duel myself for bringing all this to pass, especially now that I understand—Fleming's—motivation. If anyone should run Mr. Dailey through or put a ball in him, it should be me. I *wish* it might be me!"

This bloodthirsty speech made Mrs. Wright pale, but her mother did not appear similarly dismayed.

"To be perfectly honest, Miss Ellsworth," said the dean's wife, "I share your preference. I would back you against this Mr. Dailey without hesitation."

"Are you saying you wouldn't back Gilbert?" demanded Mrs. Wright, shooting her mother a reproachful look.

"I don't want Gilbert anywhere near him, Jane, and neither should you." She turned back to Lily. "Gilbert will not listen to us, Miss Ellsworth. You perhaps already guessed that, seeing as his own wishes about your engagement prevailed in the face of...warning."

"Mrs. Fellowes, Mrs. Wright, if you have come today in order to ask me to use my powers of persuasion upon him, you have been anticipated."

"Has Gilbert already consulted you?" wondered his mother. "How can that be, if you did not know he challenged Mr. Dailey?"

"Not Gil—not Mr. Wright, no," said Lily. "But Mr. and Miss Kenner called yesterday to say much the same thing: would I try to convince their cousin not to do anything reckless? I do not think the

Kenners imagined he would call Mr. Dailey out—they pictured no more than fisticuffs, I suspect. A brawl."

"Bless Simon," beamed Mrs. Fellowes. "My wise peacemaker."

This praise of her nephew appeared to rile Mrs. Wright, and she almost snapped, "Yes, yes, we know that with Simon cool reason always prevails, if only because he lacks Gilbert's passionate nature."

"And I told the Kenners I would make the attempt," Lily resumed. Entertaining as it might prove to have Mrs. Wright and Mrs. Fellowes snap at each other, Lily felt a little pang upon hearing Mr. Kenner's coldness of heart described.

Mrs. Fellowes cast a quelling eye at her daughter before continuing, "I am glad to hear Gilbert's cousins have acted in his best interests, Miss Ellsworth, and glad as well to hear of your willingness to 'make the attempt.' However—I hope you will forgive me for venturing—I do not believe you will have any more success in dissuading my grandson than any of us, much as he may respect your opinion. What do you think?"

Lily hesitated. If they thought she would not succeed, why were they here?

"Well...in truth, Mrs. Fellowes, while I promised to speak with Mr. Wright, I did not have very great expectations of success. He—he and Mr. Dailey have already had one encounter, where there would have been blows, had I not physically inserted myself between them. Something I do not know how I could repeat at a duel, even if I could find my way there, with my ankle."

Again mother and daughter regarded each other, and Lily felt a twitch of impatience. *What?* What were they after? Did they just seek a companion in anxiety?

At length: "Shall I, Jane?" prompted Mrs. Fellowes.

Mrs. Wright bit her lips. Nodded.

"There is *one* way Gilbert might be convinced to give up this duel," said the dean's wife slowly. "That being...if he no longer had the *right* to challenge Mr. Dailey."

"I don't understand."

"As your intended husband, Miss Ellsworth, my grandson has the right to champion you. He has the right to defend your name as he sees fit, just as any of the male members of your family have that right. But if—if he were...no longer...your intended husband, he would lose that right, and the duel would have to be called off."

"But how—?"

"I mean to say, Miss Ellsworth, in so many words: if you were to jilt him, Gilbert would have to withdraw his challenge."

Lily's eyes grew round as guineas. "You're asking me to *jilt* your grandson?"

"Yes."

"But why ever would I do that?" she demanded, her mind beginning to race and her heart to pound. It couldn't be—could it? A sign from heaven, as it were, a confirmation of and a blessing upon the decision Lily had already made. Heaven wanted her to jilt him! Heaven offered this escape—this bolt-hole. In jilting Mr. Wright, she would not only please herself, but she would please his family and possibly save his life!

Mrs. Fellowes was speaking again, and Lily hoped she had not missed more than a few words.

"—A good match. An exemplary match, from your perspective. He is handsome, rich, of good family. But, Miss Ellsworth, you are by no means a young lady without resources, I need not tell you. You are no penniless, plain creature approaching the danger years. There will be other opportunities for you to do as well, if not better. Why, you might catch yourself a lord! I saw how every gentleman of your acquaintance was charmed."

Lily was silent, keeping her lashes lowered and her hands quiet. Oh, it would require no persuasion for her to release Mr. Wright. Especially if he might possibly get himself killed, in addition to dragging her reputation once more through the mud. She was more than willing to release him earlier than she had planned.

If only being free would get her Mr. Kenner!

She held very, very still, thinking with all her might. Because—yes—

Perhaps she could work this situation to her benefit.

"It is all very well, Mrs. Fellowes, to say I am young and will fall upon my feet," said Lily slowly, "but what of my own affections for Mr. Wright?"

"Yes," cried Mrs. Wright, "that is precisely what I told my mother! That surely your own feelings for my son would make it impossible for you to give him up!"

"Even if keeping him would be to risk his life?" retorted Mrs. Fellowes.

Lily inhaled sharply. But, it must be confessed, not over the thought of risking Mr. Wright's life. No—she was thinking, *What if this were about Mr. Kenner*? If she had been engaged to Mr. Kenner, would she have given him up, in order to protect him? *At once*, she realized. But that was ludicrous, of course, for a dozen reasons, chief among them that she was *not* engaged to Simon Kenner, nor was he the sort of man who went around challenging people to duels. That coldness of heart again...

Mrs. Wright began to sniffle, picturing Miss Ellsworth weeping over Gilbert's cold, still corpse, but soon enough her mother said, "Now, hush, Jane, and let me handle this. Your own commendable love for your son clouds your judgment. Tell me the truth, Miss Ellsworth. You seem like a commonsensical girl. Is it possible that you are fond of Gilbert, without being already head over heels in love with him?"

Lily looked up then, and she was unable to prevent a glint of respect from lighting her eye. Mrs. Fellowes was a sharp one, no doubt.

"I thought it might be," the dean's wife said. "And therefore I hoped you might be reasoned with."

Carefully, weighing each word, Lily replied, "When you put it as you have, I would indeed not want to risk Mr. Wright's life. But I will be very, very sorry to part with him. I might not love him to distraction—yet—but I did hope to, one day. Moreover, if I ended our engagement, I am not as confident as you, Mrs. Fellowes, that I would ever find another gentleman I liked so well."

"You must give them a try," Mrs. Fellowes answered robustly. "It is understandable that you would give Gilbert the preference at first, but I daresay there are others as eligible and winning. If I remember aright, you had many beaux to choose from."

Lily sighed. "But I preferred Mr. Wright to them all. And even if I hadn't, they all went away, once I became engaged. Every last one of them. Most of them to clamor about Miss Carlingford, the bishop's grandniece. If I—gave up—Mr. Wright, I would have to begin anew with whomever I could find."

"There will surely be many handsome officers who will winter in town. So dashing in their red coats!"

"Oh—soldiers." Lily gave a little shudder. "I'm afraid I don't much care for soldiers. No. I would have to seek elsewhere. But—I suppose—Winchester does have an abundance of...clergymen."

Mrs. Fellowes arched a skeptical brow. "That it does. But I was not aware you had any interest in clergymen, Miss Ellsworth, unlike your older sister."

"Oh, I do, though," said Lily, smoothing out Tyrone's robe on her lap. "It is too bad I cannot compete with Miss Carlingford, however. I haven't any bishops in the family. Whoever wins her wins preferments."

"You have your beauty and your wealth," countered Mrs. Fellowes. "And forgive me, but I suspect, nine times out of ten, a man would choose such birds in the hand over the tenuous possibility of ever rising to an archdeaconry or bishopric."

Ah, but it was that tenth time that troubled Lily, and she did not have to make a pretense of sounding doubtful. "Added to Miss Carlingford's bishop, Mrs. Fellowes, there is the equally vexing matter that I am in danger of falling to the ground between two stools if I end my engagement. You see, if I keep it, it poses a danger to Mr. Wright and adds to the talk about me. But if I end it, then I am called a jilt, and there is still more talk about me. Perhaps doing irreparable injury."

If Mrs. Fellowes' wiliness had won grudging respect from Lily, Lily was fast winning the same from the dean's wife.

"What would you have of us, if you were to end the engagement?" asked Mrs. Fellowes. "I—would be glad to put it about that it was entirely amicable and that you were a good girl who decided you would not suit. I would let it be known, moreover, that we none of us bore any ill will about it and thought as—highly of you as ever."

Mrs. Wright, quite beyond her depth with these negotiations, looked from one to the other, not daring to interject.

"That might do very well," Lily replied at last. "And, perhaps, just one, single, other thing."

Mrs. Fellowes waited, spreading her hands palms upward.

Lily's smile was demure. "If I were to decide upon a clergyman, I would not want any of my little history to be held against me. That is, if I were to decide upon a clergyman, Mrs. Fellowes, I ask only that you would back me."

There was a long pause while the dean's wife weighed the risks of this. She did not particularly place deep faith in Miss Ellsworth, but what would be the harm in passing her word? Winchester was awash in clergymen, and to allow any one of them to be enchanted by this young lady was better than letting Gilbert fall to her, at risk of his life.

There was no question.

An answering smile lit Mrs. Fellowes face, and she held out her hand.

"I think, Miss Ellsworth, we understand each other. Now may we count on you when you see Gilbert today?"

Lily met the old lady's firm grip with one of her own.

"You may."

Chapter Twenty-Five

Resolve on this, thou shalt be fortunate,

If thou receive me for thy warlike mate.

— Shakespeare, *Henry VI, Part One,* I.ii.269 (c.1590)

It would not be an exaggeration to say there was much anxiety at the rectory. Kenner read the same page of his open book over and over, and the sheet of paper before him held no more than a paragraph, lined through. Sophie had been pacing the parlor much of the morning, when she was not pacing the garden and stealing over to the gate to glance up and down the road.

When she came in again after another of these surveys, she found her brother had removed to the parlor as well, abandoning the pretense of working on his sermon. Instead he was tuning his fiddle. But he put it down when he saw her.

"Any sign of him?"

"No. But surely he must come soon. He wouldn't ignore her note. I told Vickery to watch for him, but the maid can hardly spend the day standing at the gate either. I don't suppose it would do for us to walk over to Hollowgate?"

"Better not. Gil would know something was in the wind if we did. We had better just intercept him after he has seen her."

With a sigh, Sophie took a seat in her favorite armchair, taking up her mending, while her brother began to play.

"Why, that's 'True Lover's Farewell,' Simon," said Sophie after a minute. "The song little Miss Beatrice was playing, and the Ellsworths all sang."

"Yes. I asked Miss Araminta for the music, and she copied it for me."

"What a pleasant evening that was. I wish there might be many more in the future." Sophie's nose crinkled in a sudden giggle. "Little Beatrice—she made Lily fire up when you were still drinking your port with Mr. Ellsworth."

"Oh?" He stopped playing and gave the peg of the top string a turn. "What could that harmless young girl possibly have done?"

"It wasn't anything she *did*, Simon. It was that she asked Lily in complete innocence whether Lily was being good—you know—well-behaved—in order to make you fall in love with her."

Kenner's long finger slipped against the catgut with a squeak. "And that made her angry?" His voice was level, and he even managed to add lightly, "Younger sisters can be so provoking."

"So we can," Sophie agreed. "Yes, she was vexed, but also...embarrassed, I think, because she turned colours. It must have been because she knew—though no one else did—that she was already engaged."

"So she was and is," said Kenner. Laying his instrument aside, he rose and went to the window.

"Sometimes I have thought—" Sophie broke off. Pressed her lips together and went back to her mending.

His head swung around. "Thought what? Do finish your sentences, Sophie."

"All right, then. Sometimes I have thought that—if not for Gilbert, of course—Miss Ellsworth might have been the sort for you, Simon."

"Indeed? And why would you think such a thing?" He was at his most remote and expressionless, but having had few people to speak to at Miss Carlingford's birthday the previous afternoon, Sophie had leisure to observe the fortunate young lady herself. And in doing so, she had made a discovery. Or, at least, she formed a hypothesis, which she was now interested in testing. Miss Carlingford had been most friendly and gracious to Sophie, but even in speaking with her, that young lady's eyes slid continually to Simon, so she knew Miss Carlingford's cordiality was not meant for her. In return, Simon was easy and courteous with Miss Carlingford. Attentive, yet detached. In fact, he was just as he was with the Miss Weekses or Miss Terman or Miss Beckford. Just as he was, that is, with everyone save Miss Lily Ellsworth. With Lily he was different, Sophie decided. With Lily he was cool and contained; his eyes were hooded; he held himself on a tight rein. Hard as it was to imagine, she thought, could it possibly be just possibly, *possibly* possible that Simon was the littlest bit *épris* with their beautiful neighbor? If it was—possibly possibly possible—how sad and ironic that would be. Both Kenners in love with two people who not only did not love them back, but who loved each other!

Of course, Sophie reminded herself, *I am not in love with Gil any longer, so the situation is only half as sad and ironic as it might have been*. Furthermore, Sophie shared her family's belief that, with Simon, cool reason generally prevailed. So, whatever his feelings for Miss Ellsworth, they were not likely to trouble him overlong. Still, the situation bore traces of tragedy for a susceptible imagination like hers.

"I thought Miss Ellsworth might have been the sort for you," Sophie resumed with unwonted daring, "because she doesn't *prostrate herself* before you, Simon. You know how everyone thinks you're so clever and marvelous—"

This drew a grin. "You mean to say it is her low opinion of me which makes her a promising candidate?"

"Because you don't *overawe* her, is what I'm trying to say, rather. And she—doesn't overawe you."

"Doesn't she?" he muttered under his breath.

"Miss Kenner! Miss Kenner!" gasped the maid Vickery, thrusting her head in the doorway, her prominent eyes bulging even more in her excitement. "I see your cousin in the road! He's on horseback but riding slowly like."

Both Kenners sprang up, slipping past Vickery to spill out of the rectory and down the step. At the gate they slowed, in an unconvincing attempt at nonchalance.

"Why, Gil," called out Kenner with a wave, "have you been calling at Hollowgate? If you mean to go home now, you're all turned around. Miss Ellsworth must have dazzled you, for Meadowsweep lies the other way."

"Or are you going to the deanery?" asked Sophie.

"I hardly know," replied their cousin. "No. I don't want to go to the deanery. Except I must." Even as he spoke he drew rein. Sophie thought he would alight from Thunder, but he did not.

Brother and sister glanced at each other, brows lifting.

"You *have* been at Hollowgate, have you not?" Kenner ventured.

"I have."

It was a warm day but not hot; otherwise Kenner might have suspected sunstroke. What on earth passed between Gil and Miss Ellsworth to put him in such a stupor?

Before Kenner could think of the best way to broach the subject, his cousin took hold of the pommel, sagging over Thunder's neck as if he had had too much to drink. Then he swung his leg clumsily over, and slid all the way down.

"Good God, man," Kenner said before he could help himself, "was that your first time getting off a horse?"

"Simon," reproved his sister, hurrying forward to place a bracing hand on her cousin's arm. "Gil—are you all right? Won't you come in for a minute until you feel better?"

Numbly, Wright obeyed. Not even catching up Thunder's reins—leaving Kenner to do it—he followed Sophie into the rectory.

"You're—you're a dear, Sophie," Wright mumbled, when she directed him to a seat and told Vickery to bring Mr. Wright a measure of currant-juice.

"I am?"

"—But have you got anything stronger?"

"We'll mix it with some brandy," Kenner offered.

This elixir administered, the young man began to revive, his dazed expression gradually yielding to one of set misery.

"I may as well tell you," Wright muttered. He tipped back the glass to drain the last drop. "Let me have another, if you please."

Twitching with impatience, the Kenners waited for him to toss off a second glass of brandy-laced juice.

With a decisive *clink*, Wright set the glass down. Then he rested against the back of the chair, shutting his eyes.

"I'll have Vickery make you a sandwich," suggested Kenner.

A jerk of a nod.

Kenner slipped out to pass the word to the maid, and when he returned he paused in the doorway because Gil had opened his eyes again and was looking at Sophie.

"She's jilted me," he announced curtly.

Sophie gasped and took hold of his arm again, and so in need of comfort was he that he didn't object. No—to everyone's horror and amazement (including Gilbert Wright's own), his face contorted with the struggle to fight back tears.

Kenner said nothing. He didn't so much as move. If he could have backed unnoticed from the room and simply eavesdropped for the remainder of the conversation, he would have, if only to save his cousin embarrassment and so that Gil would divulge the full story without distraction.

She jilted him?

"I was—I was going to defend her. You know about that wretch Dailey—what he'd already done. And then to—it was his fault that man Fleming attacked her!" Wright's fists clenched, and the burst of rage helped stave off more embarrassing emotions. But soon enough his face darkened again, and he took hold of Sophie's hand without even realizing it, clutching it so hard that she winced. "I should not have left her the past few days. That was my downfall. My mistake. But there was the corn harvest to oversee—I couldn't leave it all to Father—and there was Slapbang—"

"Of course, of course," soothed Sophie, wishing she might withdraw her hand.

"She told me it would have made no difference, if I had been beside her every minute these last few days," he went on hoarsely, "but of course it would have. It must have." He tugged on his forelock. "She said we would not suit and thanked me. She said she would prefer to leave her defense—if any defense was necessary—to her family. 'If any defense was necessary'! What will that ineffectual old father or young brother do to defend her? And how much less could her old uncle or younger cousins deal with Dailey? I was going to shoot the man. That would have put him in his place! But now—now—now Miss Ellsworth says no, thank you, and I haven't the right and would I please go with her good wishes and—by the by—deliver some bottle of something-or-other to the deanery with this note from her?" With a groan, he released Sophie to bury his face in his hands. "I have gone from her intended husband to her errand boy!"

"Oh, Gil," Sophie sighed. She would have patted him with the hand that still worked, but she was afraid of him grabbing it and crushing it as he had the other. But her voice was tender, sorry. A balm to him.

At the sound of it, the sweetness of it, he raised his head and looked at her. Really *looked* at her.

Discomfited, she blushed faintly and shrunk back.

"I should have loved you, Sophie," said Gilbert Wright.

She went a glowing red, as if she had ignited, and Kenner thanked God that embarrassment prevented her glancing at him. What was happening? Was Sophie about to get everything she ever wanted? Her brother could hardly sustain interest in the question, though, because his legs had gone weak for altogether different reasons. If it would not have drawn attention to himself, he would have been glad to collapse into a chair.

Because Miss Ellsworth was...free.

Free!

"I should have loved you, Sophie," Wright repeated, his voice growing stronger. "Miss Ellsworth turned my head all right, but it's been you who's loved me all along."

"Gil—"

"—And been faithful to that love—unlike her—"

"Gil—!" cried Sophie more sternly, for her cousin had slid from his chair onto one knee, seizing her mangled hand between both his own. "Gil, do stop."

"No, Sophie. I won't now. I know I've been cruel to you. I've taken you for granted and ignored you because you've always been there. I've pretended not to know what you felt for me—not to see what was plain for all the world to see—"

With a strength that belied her smaller frame, Sophie ripped her hand from his and shot to her feet. "*Stop*, Gil. I won't hear this. You're out of your mind because Miss Ellsworth won't marry you, but that doesn't mean you should go proposing to the very next person you run across. Now, I'm sorry for you, but I would not be your friend if I let you do this now."

Kenner was torn between admiration for Sophie's unexpected spirit and dismay that she would lose her opportunity. It was natural that she would resent the timing of her cousin's proposal, but if she did not give Gil *some* encouragement, his impulse would surely pass.

Therefore Kenner broke his silence. "Soph," he murmured.

It was enough.

Wright's head snapped around. "Oh—come back, have you?" Colouring, he clambered to his feet. "If you were listening to that, you, for one, must be delighted."

"Delighted that you're finally being kinder to my sister?" asked Kenner mildly.

"Delighted that Miss Ellsworth has sent me packing."

"What do you mean by that, Gil?" demanded Sophie. "I know you and Simon don't always get along, but that doesn't mean he wishes ill upon you."

"Never mind that now," Kenner said tightly. "That's between Gil and me. But listen to me, Sophie: are you very certain you don't want to hear him out?"

"I don't need you making my proposals for me," bit out Wright, his chest swelling.

"Nor do I need you *accepting* any for *me*, Simon," Sophie added, taking her brother by surprise. She crossed her arms over her chest and almost glared at him.

Kenner held up his hands to her in placation. "I only thought—"

"You thought," jeered Wright. "It sounds like you can keep your thoughts to yourself, Simon, or save them for the pulpit. Because Sophie can accept her own proposals."

And then Sophia Katherine Kenner took both brother and cousin aback, emitting a yelp of pure frustration, her mild brown eyes glowing with unfamiliar fire. "Yes, *Gilbert*. I can accept my own proposals. And I can *refuse* them, too. Look—I don't mean to be unkind about it, especially since you are down in the mouth at present, but once you come to your senses I think you'll be just fine, Gil—if not outright relieved—that I am refusing."

He sputtered for some moments, going alternately red, then pale, then red again. "You—can't mean that, Sophie!"

At his dumbstruck dismay, the anger which had flooded her soon ebbed. She was utterly unused to hurting people's feelings and wondered how a girl like Lily Ellsworth stood it. "I'm sorry, Gil. I'm afraid I do mean it. I thank you, but I don't want to marry you."

"But—but you've loved me all your life!"

"I have—or, I thought I did," she admitted. "But I suppose Miss Ellsworth is not the only person who has grown to understand her own heart better recently."

His brow grew thunderous, his famous sweet temper giving way to belligerence again. "That's fine, Sophie. Just fine. But be warned: I won't ask again."

"I know, Gil. I don't expect you to." She reached for him but thought better of it. Her hand dropped back to her side.

Vickery appeared with sandwiches on a plate, and Wright rejected them with an angry wave.

"Oh, Gil," mourned Sophie. "What—will you do now?"

"Do?" He clapped his hat back on his head so hard it pressed his hair in his eyes, and he was forced to adjust it. "Why, I'll leave you to marry who you will, Sophie."

"Thank you," she said meekly.

He was already moving to the door, Vickery scooting out of his way. "And I'll go back to Meadowsweep and help my father finish the corn harvest, and I'll see all those people coming to talk to me about stud fees for Slapbang in the spring, and I'll leave the Ellsworths to salvage what is left of Miss Ellsworth's reputation however they see fit. It's nothing to me. I wash my hands of the entire business."

"Of course," said Sophie.

"But first," snarled her cousin, "I'll deliver that damned bottle of whatever-it-is and the confounded note to the deanery."

With that, he pushed his way out, not waiting for Vickery to open the door and shutting it behind himself with a reverberating slam.

Chapter Twenty-Six

A Prebendary was offered me, as they call it, it was a good fat Benefice, and I accepted it.
— Erasmus, *All the familiar colloquies of Desiderius Erasmus,* trans. N. Bailey (1725)

Unbelievable," repeated Lily. She read the first paragraph of the very long letter again and then rotated the sheet to read its crossed conclusion. "The man will not listen to me, and you must answer him, Papa."

"Who is it from, my dear? Mr. Wright?"

The Ellsworths were gathered at breakfast. Their last breakfast all together, for it was the day all of them but Lily would return Tyrone to Winchester College to begin his fourth year.

With a scoffing sound, Lily crumpled the letter in a ball and tossed it down the table to him. "*Not* Mr. Wright. Mr. Wright has too much pride to ask me again, not to mention I do not think he could write a letter this long if his life depended on it. No, Papa—it's from that Mr. Dailey, of course! He insists that if I am not going to marry Mr. Wright, I must marry *him*, because he feels responsible for all that has happened."

"He's right about that," interjected Araminta, picking tea leaves out of her cup with her spoon.

"I don't care if he's right about it. I won't marry him. I never want to see the man again. And I won't even answer him. Please, Papa, can you do it? And be very firm and ask him never to trouble me again? Please?"

"Better do it, Father, or Lily will make me run him through," said Tyrone.

Thus appealed too, a chivalric light kindled in Mr. Ellsworth's countenance. "My dear girl, you may depend on me. I will be very plain with him. And Bobbins—" he addressed the footman "—if any further correspondence comes from this Dailey fellow, Miss Ellsworth is not even to know of it. It must come directly to me."

Bobbins bowed in acknowledgement, and the Ellsworth patriarch beamed around the table as if looking for another damsel to save from distress. Happily for him, Mrs. Ellsworth was reading her own correspondence and began to shake her head and click her tongue over the note she had received.

"Oh, my. My, my. I am glad Mr. Dailey is settled, for here is more news."

"What is it, my love?" prompted Mr. Ellsworth with a fond smile.

She lay the paper down. "My brother Clifford writes to me to say that Mr. Whisp the prebendary has died."

At this, the younger Ellsworths gawped at her, for the name of Whisp was infamous among them at Hollowgate, following the events surrounding Florence's and her father's broken engagements the previous year.

"Do you mean *old* Mr. Whisp?" asked Lily. "The father-in-law of *that woman*?"

"Yes," answered her stepmother hastily, throwing her a cautioning glance. The less said about *that woman,* the better. "The older Mr. Whisp, who has held one of the prebendarical stalls for decades and yet has been absent in Weymouth for—oh—years and years. He has died."

"The rest of the family won't come back to Winchester, will they?" was Lily's next horrified question.

"Who knows? Perhaps the bereaved dowager Mrs. Whisp and her other son might—the one not married to...that woman, I mean. If they don't, they will have to do something about the house, or it will go to wrack and ruin."

Some conjecture followed, about whether the younger Mr. Whisp—was his name Mr. Edmund Whisp?—would indeed return, and whether he was married or had children, and so on. But it was Lily who said after a few minutes, "Will the bishop appoint a new prebendary to replace the deceased Mr. Whisp?"

"He will. There must be twelve in total, as each one is required to be in residence at the cathedral for one month of the year at least."

"But the late Mr. Whisp was never there!" Araminta protested.

Mrs. Ellsworth sighed. "No, he wasn't. He had a dispensation from the king because of his wife's ailments. It allowed him to be excused, but still to collect all the 'power, profits, emoluments, and advantages' the position granted him. It was a sore point with the dean and chapter that others must do Mr. Whisp's work for him, and I imagine the bishop will choose his replacement carefully."

Lily crumbled her toast as she thought. "Mama—does Mr. Gregory have any guesses whom the bishop will appoint?"

"What do we care?" asked Araminta, tossing a scrap of cured kipper into the air for Snap to catch. "We never attend service there."

"My brother hopes Mr. Grimley the deacon will be considered," Mrs. Ellsworth mused, "but Bishop North is known for distributing much of his patronage to family members."

"Ah," said Lily. "Then it will go to whoever marries Miss Carlingford."

"Most likely." Mrs. Ellsworth refilled her husband's teacup. "To be frank, I am going to encourage my brother to try his luck with her, although she is quite young and will have many to choose from."

Lily having been the only one besides Mrs. Ellsworth to lay eyes on Miss Carlingford, she was the only one compelled to hide her skepticism at this suggestion. Indeed, what young lady with eyes to her would choose Mr. Gregory—surely twenty years her senior and bluff and slightly ridiculous—when she might have someone closer in age? Someone whip-thin and graceful—a man clever and keen, on whose words his congregation hung?

When her family had gone, along with two under-footmen to carry Tyrone's trunk, Lily made her laborious way to the drawing room, bored at the thought of sewing (after so much sewing for her brother) and wishing for the thousandth time that her ankle didn't prevent her from walking out. It was not that she was particularly desirous of going into town with her family—with news of her broken engagement so fresh, as well as the nine days' wonder of the attack on her, the Ellsworths were not without courage to be seen in public. But Lily wouldn't have minded wandering the grounds of Hollowgate. As it was, she leaned her crutches against the pianoforte and sat down to play.

The sheet music for "True Lover's Farewell" was buried under some other pieces, but Lily plucked it out and placed it on the stand. She was rusty and had to pick her way through a few times before it flowed, but when it did, she began to sing:

"'O fare you well, I must be gone
And leave you for a while:
But wherever I go, I will return,
If I go ten thousand mile, my dear,
If I go ten thousand mile.'"

During the second verse her fingers stumbled, and there was a moment when only her voice was heard: "'Ten thousand miles it is so far—"

But not only her voice.

A second one. A clear, warm tenor. "—To leave me here alone..."

Lily spun around. "Mr. Kenner!"

It was indeed he, leaning negligently in the doorway. How long he had been there was impossible to tell, but a corner of his mouth curved, and he gave her a little bow "I beg your pardon for intruding, Miss Ellsworth. I heard the music and told your footman I would announce myself."

"Oh?" Her voice was not as steady as she would have liked. "That seems a decision Bobbins should have allowed me to make. Supposing I did not want to receive callers?"

"Have you ever turned callers away?" he asked mildly. "I am far more used to finding a full room when I visit, so if I were refused entrance, the rejection would feel deeply...*personal.*"

"I am part of a large family," Lily replied, closing the lid on the piano keys. Her heart was drumming, and she found it difficult to meet his gaze. "Which means half of those present are *always* present. And therefore the rooms always seem full."

"And yet not today."

"And yet not today," she agreed. "They have gone to take Tyrone back to school. We always do go—all of us. Even Snap. If not for my ankle, I would have been with them, and Bobbins would have told you quite honestly that no one was home." She threw him a challenging look. "And perhaps, now that you know they are gone, you would rather not stay?"

He appeared to be weighing something in his mind but then said, "I'm indeed sorry to miss them, but as a matter of fact, I did particularly hope to speak with you today. To see how you were doing."

The kindness in his words made her insides clench most painfully with hope, and it was all she could do to keep her face impassive. She mustn't hope. She had no reason to hope. Hoping hurt.

Lily took up her crutches again (shaking her head when she saw him take a step toward her) and made her careful way to the sofa. She had hoped before, when he and Sophie brought the crutches, only to learn she was their good deed for the day, before they went to dance attendance on Miss Carlingford. Why would today be any different? To suppose she was anything more than another one of the curate's clerical calls would be dangerous. Dangerous to her heart and her peace of mind because, most likely, she was just a name on his list of the day's obligations, just after Mr. Harvey and just before Mrs. Hambly.

It was the bitterness of this thought which made her say ungraciously, "Won't you sit down, or do you prefer to loom over me?"

He raised his eyebrows in mock astonishment. "Such a peculiar word choice. But, when one is my height, 'looming' is often an unintentional consequence. I suppose tall men are accused of 'looming' and short men of 'lurking.' However, I will accept your kind offer and be seated."

But Lily was still resenting his possible pity. Would he skip off to Miss Carlingford's side, when his duties were done?

"Mr. Beckford came to assess my progress yesterday," she announced, "and he says I am coming along nicely, so you needn't be concerned. I don't mean to sound discourteous, but I confess to disliking heartily calls motivated by clerical kindness."

"Splendid," he returned, "because I am not making one."

This took her up short. "You're not?"

"No, Miss Ellsworth. I was calling as a friend. But perhaps you have no liking for those visits either?"

"No—no—visits from friends are—they're quite all right."

She was right to be suspicious, Kenner thought. He had asked himself the same question as he walked over from the rectory: *why* was he calling on her now? He would do better by far to keep his distance at present. There was a tricky labyrinth to be threaded, and no step in his planned route would be aided by calling on Miss Ellsworth.

And yet here he was.

Because he could not resist. Resist seeing her again, knowing she was free and that he was free to do everything in his power to win her.

Of course, seeing her and threading a tricky labyrinth with success would mean nothing if she didn't like him at all. But even if she thought she did not like him, she had to *feel* it, didn't she? That there was something in the air between them, in the friction between them. When he nettled her and her blue eyes flung sparks, he could hardly be criticized for wanting to do it again. And again.

He heard himself say, "I come, therefore, as a friend, to see how you fare after your broken engagement."

Lily drew herself up. "We might be...friends, Mr. Kenner, but you touch upon a very private matter, even if Mr. Wright is your cousin."

"You're probably right. I beg your pardon." He smiled at her beneficently.

While he looked at her, Lily looked at the carpet. And then at the (empty) fireplace. And then at her hands.

It would be her turn to introduce a subject she thought more acceptable, but Lily's curiosity overcame her, as he hoped it would.

"I suppose there is a lot of talk about it—my broken engagement? My family doesn't mention it, naturally."

"Oh, I don't know about 'a lot' of talk. It isn't in the *Chronicle* this time; nor have I seen any hand-bills posted on the matter, so one might almost call the level of gossip a falling-off from your zenith."

An unexpected giggle took her, and she raised her eyes to his again. "I've become somewhat notorious, I'm afraid. Have you considered it might be dangerous to call yourself my friend?"

"I have, as a matter of fact."

The honesty of this reply sobered her soon enough, it being exactly what she feared, and her reply was stiff. "Well, then. I am surprised you've come."

"Are you?" His tone was bland. "That's a hit at my courage, I suppose."

"No. I think you courageous enough," she rejoined. "If it was anything, it was a hit at your wiliness. I think of you as a person who makes calculations, and I do not see how...continuing to look kindly on someone who has been in as much trouble as I have of late will aid your cause."

It was his turn to be uncomfortable, and he shifted in his chair. Then he rose and wandered the room, skirting the furniture and pausing at one of the windows before settling at the mantel.

"What cause would that be, Miss Ellsworth?" he ventured at last. His pale eyes met hers in the looking glass.

Her chin rose. "Why, the cause of climbing high in your profession, sir. I am not the only person in Winchester people like to talk about, I'm afraid. Perhaps others don't speak of it to your face, but I can assure you that your ambitions interest those around you nearly as much as my misadventures. They say you might end in a bishopric, if you play your best card."

"Hmm." He tapped the glass cover of the ormolu clock face. "Very helpful to know. And which 'best card' did everyone have in mind?"

Lily threw caution to the winds. "Can't you guess? You must not be as clever as I gave you credit for. Your best card, sir, is to woo and win Bishop North's grandniece. Miss Carlingford. Only imagine the doors which would fly open for you! My stepmother tells me the bishop makes a firm practice of advancing his relations. If you say you have not considered it, no one would believe you."

Slowly, reluctantly, he said, "I have considered it."

The admission infuriated her. It was unjust, she knew. What unmarried clergyman in all Hampshire had not considered it, if he had two wits to rub together? But she wanted him to deny it! To declare himself above such things, even if it wasn't true! What devil had prompted her to bring it up at all, except that she wanted to hear from his own lips that he cared nothing for bishoprics and bishop's grandnieces?

Her laugh was brittle. "If young ladies were allowed to place bets on anything and everything as young men may, I would put a hundred guineas on *you*, Mr. Kenner, to carry away the prize."

"Only a hundred guineas?" he growled. "Do you think my odds so slim?"

Angrier and angrier with herself and with him, Lily's fingernails dug into the sofa brocade. "Well, you *are* a mere curate, sir. So if she is ambitious for her future husband, she might like to begin a rung or two higher on the ladder. Say, with—with Mr. Gregory or Mr. Fields—both rectors in their own right. But I daresay you are younger and better looking, and she might weigh those more heavily."

"You have given this a great deal of thought, Miss Ellsworth," he said, his voice smooth again.

"Everyone has!" she retorted, reddening.

"No, no. I don't say it as a criticism," soothed Mr. Kenner. He abandoned the mantel and returned to his chair, at once too close and too disconcerting. "Please—tell me more. If I did indeed aspire to be a bishop and sit in the House of Lords one day, tell me the exact steps I should take."

Her bosom swelled, and Lily did not know whether she would rather have a good cry or bring one of her crutches down on his instep. Horrid man!

Glaring at his unreadable expression, Lily little suspected Kenner was thinking how like a wrathful angel she looked, come to pour her golden vial upon the earth. Which angel would she be? he mused.

The fourth, perhaps. The one whose vial, poured out on the sun, would "scorch men with fire."

"I don't suppose you need any advice, Mr. Kenner," Lily said crisply, "on how to go about winning Miss Carlingford. You know how to dance and speak and play your violin. It's more than most men can do. You might even arrange for her to see you shooting your arrows—"

"—Though I would never dream of shooting one anywhere near her lovely head," he interjected.

And then Lily's hand did jerk toward her crutches, but she drew it back in time. Mr. Kenner had placed no especial emphasis on the word *her*, but he did not need to—Lily caught the allusion clearly enough. Briefly, her cheek worked. Oh, so Miss Carlingford also had a "lovely" head, did she?

"No, indeed," she answered sweetly. "What need could there be for so brutish an action? Miss Carlingford appears to be all that is charming and amiable. Therefore threats would not be required, though I might warn you to keep some of your more villainous thoughts to yourself."

"My 'villainous thoughts'?" repeated Kenner. "As I have said before, every man, being born to trouble is guilty of such. But when one is in the company of an angel like Miss Carlingford, I declare, all wicked thoughts fly straight out of my head."

"Isn't that curious?" Lily said archly. "Because when you are in my company, sir, your wicked thoughts seem rather to fly straight out of your *mouth*."

That made him chuckle in genuine amusement and grin at her, looking so boyish for a moment that she felt her temper abruptly abandon her. Oh, dear.

"Ah, Miss Ellsworth—what is it about you that makes me such a reprobate? The Good Book says, 'When the wicked are multiplied, transgression increaseth.' Miss Ellsworth, I must beg you not to increase my transgression."

Though his words were teasing, a shadow came over her face.

"Yes, well," she fumbled, pretending to adjust the light blanket she had placed for modesty over her legs. "That is precisely it. As your...friend, I would not like to increase your transgression. It would be—*I* would be—an obstacle in the path to your eventual bishopric."

Bishopric be damned, Kenner almost declared, chagrined to see her withdraw from him.

"Therefore," Lily continued, steeling herself, "my first recommendation would be that you stay away from Hollowgate. For a time, at least. You and Sophie both. My continual scrapes and scandals will do you no end of mischief if you do not distance yourself from them." When he was about to speak, she held up an imperious hand. "No, no—you may not interrupt. You asked for the steps you should take to ascend the bishop's throne, so it is only courteous that you hear me out while I give them. Firstly, then, stay away from Hollowgate. Secondly, flatter and dance attendance on Miss Carlingford. By doing so, you might be named a prebendary of the cathedral, in place of the late Mr. Whisp. You have heard of the opening?"

Kenner sat back in his chair, one leg crossed over the other and his eyes now hooded. "I have."

"When you are no longer a mere curate and have been graced with a considerable income and a house in the close, you will be deemed by all and sundry a Promising Young Man, and the ripe plum that is the bishop's grandniece will tumble into your lap."

Nodding slowly, he regarded her another moment. "That's all? Those are my three steps? Stay away from you and your evil reputation; win the well-connected Miss Carlingford; secure the prebendary position. These things done, my ascent will dazzle and end in a bishop's chair?"

"Those are my recommendations. If you succeed in winning Miss Carlingford, your path thereafter will be smooth and clear, and you will enjoy as much as Bishop North's patronage can do for you."

"But supposing Miss Carlingford and I don't suit? We've only spoken a few times in company, you know."

"Pooh!" Lily dismissed this.

"You scoff, and yet, if I am not mistaken, this was the reason you gave for not marrying my cousin."

She shot him a sharp look. "Well, and what if it was? I spent enough time with Mr. Wright in enough circumstances to judge that we would not—make each other happy, ultimately." She smoothed the blanket another time and picked a strand of hair from it. "Did—he tell you that, or is it a matter of public record?"

"Gil said so."

"Oh. I did not know—you were so confidential."

Kenner shrugged. Then he uncrossed his legs and sat forward again, elbows on his knees. "And there are so many ways in which couples may not suit! Even adequate time spent in each other's company might not reveal all. To turn the subject slightly—has it ever struck you as odd, Miss Ellsworth, that, Mr. Dailey aside, men and women of our class generally refrain from...intimate embraces...until we are engaged?"

She certainly never expected this direction for the conversation, and she felt her face warm. The question could only be rhetorical. Watching him warily, Lily said, "That is turning the subject with a will, I would say!"

"Is it? Bear with me, then. You see, I mean to point out your unusual situation. That is, Miss Ellsworth, unlike most of your peers, you have had the opportunity to compare the—caresses—of two gentlemen already. And, were you to become engaged a second time—"

"You are certainly right in saying such—activities—can be revealing, Mr. Kenner," she interrupted quickly. "Though in Mr. Dailey's case, I did not need his advances to show me he would never do. And in Mr. Wright's—" she broke off, swallowing. "But this is none of your business, sir. I cannot imagine where you are possibly going with these musings."

"Oh, nowhere. Nowhere at all. I was just thinking of myself and Miss Carlingford, I suppose. What would happen if I engaged myself to her, and I then traded on the privileges that granted, only to find that...kissing her...was not so pleasurable as I imagined? I wish

I, like you, might have some other examples from which to draw comparisons."

"Hard luck for you, I suppose," she answered ruthlessly, praying he didn't notice the tremble that shook her. "And I must say, I think we have spent enough time on this most inappropriate subject."

"Mm. You're probably right, Miss Ellsworth. It must be our transgression increasing again."

"*I* didn't bring up the subject of kissing!" she protested. "So I am in no way to blame for where we find ourselves."

His eyes dropped briefly to her lips. "Aren't you?"

Those rosy lips parted, nonplussed.

But Kenner then gave a light sigh and rose to his feet. "Well, I have no more excuse for lingering. You have given me my orders, and now I must carry them out. But, Miss Ellsworth, if I am not to see you for some time—until I am safely made a prebendary or engaged to Miss Carlingford—whichever comes first—allow me to say I cherish our disinterested friendship more than ever. I can do nothing for you, and you can do nothing for me (nothing helpful, at least); therefore we may trust each other's motives as entirely of the purest."

"Yes," said Lily, her spirits sinking to see him go. And was he really going to take her advice? Could he not tell she spoke in sarcasm and irritation?

"And therefore," he went on, "you will not suspect me of anything, will you, if I ask that we shake hands on our friendship?"

"No-o-o...I guess not."

Hesitantly, she extended her pretty little hand to him, expecting him to seize it in a firm grip. But he took it gently, lightly, and, before she knew what he was about, he had turned it and carried it to his lips.

And then, before she could recover, he went, throwing over his shoulder a soft, “Good-bye, Miss Ellsworth.”

Chapter Twenty-Seven

Should her destination be to remain an inhabitant of her father's house, cheerfulness, good temper, and obliging resignation of her will to that of others, will be there equally her duty, and her interest.
— Priscilla Wakefield, *Reflections in the Present Condition of the Female Sex with Suggestions for Its Improvement* (1798)

Lily would remember that month of September, 1801, as the most dismal of her young life. Tyrone was gone; Minta spent her days at school; her stepmother taught Beatrice most mornings. Lily sat, sat, sat, or crutched around the house and grounds, but never very long or very far. Florence and her aunt Jeanne visited from time to time, but having their own busy lives, they did not come more than a couple times in a week, and that left many hours to fill. Out of sheer boredom, Lily asked her father to show her how he kept the estate's account books, with its income of rents and farm produce, and its outgoings of tithes and taxes and wages, along with the household expenses which he transferred monthly from Mrs. Ellsworth's house book. Her interest pleased him, as did her aptitude with numbers, and it was both agreeable and unusual to spend time together. She then took to reading with Beatrice or accompanying her sisters as they practiced dancing. She made Florence a matching cushion and Snap a new dog bed. She lived very, very quietly, that all the whispers about her might die away from lack of fuel. And if her goal in life had been to become the pleasant spinster daughter and sister on whom the family could rely, she would have been supremely satisfied with her progress.

However, such was not Lily's goal. Nor had it ever been. It was not that she still cherished any ambition to be the Belle of Winchester—that had not proved the unqualified delight she hoped. But she wanted more than this invisible, uneventful, immobile life.

Therefore September was dismal.

And worst of all, Mr. Kenner heeded her advice and kept away. He and Sophie both.

The rest of the Ellsworths saw the Kenners at church, of course, and still spoke of his marvelous sermons and puzzled over why they had not called at Hollowgate in so long—"Mr. Kenner even refused to come and play music with me again!" Araminta complained—but Lily neither saw them nor spoke of them.

She thought of Mr. Kenner, though. Plenty.

She wished she had not been so touchy the last time she saw him, when by his own admission he had called there in friendship. Suppose she did not see him again until he was already engaged to Miss Carlingford? And why on earth had she encouraged him in that pursuit and told him exactly how to go about it? Ten to one, if she had left him alone, he would have bungled the business, and then, with the bishop's grandniece out of the picture, he might eventually—when all the sensation Lily had caused died away to nothing, or nearly nothing—have come to see her in a different light. A bridal light. While it was true Lily could not bring him "power, profits, emoluments, and advantages" in the Church, it was nevertheless within her abilities to bring him profits and advantages of a worldly variety. *I can keep household account books too now*, she mourned to herself. *And pay visits to the poor without too much complaining. And my dratted ankle has taught me more patience. My sisters would tell him I have got better—kinder to them and more helpful! All this, when it's too late.*

Mr. Kenner would never reap these benefits now.

It was nearly Michaelmas when Florence rushed in one morning after breakfast, her normally pale cheeks rosy with fresh air and excitement, and Mrs. Ellsworth on her heels.

"Lily, dearest, look what we've brought you!" With a flourish, she stood aside to reveal a rickety wheeled chair. "I begged Miss Hambly to lend it to us, just for the day, even though old Mrs. Hambly never goes anywhere that I know of."

"Am *I* going somewhere?" Lily asked, her eyes lighting.

"Yes! To Haskins'—you know, the mercer in the Square. Our stepmother and I have need of your opinion."

"Oh—not Haskins'," Lily protested. "He's the one who wanted me to patronize him when I was engaged to Mr. Wright."

"Florence and I have decided you have hidden away long enough," Mrs. Ellsworth reproved. "The gossip has quieted, and Mr. Haskins is too good a businessman to mention your engagement now. Come, come—you love to shop. I want to choose new draperies for the nursery, and Florence wants to recover some chairs."

"And we can do neither without consulting you." Taking up one of the plumper cushions from the sofa, Florence plumped it further. "We will need this, I suspect, for it may be a bumpy ride."

It was, but not all the bumps were literal.

For, just after they jostled and jolted Lily's borrowed chair into town and passed the Black Swan Inn, who should they see approaching but the dean's wife Mrs. Fellowes? It would be hard to say which woman was most discomfited by this apparition. Mrs. Ellsworth, still conscious of abandoning her brother Mr. Gregory's house to marry Mr. Ellsworth? Florence, whose jilting of Mr. Gregory had caused him to flee St. Eadburh's in the first place? Or Lily, who had done her best to drive the woman to the wall, in return for giving up Gilbert Wright?

So uneasy were the Ellsworth women that it took Lily a moment to notice the dean's wife was not entirely tranquil herself. In fact, her greetings were as flustered as their own, and, so far from resenting any of them, she seemed at pains to be affable.

"...A pleasure to see you all. You have been very quiet at Hollowgate."

Mrs. Ellsworth murmured something about Lily's ankle.

"Of course, of course. So wise of you, Miss Ellsworth, to follow the doctor's orders."

"They say 'least said, soonest mended,'" answered Lily, "but I would add that, with a sprained ankle, 'least *done*, soonest mended' applies as well."

"Yes, too true." Mrs. Fellowes gave a most uncharacteristic anxious titter. "Both are true. Miss Ellsworth, in the interest of living at peace, I have been most *constant* in putting about how amicably you and my grandson parted."

"I thank you."

"I have even expressed my—approval—of you in general and my good wishes for your future happiness, which I hope has contributed to the affair—blowing over so—er—quickly."

"Has it?"

"I believe so."

"See, Lily?" Mrs. Ellsworth interposed. "I told you so."

"Then again I thank you, Mrs. Fellowes," said Lily. Her eyes held those of the dean's wife, and the woman gave a firm nod, which Lily interpreted correctly as, *I am a woman of my word, as you see.*

Lily's smile blossomed. "Yes—thank you for being a...peacemaker. It was indeed an amicable parting, and I, too, wish Mr. Wright all the best in his future endeavors."

"Delightful. Very good of you to say, Miss Ellsworth. Very affable."

The usually formidable woman was at such pains to be gracious that Lily wished she could remind her of the second half of her promise: to back Lily in the husband of her choice. But, it being impossible in such a setting, courteous bows were exchanged and the ladies proceeded their separate ways, no more being said among the Ellsworths than a "Whew! That went better than I thought it would" from Florence.

Haskins and Company, the premier mercer in Winchester, occupied a grand showroom in the Square, with walls of shelves displaying every kind of fabric for upholstery, draperies, and personal habiliment. Lily had heretofore spent all of her visits among the silks and stuffs and crapes and woolens, and she still shuddered to think of the array of Norwich crapes, which the Ellsworths had been obliged to wear when they were in mourning. But this day, after Mrs. Ellsworth and Florence helped her back onto her crutches to enter the shop, they directed their steps toward the household linens and furnishings.

As Mrs. Ellsworth predicted, Mr. Haskins made no mention at all of Lily's former engagement, only congratulating Florence on her recent marriage and venturing a hint or two at how Mrs. Ellsworth must be looking forward to her own "happy event." (Lily marveled inwardly at this. How *did* that man know everything? There had been no announcement, and the high waistlines of the day did not betray Mrs. Ellsworth's secret as yet.)

Her stepmother only demurred modestly, returning her attention to the materials he had pulled down for her. When, after a conference among them, she selected a silk-and-cotton ivory damask,

Mr. Haskins beamed. "Ah, a fortunate choice, that damask, and a fashionable one."

"Fashionable?" laughed Lily, nudging her stepmother. "Well, we would not want our nursery to be unfashionable. Suppose the baby were to object?"

"He can have no objection, for the damask is very fashionable," insisted Mr. Haskins. "Why Mr. Compton of the cathedral close just ordered twenty yards of this very fabric for the house behind the cloister."

Mrs. Ellsworth considered, picturing the close in her mind. "The house behind the cloister? Why, that one has been unoccupied for several years. Was it not assigned to the late Mr. Whisp, who already had his own house, which he did not live in either, being always in Weymouth?"

"Yes, madam. But now Mr. Compton says the house is to be made fresh for the new prebendary Mr. Simon Kenner, who will be appointed in October at the chapter meeting."

The ladies stared at him, and Lily gave a yelp.

As with Lily's erstwhile engagement and his guess at Mrs. Ellsworth's condition, the mercer appeared pleased to be the first with the news, rubbing his hands together complacently. But then he tapped the side of his long nose with a forefinger. "I mention this in confidence, you understand. I don't believe it has been announced yet, so please do not repeat it."

Mrs. Ellsworth assured him of their discretion, but then, sadly (in Lily's opinion), steered away from the fascinating subject into a discussion of yardage and linings and such, to which Lily contributed only a few absent rejoinders before whispering to her sister, "I'm not used to standing so long on crutches. I believe I'll sit down a minute."

It was a lie, she knew. It wasn't the crutches digging into her that made her think she might collapse; it was Mr. Haskins' thunderbolt. How Lily wished with all her heart that she was home in Hollowgate in her room! Wished it as strongly as she had wished all month to be out in the world again.

So...he had received the desired appointment! Mr. Kenner was to be the new twelfth prebendary of Winchester Cathedral, with all the benefits that entailed. He had succeeded in climbing higher on the ladder of his profession, and, at his young age, obtained a lofty, comfortable place that many an older clergyman would envy. And, she feared, what could this premature apotheosis mean, except that he had also succeeded with Miss Carlingford? He was not given this plum for being the dean's grandson alone, was he?

Lily had forgotten she was going to make her way to the sofas surrounding a table heaped with pattern books. No, she stood in the center of the showroom, sagging on her crutches and biting her lip in an effort to master her expression.

And this was where she came face to face with the young lady herself.

Miss Carlingford, in other words.

They had never before been introduced, but that they knew each other by sight was plain, for Miss Carlingford halted abruptly when their eyes met, and she went as pink as Lily was sure she herself must be.

Somewhere, in a corner of Lily's mind that wasn't frozen with horror, a stray thought popped up: why should Miss Carlingford blush? What reason would she have to be embarrassed by meeting with Lily Ellsworth? For her part, Lily had a thousand reasons to be embarrassed by encountering Miss Carlingford—a thousand reasons, all whip-thin with pale blue eyes, but there could be no possible reason for Miss Carlingford's alarm. That is, not unless she *knew something of Lily Ellsworth* that she would rather Lily Ellsworth not know she knew.

Was it possible Mr. Kenner had spoken to Miss Carlingford of her? But why, and what might he have said? How would Lily even have come up as a topic of conversation? She had a vision of the young lady saying drolly, "Oh, you're the curate of St. Eadburh's, are you? Isn't that where that scandalous Ellsworth family attends? I heard Miss Ellsworth kissed a strange man in public and embroiled herself with drunken vagabonds and then jilted your cousin Mr. Gilbert Wright." And then Mr. Kenner would have replied in his dry way, "I hope you will not hold me responsible for the antics of my congregation. It would take a more forceful clergyman than I to rein in the likes of a Miss Ellsworth. But then, she comes from a wild and disreputable family."

Neither young lady had yet managed to utter a single word before the onus of it all was taken from them by Mr. Wilfrey, the chief shop-man at Haskins and Company. The bespectacled, withered assistant rushed up to them clutching a pattern book, gasping, "Miss Carlingford! How glad I am you stopped to speak with Miss

Ellsworth. For you nearly forgot the silks pattern book, and what would a trousseau be without silks, I ask you?"

"Trousseau?" breathed Lily.

"Er—thank you," muttered Miss Carlingford, seizing the book from Mr. Wilfrey as if it were contraband to be hidden.

His ingratiating smile faltered when he glanced from one to the other, and then he began to back away with a series of bows, as if he were exiting a royal throne room. "Good afternoon to you both. Do let Haskins and Company know, Miss Carlingford, if we can answer any questions or supply samples or place orders..." Then, spinning on his heel, he darted off, calling, "Dobbs! Careful with those bolts! They're four shillings the ell."

Gathering herself, Miss Carlingford now dropped Lily a hasty curtsy and hurried for the street door without a word, carrying the pattern book in front of her as a shield.

"As if I could injure her," Lily murmured, watching her go. "As if she had not everything—*everything*—in her favor. Mr. Kenner, her silly bishop, a silk trousseau, the new house in the close. She need not dread me, no matter what Mr. Kenner might have told her."

Though it niggled at her, as what did not, this day? What might he have told her?

Later Lily would feel grateful. Grateful for the serendipitous outing to the mercer. Because it would have been much, much worse to learn of Mr. Kenner's engagement and appointment from the man himself. To have had no warning when he returned to Hollowgate—if he ever called again at Hollowgate—to tell her he had carried out her instructions to a tee and met with triumph upon triumph upon triumph.

Chapter Twenty-Eight

Is not this (as we say) as plain as Pottage, as clear as Crystal, to speak in your Dialect?
— John Hay, *Sound and solid reason against the Presbyterian prints* (1703)

"Mm-hm." With gentle hands, Mr. Beckford the doctor flexed Lily's foot. "Mm-hm." He rotated her ankle. He had her place her foot flat on the floor while she moved her knee slowly to one side and then the other.

"You have done well, Miss Ellsworth," he pronounced. "You have followed my orders, and your sprain has recovered nicely. I hereby give you permission to start placing weight upon it."

"You mean I may walk again?"

"You may try it. Let the pain be your guide. Put what weight you can on it, and when it grows sore or tired, then you must rest it again. If you try to do too much too soon, you will feel it, and your recovery will be that much longer."

"Yes, sir. Thank you."

"There's a good girl. It is none too soon, Miss Ellsworth, because you have lost a great deal of colour. Though the weather turns cooler, you must be more out of doors, until we have restored the roses to your cheeks."

"Hurrah!" shouted Araminta. "It's been tedious, Lily, having you confined to the sofa or limping and moping about. May we have Flossie and Robert and Uncle Charles and Aunt Jeanne for supper and dancing, Mama?"

"I don't think Lily is supposed to dance yet," Mrs. Ellsworth said doubtfully.

"But at least she no longer needs to take up the entire sofa."

"Very well, very well. But first Lily might begin by coming with us to church this Sunday."

It would be an exaggeration to say that the Ellsworths had been waiting with bated breath to hear Mr. Kenner's promotion announced (true to her word, Mrs. Ellsworth had not even mentioned it to her husband; nor did she and Lily discuss it), but the two women did exchange a meaningful glance when the Ellsworths entered the church, Lily making careful progress on her father's arm.

Lily had counseled herself strictly, in preparation for this moment. For her own protection, she would not look at Mr. Kenner or seek him out in any way she could avoid. To do so might reveal the sadness and longing and jealousy and resentment she carried inside. If his good fortune were made public, she would smile and look about and applaud or do whatever everyone else did. And if his engagement were also announced, she would do more of the same and wish him and Miss Carlingford all imaginable happiness. And otherwise she would try not to see or hear anything. Unless—unless there were some tiny opening, wherein she might convey to him her displeasure that he had talked of her to Miss Carlingford. But even to attempt that would be dangerous—like trying to pour out a serving of the ocean into a thimble-sized cup.

Lily had the advantage of Mr. Kenner, at least. He had no preparation whatsoever for her appearance after an entire month of not seeing her, and for one dreadful minute he could remember neither the order of worship nor what he was even doing there. His flock took their seats in the usual fashion and turned expectant faces toward him—with the exception of Miss Ellsworth, who kept her bonnet lowered. But Kenner sat like a man turned to stone, his lips parted, and his eyes locked on the window scene of St. Eadburh cleaning the shoes of her fellow nuns. Puzzled, the congregation swiveled to consider the stained-glass depiction anew, and Mrs. Pease was heard to click her tongue and declare it needed a proper cleaning.

It was Sophie Kenner who finally cleared her throat lightly—and then once more, *loudly*—and jerked her head toward the lectern. Kenner sprang—lunged, almost—for the reading desk, flinging open his portfolio with such lack of control that papers flew out, and he was compelled to retrieve them. When he straightened again, he saw the concern on everyone's faces—though Miss Ellsworth continued to look at her lap.

Compose yourself, man!

A service never seemed longer, both for him who led it and for her who spent it staring at her hands. Kenner read three lines from the wrong Scripture passage and had to begin again. He lost his place in his sermon notes (Lily had sneezed). And while she had the easier task, simply keeping her head lowered, she could not shut out his warm, melodious, entrancing voice.

Would he give up his curacy, when he was a prebendary, she wondered? Would St. Eadburh's see him no more? He would remove from the rectory to the house behind the cloister, it seemed. And even had he not been going to marry Miss Carlingford, Lily would have been sad to think he would no longer be their neighbor. But if he was indeed going to marry Miss Carlingford, then sadness would be preferable to Lily having to call on the new Mrs. Kenner and Mrs. Kenner on her. No, no—he had better remove to the cathedral close.

Maybe Robert and Florence would let her pay a long visit to their house in Kingsgate Street, and she could attend St. Michael's with them. And maybe time would pass, and Lily would meet another young man—*not* a clergyman, she vowed—whom she liked as well as Mr. Kenner. After all, it had taken her quite some time to begin to like him, and it was sheer misfortune that she seemed to be making up for her delay by liking him far, far too much, in a veritable, heavy, crushing, heap of liking. That is, she liked him unbearably when he wasn't vexing her. Because—truly—what *had* the man said to Miss Carlingford, that she should be so embarrassed to meet Lily?

If only his dreaded announcements could hurry up and be announced, so their horribleness would be over and done with! It would be better than having them hang over her thus, like the sword of Damocles.

I will ask him about them myself, she decided. *Cut the single hair with my own hands and let the sword fall.*

Yes. Ask him point-blank—when no one was within earshot. If the sword was going to behead her, the sooner it happened, the better, so she could go about the business of putting her head back on.

Kenner was involved in his own internal debate. He stood at the door, bowing to his parishioners and parroting meaningless remarks like a puppet whose puppet-master was simultaneously reading a book or thinking about his dinner. And all along, he was aware of the Ellsworths and Miss Ellsworth in particular, drawing nearer.

"You have to tell her, Simon," murmured his sister beside him, following his gaze. "Someone must. We cannot just let her learn of it."

"I know it," he replied. Yes, there was much to tell Miss Ellsworth. He had succeeded, praise God, in threading his labyrinth. There was nothing now to prevent him from making a beginning. *But when? How?*

His bows grew ever more cursory and his greetings more inattentive. Mrs. Pease told him the stained glass needed cleaning, and he replied, "Yes, isn't it marvelous?" Miss Weeks said she was very,

very sorry, but she could not help with the church flowers this week, and Kenner said, "Thank you. Thank you very much." Mr. Beckford reported that, after another relapse, Mr. Harvey was up and about again, only to have the curate reply, "I noticed she was not on crutches today. Splendid."

And then the Ellsworths were before him.

"When are you ever going to call on us again?" demanded Araminta. "Was it only Tyrone you liked, and now that he is gone to school, you can't be bothered?"

"Soon, soon," he answered vaguely, even as Mrs. Ellsworth chided, "Minta…" and Sophie Kenner made an impatient movement.

"Miss Ellsworth," said Kenner, thinking he would take the bull by the horns, "we are glad to see you on your feet again."

"Thank you." For the first time that day she lifted her eyes to him. Intent, vivid blue eyes, in which he detected both challenge and accusation. Accusation?

His throat seemed to close. Mr. Ellsworth was bowing to him and beginning to lead his family away, but when Kenner tried to say something—anything—to detain them, he only coughed—choked, rather—his heart jumping and thumping as if resolved on escaping his chest.

It was Sophie who saved the day.

"Lily!" she called after her. "Wait, Lily. Will you come to the rectory just now? It has been ever so long since you have. We would love you to join us for a little luncheon and to—to talk about the flowers for the church. Miss Weeks says she cannot help us. If you are not too tired...and Simon and I will ensure you make it back to Hollowgate, even if we have to carry you pick-back in turns."

Lily turned at once. "I will come. I would be glad to." Ignoring the disappointed looks on her sisters' faces for not being included in the invitation, Lily accepted Sophie's extended arm.

"Here, Simon," said his sister, "you help Miss Ellsworth. You're stronger."

"No," Lily interjected, before he had even moved. "Thank you. It isn't far to the rectory, and I think I am perfectly able to walk unaided, if we don't walk too fast."

There were three fluttering hearts as they entered the rectory, three people trying to decide on the proper plan of attack. Sophie thought she would let Simon take the lead. Kenner thought he would indeed take the lead, if he could master himself enough to speak.

And Lily—well, Lily had already made up her mind.

No sooner was the maid Vickery dismissed and sent to make a tray of sandwiches than Lily said in a bright, bracing tone, "Mr. Kenner, I hope you will forgive me, but curiosity and eagerness threaten to consume me."

"Oh?" He gestured her toward his favorite armchair with its matching footstool.

Lily took it obediently, but instead of elevating her ankle, she sat on the very front of the chair and pushed the footstool aside.

"Yes. It is just that, the other day, we—my stepmother, my sister Florence, and I—visited the mercer's in the Square, Haskins and Company, and Mr. Haskins let slip that the house in the close behind the cloister was being refurbished for its new occupants. And he—well, Mr. Haskins—said—"

"He mentioned my name?"

"Yes. He said you were to be the new prebendary! Is it really so?"

"...Yes."

Lily gave a firm nod. "Ah. I see. Yes. Well, I do congratulate you, then, on your success. It is just as I foresaw."

"The bishop told Simon it was a pleasure to have so qualified a candidate already known to him and in residence in Winchester," Sophie said proudly.

"How lovely. Though he could hardly do worse than old Mr. Whisp," Lily added with a grimace. "The late Mr. Whisp was never in Winchester that I knew of, leaving his duties to be covered by the other prebendaries. You will certainly be an improvement, Mr. Kenner, by the mere fact that you are neither dead nor gone to Weymouth."

"I must beware your honeyed blandishments, Miss Ellsworth," he replied, the joy of hearing her candor loosening his tongue. "After all, 'a man that flattereth his neighbour spreadeth a net for his feet.'"

His eyes gleamed at her, addling her considerably, and she rushed onward. "So—you'll be removing to the close! My family will be very sorry if, with your new duties, you give up the curacy of St. Eadburh's. But you will, I suppose—won't you?"

"I—haven't decided yet," he admitted. "I was going to speak with Mr. Gregory about it. If the rectory is unoccupied, he might be interested in resuming the duties of the parish himself, unless..."

"Unless he still wishes to avoid my family," Lily supplied. "Well, I cannot speak for my parents, but I know—my siblings would beg you to stay. Your preaching is much to be preferred over poor Mr. Pennyforth—"

"Poor, *dead* Pennyforth. I triumph once more, it appears. Miss Ellsworth, your flattery quite turns my head."

"Nonsense. I meant when he was alive, of course. And you're better than Mr. Gregory ever was, as I believe I've told you."

Placing a palm to his chest, Kenner bowed his head in ironic deprecation.

"In any event, when will it be common knowledge? My step-mother and I have said nothing to anyone of the matter, though we are bursting to."

"Soon enough. They were only...waiting for me to be ready to have it known."

He paused, thinking how to proceed, but Lily had turned to his sister. "What about you, Sophie, do you look forward to removing to the close?"

Biting her lip, Sophie regarded her brother. "Oh—as a matter of fact—Simon, would you object to my telling the other news? I must, mustn't I? Say I may—I cannot be easy until it is said!"

Lily drew a sharp breath. Here it was, then.

The shears.

They would cut the single hair from which the sword above her dangled. Lily shut her eyes ever so briefly, but it was no use. It didn't matter if she wanted to hear the news or not; the news would be told all the same. Therefore, despairingly, she struck in, her voice hard and determined in its cheerfulness.

"Why, Sophie, you may be easy at once, then. Because I already know the news."

"You...do?"

"I do." Lily tapped her forehead. "I know all. Because nothing escapes the net of Haskins and Company, it seems. But even they could not surprise me with it because I foresaw it, did I not?" This last she addressed to Mr. Kenner, favoring him with a glance as hard and bright as her words.

To her annoyance, the man looked bewildered. As bewildered as ever his cousin Gilbert Wright did when Lily rallied him. Honestly—it had been a month, but could he possibly have forgotten their conversation? The three steps she had given him to success...? Had she alone spent the month pondering and regretting and ruminating, while what affected her so deeply floated straight out of Mr. Kenner's head? Maddening man!

Indignation felt better than heartbreak, however, and Lily found the words coming more easily. "I know the rest of your news, Mr. Kenner. More than that, I know you have been talking of me behind my back, and I will take this opportunity to say that you had *no right* to do so. I don't know what you might have said, but I suspect it was deeply personal and private to me, and you had no business whatsoever sharing it with any other person. It has caused embarrassment and discomfort on all sides, and I hold you entirely to blame. In fact, I demand an apology."

For a second he only sputtered, his puzzlement deepening, and his stupid expression made Lily want to throw something at him. Both of them forgot all about Sophie's presence, or Lily would have seen that Sophie was equally mystified.

"But I—I've never said anything in my life to Haskins and Company," Kenner managed at last. "And never will, now that I know what truly indiscreet workers they employ."

"Haskins and Company!" shrilled Lily, rising to her feet and in no way appeased by his jest. "Who said anything about Haskins and Company?"

Her rising forced him to his own feet. "*You* did!"

"No, I said I heard about the news *at* Haskins and Company!"

"About the house in the close? About me becoming a prebendary?"

"No! I mean—yes—but that is not what I am now referring to, sir, and therefore you are being deliberately obtuse!"

Kenner passed a hand over his forehead. "I promise you, Miss Ellsworth, this obtuseness of mine is wholly unintentional. All right, then. Leaving aside whatever I might have said, to whomever I might have said it, let us begin at the beginning: what *additional* news did you learn of at the mercer's?"

"Your engagement of course!" Lily fairly roared.

"*My* engagement?"

She uttered a groan of exasperation. "Is your hearing going as well? Or are the words I'm using too difficult to understand?"

"I'm beginning to think anything might be possible."

"Lily," spoke up Sophie, startling the other two, "who told you Simon was engaged?"

"Uh—well—the shop-man did," she admitted. She crossed her arms over her chest. "He ran after Miss Carlingford with the silks pattern book and said she would need it for her trousseau."

"Aaaaaaahhh..." both Kenners breathed, comprehension dawning.

"And Miss Carlingford was most embarrassed to see me there, by which I could only assume that you had spoken of me to her." Lily's brow creased with a new thought. "I suppose it might have been *you* who spoke of me to her, Sophie." In which case she would have to apologize to Mr. Kenner and lash out at his sister, all of which sounded like too much at present.

"Lily," said Sophie again, "Simon isn't going to marry Miss Carlingford."

"What? Of course he is," Lily said blankly. "Or has he not even told you?"

"There's nothing for him to tell me. I promise you—he is not going to marry Miss Carlingford."

Baffled, Lily whirled on the man himself. "You're not engaged to Miss Carlingford?"

He was recovering his usual aplomb and said dryly, "Not that I know of."

"She may have been shopping for her trousseau," Sophie returned, frowning reproachfully at her brother's levity, "but she is not going to marry Simon."

"Then who on earth is the woman going to marry?" demanded Lily. Conscious of her knees weakening, she collapsed back into the armchair. She was *amazed*. No—amazed and relieved. An inexplicable bubble of laughter threatened to escape her.

"It's Gil, Lily," Sophie explained with a sigh and a pitying look. "Not Simon. Miss Carlingford is going to marry *my cousin Gil*."

Lily's astonishment robbed her of words. She stared from one Kenner to the other to see if they were playing a trick on her, but Sophie only looked sad and Mr. Kenner smug.

"Marry Mr. Wright?" echoed Lily, at length. "Mercy. Mr. Wright proposed to Miss Carlingford? But—but—how on earth did he even meet her?" And then she did laugh, long and merrily, though it was tinged with hysteria. "Now I understand." That is—now she understood both Mrs. Fellowes' and Miss Carlingford's embarrassment. They were embarrassed by his rapid defection. They were embarrassed because Lily didn't know.

"They met at the deanery," Sophie hastened to explain. "I believe the very day—the day—you ended your engagement with him. Oh, Lily, I hope you aren't terribly hurt. I know it does not say much for his constancy."

"His constancy? Nonsense. No—I am glad for him. I wish him every, every happiness." Lily said, her sincerity evident. Her laughter spilled out again. "It all makes sense now. She thought I would be angry that she was marrying Mr. Wright! Oh, dear me. No—I don't know her, but I wish them long life and countless blessings. May they prove admirably suited."

At her choice of words, Kenner raised a teasing eyebrow, and Lily was conscious of a warmth spreading through her, from her middle outward. A glow. She wanted to sing and rush about and embrace everyone and dance, all at the same time. She didn't care who married Gilbert Wright. He might marry anyone and everyone he pleased.

Because Mr. Kenner was not going to marry Miss Carlingford.

Mr. Kenner was not at the moment going to marry *anyone*. Which meant, of course, that he was going to marry Lily Ellsworth, if she had anything to say or do about it.

Oh, please, don't let it show, what I'm thinking. If it shows, I am lost. She didn't dare look at him, but the warmth spread to her face and fingers and toes, as if she were a bottle filled to the very top with bubbling, sparkling, rioting champagne. And then she had to peek at him—she couldn't help herself.

As if she had been speaking her thoughts aloud, the very moment she lifted her eyes they met his hooded ones, and all the champagne inside her turned at once to boiling water. *Caught!* If Mr. Beckford had seen her at that moment, he would have declared the roses returned to her cheeks with a vengeance. *Flossie always told me I wore my heart on my sleeve.* Lily wished she had her fan at hand, but there was no relief from his regard.

A corner of his mouth lifted, just one degree. And then one more. And then his lips made the slightest motion. A butterfly movement. A pursing, so fleeting she might have imagined it. Like a blown kiss.

My fan— Her breathing shallow, she tore her eyes away. *Oh, my kingdom for a fan.*

Sophie gave a sigh of relief. "How glad I am that you aren't distressed by it, Lily! I was on tenterhooks when I learned."

"Hmm? Oh—no—don't be anxious for me," Lily murmured. "I'll be just fine."

"Sophie," drawled Kenner, "would you mind seeing Vickery about the sandwiches, or am I the only one whose appetite is...whetted?"

His sister made to answer, but something in his expression stopped her. With a quick nod, she rose and left the room, shutting the door behind her.

In one smooth, feline motion, Mr. Kenner dropped into the chair beside Lily, and she felt the hair on the back of her neck stand. A panther and his prey. She could not run.

She had no desire to.

"So," Lily breathed, her gaze trained on his hand, with its long fingers curled around the end of the chair arm. "So you aren't going to marry Miss Carlingford, as I advised you."

"I am not."

"Well, then. That's—that's your loss."

"Is it?"

"Of course. Such a—nice young lady. And you let her get away. You—let your cousin marry her."

The fingers released the chair arm. Then she saw them reach—take a fold of her dress between them—and tug ever so gently.

"But I had to 'let her get away,'' he said softly. "I couldn't marry her."

"Oh?" Her heart was in her throat. "Why—whyever not?"

"Because the only person I intend on marrying, Miss Ellsworth, is *you*."

"Wh-what?"

"You heard me."

Another tug on her skirt. Slowly she raised her eyes. She thought she might tremble into pieces.

"You want to marry—me?"

"That's right," he whispered. "What do you think of that?"

She swallowed. Blushed. "I think—that's a lovely idea."

"Then come here."

Several, several minutes later, Lily straightened on his lap, laughing and pushing him away. "We have to stop—no—stop that! Vickery and Sophie will be back with the sandwiches any moment."

"You're right." Putting both hands at her waist, he lifted her off him, that he might go and push a chair against the door. "They'll understand what that means, I trust. Now where were we...?"

"Simon," she murmured, still later, as his lips brushed the length of her neck. "I can answer your question."

A bite at her earlobe. "Which question?"

"The one about kissing." She shut her eyes luxuriously. "I would say your kisses are considerably more pleasant than your cousin's. Not *quite* as pleasant as Mr. Dailey's, but they'll do."

"Vixen," he muttered, covering her mouth again.

It was later—*much* later—when Vickery and Sophie had been readmitted and the good news told and the sandwiches eaten and Kenner was walking her back on his arm to Hollowgate that Lily said, "It's too bad for you, marrying me. I maintain that Miss Carlingford would have helped you to that bishop's chair."

"Her marrying Gil might be helpful enough. And whoever said I wanted to be a bishop? I did want more than a curacy, I'll admit, however. Because how is a fellow to propose to a wealthy, beautiful young lady, if all he has to offer is a curate's salary and somebody else's rectory? Gil had me there, with his Meadowsweep inheritance and his confounded racehorse—"

"And don't forget the pineapples."

Laughing, he swung her arm. "How could I? You won't let me forget them."

"But seriously, Simon, should a rising clergyman marry a scapegrace like me?"

"I can't speak for every rising clergyman, but this particular one will be damned if he lets anyone else marry you. I think I've loved you since I saw you stripping my garden of every last blossom." Stopping her in the very road, he gave her several proofs of his sincerity.

"Simon! We are in public."

"If the Romsey Road is good enough for Walter Dailey, it's good enough for me."

Lily shoved him, laughing, but he seized her and kissed her again. "I'll let you go when you tell me how long you've loved me."

"Hmm...a difficult question, but I think it came on about half an hour ago," she replied, earning herself a pinch. But then he took her arm again, and she leaned her head against his shoulder with a happy sigh. "That's a question I can't answer, but it might have begun when you said you were tempted to put an arrow through my head. No one has ever talked like that to me, you know. But—in all seriousness—I knew for certain when that man attacked Beatrice and me, and you were so very, very kind and comforting and safe."

Even at this late date he tensed to hear her mention that day and planted a fierce kiss on the top of her head.

When they reached the gateposts of Hollowgate and turned in, Lily said, "Only think, your family didn't want Mr. Wright to marry me—how much more will they protest at *you* doing it?"

"That's why I stayed away from you for a month. To let the uproar die down and to ensure your evil reputation didn't prevent me from getting the prebendaryship that would allow me to marry you."

"Cunning, sir. Very cunning. I thought you had forgotten me and were camped at Miss Carlingford's door."

"Don't look for sympathy from me there, when I had to watch you courted by every man in Hampshire, only to then engage yourself to my blunder-headed cousin."

"I hope your blunder-headed cousin will look as contentedly on our engagement as I do on his."

Kenner only shrugged. "We may have another wrestling match to settle the matter, but that doesn't worry me. I only wish I could wrestle the whole lot of them into submission! Promise me you won't let any resistance from my family discourage you, Lily. We'll prevail in the end."

"*You* were the one whose resistance discouraged me, when I was engaged to Mr. Wright," she protested. "As long as *you* don't change your mind and wish you had chosen otherwise, I'll be content."

And then he had no choice but to offer additional proofs of his staunchness, but at least they were well up the drive by this point.

Breathless, she glowed up at him. “I hope they will all be happy for us soon enough. And Simon, I think our marriage will have at least one ally in your family.”

“My father, perhaps?”

“Perhaps. But I meant your grandmother Mrs. Fellowes.”

“Granny!”

“Yes. Have I ever told you I’ve come to admire her? We understand each other, I think.”

“Because I am the favorite of both your hearts?”

“That, you conceited man, to be sure. But even more to the point, because I think she can be counted on to be a woman of her word.”

And so she was.

The adventures of the Ellsworth Assortment continue with Minta's story in *Minta in Spite of Herself.*

THE HAPGOODS OF BRAMLEIGH

The Naturalist
A Very Plain Young Man
School for Love
Matchless Margaret
The Purloined Portrait
A Fickle Fortune

THE ELLSWORTH ASSORTMENT

Tempted by Folly
The Belle of Winchester
Minta in Spite of Herself
A Scholarly Pursuit
Miranda at Heart
A Capital Arrangement

PRIDE AND PRESTON LIN

www.christinadudley.com

Printed in the USA
CPSIA information can be obtained
at www.ICGtesting.com
LVHW041319261024
794892LV00041B/614

9 781963 408072